Hate Loves Games

Carleen Baker

The
X
Press

Published by:
The X Press
PO Box 25694
London N17 6FP
Tel: 020 8801 2100
Fax: 020 8885 1322
E-mail: vibes@xpress.co.uk
Website: www.xpress.co.uk

First Edition 2006

Printed by Bookmarque Ltd., Croydon, UK

Distributed in the UK by Turnaround Distribution
Unit 3, Olympia Trading Estate, Coburg Road, London N22 6TZ
Tel: 020 8829 3000
Fax: 020 8881 5088

Distributed in the U.S. by National Book Network
15200 NBN Way, Blue Ridge, PA 17214
Tel: 717 794 3800
Fax: 717 794 3804

ISBN: 1-902934-34-2

To Nadezia aka Bunnie and Jade

One

She stood over him.
What had life come to?
Her mind was blank to today but yesterday plagued her.
How had she gotten here?
She held the killer in her gloved hand.
She felt dizzy, hurt.
Her jumper was ripped, her left side bleeding hard.
She turned to leave, holding her injured side.
Blanking out her future nightmares thinking only of what was to come.
She still held tight to the bag.

"Hello stranger," a familiar kind of voice said to her from behind. Kellie turned to see a pretty boy in straight jeans and an Iceberg Mickey Mouse t-shirt. Unfamiliar, but cute. She kept walking; she was in a hurry after doing some late-night clothes shopping. The goodlooking stranger walked up beside her, looking keenly at her body wrapped tight in her new Topshop baby-blue mini dress. It was the first week of proper summer, she looked sexy and knew it.

"I like you babes, I just wanna talk to you for one minute…Please," he said still walking beside her. Gently, he pulled her arm to stop her from walking away.

Usually Kellie didn't like men invading her personal space, but as she looked at him more closely, he was definitely her type and more: tall, fit, dark; bald, with a small goatee.

"I can't stop, I'm on my way somewhere. Give me your number and I'll give you a call?" Kellie said, then immediately wished she hadn't.

"Only if you promise to call, man." He smiled, flashing a perfect set of teeth; the two canine teeth golden. He really was a honey. On the bus, she stared at his number all the way to Mo's house.

"Thanks for sitting for me love. Where are the lil' Rug-rats anyway? It's too quiet," Kellie said walking through to Mo's sitting room.

Mo had been her best friend for over ten years; they had gone to the same secondary school. Her heart was big and she was as honest as a best friend could be.

"They're both asleep thank goodness. I've been getting some peace and quiet." She smiled, looking radiant as a life grew inside of her. At six months pregnant her stomach protruded, round and healthy. She yawned and stretched a bit, then bunched her long extensions into a hair band.

"Mo, I met this well cute guy today. I got his number."
Kellie hid her smile and waited for her to pounce. Mo was always

encouraging her to find someone to settle down with, like she had, with her long-term boyfriend Tex.

"Really! What did he look like? I bet he was nice. I know you, always getting approached by boom men. You wanna drink?" She passed to enter the kitchen. Kellie followed.

"Yeah, I need something cold to cool me down," Kellie accepted, fanning herself playfully. "He's tall– about six foot, dark skinned, bald, has a gold tooth; proper, proper sexy!" Kellie pictured him in her head, she was grinning stupidly.

"Bald head? Will orange juice do you?" Mo asked.
Kellie nodded.

"So, when you gonna call him? Are you even *gonna* call him? What's his name?"

"Shit, I didn't get his name, how can I call him? He probably won't remember me anyway," she joked.

"Is that gonna be your excuse to let another honey go?" Mo raised an eyebrow.

For a minute she *had* considered 'letting this one go' as she had in the past. She didn't have the time or energy for men. But it was true that she couldn't let them *all* go. Her two-year-old son came into the kitchen rubbing his tired eyes and looking handsome, so like his dad. It would be nice to give Samuel a male role model to look up to and herself a chance to be happy.

"Maybe I *will* make the call this time."

Three days later, her reality was to become a long dream; Kellie had spoken to Sediko on the phone a few times and was due to meet him that night. In her office sitting in front of her computer, work was the last thing on her mind. She sighed and looked at her desk. Her 'work to do' pile had papers stacked high. Bill, her boss, loved to pile on the work. The more work she did, the more money he made. The phone rang, interrupting her thoughts.

"Good morning, Laymend's Fashion Company, Mr Laymend's office, Kellie speaking, can I help you?" she asked on his private phone line.

It was the same for most of the morning: audio typing; juggling the phone; calling Tracy her office junior– best used for photocopying or faxing. If it weren't for Kellie arranging Bill's whole diary, it would all crumble for him– including his personal life. She would never tell him that though, she didn't want to dent his pride and she did love her job; being around all the best clothes and shoes, knowing what was 'in' for the season. Sometimes, but not often enough, she and Bill would go away on weekend business trips; France, Italy. They had even gone to New York once for the weekend. Wherever the job took her, all expenses were paid.

At twenty-one years old and in a mere eighteen months, Kellie had managed to work her way up from administrative assistant in the accounting department, to personal assistant to the managing director. She had lost all of her friendly colleagues in the process but it had been well worth it. She looked at the clock; 2:15, hours to go. Bill came out of his office, breaking her thoughts.

"Kellie, have you typed up that audio tape? The clients are being shown up here as we speak. They're early." His dark eyes looked at her pleadingly.

"You only gave that to me this morning, you can't mean *that* one." Kellie looked up at him.

"What! I need those now I-"

"Don't panic," Kellie stopped him before he burst a vein, although he did look cute when he was angry. He resembled Al Pacino with that deep voice and sly sexy look. Kellie handed him a folder.

"Aha you're the best!" He grabbed the folder grinning from ear to ear.

"Bill, is it alright if I leave early today?" Kellie asked.

"Leave early?" He stopped in his tracks.

"Yeah. I got a date." She knew by giving him this information that it might give her a better chance. She hardly ever revealed things about her personal life, not that she had anything to tell, but she knew he would be interested.

"As long as all the new prints are up to date and ready for show." Bill didn't wait for her to answer, he knew her well, she had done that last week. She knew how to prioritise her work load.

Behind her desk, Kellie stood ready to smile and show Bill's clients into his office. She looked chic in a grey Topshop skirt suit. At 5'8" and a slim size 10, she looked good in most anything. Her long thick hair and flawless dark complexion combined to give her an unforgettable beauty that seemed to charm even the most difficult of clients.

Three forty-six. She picked up the phone and called Sediko's number.

"What?" he answered.

"Sediko?"

"Yeah."

"Is that how you always answer your phone?" Kellie smiled.

"What's up babes? Hope you're not calling to stand a man up, I won't have it."

"No. Just checking what time we were meant to meet." Kellie liked the butterflies in her stomach.

"I'm picking you up, innit? Where you live again, Bermondsey?" His voice was rough and coarse, the total opposite of how he looked.

"Yeah. Eight o'clock?" Kellie half asked, half reminded.

"Boy, man can see you now if you're free? Where are you?"

"At work; actually I'm just leaving." Kellie twirled the telephone wire and grinned.

"Can I come get you?"

She didn't think twice. She gave him the address then cradled the receiver. She sat back in front of her computer and waited.

≈≈≈≈

W hat you fucking on! Get up and get the fuck out!" He dragged Brenda by her long blonde hair and dragged her towards the door. She scrambled up, he wrenched open the door, and just before he had the chance to kick her out literally, she was gone.

All Brenda could think about was going back to him after he had calmed down. All Sediko could think about was Kellie. He hadn't even linked with her yet and he could see her eyes in his mind's own. They were calling him. That bitch Brenda had smoked his stash of Charlie, he couldn't believe it. He was pissed off; she knew better. Now he had to make do with his herb. Did Kellie smoke? he wondered.

At twenty-four, Sediko had no ideas of settling down. He played games with women– pretended to love them and when they fell in love with him, treated them like shit. He had sex with at least half of the girls every place he'd ever been and had broken hundreds of hearts. Many times he lied about his name, though in truth, he didn't really care if his women knew about each other– they were always welcome to leave. He didn't beg *any* woman to stay with him, he didn't need to, there were too many available.

Often it was the ladies that got him into trouble. Always, he wanted the women that he couldn't have. Most of the time, in the end, he got them. He showed his niggas that a ho would be a ho no matter whose she was and he'd slept with many of his friend's girlfriends to prove it. He'd slept with daughters, nieces, and aunts, and once he had slept with one of his closet bredrin's mother. Path still didn't know to this day.

But Kellie was a good girl, he could tell that she was. If he could have her on the first night, he would. But if she didn't give it up easily, like most chicks did, it would only heighten the intrigue. He lit his spliff, then left to collect Kellie from work.

≈≈≈≈

T hat was quick," Kellie said once Sediko had found his way to her office in the massive twelve storey building. She stood looking sexy in a grey lightweight pants suit. He loved her long hair, but would later have to check if it was real. If it wasn't, she and the hair could hit the road; he would be too disappointed.

"Nice space," he said to her looking around the roomy office, equipped with a desk PC and a load of work; something he had never had to worry about.

8

"Thank you," she said leaning into a closet to get her jacket.

As they walked out to the lift, a white suit winked at Kellie. Sediko was infuriated, he didn't want his woman being watched. Furthermore, he didn't want his woman to work, he would take care of her. The fact that he was thinking like this so soon, surprised him. And in the lift, he found himself lost for words, something he wasn't at all used to.

Once they reached the ground floor, Sediko's phone rang. "What?" he answered. From the corner of his eyes he could see Kellie's beautiful smile.

"Two-Face, what you sayin', nigga? What you on? Mel just belled me for a t'ing. Man's busy right now. Can you deal with it?" Path asked down the phone.

Sediko wasn't happy, he didn't like mixing business with pleasure. But, he didn't mind doing small favours for his boys. "What, rice or peas?" he asked.

"Rice, innit."

"Yeah yeah, where is he?" Sediko asked reluctantly.

"Back of Haydon's, twenty minutes," Path educated him.

Haydon's was Sediko's surprise investment. The barbershop was making more money than he had expected and it was somewhere for him and his boy's to cotch.

As they approached the car, Sediko opened Kellie's door for her. He felt foolish trying to be a gentleman but he was good at pretending. Now, how was he going to explain his moves? He didn't want her knowing too much about too much.

"We just gotta quickly fly somewhere. I gotta drop something to my cousin. Then we'll go wherever you want," Sediko explained vaguely.

"Home. So I can change out of these clothes."

"I can help you with that if you want." He grinned at her wickedly.

"I love your car," she changed the subject, "except my son couldn't ride with us in this two-seater."

"You got a son, what's his name?" Sediko asked hiding his disappointment.

"Samuel. He's two."

"Where's his dad?" Sediko didn't like the idea of competition. Not with her anyway.

Her smile fell and he wished he hadn't asked. She briefly explained to him how he had been killed in a motorbike accident after she had given birth.

"So where do you wanna go tonight?" His turn to change the subject. He turned on the engine and drove off.

"Out for a drink somewhere?" she suggested, her smile coming back.

"You hungry? I'm a boom cook." Sediko wanted to get her back to his place, he could make the stushist of women give it up on the first night.

"I'll probably be hungry in about an hour."

She buckled up.

Outside Haydon's, the car pulled up. Sediko jumped out and left Kellie sitting patiently. Quickly, he slipped around the back where Mel was waiting.

"You got my dough?" Sediko asked him.

"Yeah, fifty."

"Don't fuck about. You know you owe me two-fifty. Just gimme that plus twenty bills for this."

Sediko knew what was going to happen next. He knew these cats only too well. That's why he hated dealing with them personally. He didn't want to get angry. He didn't want this fool messing up his day.

"Please Two-Face man…alright, I'll give you a oner and the rest tomorrow." Mel - red skinned and fat as hell - panicked, sweat dripping off his fat face. Sediko looked at him, then turned to walk away. Mel pulled his shoulder.

"Don't put your hands on me. You're trying to be bad innit! You think I'm stupid? You're trying to hide from man, you thought it was gonna be Path coming! Yeah, I want my fucking dough!" Sediko punched him in the face without a second thought, and smiled as the first punch sent him to the floor. His nose gushed blood. Sediko bent to search his jacket pocket.

"What's this? You fat fuck!" Sediko pulled out a wad of bills, probably close to five hundred.

"That's my mum's! Serious, Two-Face!"

Mel tried to sit up. Sediko booted him back down.

"Ahh shit! Alright, man. I'll give you the two-fifty," he begged.

"But you're trying to knock, man. If Path would have come you wouldn't have given him my dough," Sediko said pushing the money into his pocket."

"Noooo!" Mel began to cry. "I just sold my baby mother's wide screen. I need that shit. Alright, alright, at least give me my shit. At least that. At least." Mel wiped his eyes, smearing the blood all over his face.

Sediko threw the baggie full of goods onto the floor. Mel scrambled for the bag, forgetting all about the money he had lost. Sediko kicked him again in disgust; he hated fucking cats.

Fixing his shirt, Sediko went back to the car. Seeing Kellie made him relax. "Sorry 'bout that, was I long?"

"No, you're alright." She smiled innocently. They drove straight to her house where he managed to find out mostly everything about her. Kellie was nothing like some of the crackhead ghetto girls that he knew; she was a hardworking mother on the right side of the law. And her crib was just as boom as she was: three bedrooms upstairs and a big kitchen attached to a long living room. Sediko could see himself comfortable here, except this area was mostly white– his was in the middle of Shantytown.

Kellie's doorbell rang. She ran and opened it to a pregnant black woman.

"Yes, I'm here to make you look good for your man," the girl announced laughing. She came in, then covered her mouth in surprise when she saw him.

Sediko smiled, "Is that what she calls me?"

"Mo, that's Sediko. Sediko that's Mo," Kellie introduced.
They gave each other a nod.

"I'm gonna run upstairs and get washed and changed. You two get to know each other." Kellie winked at Mo.
Sediko could see that this was the friend whose opinion would mean a lot to her.

"So what do you do with yourself?" Mo asked him. Sediko hated small talk but this girl's first impression would be what Kellie would be hearing about.

"I'm just a hustler still. But, I own half a barbershop. I look after myself. When you due?" He nodded towards her stomach as if he really wanted to know.

"She'll be a winter baby."

"You married?" he asked. Women just loved a conversation.

"Engaged, soon to be. I live just down the road with my other half and son. I've lived there for quite a while."
Mo droned on for a further twenty minutes before Kellie came back downstairs in a red skirt and a black shirt. Simple looked sexy on her.

"Ready," she announced, bouncing down the stairs.
She looked boom, Sediko couldn't wait to have her.

"So where are you two off to, leaving me behind?" Mo asked sounding desperate.

"Out for something to eat. You can come....if you must,"
Sediko replied chuckling, secretly hoping that she'd decline. But if she accepted, it would make Kellie happy and first impressions meant everything.

"Ah, I'd love to. Ain't he sweet Kel?"
They both smiled.

Sediko had it all planned; he'd dealt with clingy best friends before. As soon as they finished eating, he'd suggest alcohol. Mo was up the duff and would be forced to go home. He wondered if he would get lucky tonight. Usually he had no doubt, but with Kellie it was different. It wasn't just one night that he wanted, it was every night. He couldn't believe it, but maybe he loved her. Perhaps this was what they called love at first sight. Many girls had tried to explain the feeling to him but he had never understood.... until now.

As they left the house, Sediko's phone rang.

"What?"

"Two-Face, I need to see you."

Her voice was more annoying than an alarm clock.

"Yeah, I'll bell you."

Sediko wanted to change his number; a regular thing for him. He had three phone numbers and somehow this bitch had managed to get hold of them all.

"Where are you? Who are you with?"

"Come on now, you know better than to question me." He looked over at Kellie. At least the clingy best friend had come in handy; she was doing him the favour of keeping Kellie chatting.

"Are you with some bitch?" Her voice was almost pleading.

Sediko was angry, she was pushing her fucking luck. And after she had stolen his personal stash?

"Listen, don't piss me off. I'll bell you tomorrow bruv and we'll sort shit out. *Don't* phone me back." She kept talking; he locked off his phone.

He was gonna fucking kill the bitch. She was fuming because he hadn't been fucking her. She had begged him to go to her house last night and he had said no. His Motorola vibrated in his pocket. He took it out and switched it off too.

"How many phones have you *got*?" Kellie asked laughing.

Sediko wasn't. Brenda had really pissed him off.

Thirty minutes later, the clingy best friend did him another favour. Three couldn't fit in his car, so he left it in Kellie's garage and they took a cab instead.

They walked into Whyno's, Sediko's favourite restaurant/bar in Brixton. Inside, the place was packed with all sorts of people. It had a Caribbean feel, with fake palm trees, and tables and chairs made out of raw wood, polished down smooth. Soursop, Guinness and Pineapple punch were typical drinks on the menu.

"What you ladies having? Rice and peas, mutton, curry goat? It's on me."

"It's alright. You can spend your money on me next time."

Kellie just wanted him to see that she was an independent woman.

"Babes, I'll take it as a sign of disrespect if I can't treat my lady and her friend. I know you women, as soon as I turn my back you're like, 'that broke pocket nigga couldn't even pay the bill. Scrub!'" Sediko joked, mimicking Kellie's voice.

Kellie and Mo both laughed. The ice was broken.

≈≈≈

K ellie felt on cloud nine as the cab pulled up outside Mo's house. Sediko had called her his lady. That was definitely the title she wanted to carry.

Mo winked good luck to her as she left them alone for the night.

"Where to now?" Sediko asked her.

"Out for some hard liquor!" Kellie found herself saying though she very rarely drank.

"Kellie, before we go any further.... can I kiss you?" He knew all about respecting a woman's personal space but usually he didn't care and he had never *asked* first.

"Since you have informed me that I am your lady then I think you're entitled," Kellie answered.

Sediko leaned in to kiss her; his hand caressed her face. He desperately wanted to spread his hands all over her body but he knew that patience always paid off with good girls. The kiss was as special for him as it was for her and lasted as long as they both wanted it to.

≈≈≈≈

M uch to Sediko's annoyance, Kellie awoke alone in her own bed. She yawned, stretched, then rolled out and went downstairs to the living room where it was still dark. She looked up at the giant clock on the wall: 5:57 am. She just couldn't shake the 'up-for-work-early' routine. She sank into her large cream sofa, feeling relaxed. Kellie loved her home, it had that cozy feel that made others feel at home even though they weren't. Mo had often said so. Sighing, she closed her eyes and retraced the previous evening's events.

They had gone to the Della wine bar in Ladbroke Grove about 10:00 pm. After about four drinks each they were talking like they had known each other for years. Sediko intrigued her. He was a good listener. He didn't talk about himself much but Kellie just saw it as a challenge. She had excused herself to use the bathroom. On her return, a man had called her over to him. She was used to being approached by unwanted men so she nodded toward Sediko, gesturing that she already had a date. The guy had approached her regardless.

"Can I buy you a drink?" the man asked without smiling. He was handsome, but only a '4' on the Sediko scale.

"Actually, I'm with someone."

Kellie turned to continue walking to where Sediko was waiting, watching them. Fuming.

The guy had grabbed her arm. "Don't walk away from me," he said and held her tight.

"Get your dirty hands off me. I don't wanna talk to you." Kellie had raised her voice slightly; he let go.

13

"What, you think you're too nice? Look, here comes your boy," he had gestured towards Sediko, laughing.

"Who you calling boy? Why you trying to dis' a nigga for, you know better than that."

"Shit. You think you're bad cos your name's Two-Face. You ain't no one. No one to Mia or me. Now I'm all up on *your* bitch, you don't like it!" The guy had started to get rowdy. His arms flared up with every word.

"Two-Face," he had called him. Kellie wondered about Sediko's nickname; hoping it wasn't the obvious. She'd stood and watched as beef began to show its ugly head.

"Come, let's just go finish our drinks. Forget this."

Kellie had tried to pull him gently away but he was standing rigid.

"Shut the fuck up bitch! This-" the guy began.

"NIGGA SAY THAT AGAIN!" Sediko almost pleaded. His eyes seemed to cloud over. This didn't seem like the same calm person that she had just spent half the day with.

Two men came up behind the other guy.

"Yeah, what now? I got my boys, you got your bitch. Lets go!" he challenged.

The man behind him spoke up.

"Y-yo Kirk. W-what's h-h-happening? Y-you ain't g-go-got no beef w-with Two-Face h-have you?"

The stuttering man sounded so scared that Kellie almost felt sorry for him. She looked at Sediko, he looked angry.

"Yeah James, you stuttering bastard! What you think's going on?! You better tell your pussy boy to back up. Just watch! It's true I'm with my woman, why I don't slap yuh na." Sediko's voice had calmed but still sounded deadly.

Kellie had looked around the bar, everyone was silent and trying not to stare; no one dared try and stop the argument or get involved.

"Y-y-you kn- know I don't w-w-want no beef T-t-t-Two-Face. K-Kirk you on your o-o-own."

The man with the stutter backed off into the crowd with the other. Sediko's eyes blazed into Kirk's, who was now shrivelling like a prune.

"Tell Mia that I'll see her soon. I'll pay her a little visit," Sediko promised and grinned.

"Just leave her....This doesn't involve her....alright, alright, I'm sorry. No disrespect," he pleaded.

Sediko had put his arm around Kellie's waist and turned, leaving Kirk almost in tears. They went back to their table. The guy left.

Kellie had quickly decided that she wasn't going to interrogate him about this 'Mia' even though she really wanted to know. She didn't want to make him angrier than he already was.

"Where's my bag?" Kellie looked around where they'd been sitting. "I left it with you when I went to the bathroom!" Tears welled up in her eyes.

"Don't worry about it babes. I'll buy back your bag," Sediko had said to her, not really paying attention.

"My phone. My purse. Luckily my keys were in my pocket. Shit!" Kellie looked around at the packed bar, it could have been anyone.

"Here, take this." Sediko had taken a roll of bills out of his pocket. "Tomorrow, replace everything you lost today. It was my fault. I'm sorry." He looked into her eyes apologetically.

Kellie hadn't blamed him but if he wanted to blame himself and pay damages, who was she to stop him? She couldn't remember the last time she had been given free money. She had to work her ass off to make half of what he had handed her.

"It's okay; I don't need your money."
She couldn't believe what she had said. It was more than £500. That was more than enough. Enough, plus a pair of shoes.

Sediko had rolled the money tight and pushed it gently between her cleavage.

Kellie awoke realising that she had fallen back to sleep. It was 11:15 am and the sun beamed into the room, turning the cream coloured walls into orange. The landline rang. Kellie rubbed her eyes and let it ring three times before answering.

"Hello?"

"Hi sexy," Sediko's voice greeted gently in her ear. "What you doing today?"

"Actually I don't know, I just woke up." Kellie yawned and stretched.

"Am I boring you?"

"Don't be silly. You were the last thing on my mind when I fell asleep and the first thing on my mind when I woke up," Kellie admitted.

"Alright. So what, can I come get you?"

"OK, around two-ish alright?" Kellie liked the butterflies continuously flapping around in her stomach.

≈≈≈

As Sediko finished his call to Kellie, his doorbell rang. He switched on his television to observe on his surveillance camera.

"Come on, I know that you see me."
It was Brenda. Sediko answered the door; she barged in.

"I thought you said you were going to phone me last night. I waited."

"When did I say I was gonna call you?"
Sediko walked past her into his newly painted, deep red front room.

"You didn't say, but it was Friday night. I always roll with you Friday nights."
She threw herself onto his sofa. Sediko was fuming. This bitch liked to

15

get into too much of his business.

"Listen, don't come in here trying to piss me off and don't get comfy cos I'm going out."

Sediko sat with his weed box in his lap. Since he had met Kellie he hadn't really been doing Charlie, more burning weed. She made him high enough, but he would never say that out loud. He started rolling a weed spliff.

"So you got someone else now? Some other bitch? You're acting all funny. I always meet you on Fridays, the past seven months," Brenda whined.

"And what is it to you if I get another bitch? Keep yourself out of my fucking business. And anyhow, I hear you been tryin' to get information about me from people, like you did before I swore I'd bust your face. It's long over fucking due; going off like you're my fucking woman. Bitch, you should be glad you still see me!" Sediko shouted. She was fucking unbearable.

A tear fell from her eye.

He was meant to be keeping her sweet. Although she had just turned 18, she'd helped him out more than once already. Never financially, but she was there when he needed a place to lie low. Brenda and her parents were rich and stupid. In the game that he was in, it was essential that you had a girl like Brenda, as times came high and low. Anytime you needed money, a bed for the night, an alibi, a place to stash, or maybe just a place to do a quick shit after some run belly take-away, whatever the weather, she was it. If her parents ever found out that their precious daughter loved sucking his big black cock they would probably send her to the priest then collapse from a heart attack.

"Listen. I ain't got no bitch," he said licking the Rizla paper. "I got a wifey. A black queen. But... but don't cry. You always be my number one shiner. You know that. Be a good girl and go on down. Go on," he coaxed. He approached her and she fell to her knees.

Two

IT WAS MONDAY morning and Kellie awoke at her usual time, 6:00 am. She showered then dressed for work, choosing a camel coloured pants suit. She then went to Samuel's room; he was already awake and playing quietly.

"Come on little man, it's 8:00." He looked up from playing with his trucks and ran towards her.

"Morning mummy," he sang.

As he ran towards her on chubby little legs, Kellie held out her arms. "Come on, let's get you into the kitchen, Buffie will be here in a minute." She scooped him up into her arms and carried him downstairs just as the doorbell rang. Buffie was always on time.

Kellie sat Samuel on the chair and went to answer the door. Buffie had been looking after Samuel for nearly a year now. She had just finished school and was now doing a modern apprenticeship in child care. Samuel loved her.

"Right, I'm going now. Off to stand packed like a sardine on the late sweaty tube." Kellie picked up her briefcase.

"Buy a car Kellie. It's not like you can't afford it," said Buffie as she began to make breakfast.

"Bye," replied a smiling Kellie as she turned and hurried toward the door.

Kellie got to work on time as usual. While waiting for the lift she was joined by Sally Weavers, one of the many inside candidates that had gone for her PA job. Sally openly hated Kellie for getting the job over her.

"Good morning, Kellie. How is Mr Laymend this morning?"

"I don't know Sally, I've just got here," Kellie mumbled.

"Well let me tell you, he's livid. I've been here since seven this morning, met him in the lift actually."

The lift finally approached. They both got in.

"Maybe you should try to get in a little earlier. Mr Laymend does need 101% commitment and you know what they say about the early bird," Sally remarked looking smug.

Kellie stayed silent at first, she didn't want to give her anything to gossip about in the cafeteria. But as the lift neared the fifth floor she couldn't help herself. "You *have* to come in early, you need to keep up with your photocopying; you junior receptionists have varied roles. Senior secretaries haven't got time to play around making coffee. And to think, you're what, twenty years older than me and less experienced. Oh, that reminds me, when you've got time I need you to do some running around for me; Tracey's off sick."

Sally got out and hurried to her small office as Kellie continued up to

17

her much larger one.

"Morning, Bill."

Kellie walked through to her boss's office. He looked up from behind his desk. Phone in one hand, the other madly tapping the keyboard of his laptop.

"Kellie, I'm glad you're here. Come take this call. It's Mr Patel from the Kenning's. He's demanding a meeting today. He lost his contract. I can't meet with him today, I'm sure I've got meetings all morning." He pushed the phone towards her.

"Is the phone on hold?" Kellie whispered.

"What's that?" He looked at her baffled.

"Let me."

Kellie moved papers and sat on his desk in front of him. She took the phone then put it on loud speaker.

"Good morning, Mr Patel, my name is Kellie, Mr Laymend's personal secretary, can I help you?"

"Ello, don put mi on ole again. Meeting today what time?" Mr Patel shouted angrily.

"Mr Patel, I'm afraid that Mr Laymend will not be able to meet with you this morning on such short notice. I'm sure you understand, with him being such a good and busy businessman, like yourself. I can personally make you an lunch date with-"

"That pretty black girl?" Mr Patel cut in.

"Yes, this is Kellie, Mr Laymend's personal secretary."

Kellie flipped through Bill's diary. Bill pointed to a date three months away.

"How about the week commencing the end of next month?" Kellie played with her words.

"Yes, yes, you be there?" he asked eagerly.

"Yes, Mr Patel, I will be present at the meeting. I'll look forward to seeing you then. Bye." Kellie cut the call before he had the chance to say any more. She got up and sat in the big brown leather chair opposite his desk.

"Thank you Kellie, I was on the phone damn near twenty minutes. Anyway, what's my schedule for today?"

"You have a meeting with Mr Fish in approximately twenty minutes; early lunch with Lisa at 11:00 am. You've got to be back here by 1:00 pm for the photo shoots that you never miss. Then, you're meeting your wife to discuss plans for your daughter's wedding; that's at 2:30 pm. Then later you're going by Virgin trains to Slough. I'm afraid I can't accompany you this time."

Kellie had his diary in her head. His life was more in order than her own.

"Forget Mr Fish, he cancelled– the bastard. If he phones, don't give him another appointment for another six months. Anyway, how did your date go?"

"Let's not get wrapped up in my personal life. How about yours? Planned what you're going to say to the wife?"

"Well first let me remind you that the only reason I tell you details of my personal life is that all the other women hate you, so you can't go around gossiping."

"Ha, ha, spit it out."

Bill had always trusted her and asked her opinion often. She always gave it to him straight, whether he liked it or not.

"This wedding Kellie, what am I going to do? He's a tramp, a punk. He's uneducated and worst of all unemployed. Marie thinks they will be happy, it's starting to come between us for christsake. I refuse to spend thousands of pounds on a short term marriage and it *will* be short term, mark my words."

Bill looked stressed out. His Italian accent thickened in frustration.

"Come on, it won't exactly break your bank balance. What harm can it do except teach her a lesson?"

"I wish it were that simple. I hate the bastard, he will not marry my little girl and he will not spend a pound of my money."

"You're not giving yourself any options. Here's an idea. Give Carrie a choice. A big expensive white wedding, all the trimmings, but no financial help whatsoever after the wedding. Or, they postpone the wedding for a year and Jeff can move in with you."

"What? An expensive wedding or a doss in my house! What's in this for me Kellie?"

"Do I have to spell everything out? If she chooses to get married now, with no financial help, where are they going to live? Who's going to give Carrie her weekly allowance? I'm sure you said Jeff hasn't got a job. How long do you think Carrie will last without her Donna Karan shopping sprees? If she goes for plan B, to wait for a year, then at least you can keep an eye on him and hopefully in a year's time Carrie will see that he's a leach and it will all end in tears."

"Perfect!" he shouted and began to dial his home number. Kellie excused herself back to her office.

Leaning back in her black swivel office chair, Kellie switched on her computer. Just as the boot-up tone chimed, Bill buzzed her phone.

"Marie's liking the idea, at least we agree on something."

"Good, remember you have an early lunch with Lisa Brooks, I booked you into a restaurant on Regent Street. Italian. Be there by 11:00 and don't be late, you know models hate waiting."

Kellie sorted through the papers Bill had dumped on her desk this morning. After only a few moments, another buzz and Bill's voice broke the momentary silence.

"Kellie, can you come in here please?"

She sighed and went through to his office, which was a bigger extension of hers.

"Bill, what is it that you couldn't say over the phone? I do have work to do, and so do you; I need those letters signed for starters." Again she sat opposite him in the brown leather chair.

"Well, Mrs Brooks has informed me that she will be bringing a partner to the meeting, and, well, it's too late to call Marie, so I'd like you to come. Not for a business meeting, I'd like you to come as my date."

He looked vulnerable.

"Why can't you ask one of the Barbies in the canteen? I'm sure one of them will be more suitable."

"Maybe, but I want class, beauty and brains not silicone, small talk and migraine."

They both laughed.

"In that case, I'd love to then. Be your date for the morning. When did you find out that you didn't want to take Marie?" Kellie asked with a grin.

"About two weeks ago," Bill confessed.

"You bad boy, didn't think wifey was suitable?"

"Don't patronise me. I just want to make a good impression; I want her in my clothes. I know she'll like you.

At 10:58 am, they pulled up outside the posh restaurant. In truth, Kellie didn't want to be there. Whenever she accompanied him on business she prefered to keep a low profile. She always sat at the back and never went out for after business drinks with Bill and his associates. She braced herself; this would be a bit awkward

Inside the restaurant they were shown to their table where Mrs Brooks sat with her partner. She was beautiful. Her hair was bright-red, long, and curly and her face was peppered with small faded freckles. She looked tall even sitting and was model thin. Her partner on the other hand, was the total opposite. He was extremely ugly, had dark hair and was stumpy looking.

"Good morning," Lisa beamed, standing to shake hands with them both.

Kellie and Bill sat beside each other; Lisa opposite Kellie.

"Lisa, you remember Kellie. Kellie...Lisa," Bill introduced.

"And this is my latest accessory– Mike," Lisa joked, wishing that she had brought someone more interesting. She had only brought Mike because she had thought Bill would bring his boring wife. But instead he had brought Kellie, a black woman. Lisa was intrigued.

A waiter came with their menu. Kellie could see Lisa staring at her.

"What you having, sweetie?" Kellie teased, smiling at Bill.

"Whatever you order, honey." Bill didn't know what Kellie was playing at but liked the game and played along. The squirm on Lisa's face was a sight.

"How's your wife these days, Bill?" Lisa spat.

"She's fine thank you. And where's your husband these days? Don't see much of him, is he retired?"

Quickly, Kellie squashed the tit-for-tat that she'd started. "Let's not get into marital talk. Let's order first, then we can talk business," she suggested.

"Why Bill, would you want me to model your clothes when you have a beauty right beside you? I'm sure you agree. She's fresh, young and pretty," Lisa said looking at Kellie. Bill's wife hadn't been competition but this woman was a threat to her affairs, she thought.

"Actually, I'm not into modelling. It's definitely not my thing," Kellie replied, flattered. Lisa's staring was getting out of control.

Bill turned to her, amused.

"I'll do it for you, Bill. But, under one condition. I'll only do it if Kellie joins me."

Lisa felt like playing hard to get. Laymend's had had a lot of low-key models in their designs but never a super model, as she no doubt was. Bill needed her. She was only considering it because she and Bill had been having an on and off affair for three years.

"Well Kellie, it doesn't sound so bad. Like Lisa said, you definitely have the looks." The idea grew on Bill immediately.

"No, no I couldn't, it's really not me." Kellie wanted a fast exit. She wanted to tell them that she was a professional, not a piece of meat. She wanted to tell Bill, especially, to fuck off. Instead she said, "Really, Lisa, this is *your* career."

"So you do a one-off modelling job; it may make you famous but it won't kill you. Most girls would jump at the chance."

Lisa began to look offended. Bill just looked at Kellie with a grin, waiting to see how she would get herself out of this one.

"Okay, just a few shots. I'll only be doing it to get you behind the lens; I will not be enjoying it," Kellie gave in. The idea made her feel sick.

"Good!" Bill clapped his hands. "So you'll both be cover models. What will it be, evening wear? But the trouble may come with Kellie, FHM won't be expecting two."

"Don't worry about that Bill, leave this with me, they'll be ecstatic. Two sexy scantily clad women, they're getting two for the price of one. Anyway, telephone me with the details, Bill." Lisa stood to leave.

"You're not staying to eat?" Bill asked, also standing.

"No, the two of you look like you need quality time. To talk business of course. I'll just fade into the background until you need me again." She left without waiting for her silent partner.

"Nice to meet you," he said before rushing off to catch up with her.

"She is definitely a weird one, Bill, where did you find her?" Kellie shook her head.

"So, you're going ahead with it?"

"Well I said I would, didn't I?"

"Shall we order?" His eyes twinkled.

≈≈≈

Come Path, you idiot." Sediko laughed hard as he tried to pick Path up from the floor. They were both high as kites. Sediko couldn't remember how Path had fallen but he knew that it had been funny as hell. They were in the so-called 'office', a room above Haydon's barbershop, about to link up with two ladies from Florida.

"Come on nigga, straighten up," said Sediko laughing as Path slowly stood up, using the chair for support. A car tooted its horn outside and Sediko looked out the window to see a long, shiny, white Limousine.

"Shit Path look, that *can't* be the bitches from Florida."

Path staggered over to the window to see. The car window wound down and there they were.

Downstairs, the rest of the men were giving Path and Two-Face their props, because although they could all afford to hire a limousine, it was better to have a female pay for it.

"You guys coming or what?!" one called up to their open window. They turned to each other, smiled, then left the room.

The girls watched them cross the road. Sediko in a twisted Levi's Jean suit and Path in a new Nike track suit, his hair freshly plaited. They climbed in. Sediko couldn't even remember which one he had chirpsed, they looked the same.

"Hey Two-Face, what's up?" one said. He remembered her name to be Sammy, or Shanice. Some shit beginning with 'S'. She sat up close to him. He was the most gorgeous black man she had ever seen. The only black man she had ever kissed.

"I'm cool. What you two ladies up to tonight?" Sediko asked.

"Whatever you want. Me and Stacey just looking for fun," Samantha said. She and her sister were on vacation. Sort of like a long hen night. Sammy was getting married in a week. She had heard all about the English black men and had decided she would have to sow her oats before taking the big plunge.

"You ladies smoke weed?" Path asked.

"Yeah what, like a blunt? Yeah." They looked at each other. They were both happy to do anything illegal and Stacey had tried it a few times.

Two-Face didn't believe in wasting time with these sorts of chicks, they liked it fast and rough. He leaned over and kissed her neck; she responded eagerly. He knew he would get to fuck her tonight, but it was Kellie that he really wanted.

"Where's the champs ladies?" Path laughed.

Sammy lent over to the coolers and took out some cool champagne. She poured it into four tall glasses.

"So what hotel you at?" asked Sediko.

"The Hilton in Paddington, you know that one?"
Sediko nodded, moving his hand up between her legs.
"Back to the hotel Jeff!" Stacey sang.

Sammy lapped him up, kissing his neck and forcing his hand down her top. Sediko looked into her eyes just the way he knew she would love and always remember. He couldn't wait to get her back to the hotel. She was proper fit– big breasted, slim. But first he would use the room phone to make a few international calls, order everything in room service, and demand a full drink cabinet.

Sediko looked over to Path who already had Stacey's bra off. "Ah, you dat," he laughed, still reeling from the crack they had smoked earlier. Sediko had decided to tease Sammy and wait, though she was dying to get to her friend's stage.

They pulled up to the hotel and were treated like royalty. Their room was the top floor penthouse suite with a balcony. Sediko strolled around and took in his surroundings. Sammy called him into the bathroom. He followed her where she sat naked in the bubbling jacuzzi. She called to him again. Sediko went in, closed the door behind him and stripped off his clothes.

Sediko awoke in the large hotel bed with Kellie on his mind. He looked at his watch: 7:00 am. He unwrapped himself from Sammy's embrace careful not to wake her. He tiptoed through to the other room to wake Path, who struggled to get out of Stacey's killer hold. Every time he tried to move her arm, she held tighter. Sediko stifled a laugh. They were unlikely to wake up. Sediko and Path had given them enough drink and drugs to keep them asleep all week. Finally, Path rolled out of the bed. They both dressed quickly and called to get their ride.

In the limo, they both laughed and joked about the previous night's events. Sediko admitted to Path that he had not had sex with Sammy, he hadn't even kissed her on the lips. He hated her already and hoped she didn't call him again.

"All that went down was a shiners, bruv." Sediko didn't admit the reason why. All he could see was Kellie's face, begging him to save it for her.

"Come we go to my mans, BC's. We need the heat if we gonna do that shit. It's perfect, boy dem won't stop a limo."

Sediko smiled at his revelation; he had big plans. Though he had power over a lot of people, he didn't have the money that he really wanted. This move that he and Path had been planning would put him up there with the high rollers. He just needed to do this one last thing, then he would be where he wanted to be.

"Yeah come, we go," agreed Path.

Path was Two-Face's was Path tightest nigga. They had grown up together from nursery, to primary, to secondary school. Then they had both been sent to the school for the out of control kids. No one could tell them what to do or how to do it. Path had been the bigger of the two then, the strongest he would say. He used to push Sediko and the rest of the boys around playfully. Sediko was always the one they made climb through the windows of the school buildings in the dead of the night and open doors for them or squeeze through railings; he was the smallest back then.

One day they were almost caught and they had to run. And for some reason he had gotten into a fight with Path. Sediko, as small as he was, had kicked Path's ass. From that day on, neither Path nor anyone else, ever fucked with him again. Those that did found themselves in a hospital bed.

Jeff, the limousine driver, looked around nervously as he approached the area he had been asked to take them. So many black people. Any one of them could highjack the limousine. He would get beaten up and then sacked. To make it worse they had been inside the shop for four minutes and he had to wait for them. Those American tarts had better give him a big tip for risking his life.

"So 13 guns, that would be about 13g's," Malcolm slurred.

"Ha, what, come on Mal, don't piss about, this ain't TV, man ain't got time for games. Two g's and you're lucky you're getting that," Sediko said as Path produced some money that they had 'borrowed' from the Florida chicks.

"Here, now pass that shit. They loaded?" Path asked.

"Don't be stupid. I put about 1000 pegs in the bag. Be careful now boys," Malcolm slurred again. It looked as if half his face was paralysed. He took the money, eyeing the little extra Path had slipped between the bills; he would get high tonight.

They returned to the limousine. Sediko called Sparrow.

"Yo what's up son," Sediko greeted.

"Yo what's up, you two still with those chicks?"

"Na, fun's over. Business calls now. You and the mans meet us at Haydon's."

Sediko cut the call and looked at Path. He knew that he was thinking the same thing. Now that they had this shit no one could stop them. Anyone that tried to cross him he would simply shoot down like a dog. No remorse. They pulled up outside Haydon's in Battersea. Sediko watched as the limousine sped away.

≈≈≈≈

M arie was getting on his last nerve.   "So that's why we absolutely have to have this dinner party. Ten people including me and you... please Bill?" she whined. She always wanted to waste money.

"The girls in my yoga class," she continued, "want to meet Jeff."

"I thought you wanted to keep Jeff low key?" Bill cut in, trying to stay calm.

"Jeff will be gossip if we hide him. A few close friends that's all."

"Is Jennifer a close friend? Is Kate?" Bill moved around their bedroom. Bigger than most average living rooms.

"I have to invite Jenny, and Kate. Well if I don't they'll only be offended. I'll just die if she thinks she's not good enough for my dinner party." Marie looked in his eyes pleadingly.

"So if I were to say yes, exactly how much cash will you be needing?" Bill sighed pulling his tie.

"Well I've already taken the liberty of making some preparations." She darted downstairs to the kitchen. Bill followed her, briefcase in arm. Marie rummaged through the many mahogany style kitchen units. Obviously she had hidden it from him and now couldn't find it herself.

"I did have a few brochures but-"

"Look, I'm not interested in the details."

"Around £4000 to begin with," she said quickly. "It sounds a lot but there is a lot involved. You can't expect me to cook and serve for ten guests!" She recovered the brochures and held tight to them.

"Well okay, maybe. If I do agree maybe *I'd* like to invite a few people."

"Yes, yes of course that was my next question. It almost slipped my mind darling," she said smiling, then turned, mumbling about having more things to do.

Bill walked around his beautiful home, a six bedroom Georgian style palace. Spacious ensuite bedrooms, real red brick, massive fireplaces, attached double width garage, and his office– the best room in the house. He found himself standing outside its door.

His two offices, home and work, were exactly the same layout and colour scheme. Same furniture, same window position, only the views were different. The consistency made him work better. At home, the door to Kellie's office was really the door leading to the passageway, and working late into the night after having had a few drinks, he'd sometimes get confused. He'd open the door ready to go home and find that he already was.

Bill went in and sat behind his desk. He decided to invite Kellie and Lisa to the dinner party. It would be a bit of dangerous fun. First, he called Lisa.

"Hello, Lisa's line."

"Hi, it's Bill." His voice was extra gruff this evening.

"Well, to what do I owe the pleasure?" she said with slight sarcasm.

"Dinner party, two weeks." He had decided to get straight to the point.

"What, not at your home?" she asked sounding surprised.

"Uh huh."

"Well well, dicing with death. Of course I'll come, I'm flattered that you asked. I've heard all about your wife's dinner parties. Shall I bring a partner?"

"I would prefer if you didn't. Actually, I was thinking you could come with Kellie."

"Now wouldn't that just please you Bill," she half moaned, half laughed.

"You've inherited a dirty mind from somewhere," Bill responded, then continued, "It would be good for you and Kellie to get to know each other."

"Have you asked her?"

"She said that she couldn't wait," Bill lied easily.

"I doubt that, but yes, I'll come with Kellie."

"Good. I'll send you the official invitations when they arrive."

Bill smiled to himself, sitting back comfortably. Lisa had a hard exterior, but with him she would always melt into this sweet little thing.

"Okay Bill, I can't wait," Lisa giggled.

Bill said goodbye, then cradled the receiver. He paused for a moment before dialling Kellie's number; he would have to approach her quite differently.

"What?" Kellie answered sluggishly.

"That's no way to answer your phone," Bill toyed with her.

"Bill, what's wrong?" Kellie's voice now seemed full of concern; or maybe annoyance.

"No, nothing's wrong. I just wanted to ask you a business favour." Bill tapped his new pen on his desk. He was now sitting forward.

"And what would that be?"

"Well, I'm having a dinner party, to er, celebrate our designs. I want you and Lisa to come wearing the dresses from the new range. It's just a few of Marie's girlfriends and their husbands. What do you say?" Bill waited. If she said no, he would ask her again at work.

"Oh, alright," she agreed with a sigh.

"Good!" Bill grinned triumphantly. It was easier than he had thought. He finished his call then shouted to Marie. She came in instantly. His door was sound proof, why she always still tried to eavesdrop was beyond him.

"Yes darling?" She looked around his office as if it was her first time entering. She snooped in here every chance that he gave her.

"My two guests will be models," he said simply.

"Models? I'm sorry, I don't follow." She stood with her hands clasped in front of her.

26

"Well, I've had a brainstorm. We're celebrating, or rather promoting my new range. You could even put that on the invitations. This way the light will be off Jeff and onto my favourite subject: fashion." Oh, so smooth, he thought.

"Well alright. But why *two* models?"

"They will be wearing my dresses. Don't worry, they're not a patch on you."

"I know darling, I am not worried. It's a fantastic idea, I'll get on the phone to get the ball rolling."

She turned and left his office, her face flushed red. Her long brown hair was in its usual bun. She didn't have to worry; she was still very sexy. A beautiful face with perfect little features. Small but firm breasts, short but fine legs. She had a grace about her and he had never regretted the day that he'd married her.

Carrie barged into his office.

"Don't you know how to knock first?" Bill sighed.

"I'm 19, I don't have to knock any more. Anyway, I've come to tell you that I want you to like Jeff. He has a good background and despite what you think; he just doesn't want to live off his parents. He's got a job now– a limousine driver," Carrie defended proudly.

Carrie looked at her father expectantly and sat down on the leather chair in front of him. Her long dark hair fell down her back; it looked as if it hadn't been combed in years. She wore the biggest trousers he had ever seen and her top was full of holes.

"A limousine driver, a limousine driver? God give me strength. Is he going to take care of his new wife on minimum wage and tips?" Bill didn't want to loose his temper.

"Daddy, please."

Marie barged in next. That's all he needed.

"Can't you knock? What's wrong with the two of you?"

Marie ignored him and spoke to Carrie.

"So Carrie, you and Jeff looking forward to the dinner party? Soon it will all be arranged."

"I didn't ask for this stupid dinner party! What's the point if daddy refuses to get along with Jeff! He won't even *try* to like him. It's embarrassing," Carrie moaned.

"Look, your father and I are just trying to do something nice for the two of you. After a nice dinner all together, he'll be like a part of the family."

"Don't act as if this party is for me and Jeff, you're doing it for you and your bitchy friends!"

"How dare you swear, you ungrateful little thing!" Marie squealed back at her.

Carrie stood to face her.

"I'll swear at you if I want! You're not my mother! BITCHFUCKSHITBASTARD!" Carrie screamed in his office. Tears ran

27

down both faces.

"RIGHT, THAT'S ENOUGH! Both of you! Now. We will have this dinner party, not for Jeff *or* Marie's friends. We're celebrating my work and me. Me. We will all get along with Jeff, including myself, and Carrie you will apologise to Marie for the foul language; you know she hates it," Bill refereed as usual.

"Sorry," Carrie choked.

"Sorry too," Marie sniffed.

"Now both of you get out my office. Oh, and Carrie you'll wear a nice dress to the dinner party."

Bill turned to his computer. They both shuffled out silently.

Bill couldn't wait to see Kellie and Lisa stand beautifully together. Their dresses would look fabulous. Marie and the girls would be green with envy. And their husbands would be drooling in fashion heaven.

Three

IT WAS MONDAY morning and Sediko had decided last night that Kellie would take the day off work. She heard Buffie downstairs, she had let herself in after two knocks.

"Kellie!" she called out, eventually coming upstairs to Kellie's open door.

"I won't be going to work today; I'm not well," Kellie said before rolling over into Sediko's arms who slept beside her.

"Well, I'll go make breakfast," Buffie said, backing out of the room. She didn't hide the fact that she didn't like Sediko one little bit.

Kellie gazed at Sediko as he slept. She loved this man. They had been together two months. They hadn't yet slept together but he hadn't pressured her once. She felt sixteen again. With him she could let her hair down, break a few rules, and smoke some weed. Before, she had never even smoked cigarettes, but weed made her feel relaxed. Now without it she felt up-tight, boring. Sediko found her hand beneath the blanket as if he was reading her thoughts. He opened his gorgeous eyes, then kissed her gently. They both fell back asleep.

The ringing phone woke her up.

"What?" she said after the third ring. She lay back with the portable phone.

"Kellie, have you had an accident?"

In her mind Kellie scolded herself, she'd forgotten to call in sick this morning.

"Nearly, I think I'm coming down with the flu, Bill," Kellie lied.

"You could have telephoned. What will I do without you? I'll be needing a few things."

Bill was angry but couldn't complain; this was Kellie's first sick day.

"Everything you'll need for today will be in the top left filing cabinet. Your schedule for today is on my desk. Any problems, call me back."

Kellie hung up. She was always ahead of schedule. A few days off was nothing big. And Bill was lucky that she had agreed to do this stupid modelling job and the stupid dinner party. Again, she curled up in Sediko's arms. It was 11 am. She couldn't remember the last time she had slept so late on a weekday; it felt so good.

Two days later and Kellie was ready to go back to work. She'd told Sediko about the modelling shoot which had been scheduled for that day.

"Nervous ain't the word," she said drying off, having just stepped out the shower.

"Here, take this just before you go in, you'll feel much better after," he urged. "Just sniff."

29

Kellie sat in the ladies' toilet cubicle at work. She held the small amount of powder in her hand. He had showed her how to separate it; she had seen him do it plenty of times. Without fear, she lifted her briefcase onto her lap. She had already smoked weed, how much different could this feel?

The white powder stared back at her. She used her new credit card to separate one 3 cm line. She then separated that into two thinner 3 cm lines. Without a second thought she closed her eyes, opened them, bent forward and sniffed hard but slowly up each nostril. She sat upright and blinked rapidly. Her nose felt tingly, then itchy; hot and then burny. She leaned back slowly and mentally fought herself not to scratch and rub it. She squinted her eyes as they began to water.

Instantly, she felt an excitement. She was a beautiful model about to be pampered. She tried to stand but fell straight back onto the closed toilet seat. "Shit," she whispered. She shook her head, inhaled, exhaled, then stood again. This time she stood poised. Minutes later she came out of the cubicle and went to the large mirror. "Yes, I *am* beautiful," she sighed to herself.

Up in Bill's office, Lisa stood between his legs as he sat at his desk. Kellie felt an unnecessary pang of jealously.

"Hope I'm not interrupting, Mr Laymend."

Kellie sat opposite them in his brown leather chair. Lisa looked strangely happy to see her.

"Well hiya, Miss model for the day." Lisa couldn't decide whether she loved or hated Kellie.

"Good morning Lisa, you look 'different' today," Kellie teased. She felt much braver than usual.

Lisa shot her a dirty look.

"Right ladies. Let's go downstairs. We have no time to waste."

Bill pushed his chair back. Lisa reluctantly moved to a position closer to Kellie.

"So will we definitely be doing the shoots today?" Kellie asked remembering that she hadn't been feeling the idea from day one.

"Come on Kellie, we're all pros here, we'll need practice shots too." Lisa couldn't wait to get this smart alec behind the camera. She could show her a few things.

With a smug look on his face, Bill stood and led them both towards the door.

Down at the studio it looked as if Bill had pre-arranged everything from make-up artists to light engineers. That was usually Kellie's job. She spotted Sally and Gwen in the corner staring at her, waiting for her to make a mistake or trip and break her neck. She decided to stick close to Lisa; after all, this was her line of work.

"Come on, hair and make up."

Lisa took her hand. No one touches my hair, Kellie thought. She sat herself down. People buzzed around her. The same people that worked below her. They looked different somehow. Kellie's head still rolled.

An hour later, everyone was telling her how beautiful she looked. She smiled at Lisa, who too, looked perfect. Bill had chosen a black halter neck backless dress for Lisa. For Kellie, a black dress with a neckline plunging almost to her belly button. Lisa jumped into her dress while Kellie struggled to put hers on before Lisa began helping her.

"You'll be great, you look great," Lisa reassured her.

"Thank you, you too." Kellie felt ready.

They went onto the set. A brilliant white sheet draped over a massive board.

"Ladies, you look gorgeous!" the cameraman shouted.

"Right Kellie, try not to look at the lights, let's make this quick and easy! I want you to concentrate on each other. I want sex kittens. Innocent sexy, sex kittens! You with me?" he shouted.

"Alright, alright," Lisa waved. "Come on Kellie, put your arms around me, onto my back," Lisa said while flicking her nipples.

Kellie did as she was told.

"Yes that's it!" The camera started clicking furiously.

Lisa threaded her arms through Kellie's and laid her head on her shoulder, her ginger curls fell gently over Kellie's shoulder and spilled gracefully onto her chest. Next, both facing the camera, they stood opposite each other clasped in a tight embrace. They had tears spayed on. They had benches brought on. And their make-up was redone every 5 minutes. After an hour-and-a-half Kellie was ready to drop.

At last, Bill shouted "Enough!" Kellie had already decided that she was going home.

An hour later, with help from Lisa, Kellie was in the car with Sediko and on her way home. A big spliff of weed rested on her lips and she was grinning stupidly.

"So how was your day, babe?"

"It was different. I think I did well. I had to keep-"

"Hold on," he interrupted as his phone rang. He talked on the phone more than he talked to her.

Kellie sat in a daze.

Twenty minutes later, he came off the phone; he rested his hand on her leg. "Let's go to my house. I'll make us something to eat. I'm a boom cook, I told you before," he coaxed.

"No, let's go to my house and forget lunch."

≈≈≈≈

Sediko's heart was racing. He felt the same excitement that he did his very first time. She had the tightness of the very first time. It hadn't happened when he had wanted it to - they had had many false starts - but he had decided that it had been well worth the wait. For three months he had waited patiently and faithfully.

After they had both satisfied each other, Sediko looked deeply and lovingly into her eyes. Gently he rolled off of her and took two ready-made spliffs from her dresser.

"How you feeling babe?" he asked. It was the first time that he had ever asked a girl if she was alright.

"Cool. Perfect. Satisfied. And hungry for more."
She climbed on top of him.

"You hungry? Let's go out to eat," suggested Sediko two hours later as he jumped up from her bed. He felt great.

They pulled up outside Whyno's just after 8 pm. Sediko spotted her as soon as they approached the bar. Light skinned, short, cute small frame, short boyish hair– she looked as sexy as ever. She had put on a little weight and her hair looked freshly cut. Smooth and straight.

"What you having?" Kellie asked.

Sediko watched her, dressed in jeans and shirt, simple but sexy. She was looking around, her eyes darted and scanned the packed bar. Was she looking for him? She hadn't spotted him yet.

"What you having?" Kellie asked again.

"What?" he asked, deep in thought.

Sediko thought about leaving. This girl was forbidden fruit right now. Shit, there it was, she had seen him across the room and briefly their eyes had locked.

"What you staring at? Sediko, you'd better stop drooling, if you wanna go talk to someone go do it," Kellie said annoyed.

The woman was walking over. Kellie watched her approaching them and looked at him for answers.

"Just chill, that's my bredrin's t'ing," Sediko barked without shouting. *What the fuck was she doing coming over to them when Kellie was standing protectively beside him?*

"Two-Face, you alright?" Her voice showed no emotion as she finally stood beside him. Sediko just nodded cooly. "I need to talk to you, it's about Kirk," she lied, her voice still sweet.

She looked no more than 18. Kellie let out some steam.

"I'll go get us a table," Kellie said before kissing him fully on the lips. He responded. She walked off without looking back.

"I haven't seen you in months, I was hoping that I'd bump into you," the girl said. Her obsession for him was boiling inside of her.

"What you want? I'm busy as you can see." His tone was harsh.

"How are you?" she asked him.

"I'm busy. What is it?"

"I just wanted to tell you that I got myself together. I'm fixed up and back in my place on Gypsy Hill."

Her heart was skipping beats. Sediko stayed silent.

"Alright, well, I'll see you around then." Her face seemed to crumble and she turned and walked away.

Sediko liked Kellie, maybe even loved her, but he couldn't let this girl walk away. He followed her out the back door, leaving Kellie waiting for their drinks. He went out to the car park and spotted her standing by his car. She knew him too well. He jogged over to her, looking left and right and stopped in front of her. She walked into him slowly and her arms went up around his neck.

"Mia," Sediko breathed into her hair as her name rolled off his tongue.

They both jumped into his car.

"So..so is that your girl?" she asked as he sped towards Battersea.

"Where's your boy Kirk?" Sediko skipped his fourth traffic light.

"Out with his boys," she answered.

He still only answers questions with questions, Mia thought.

"You miss me?" Sediko asked. He couldn't resist. He knew what her answer would be because no matter what he did, how he treated her, or who he was, Mia accepted him. She loved him unconditionally. This had been the longest time they'd spent apart since they had been young teens.

She bowed her head. "I always think about you. Wait for you..." she trailed her words. Already she had said too much. She had planned this moment for ages and she didn't want to distance herself by getting too close. Sediko was a puzzle that only she could understand. He rested his hand on her leg.

"Kirk told me about the beef you had in Della bar," she said, quickly changing the subject.

Sediko's phone rang.

"Listen babe, I gotta run somewhere to sort some business. My battery's low, I'll come straight to your yard when I'm over." He hung up his phone and felt a strange pang of guilt.

Just hours earlier, he and Kellie had slept together for the first time and it had been something special. Now, he and Mia had done the same and it had been just as sweet. It had been ages since they'd been together. While Kellie was something new and exciting, with Mia it was all familiar feelings. But it was Mia he made leave, straight away. He actually felt guilty.

The next day Sediko met up with his boys at Haydon's barbershop. They all sat in the business box above the shop. It was a small room with a dirty sink to the left, a dusty broken toilet to the right, a window ahead and a wooden half-decent table. Ten rickety wooden chairs were scattered around the room. Path, Bones, Sparrow and Image sat around him.

"Yo, what's up?" Sediko touched them all with his closed fist.

"Yeah yeah, Two-Face, lets start this shit," Sparrow said eagerly.

Sparrow was short, dark, and stocky. He spent most of his time in the gym. He loved trouble and would do anything for money. Image was tall and slim. His hair was faded almost bald. He was trustworthy if he was your boy, deadly if he was your enemy. Bones was at his heaviest, at 20 stones. He was the joker of the pack and the closest to Sediko even though Path thought that he was.

The five of them sat upstairs where not even the partner of the business could enter. *His* name was Jayson. He was a regular hardworking black man. He had owed Sediko money a few years back because he had shacked up with a pretty crack chick who had gotten him into more trouble than she was worth. Jayson couldn't even to begin to pay Sediko back the money she'd owed him. He'd just used the last of his savings to open up his barber shop and it hadn't been doing too well– only one, maybe two, customers a day. So giving Sediko half the shop seemed the only way out for him.

Sediko had settled the debt by taking half of the shop, all legally. Since then, the shop's always packed. Some just came to smoke and socialise, but that was cool, because Jayson still had had to employ three other barbers; someone always wanted a trim.

Sediko lifted a bag onto the table.

"Right my niggas, plenty to go round. I've taken out my shit, so the rest is for you niggas. And 'member, it's business not pleasure, I don't want none of you fools waving that shit round baiting yourselves up."

Sediko emptied the bag. A range of guns spilled out onto the table. Sediko now owned more guns than he needed adding more to his collection; some old, some new. His favourites: the Glock, a 9mm, a 45, a 38 and his ex- automatic. He had also bought one for Kellie, a 22 slug; it fit right under her g-string.

He watched his niggas take their guns off the table.

"I'll take the 9mm." Path couldn't hide his grin.

Sparrow picked up the pump rifle.

"How did I know you were gonna choose that shit! Nigga you fucked up," Sediko said laughing.

Image chose a Slug.

"You little bitch. You got the small shit to match your dick," Bones joked.

Everyone started laughing. Image just nodded, grinning, waiting for the laughter to stop. Sparrow continued to laugh long after the joke.

"Shut up you pussy, joke done," Image said to him.

"What! Don't try call man pussy, you got dissed, innit. What, Bones

34

talking too much truth?" They started laughing all over again.

"Sparrow, you're a pussy. You're always trying to test man," Image spat.

"What?"

Sparrow stood and stepped up to him. He held his gun up to Image's face.

"This shit loaded Two-Face?" Sparrow asked without moving the gun.

"You better move that shit out my face." Image had left his gun on the table, out of reach.

"See how I hook you niggas up with that shit and you're waving them shits around unnecessarily! What did I just fucking say!" Sediko shouted.

"I'm only playing nigga." Sparrow laughed and dropped his hand. Path and Bones watched the drama of the day in play. They would all have a laugh about it tomorrow.

"You know what, I ain't saying shit to you."

Image sat back in his seat.

≈≈≈≈

B ill, the waiters haven't arrived yet," Marie panicked, running around in her curlers and dressing gown. "Waiters?"

Bill had chosen a simple grey suit. Kellie had helped him spend all £800 for a successful business meeting some months ago. He wondered if she would remember it.

"Look, only three and the chefs can't exactly do it, can they?"

"Look darling, just calm down please, you're making me nervous," Bill urged.

Marie hurried off to the phone.

It was almost 6 pm, the dinner was to start at 7:30 pm. Carrie and Jeff entered the living room.

"Hi honey.... Jeff."

Carrie smiled hard.

"I really appreciate you giving me and Carrie a chance Mr Laymend. I do love your daughter," Jeff sucked.

"Well, that's good." Bill squeezed out a friendly smile. *Fucking dumb prick.* He held back his truer words.

At 7:10 pm, Jennifer and Kate arrived with their husbands Pete and Alister .

"Bill, my good man." Pete shook his hand vigorously.

Marie carried out her normal pre-dinner party routine. Everyone kissed everyone. All men shook hands. They then went into the living room for pre-dinner party drinks, which consisted of one drink each.

"You boys talk, we'll go help Marie with last minute details."

They rushed out to follow Marie.

By 8:07 pm, Bill and Marie sat at the two heads of the table. The two chairs to the left of Bill were empty, then sat Pete, Alister and Jeff. To Marie's left sat Jennifer, Kate and Carrie. The doorbell rang just as it looked as if Marie was going to cry.

"Here they are," Bill said rising from his chair smiling.

"Yes and 35 minutes late," Kate observed.

"Yes, very fashionable," Bill quickly remarked.

Lisa and Kellie glided into the dining room wearing the black next-to-nothing evening gowns from the photo shoot. Kellie was holding a very old bottle of French wine.

"Welcome," greeted Marie now also standing, unable to avert her stare. "Welcome," she said again looking down at her own dress– a sickly mauve, tightly fitting, floor length; not one of his. Her hair was styled in its usual bun. "Lets have the starters," she said before sitting.

"So who are these models Marie?" Kate whispered while they stood talking to Bill.

"Lisa somebody I think, I don't know the other," she whispered back between her smile.

"Let me introduce our models for the evening. My left side, Mrs Lisa Brooks."

Bill motioned for her to stand beside him. He snaked his hand around her waist. He could have sworn he had seen a lump in Marie's throat.

"To my right, is Miss Kellie Palmer."

Kellie stood. Bill found her waist also.

"These splendid dresses are of course property of Laymend's Fashion Company." He laughed lightly at his lame introduction.

"Please ladies, give us a twirl." He held both their hands up as they spun slowly.

Pete and Alister smiled appreciatively as Kellie and Lisa took the seat bedside the husbands. Jenny and Kate watched their husband's mouths drop to the floor, just as he had predicted.

"Marie, who arranged the seating," Kate whispered to her.

"Is there a problem with the seating ladies?" Bill asked as crab leek soup was served.

"No, no it's fine." Kate waved a hand.

"Kellie..Lisa, that's Pete and Alister; that's my daughter Carrie, and her partner Jeff; that's Kate and Jennifer and I'm sure you both know my lovely wife Marie," Bill introduced.

"And I'd like to say congratulations to the future husband and bride," Kellie said smiling in Carrie's direction and holding up the bottle of wine as a pre-wedding present.

"Thank you." Carrie smiled.

Jeff's eyes were fixed on Lisa; he was almost dribbling.

"Jeff, like to swap places?" Pete joked, noticing his fixation. Carrie's eyes began watering. Great! Bill thought.

"Why didn't you tell us she was coming? She's in Jeff favourite porno magazine!" Carrie whined before pushing herself up from the table.

"Carrie! Sit down now," Bill said as sternly as he could without bellowing.

"But Daddy.."

"Sit." His eyes blazed.

She sat down slowly. Bill looked to Lisa who was trying her best not to laugh.

"It's okay dear, men drool over me all the time. But he loves you I'm sure," Lisa reassured her tactlessly.

Kate broke the silence,"So Bill, the dresses are beautiful."

"Thank you, Kate. The ladies compliment them too, don't you think? Absolutely stunning."

Conversation and laughter drifted around the table. At least everyone was smiling and nodding. Bill leaned in to listen to Kellie and Alister.

"So what's your profession?" Kellie asked him.

"Er, I'm a bank manager. A chain of banks," he boasted.

"Sound like a busy man. What are your pleasures? Can't be all work and no play," Kellie toyed with her words.

"My, my pleasures?" Alister stuttered.

What an idiot.

"Your hobbies, what do you enjoy when you're not being a bank manager to a chain of banks?"

"I enjoy tennis, golf. You play?"

"I play any game that I'm taught Alister," Kellie purred back to him.

"So Kellie," Kate called from across the table. "How long have you been modelling?" She gave Alister that burning 'you just wait until we get home' look.

"Well actually, I'm not a model but a private secretary to a very important rival fashion company," Kellie exclaimed.

Bill and Lisa laughed lightly.

"Did I miss the joke?" Kate hated missing jokes.

"She works for my dad; are you dumb or what?" Carrie groaned keeping her eyes on Jeff.

"I mean really Carrie, do you have to be so crude?" Kate asked her. Carrie ignored her.

"So, are you looking forward to marriage?" Pete asked Jeff.

"Yes, I am very much, sir."

"Where are you from?" Pete asked.

"My parents live southeast," Jeff said vaguely.

"By any chance does your father have a medical centre on Harley Street? You look much like the Newman family."

"Yes, he's Jeff Newman," Carrie cut in.

"Really?" Pete looked from Jeff to Bill.

37

Bill looked none the wiser.

"Bill, the Newmans. Cape and Janice Newman."

"Oh my gosh yes, the Newmans! How could I possibly forget?" Bill sat up to attention.

"Bill?" Marie asked baffled.

"Daddy?" Carrie looked to him for answers.

"Jeff, does your father know that you're getting married? And who to?" Bill asked him carefully.

Bill had met Cape through a mutual friend of theirs. His youngest daughter Cecile, 15 at the time, had come to the studio asking if she could use the equipment for a school project. She had given him a cheque from her father as a "thank you." Bill had accepted, provided they not make a mess.

A few hours later, he and Kellie had gone down to the studio to make sure the girls were doing okay. When they got there they both got the shock of their lives. Instead of a school project, the three of them - all girls - had taken explicit photographs of one another. They had caught them in the act. Apparently their school project had gotten a little too complex and out of hand.

Cecile had begged him not to call her father. He had. Cape had apologised and sent a limousine to pick the girls up along with all pictures and negatives. Then four months later, with not a word from Cape, he had e-mailed Bill to say that the cameraman had been blackmailing him over pictures that had been left behind.

All Bill would and could do was sack the cameraman and advise Cape to inform the police. Cape then had to pay the police to keep this information out of the papers. In the meantime, the cameraman had disappeared and Cape had blamed Bill for the whole thing. Now eight years on, his son wanted his daughter's hand in marriage? No way!

"No, I haven't told him. He and I don't keep in contact." Jeff kept his head down.

"I'll tell you now Jeff, no one is taking my daughter's hand into secret marriage."

"Daddy what's going on?" Carrie was again on the verge of tears.

"Jeff can explain to you why he hasn't told his father at a more appropriate time," Bill replied.

Bill couldn't believe this tramp was from a well-respected family. Cape was a surgeon for christsakes.

"So to sum this all up for the other guests Jeff, you're the rich spoilt brat that disappointed his father. So now you're marrying his enemy's daughter to piss him off," Lisa added with her usual lack of tact.

Laughter came from somewhere. Carrie jumped up and left the room. Marie followed her. Jeff stood.

"Sit down!" Bill bellowed.

Kellie and Lisa excused themselves to the bathroom.

"You seen Cape since then?" Pete asked Bill.

"No, haven't even spoken to him." Bill stood. "Who's for a little something stronger?" He motioned to the wine.

"Yes," the men chorused.

"What about dessert?" Jeff asked.

"Fuck dessert! What about Carrie? I'm calling your father."

Bill turned and left to the living room. They all followed. Kellie and Lisa were already in there helping themselves to his scotch.

"What are you men drinking?" Bill offered. "Same as usual?"

They both nodded.

Jeff stood waiting to be offered.

≈≈≈≈

W hat the fuck is going on with you? You'd better fix up before Tex gets back!" Mo sat on the side of the bath rubbing Kellie back while she threw up into the toilet.

"I'm alright," Kellie said between heaves.

"Drink some water." Mo held the glass to her best friend's mouth. Kellie moved and sat on the floor, she drunk some more water then bowed her head in her hands.

"I'm alright, I just feel sick."

"I would say that you look high; it's either that or you're pregnant," said Mo.

"I'm not pregnant, I'm on," Kellie groaned.

Mo sat down beside her, her massive stomach one day overdue.

"Kel, I hope you're not doing anything stupid. Just think of Samuel, he's been with his grandmother for over a week-"

"Just back off Mo, everything's okay," Kellie cut in.

"Alright let me help you up."

Mo stood to help her

"Kellie listen, you know you can talk to me, help me to understand you. You're changing, you seem different."

"Mo!" she cried into her arms, her shoulder really.

Mo took her into her bedroom where they sat on her bed.

"What is it Kellie? What you taking?" Mo asked softly.

Kellie shook her head.

"Kellie to you it might sound stupid, but I wanna know what it is? How you take it? Why? If it's needles?" Mo looked her dead in the eye.

"It's cocaine, Mo."

Kellie couldn't believe how shit she sounded.

"So how do you take it?" Mo asked intrigued by her friend's sudden addiction.

"I smoke or sniff. I've never used needles," Kellie admitted.

"Oh, so that's alright then is it? You addicted?"

"How can I be addicted already?"

"You tell me, *I* don't know. But why Kellie, what does it do for you?" Mo's voice couldn't hide her anger.

"It makes me feel confident," Kellie said quickly.

"You were a very confident person before," Mo challenged her.

"You feel strong; ready for your day."

"So what you're saying is, you couldn't do shit with your days before you started drugs?"

"No. I don't know." Kellie began to cry again. Her shoulders heaved up and down. "Now I feel like if I don't have it, then I can't function, I can't go out without it!"

"How many times a day would you say you do it?"

"I don't know, it wears off, you know."

"No, I don't know, I don't *want* to know. Kellie you got to fix up. I don't like what you're doing and your reasons for doing it are shady. You're forgetting about your son. Kellie you're taking cocaine for fuck sake. You could have had a fit or overdose or something."

"Mo, I'm sorry," Kellie cried.

"No, I'm sorry *for* you," Mo said quietly.

They sat in silence for a further 10 minutes.

"So, you seen Sediko?" Mo only half changed the subject.

"Na, he hasn't even phoned me."

Kellie felt sick again.

"So where did he disappear to that night?" Mo asked.

"Look, I gotta go," Kellie said standing unsteadily.

"Where you going?" Mo asked. She didn't want to run her friend away she wanted to help her.

"I got some work to catch up on," she lied.

"You still doing the modelling?" Mo tried to make her stay. She didn't look as if she could make it down the road.

"Yeah, it's been exciting, it's a lot different than my other job. I done a few catalogue shoots, yeah, it's been good."

"I can't wait to see them. So who was that woman you done the first ones with?" Mo asked.

"This chick called Lisa Brooks, you know that one from the bra advert?"

"Oh her yeah, what's she like, she's like famous!" Mo squealed.

"She's alright." Kellie could hear her phone ringing quietly somewhere. "That my phone?" She looked around for her bag. Mo took it from beside the bed and gave it to her.

"What?" Kellie answered the private number call.

"Where you at babe?" Sediko's voice sang into her ear.

"I'm at Mo's."

"Can I come get you?"

"Whatever."

Kellie wanted him to come and get her now more than ever .

"I'll be there in 10 minutes."

"Alright," Kellie answered.

Mo was staring at her.

"Sorry Mo, I've got to go…. Thank you." Kellie stood to leave.

"Kellie, I was gonna tell you. Tex heard some talk about someone called Mia. Apparently she and Sediko are playing around."

"Really?" Kellie sighed.

"So they're saying."

"Well you tell Tex to tell that bitch if she wants my man come get him, tell her to come to my face and tell me they're playing."

"Alright calm down; I'm just letting you know what I heard," Mo defended.

"Whatever, I'll see you later. I'll talk to him." Kellie pulled on her jacket. "And thanks again Mo, I love you girl."

Kellie left and waited outside for Sediko.

Five minutes later, Sediko pulled up. He wound down the window; music and smoke flowed out. Kellie got in the car and looked at him from the corner of her eye. He was so handsome, so fine, so sexy. Such a bastard!

"I'm sorry baby," he whispered. "I brought you something." He grinned as they drove away.

"What is it?" Kellie asked.

"It's for our fifth month anniversary. Tonight, I'm taking you out." He drove fast, weaving in and out of traffic.

"Where are we going?" she asked. *Only five months?*

"What's with all the questions, wait and see." He looked at his watch. "Right, it's after seven, we gotta hurry up." He drove even faster, like a madman but with ease.

They reached his house.

"If we're going out, I'll need some things."

Kellie laughed happily. He had surprised her remembering the day that they had met. It was sweet.

"Don't worry about that. Come on."

They went inside where Sediko punched in his security code. Kellie walked through to the front room. There were gift-wrapped white boxes everywhere. A fat white rose on top of each.

"Sediko what's this?" She laughed, throwing her arms up in the air.

"They're all for you. For tonight." He sat in his chair. "Go on, they're all numbered."

He sat back to watch her.

Slowly, Kellie sat on the floor. He certainly knew how to romance a woman. The first box was small and light. She took of the rose and lifted the lid. It was a black lace g-string and bra set from Agent Provocateur. It was beautiful. He had taste and he had bought exactly the right size.

"Sediko this is real nice. I can't wait to slip it on for you."
She leaned in and kissed him. He pulled her to him. She hadn't seen him in a while, she had missed his kiss, but pulled away. She did love him but she loved surprises even more.

The second box was long, light. She took out a black Armani strapless dress. Kellie squealed. She had shown it to him a few weeks back while he shopped in Harrod's.

"Speed up; remember we got to go out."
She laid the dress back in the box.

Number 3: a light fitted black DKNY jacket; number 4: thigh high brown leather and suede Prada boots– spike heel, pointed toe. Kellie stared at them. She loved them. She pulled her black Dolcis off and slid one boot on. Sediko watched her like she was crazy as she hugged the other boot tight. She just loved the boots.

"You are a god," she joked. Kellie forgot about the numbers and just grabbed the closest box: the biggest bottle of Poison Christian Dior perfume. The next was a studded ice earring, chain and bracelet set. Kellie gasped as it sparkled up at her.

"You didn't buy me this?" Kellie couldn't believe it.

"Actually, no I didn't, it was what I call a trade, do you like it?"

"I love it." Kellie shut the big velvet box and put it close beside her.

"One more." Sediko smiled.

"What more could there be?" Kellie asked overwhelmed by the attention she had longed for. He took a box from behind the chair and opened it to reveal a sapphire and ruby ring. Kellie looked from it to him and back before she realised what was going on.

"Will you marry me one day?" he asked her.
Without waiting for an answer he slid it onto her finger. Kellie was speechless.

"Come on lets get showered and dressed, we gotta move."
Kellie looked into his eyes.

"Sediko, I love you."

Two hours later they were in his car driving to a secret destination. They eventually got to the dock where it looked as if a private party was being held.

"What's this, boat party?" Kellie asked looking up at the beautiful giant boat.

"Yep. Come." He led her up the entrance and gave a bouncer two tickets.

"Whose party is it?" Kellie was excited.

"Denzell Jones. Should be quite a few other celebs as well I hear. Come on babes, you look boom." He held her hand and went inside.

They pushed their way to one of the bars. Kellie looked around for famous faces. She spotted Ian White; Joan from Damage, he looked cute; Shelly La Rock– Kellie wanted to ask her why she hadn't recorded another album, she had quite liked her last. Sediko poured them both champagne. Kellie could have sworn she had just seen Roger Blackwood. She had, he was coming over. She did look boom. If Sediko hadn't been here she would have definitely accepted his number. He looked at her as he approached them.

"Yo what's up nigga?!" Sediko laughed to him spudding him, then patting his shoulder.

Oh, Kellie thought.

"Yeah Sediko, long time no see. What's going on?" Roger greeted him. His eyes again fell on Kellie. "And who's this fine young thing?"

"Yeah, slow down Woody, dis here's my wife." Sediko put his arm around Kellie's waist. "Kellie....Roger," Sediko introduced. Roger found her hand and kissed it.

"Nice to meet you, Kellie."

"Alright nigga we're off to look for some *real* celebrities," Sediko joked. Roger laughed and took a card from his pocket.

"Call me nigga we got to hook up."

"How do you know him?" Kellie asked as they moved away from the bar. She was surprised that he would know *anyone* in here.

"What's up Noni?" Sediko said to who looked like a very tall Naomi Campbell.

"Hiya Sediko! How are you?"

"Yeah, I'm cool. I know you're cool." Sediko hugged her. "This here is Mrs Sediko." He turned to Kellie.

"About time, it's nice to meet the woman who could tame him. You seen Roger?" she asked him.

"Yeah, he's around somewhere."

"Alright, got to mingle, bye." She kissed Sediko's cheek then Kellie's and rushed off.

Sediko led her outside to stand on the deck. With both his arms around her they looked out into the night. The boat had drifted out onto the river. There were a few people outside drinking, smoking, laughing or talking. Sediko pulled out a spliff and lit it. It did seem like the perfect time to ask him a few burning questions. Her heart patted rapidly in her chest.

"So, who is Mia?"

"I told you, my ex- innit," he replied with a sigh.

Kellie could see feel his mind seize up. He wasn't used to being questioned.

"Kellie listen, you still got a lot to learn about me. My motto is, the world is against me, so I make bare dough and get as high as I like. That's it." He passed her the spliff as she turned to face him.

"What? So is that an explanation for why the girl is going around telling people you two are back together?" Kellie asked.

"That girl is sick. We got a history. Put that together and you figure the rest out."

43

"What happened between you two? When did you break up?" Kellie asked. *This girl's name has been brought up too many times. Something must have happened between them. Why all the secrets*?

"Number one: Don't chat me to anyone; two: Don't come to me with fucking hearsay; three: Don't ever question me!" Sediko went inside, leaving her standing alone. A few people turned to stare.

Kellie looked up to the sky. She didn't believe Tex anyway. Whoever wanted Sediko she would let know that he was hers. Straight.

"Hello there." A handsome tall white suit. "Here alone?"

"No, actually I'm with someone." She wasn't in the mood for play.

"Can I buy you a drink until her return?"

"That's *his* return." She inhaled on her spliff and blew smoke into the black night air.

"You're a very sexy lady. Beautiful skin." His finger gently trailed her arm.

Kellie jerked away, looking at him with disgust. At that moment, Sediko came back outside.

"Who the fuck are you?" he demanded angrily.

"I'm sorry, I was just admiring. She did say she was with somebody."

"So then why you still here?" Sediko stood in front of Kellie pushing him out with his arm. The suit backed off quickly.

"Can I have this dance?" Sediko held out his hand to her. She paused for a second and looked into his eyes. She saw nothing. That's exactly what she knew about him in all of their months together. She took his hand slowly.

"Having doubts?"

"Never," she whispered. He was hers.

Four

FOR GOD SAKES Sally, call Kellie and have her fax you the instructions!" Bill shouted.

"Can't you just show me?" Sally was refusing to call Kellie for help, it just wasn't right.

"Sally, Kellie is your boss, you answer to her. She answers to me. I don't have time to sit and show you how to perform your administrative duties. Understand?"

Bill slammed his door on his way back to his office. He phoned Kellie.

"Hello, Kellie. Are you there, it's Bill?"

"Oh, hi Bill, I'm not due in today am I?" Kelly asked over a background of laughter.

"No, unfortunately you're not. Kellie, I can't cope with Sally. Sack her and get someone else," Bill instructed without a hint of humor.

"There's no point Bill, we already talked about this. It's only three days a week. Plus, I don't want to train someone from scratch; do you? Do you want some nosy office junior working for you selling your best work to rival companies. Or spilling coffee in your lap? Photocopying pages of your diary instead of work correspondence? Accuse me for exaggerating, but that's what it is these days. At least Sally knows the company; she's part of our team," Kellie tried to reassure him, overdoing it slightly.

There was certainly no love lost between she and Sally but at this stage she really couldn't face having to show someone new the ropes.

"Alright, why can't you come in three days a week instead of two. It would be a little more bearable."

"Sorry, I would never have the time. It was *your* idea to make me your main feature," Kellie reminded him. Bill had made her the new model for Laymend's Fashions, instead of Lisa, who had been livid.

"Okay then, I'll put you through to her."

Bill had missed Kellie since she'd cut down her hours at the office. It was understandable though, her new career was getting off to a busy start. Sally just didn't cut it. At first she had worked fine, but that was only because Kellie had worked ahead. Sally had double booked him, forgotten Marie's birthday, left his favourite suit in the dry cleaners where they then sold it; she'd messed up all his things and she could never understand his writing or his voice on audiotape.

Bill decided that he couldn't spend one more second in his office, with Sally coming in every minute asking him about one thing or another. He couldn't spend one more second at home, with Carrie and Marie both talking him to death, both wanting money for this or money for that. He dialled Lisa's number.

"Hello, Lisa's line."

"It's Bill."

He sat back in his chair.

"Is this a business or pleasure phone call?"

"Pleasure if you don't mind."

She wouldn't mind one bit. She had split with her husband and she was needing him more than ever now.

"You sound stressed Bill. Why don't you come over and I'll give you a long rub down. Full body," she lured him.

"I'll be there," Bill said before looking up to see Sally standing in his office.

Bill slammed down the phone.

"What are you doing! Were you eavesdropping?!" Bill shouted standing up.

"No, I- I just. I just came in, I was-" She stood rigid. She had never heard him speak to Kellie that way.

"You're lying! Barging in here like god almighty!" Bill was definitely stressed.

"I'm sorry Bill, I just came in here so I could ask you to sign some papers. I honestly didn't think you'd mind. I'm sorry Bill," Sally almost begged. She didn't want to blow this job. The other girls would tear her to shreds. If Kellie could do it so could she!

"Well I do mind, I mind very much! Just leave the papers and get out! Oh and I'm leaving. Cancel all my appointments in disguise of an excuse. Think you can do that?"

"Yes Bill, what shall I say?"

"Whatever, just don't tell them the truth and don't be too creative." He packed his briefcase.

"Yes Bill, I'll do that right away."

"And stop calling me Bill, you're my receptionist for christsake, what is this world coming to?"

He left her standing in his office, visibly upset.

Bill drove straight to Lisa's at a slow, steady pace. Patience was a virtue his father had told him. He pulled into her driveway and saw her bedroom curtain shuffle. She couldn't wait, she was desperate to see him.

"Well hello," she greeted him, followed with a kiss.

Marie used to be the one to show him a bit of love after a hard day's work. She took his hand and he followed her up to her bedroom.

"Before I give you that body massage, I've got something to tell you. Don't go getting upset, Bill." She sat him on her bed then continued. "Marie called me," she said casually.

"What?" He obviously hadn't heard right.

"Bill, Marie called me," she repeated confirming his fear.

"What? When? Why didn't you tell me? What did she say!?"

"If you give me a chance, I will tell." She crossed her legs in front of him. He stood up. Literally threw himself off the bed.

"Come on then! This isn't a joke, Lisa! This is my marriage!" He was panicking. He sat back down and waited for the worst to come from her lips.

"It was last week. She asked me if we were having an affair."

"Just like that? Come on, be specific."

"Just like that. I told her that she was being totally ridiculous, that you and I were just business associates and that I would never do such a thing… You see, it's okay."

She stood up to kiss him. He backed off and looked at her in disgust. What was she thinking at a time like this? She tried again to kiss him; he was forced to pushed her gently back.

"Did she believe you?" he asked her.

She nodded.

"How do you know?"

"Because I also told her that she should be ashamed for accusing a good man such as yourself."

"Why are you telling me this in bits! Lisa, what else was said? I'm very quickly losing my patience with you!" He was shouting but he wasn't bellowing. That's what he really wanted to do– frighten her; shake her bones a bit; force it out of her if he had to.

"Well, it was last week and she begged me not to tell you. She said sorry about five times. She said that she'd realised that she'd made a mistake. I forgave her."

Lisa was wishing now that she had told him afterwards.

"Then what?"

"That's it. She apologised, I forgave."

"Well that sneaky little bitch!" Bill couldn't believe this. How had she gotten the number?

"It's okay Bill, all that's matters is she's none the wiser. Come on. Let's not let this spoil our evening."

"I think I'll go," he said still standing.

"You're not, er, feeling guilty are you Bill?" She pulled at his tie.

He paused…."I've nothing to feel guilty of remember?"

He kissed her. He had missed her.

≈≈≈

Sediko stood firm.   "Just hurry up and take whatever it is you want," the man said bent in Sediko's headlock. Sediko held a 45 to his head with his free hand.

Eight men, all as naked as the day they were born, had weapons - mostly bats - pointing in Sediko and Path's direction. Three hundred thousand pounds worth of crack was at stake and Sediko wasn't leaving without it. The long twelve person table stood between them. Big scales, small scales, sieves, funnels, foil, bottles, needles, baggies, balloons, spoons, pipes, razor blades, about 3 kilos of skunk and bags and bags of fresh uncut crack.

"Don't rush me, I'm gonna take that shit just as soon as you tell your boys to throw down their toy weapons. What you gonna do if man shoots you in the balls? Bat me?" Sediko joked.

Path laughed loudly.

"You deaf?" Sediko pushed the gun deep into his skull.

"Drop your shit you lot," he instructed them. One by one, they dropped their bats. "You can fuck with us, we're just the middle men; Fixer will fuck you up!"

"WHAT?!" Sediko shouted.

BANG!

Sediko shot him in the foot. Blood squirted from his trainer.

"Ahhh my foot, man! Shit fuck!"

He cried real tears now. Sediko still held him tight around the neck as he squirmed around in pain.

At that moment, Sparrow blasted through the garage door in his shiny new Jeep. Everyone but he and Path ducked down.

"Shit, you took your time!" Sediko shouted to him.

He and Path had come in alone, not knowing what to expect. There could have been 50 men with machine guns but they had been lucky. Sediko had done his homework.

"Shit, I need a fucking doctor!" the captive moaned.

Sediko waved his gun towards the naked men. "Load that shit up. You! Load that shit up."

Slowly, they put bags onto the back seat. All were looking to one another, looking to see if anyone, but themselves was brave enough to play hero and try and stop him.

"Everything, equipment everything!"

Sediko waited for the last bag and balloon to be loaded.

"And you," Sediko released his hold on the naked leader, "give this to that pussy, Fixer." Sediko gun butted him with one almighty blow. He spun twice and passed out on the floor.

Sparrow backed out just as Sediko jumped into the passenger seat. They sped away from their biggest hit in a long while. They had never expected to get such a big turn out.

"Did you man see Two-Face gun butt that fool. Ahh!" Image laughed in the back.

"Open that shit up," Sediko growled.

"So where shall we go? That's too much to leave at Haydon's. Shit dis is hot, we can't leave that shit where anyone can get to it," said Sparrow as he drove past the barbershop.

"Don't worry about a thing baby, I got that shit covered. Drive to Wimbledon. You came true this time nigga." Sediko eyes lit up as Path slit one of the bags.

"Wimbledon? Why there?" Sparrow looked panicky.

Sediko ignored him, licked his finger and dipped and tasted, rubbing it onto his gums. They all awaited his verdict.

"Shit's cool."

They all smiled victorious smiles.

Sediko called Brenda.

"What's up sexy?"

"Two-Face, have you changed your numbers?" Brenda droned.

"Forget that. Where are you?" He hoped she was home, if not he would have to gain his own entry.

"Why? How come you-"

"Don't fuck about! Are you home?" This bitch only responded to rough treatment.

"Yes, calm down."

"Is mummy and daddy home?" he asked patronisingly.

"No."

Sediko cut the call.

Twenty-six minutes later they pulled up on Brenda's road.

"Drive to the door nigga," Sediko instructed. "Come Path, you niggas stay in the car."

He and Path pushed the drugs into two big, blue, Nike sports bags.

Sediko banged on the door. Brenda opened it. They walked straight through and up to her bedroom. They made two silent trips from the car bringing in all the equipment as well.

"So tell me now what's going on? What's in the bag?" she asked excitedly. She loved it when Sediko came to her house. It was the ultimate rule breaker.

"I'm gonna leave this here. Listen to me. Don't touch my shit. Do it and I'll leave you parentless. Understand?" He grabbed her arms tight. Her hands were sticky when it came to rice.

"Ok ok, what is it?"

"The white stuff."

Sediko watched her eyes light up. He threw her on to the bed.

"Don't smile with me, I ain't playing," he said angrily.

"So what, you gonna give me?" She leaned back on the bed.

"I'll come back later." He wanted a fast exit.

"No! If you leave, I'll flush it, all of it," she threatened. She jumped off the bed away from him.

"You got some horny bitch." Path laughed. "I'll meet you in the car. Ten minutes, that should be enough for you." He laughed again and left the room.

"Why you trying to get fucking smart? You think that's funny?! You think that's funny?! You know how much money that is?!" Sediko circled the bed. She jumped over to the other side.

"Like I would really do it?" She panicked as Sediko tried to corner her.

"So then why you trying to get me mad? And you wonder why you don't see me."

"Alright. Please, I won't touch it. But why can't you stay for ten minutes?" she begged. Sediko wanted to laugh. "It's just that I miss you sometimes." She edged closer to him.

"Alright, if I come back tonight and you've touched my shit, I'm warning you from now, Brenda, I will fucking batter you; no man would want you after that. You hear me?" Sediko walked out of her room.

"Wait Two-Face, can't you just stay a little longer? What time you coming back?" She followed him down the stairs.

"What's with all the fucking questions? Shit. Sounding like boy dem!" He got to her front door and turned around to kiss her. "I'll be back later."

She opened the door for him.

Sediko jumped back into the jeep. "Back to my yard now soldier," he said to Sparrow.

The drive back was silent. Sediko's mind went places he hadn't dreamed of before. He now had the money he needed to make *real* money. He had passed the first hurdle towards his dreams. Soon they could finally be brought to life.

As the jeep neared Sediko's house they could hear commotion.

"Shit, ain't that Kellie and Mia?" Sparrow shouted laughing loudly. Everyone leaned closer to see through the rain soaked window. As they pulled up outside his house they could see Kellie and Mia both stood soaked through with rain, arguing. Neither noticed them approach.

"Aha you got sprung!" Image laughed.

Sediko slowly got out the car as he pulled his hood ends.

"Stop calling his phone every fucking minute! He doesn't want you! You been running down my man for two years and he's still with me!"

"He told me that he loves me."

"And! That's your fucking business if you want to listen to his bullshit lies! He don't love you! Maybe he did once but what's now is now! He.. is.. with.. me!" Kellie shouted. Her arms rising and falling.

"You two are so together. Is that why he turns to me? He comes to me. You need to check yourself!" Mia screamed back at her.

Kellie towered over her. "Don't come up to me with all this shit Mia, from the time I saw you in the bar, heard your name called, I knew you were a little man thieving ho!"

"Who's a ho? Do you know me?" Mia's face was burning red. Still, neither had felt his presence.

"No bitch, I don't fucking know you! I don't want to know you, so come out of my life, step away from my relationship! Sediko will use girls like you to suck his dick and fuck when he's bored, so do *yourself* a favour!"

Kellie had reached the end of her rope. Sediko watched her in action, he hadn't seen her like this before. She very rarely shouted. Never lost control.

"BUT I LOVE HIM!" Mia screamed.

"Bitch is you deaf?!" Kellie stepped closer to her. Mia swung clumsily at Kellie, Kellie stepped back and kicked Mia hard into her stomach. Mia fell back towards Sediko who stepped swiftly out of her way. She staggered onto the jeep's bonnet, then fell to the floor.

Sediko turned to the car, the boys were in stitches, laughing hysterically while watching Mia, now crying hysterics, on the floor in front of the car.

"Come on get up you little Jessie! Look, you can fight for your man now! Long time I wanted to see you and fuck you up!" Kellie pulled her up by the collar; Mia screamed out. Kellie punched her twice in the face.

"Two-Face! Get her off me!"

"Don't talk to my fucking man! Don't bring yourself back to our yard. Don't even think about my man!" Kellie boxed her face again.

Sediko had seen enough. He held Kellie's arm, as she was about to send another punch.

"Alright ladies, break it up." He pulled Kellie towards his front door. "Yo nigga, drop Mia home?" Sediko called to Sparrow.

"Hell no." He reversed his jeep.

Sediko watched them all still laughing. He hid his amusement.

"Good bitch, walk! Walk in the rain! Go to your yard!" Kellie shouted to her.

"Bell me later, nigga!" Sparrow shouted to him. Sparrow was still laughing as he sped off.

"Sediko?" Mia almost begged.

"Go home, man," he told her.

Sediko felt no remorse.

"Fuck you!" she screamed.

The stupid bitch. Kellie picked up Mia's bag and threw it in her direction. It flew over and hit her head.

"Take your shit, you broke bitch!"

"Fuck you, my man will pick me up! Kirk will pick me up!" she replied, looking like a wet cat just dragged in.

Sediko walked past Kellie to his door. As he punched in his security code, he could feel Kellie's eyes burning into his nape.

"You got nothing to say? This bitch telling me shit about my man, about you. Sediko, you'd better find your speech!" She stood hands on

51

hips in front of him breathing heavy and livid.

Sediko sat down.

"You're right, I ain't got nothing to say. All you should care is that it's you standing here and not her," he told her.

"What?! She's telling me she's been seeing you for over a year. Me and you been together two years, so how does that work out?" she demanded. She wasn't letting go.

"She's a crack ho, I told you this long time. Even Path told you that shit."

"Don't fuck about with me Sediko! I've had enough of all this secretiveness bullshit! The girl said she's fucking you! So, what?" She was shouting now.

"Who you talking to?!" Sediko shouted twice as loud as her loudest voice. He saw her flinch. He stood up in front of her. She stepped back slightly and stood silent. "Who the *fuck* you talking to?!" he shouted again. She flinched again. He could see fear in her eyes for she very rarely saw him 'skies the limit' angry. He didn't want to scare her away. But now she stood eyes wide, he had never shouted at her that way in the whole two years.

Finally she spoke, in a low calm tone. "Alright, you know what, I'm gonna go home, leave you to think. It seems that you're caught up between two women. Don't know what it is you want right now. That's cool. I'll just go and let you choose. I'll be right at home waiting for you. You just let me know who you want. When you're ready of course, Mr big man, Two-Face," she said sarcastically with a grin. She went to move. He blocked her.

"You're just gonna go now, just like that?" His voice softened. She stood silent. "Well!?" he shouted when she didn't answer.

She jumped.

"Alright I'll stay, only if we can talk." Her shaking hands lifted, then dropped.

"Go then."

He sat down. She stood silent. Then slowly, Kellie sat down. Minutes later, she sniffed four lines as he watched.

"Oh yeah, I brought you a present," he said with a smile.

≈≈≈≈

Miss Launders, you're due in November. I'm sorry, isn't this good news? You say you've been together what, three years?" The black nurse sat opposite her across the table. Her friendly, familiar face awaited explanation.

"Er yeah, it's just…" Tears fell from Mia's eyes. She sat with her hands in her lap.

"Mia," the nurse started unsure whether to continue. She chose her words carefully. "If there is anything that you'd like to discuss, a

52

termination maybe, anything at all, it would be strictly confidential. I could call the doctor to have a word with you?"

"No no, it's not that, me and Kirk..." Mia couldn't even continue.

"Stop me if I'm saying too much, but Kirk I think can't have children, maybe you're worried about how he will take it? Bigger miracles have happened," the nurse said gently.

Mia bowed her head. "I wish that it was that simple. It goes so much deeper than that," Mia whispered. She did need someone to talk to, someone who wouldn't judge her. "I....well, I've been with someone else," she confessed, tears still rolling down her cheeks. She continued, "Kirk will know that the baby isn't his because it isn't." Mia looked up to see that the nurse's face of pity and apologies had turned into a face of 'Well, you made your bed.'

Mia cried even harder.

"Okay well, are you going to tell Kirk? Give him the choice? He seems like a good man, he'll stick by you."

"No, yes, well it's not like that. I do love Kirk, but um, I'm *in love* with another man...Sediko."

"Well." The nurse sat back.

She was judging her now. Poor Kirk, she must be thinking. What about poor her.

Mia stood up. "Thank you. Bye."

"Okay, well Mia you know I'm always here if you want to talk. Just book an appointment any time and I'll see you alright?"

Mia left the room and rejoined Charlene who was sitting in the small waiting room.

"Well?" she asked, standing to greet her with a big smile on her face. Mia tried to smile back and succeeded. The white walls spun around her.

"Congratulations girl!" Char hugged her tight. She was mixed race, tall, slim, and had short hair. They had been friends for about four years; she was Kirk's cousin.

"I don't want anyone knowing yet, not even Kirk. It's way too early." Mia wanted to throw up again.

They left Thomas Hospital and travelled back to Mia's Gypsy Hill flat in silence.

"So what you wanna do tonight girl? Celebration time, no alcohol though." Charlene wondered why Mia was quiet and looking so pissed off.

"Listen Charlene, I want you to go."

Mia stood up.

"What?"

"I forgot, I gotta meet someone."

"Who?"

"Why do you want to know?"

53

Mia walked towards the door. Charlene didn't follow.

"Who you meeting?" Charlene pushed.

"Just go! Go get out!" Mia shouted suddenly uncontrollably.

"Mia. What's a matter?" she said, slowly standing.

"Why you here? What, what you trying to get brownie points with Kirk? How much of my business you can chat!" Mia was confusing even herself.

"Mia?" Charlene looked at her in confusion.

Mia opened the front door. Charlene closed it shut.

"I'm just worried about ya innit. Two-Face fucked your life up once and now you're dealing with him again. I can't just watch ya let him fuck you up all over again. No, I can't," Charlene said high pitched and stern.

"I'm not messing with him. You know he's got a girl." The lie burned Mia's lips. She hadn't told Charlene that she had been seeing him irregularly behind Kirk's back.

"Good, so let him fuck '*er* up. And next time if you want to be alone you can come better than that. I'm off." She reopened the front door. "But Mia, remember how long it took ya to get on your feet and who helped ya to get there yeah," Charlene said before leaving.

"Who said I ever *did* get back on my feet?" Mia said to the closed door.

She phoned Sediko.

"I need to see you," Mia told him.

"I need to see you too, I need you to hold onto some things for me. The coast is clear, come to my yard."

"Alright. I'm on my way." She cut the call. How was he going to react when she told him? Would he be angry, happy? Only god knew with him.

"What's up with you? You been crying?" he asked, letting her in.

She followed him into his front room. Mia could see Kellie everywhere. Her slippers, two tea cups, slow jam CDs on the table and a massive cream rug that definitely wasn't Sediko's style.

"I got something to tell you." Mia was shaking.

"What?" Sediko asked looking serious.

"I'm pregnant," she blurted out.

She watched his eyes his body language and awaited his reaction. His eyes were burning into hers. Then suddenly, he scooped her up in his arms.

"Kellie, that's the best news I've heard all my fucking life!"

"Put me down. Put me down!" Mia shouted.

"What's wrong?" He dropped her, looking baffled.

"You, you just called me Kellie. I'm Mia, fucking Mia!"

"Did I? I'm sorry, must have been slip of the tongue. I'm happy. You're giving me my first born. Shit. I'm happy!"

54

"Really, really Sediko? Listen, I'll tell Kirk; I'll leave him. Just tell me to and I will, it will be me, you and our son."

"Don't be going over the top Mia, I can't leave Kellie."

"Why? Do you love her? Is big bad Two-Face pussy whipped?" Mia spat. *What did he want her to do? She hadn't gotten herself pregnant.* "You just said that you were happy."

"Don't try mess up a man's words. I said that I was happy you were giving me my first born. That's it, I'll look after mine, there ain't no more you and me like that any more. We done a t'ing, you got pregnant. If I was you I'd stick with Kirk."

"What? I thought that this was what you would have wanted."

"Come on, I didn't tell you that. You come in here telling me you're pregnant, how I know that baby is even mine?"

"Kirk can't have kids and I wouldn't do that to you. I would never," she reassured him.

"You wouldn't do it cos you couldn't! If I ever..." Sediko sat down to build a spliff.

"So what am I gonna say to Kirk?" She looked to him for answers.

"I don't give a fuck."

"What you gonna say to her?"

"Don't you worry about that, that's *my* business." He licked, then tore his Rizla paper.

"Kirk will kill me." Mia's problems were piling high and fast.

"Kirk ain't gonna kill any one. Anything happens to that baby, I'll kill you both! I'm serious." He rolled a small roach.

"Why can't it just be me and you, like it was before. Remember? I will have your real son, I won't be pushing jacket onto you!"

"Keep your big fucking nose out of Kellie's business! What the fuck is wrong with you?" He crumbled tobacco into the Rizla placing the roach at one end.

"I want me and you."

"Yeah, we see each other already, what more do you want?!"

"That's not enough, I see you once a month if I'm lucky. It's something about you, about our past. I would have never taken second best before. I was number one. Sediko you must feel me, you're risking you and Kellie for us."

"I ain't risking nothing. Kellie would beat you down, again. Not leave me, you dick head." He laughed lightly now, breaking herb up in his palm.

Everything was a big joke to him. A life, their life, was growing inside of her and he didn't care.

"Do you care about me?" She had to hear him say so.

"Stop running man down, you can't have me. Simple." He crumbled the herb evenly over the tobacco.

"Alright, but do you care for me?"

"I don't think you'll like my answer. You can't have me, like I said, so what does it matter?"

"But look how tight we used to be. I know that you loved me. Even if you never said it, I knew."

"That was then. Read my lips. You can't-"

"I can't have you but I can have your child?"

"You finally got it." He rolled the spliff and searched for a light.

Five

SAMUEL, WANNA COME talk to mummy?" Kellie held her arms out to her son. He shook his head and stayed put.   "I just about made his gran agree to let him come and stay," Kellie told Mo.

Mo stepped back to give Kellie and her son space.

"You should never have let him go," Mo said, walking out of the room.

Kellie stood silent. Samuel looked much like her older brother Kerion. He'd been in America since she was 12 years old. She sat on the chair. "Want to sit?" She patted the empty space beside her. Samuel stood unsure. He had a right to be so distant. In the past year Kellie had neglected him; he had been living with his grandmother. She had left him there for the weekend; the weekend turned into a week, then a month, then six. She blinked and it had turned into a year. And in all those months she had hardly seen him.

"Mummy's sorry."

Kellie watched her distant son. Not even a grin, a glimmer of love. He hadn't missed her.

"Have you seen Buffie?" Kellie asked. He cracked a smile and nodded.

"Want to go home," he said quietly without looking her in the eye. At three, he had grown so much. He was taller and his speech was much better.

"Home with mummy?" Kellie's heart was breaking slowly.

Samuel shook his head no.

"Can mummy come and see you next week?" She wiped her eyes and tried to smile.

He nodded.

"Okay, lets go see Andy, you can play for a bit then I'll take you home to Gran."

Kellie stood, took his hand, then kissed and hugged her boy, her only son.

"Feeling guilty?" Mo had crept up on her.

"Go on Sam, go play." He ran out of the room to Andy who was waiting patiently for his best friend to come back.

Kellie sat herself down hard on the chair. Somewhere along the line she had lost her family values. Her mother and father had returned to Jamaica six years ago, her brother had his own life in America, and now her son had found a new family. Had she put work and Sediko in their place? Had she forgotten her priorities?

With Samuel sitting up front with his seat belt tightly strapped, Kellie drove back to Sutton. He sat silent and confused. A year had gone by and he had hardly seen mummy, then suddenly mummy wanted to shower him with gifts. Kellie needed Sediko, needed him to reassure her that she wasn't a bad mother but a headstrong career woman. Her phone rang.

"I thought you were meeting me? I'm waiting."

"Oh shit, yes sorry. I'm a bit tied up at the moment, give me about an hour."

Kellie had forgotten, totally. She indicated left onto Samuel's road, not hers.

"Alright, can't wait to see you."

"Listen, I'm gonna drop it, then go," Kellie said, grinning at this new found attention.

"You can't spare five minutes? I'm spending my P's on you."

"No. Sediko's expecting me back."

She pulled up into the driveway.

"Alright safe, I'll see you soon."

All Kellie could think about right now was Samuel and how she had failed as a mother.

Samuel's gran, Carol, came out to the car and opened Samuel's door. He smiled widely when he saw her– a welcome he had denied his mother. Samuel turned to her. "Bye Kellie," he said quickly, then ran into the arms of his awaiting grandmother. As the door slammed shut, Kellie quickly backed out and waved before speeding off.

As soon as she got to the next red light she dipped her finger into her car stash. She had converted what had been an ashtray, into a crack tray. Instantly, she felt better. She would get her son back. Crying did no good.

Kellie tried to concentrate on Shawn as she quickly drove towards Battersea. Shawn. She just couldn't work him out. He liked her and made it obvious, but kept his distance. He was her first, best and only customer.

Kellie reached Battersea; Falcon Road to Haydon's Barbershop.

"What's up you?" she greeted Jayson half smiling as she looked at herself in the many mirrors. Her hair fell on her shoulders and she wore a beige pants suit with only a bra beneath her jacket.

"Your shit's upstairs." Jayson kept his eyes on the nappy head he was cutting.

"Path up there?" she asked stopping at the foot of the stairs.

"Na. Sediko and some girl," he said still cutting.

Anyhow! Anyhow, he had that bitch Mia up in there! Mia would leave via the window!

Slowly, Kellie walked upstairs and opened the door. She saw Sediko standing with a pretty white girl. Her strawberry blonde hair fell near her bum. Kellie grabbed the bag that she had left earlier, off the table. Quietly she took out the small handgun that Sediko had given her. The two stood in deep conversation, their backs to her. In the background a small stereo played the radio. Kellie could see the flirting. She pointed the gun at them.

"Who the fuck are you?" she asked her calmly. Even she was shocked by her sudden madness.

"Ohmygod!" The girl jumped into Sediko's arms as they both turned to her.

Sediko was driving her crazy. She was constantly trying to keep a lead on him and keep the females away. Women were constantly ringing his phones, especially Mia. This one was pretty. Slim, blonde and pretty.

"Kellie! What the fuck are you on?! Are you high?" he shouted coming towards her. He quickly and easily grabbed the gun from her hand. "Are you high?"

"No. Maybe a bit." She had needed a pick-me-up after the day she'd been having.

"Didn't I fucking tell you to slow down on that shit?!"

"Gimme my shit, so I can slap it across that bitch's face," Kellie spat towards her.
The girl backed up to the window, looking scared.

"You want this across your face, you stupid bitch!" Sediko was angry. "You think this is a fucking toy? I told you to leave that shit at home. You can't just wave that shit around in man's face! And what did I tell you about leaving your shit here? It's hot I told you!"

"Oh fuck you," Kellie sighed. He wasn't going to tell her who the blonde was, he never did.

"No fuck you, you mad bitch. Here, go do your shit elsewhere." He gave her back the gun. "I'll see you later at my yard. Make sure, yeah," he ordered.
Kellie nodded.

"Come here," he ordered again.
Kellie went to him. He kissed her hard and passionately, then went back to his conversation with the blonde.

Kellie left the room with her emotions in tangles. Was she angry with him for flirting with another woman? Was she angry at the way that he regularly shouted at her now? Or was she happy that he had showed her affection in front of the blonde? Happy that they could argue, then make up, quick enough for it not to hurt.

She drove straight to Brockwell Park, Brixton.

Kellie parked, then walked to the spot with her small package. He stood waiting. Dark, tall and handsome in a Kangol hat and a black linen shirt, he had all the qualities that Sediko had when they had first met two years ago.

"Hello. You look nice," he complimented. It was their second meeting.

"Why thank you." Kellie nodded and laughed.

"I'm serious." He looked at her nervously. "I know that you got your man, but I like you. I just thought that you should know," he almost whispered.

"Well, okay. Like you said I have a man and I told you on the phone that I couldn't stop."

"Does he know where you are?"

"Why?" Kellie pretended to look annoyed.

"Just wanted to know if he knew who you were meeting."

"Why? He gave you my number didn't he?"

"Yeah. Alright. Just keep our meetings between us yeah, you know how he stays."

"Yeah, don't I?"

"So, can I invite you out for a drink?"

"Hello? You listening? I can't stop; you want this or not?" She lifted the package to his attention.

"I want you, but I'll make do with this." He smiled, dipped into his pockets and took out a brown snakeskin wallet. "There's a little extra in there, buy yourself something nice, from me."

"No thank you." Kellie took the money and began to count out the right amount. When she looked up with the extra £200, he was gone, walking away from her down the pathway. Kellie watched him go.

Did Sediko really give him her number? He'd never mentioned him. Why didn't he want Sediko to know about their meetings? Shawn had given her his number once; it was locked off after a week. Every number he had given her since then was disconnected in days. He contacted her if he wanted anything, but always with a new number. Shawn was right about one thing though, telling Sediko of every single meeting would only get him into a fit of jealous rage. She'd keep it on the low. As long as she was making money, who cared?

The next day, Kellie drove to work to check on Sally.

"Here to check on me are you? Still?" Sally sighed, looking up from her desk.

"No, not at all," Kellie fibbed and strode straight past her.

Bill sat turned toward the window. Kellie shut the door behind her. "Morning Bill."

"Hi," he replied smiling, then turned to face her.

"Just came to check on the two of you." Kellie sat across from him.

"Well, we've got a understanding. It took time; now it's like this– Sally?" He buzzed through to her with an 'up to something' look on his face. He sat back and waited. There were two knocks on the door. Bill waited twenty seconds before saying,"Come in Sally."

She came in slowly, stood by his desk and avoided eye contact with Kellie.

"Yes, sir?" she murmured.

"Kindly show Kellie her mini portfolio."

"Yes, sir. Don't you have that, sir."

"Oh yes, you're right, I see. That's all then, off you go." He spoke to her as he did his daughter. Sally left quickly.

"Nothing but respect."

"What's all this 'sir' business?" Kellie began to laugh, but instead she rushed to the bathroom. She was going to be sick.

Two weeks into May, Kellie was throwing up every morning. She laid in bed staring up to the ceiling. She hadn't seen Sediko in over a week. She was used to that now. He never told her where he was so she had just stopped asking. He would probably call her just now. He would always call at the same sort of time on the same sort of days.

Twenty minutes later her phone rang. She knew it would be him. Full of stories, apologies and gifts.

"What's up?" he breathed.

Kellie stayed silent.

He continued. "I'm sorry, I been tied up babe, you know what man has to deal with. But listen, I got a surprise for you," he mimicked her thoughts.

Sediko would always buy her gifts. Jewellry mostly. Her car had been the biggest bribe for her silence. She recalled the conversation:

"Don't ask me any questions, I just brought you a car."

"Really?" she'd said flatly.

"Don't be like that babes, I said that I was sorry didn't I?"

"It's all good. What's the surprise *this* time?"

"Well, the mans dem are taking the wifeys out."

"What? That's not a surprise. I ain't going," Kellie said adamant.

"What? Boy, if you don't wanna come— safe, but don't screw when I take someone else," Sediko threatened and she knew that he would.

"Whatever. When is it, tonight?" There was no way she was letting him take another girl.

"Yeah, you down?"

"Alright, what time?" Kellie asked. *Was that a woman's laughter?*

"I'll bell you later." He cut the call.

Kellie threw the phone across the room. He had her on emotional lock down. He was telling her that he would take other girls out and it was making her cling to him more when it should have been making her run a mile. Whatever he did or said was alright with her. He would fire questions at her but wouldn't be questioned. How had she made it that way? How had she learned to accept it? She looked at the half-smoked Charlie spliff between her fingers then ran to the bathroom and threw up in the sink.

By 6 pm Kellie had every designer dress that she owned spread out across her bed. If she was going out tonight with the 'wifeys' as Sediko called them, she would have to look extra glamourous. They all had a habit of watching her, studying her.

Kellie stepped into her bath and leaned back. Sediko still hadn't called. Lately she had just been feeling so tired, and she had been feeling sick all the time. She had considered the possibility of being pregnant but the pill was her morning ritual. It was probably food poisoning taking its course. She didn't have time to go to the doctor. She had two careers, a fight for her son and Sediko. That was enough.

Kellie looked up as she heard a noise coming from downstairs. She sat up and listened. She heard it again. She got out the bath, took her towel off the heater and tiptoed, dripping wet and slightly nervous, into her bedroom. Slowly and quietly she opened her knickers drawer for the gun that Sediko had given her. She fingered beneath the clothes. It was gone. She stood up as the noise moved upstairs. Soft creeping along the hallway. Kellie's heart began to really beat now. She opened her wardrobe and took out Sediko's metal bat. Shaking, she tiptoed towards her door and stood with her back to the wall. She waited. She could hear breathing on the other side. Holding tight to the bat, she held it up in the air, baseball style.

A figure stepped into the room. Kellie stepped out and swung the bat as hard as she could.

"What the fuck!" Sediko shouted ducking down quickly. Kellie swung a full 360 degrees with the force of the blow and fell clumsily onto her bottom.

Sediko began to laugh.

"It's not fucking funny! You frightened the shit out of me!" Her towel dropped to the floor.

"A burglar would be happy to be knocked out if your body is the last thing he's gonna see," Sediko joked sitting on her bed. "Come here babe, come." He held out his arms for her to come. She sat astride him.

"What's up babe? You look sick."

"Gee, thanks. I'm alright." Kellie looked hurt for a few seconds.

"No for real, what's wrong?" He pulled the clip from her hair and watched it fall to her shoulders.

"Well, I have been feeling kinda sick," Kellie admitted.

"Feeling sick, being sick or both?"

"Who are you, my doctor? I said I'm alright." Kellie kissed his lips then stood and went back to the bath.

Her followed her and sat on the closed toilet seat, watching her.

"So, where and who?" Kellie asked pinning back her hair.

"Bones with Keisha, Path with Mandy I think and Sparrow and Image with their bitches."

"I thought you said wifeys. Them man are gonna bring some scabby hoes. I can't be seen with them girls, shit," Kellie half joked.

"Boy, Image and Sparrow don't know the meaning of wifey trust me. Don't worry, I told them about them broke bitches. You don't need to worry about them girls anyway, you're coming with me, innit?"

"Right, so you're not gonna leave me with them?"

"Yeah but-"

"Exactly. I've never seen one of them with a decent woman."

Kellie shook her head. She wasn't looking forward to her surprise. Sediko used her sponge to wash her back.

By 10 pm they were on their way to Haydon's to meet everyone. Kellie looked sexy in a Gucci Victorian style shirt with ruffles up to her neck and a similar style thin denim skirt. It was her favourite buy for the moment. She had been making a little extra cash and was shopping uncontrollably.

Her phone rang as Sediko passed the speed limit as usual. 'Shawna' flashed up on her phone. He didn't usually ring her at these times times. She answered shakily.

"What's up girl?" Kellie felt more than stupid.

"I guess you're telling me to call back later?"

"Yeah, Monday's cool."

Kellie shifted in her seat and cut the call quickly.

"Who was that?" Sediko asked turning left onto a no left turn road.

"Shawna."

"Who's that?"

"My friend, I do have them you know." She kissed her teeth pretending to be annoyed.

"Is that the one you been selling to?"

"It's not really selling, she just smokes a lot that all. What's all the questions?" Kellie sighed. She couldn't wait to get to Haydon's.

"Why, what you hiding?"

"When you tell me to stop questioning you, does that mean that *you've* got something to hide?" Kellie tried to catch him out.

"Most of the time." He grinned to her. "No really, I just wanna know who's putting they money in my woman's hands, that's all."

He honked his horn to a green Punto that swerved in front of him. Sediko leaned out of his window.

"WHAT THE FUCK YOU DOING! GET OFF THE FUCKING ROAD PUSSY!" Sediko cursed, trying to pass the swerving car.

"Sediko, slow down!" Kellie panicked. She could almost see an accident.

Sediko pressed his horn in a constant bid to drive up beside him.

"You fucking idiot! Scratch my shit and see if I don't drag you out of yours!"

Both cars kept racing head to head, going up to 70 mph. Sediko cursed some more as they came to a single lane. Traffic approached from the other direction. Finally, the Punto slowed down to second place.

"Was that really worth it?"

"Yeah, that was fucking great! You see my shit tear? I'll knock any pussy off the road!" He laughed.

Eventually they pulled up outside Haydon's behind a silver X5 BMW.

"Come, we'll talk later about Shawna."

"Can we talk later about Mia?"

Sediko got out of the car.

In the Space Cruiser, Kellie took a seat at the back beside the window. Four women - two familiar - sat in the back with her.

"Hiya Kel," Keisha sang. Kel? Who was she to call her Kel? Annoying bitch number one, Bones's long time woman, the queen of irritating– Keisha. She was 28, but acted more like 18.

"Hi. What you been up to? Haven't seen you in a few months," Kellie greeted with a manufactured smile.

"I been alright, you know, working and stuff."

More like 'and stuff', she ain't never had a job.

"I saw you in *Now* magazine with that what's her name, Lisa Brooks." Keisha smiled a chubby smile. She was a least a size eighteen. It would suit her, if she would just accept her size and stop buying size twelves to squeeze herself into.

"Yeah, I saw that one! Was that you?" a slim Asian girl asked from the front.

"Look, them man ain't got no manners. Keisha pointed to the Asian girl with long thin hair. "That's Sophia, Kellie, she's with Image." She then pointed to a skinny light skinned girl. "That's Melinda, Sparrow's new t'ing."

"His new t'ing? I'm his personal," Melinda said.

She looked and spoke like a Jesse. These were the kind of chicks that she hated to be around. Melinda looked cheap in a market jean skirt suit. At least it was meant to be a suit, and she had on more make up than a black Barbie doll.

"And that's Mandy. She's back with Path, again. I think you two met, last year."

Kellie leaned forward to see Sediko and the rest of the boys laughing and catching a joke and here she was stuck at the back with a load of dumb bitches. She needed a spliff.

"I saw you in one next magazine with that Lisa, you were in a restaurant up London. It looked as if you didn't know the camera was there. All up in your morning when you were eating," Mandy said from beside her.

"Na I didn't know. When I saw the picture it spooked me out a bit, but it was Lisa they were taking the pictures of."

"So what's that woman like? She looks like one of those J-Lo type bitches, wants every shit up in her star dressing room for them and their entourage." Mandy looked relieved to have some real conversation.

"She's alright, I seen much worse. Monday my pictures will be all over the place– in bikini wear." Kellie accidentally began to relax as she fell into conversation with Mandy while on their way to a secret destination.

"For real?" Melinda spun towards Kellie, her head tilted to the side waiting for an answer.

"Who are you modelling for?" Mandy asked interested and truly glad to have a real woman to talk to. They both ignored Melinda.

"Well I work for Laymend's Fashion Company, you know that range?"

"Yeah, I got the catalogue," Mandy said surprised.

"For real? You work for Laymend's?" Melinda chimed in. Kellie couldn't take her for much longer.

"I can't wait to see it." Mandy smiled. Kellie smiled in return. She liked her. She was pretty with short-cropped hair. Her skin was dark and she was slightly podgy. Kellie knew that they had at least one thing in common– their taste in clothes. Kellie owned the same dress that she was wearing.

"So what did Two-Face say about you doing bikini modelling?" Sophia asked. All women leaned in to hear her answer.

"I haven't told him yet."

"Oh my god, you're good star; Image would kill me," she said laughing, covering her mouth.

This girl was beyond dumb. Kellie wouldn't even try to have an intellectual conversation with her. It would only cause mass destruction in her small head.

"So what you gonna do Kellie?" Keisha probed.

"What do you mean 'what am I gonna do'? It's *my* body, he knows that I model."

"Well I couldn't do it, obviously. I'm about 6 sizes too big. But I would never do it anyway. Bones would screw every man looking at my body." Keisha gave Melinda obvious eye contact.

Kellie looked straight at her. "Keisha, what you're wearing now is almost less than the bikini. You're wearing a mini skirt and a tiny belly top that ain't holding you in."

Mandy stifled a laugh.

"It's true," Mandy defended. "Not about you Keisha, but why should she tell him, since when did he become her dad? Come on girls, you're letting man run your life?"

"So anyway, Mandy, you know where we're going?" Kellie asked.

Melinda laughed, 5 seconds late. "Oh, I get what you just said."

Finally, they parked up.

"Come on ladies!" Path called. They all got out and stood by the car.

"Where are we?"

"Edgware Road. People, welcome to my new venue!" Sediko shouted. Kellie looked around the deserted area baffled.

"Sediko, I know you didn't make me get all dressed up for this shit." Kellie looked to him.

"Exactly. Path?" Mandy looked to her man.

"I brought you here to show you what I've been trying to do. All those times when I've been away knocking a hustle, I've been saving up for one thing. This is where mans dream starts. My new club. Where all your new jobs will be." He grinned.

"Whose job?" Kellie frowned. She was shocked. A club. "Sediko, when did you decide this? Have you bought the property?"

"Yep, it's all mine babe." He smiled proudly.

"Oh Sediko, congratulations then! Mr bar manager." Kellie hugged him. She could get to like the idea.

"Will I get a job Two-Face?" Melinda asked excitedly.

"Yeah Melinda, we got special jobs for girls like you."
She squealed. Sparrow laughed behind her back.

"So you gonna take me inside?" Kellie asked Sediko.

"All in good time. We're going out somewhere else to celebrate. Come." Sediko looked up to the derelict building, then over to Kellie, as if they were both the loves of his life.

Kellie walked away from the group to light up a Charlie spliff. Mandy wandered over to her.

"What's that smell?" Mandy asked.
Here we go. She realised now that it wasn't everyone's thing. It wasn't her thing, at one point.

"It's a Charlie spliff."

"It looks like history repeating itself."
Mandy went back to the car and got in while everyone else stood outside and chatted. Kellie put out the spliff and joined Mandy.

"What did you mean by that, 'history repeating itself'?"

"Addicted yet?"

"Why don't you just mind your own business. I was beginning to like you." Kellie kissed her teeth. This was going to be a long night.

"I don't wanna fall out. But facts are facts. It's just-"

"Oh don't hold back, just say what it is you wanna say. You will eventually anyway."
Kellie was intrigued, what connections did she have with this nosy stranger.

"You know I used to go out with Path a few years back. Way before you and Sediko."

"Please, just get to the point. Hurry before someone comes," Kellie urged.

"I will if you give me a chance. Two-Face was with a girl called Mia, and before I continue, I heard about you two's ruckus outside Two-Face's flat-" Mandy stopped as Keisha and Melinda climbed in.

"Later," Mandy mouthed.
Kellie couldn't wait. This Mia. That bitch. Why was she pushing up

herself onto Sediko? She would soon find out.

They all ended up in a bar called Thongs & Things in East London. As soon as they got in, Kellie excused herself to the toilet. Mandy followed.

"Carry on." Kellie tried not to sound too desperate.

"Right. They were together from when they were in school. Everyone knew about Two-Face and Mia, she loved him nuff. They were both into that shit, what you're doing. Mia started selling it for him and ended up on it herself. She lost her looks, lost weight and lost her flat. When Two-Face saw that she was going down hill he kicked her straight the to the curb. Mia though, wouldn't let him go. But Two-Face didn't want her because she was hooked on drugs and hooked on him. He used her for as long as he could— sending her on errands, he even made her bring back drugs from Jamaica a few times. Then when she was all used up, he was gone. Then she met Kirk. Kirk fixed her up and got her off the poison. She was all good for about 6 months, but then she left Kirk and went back to Two-Face. Boom. She was hooked again, this time she looked like a skeleton, all marga. I remember once when I was with Sediko and Path in Whyno's, my girl came in there and begged for him to take her back. Literally begged. Once again Two-Face dissed her, in front of every one. I saw her quite a few times after that. She was fucked. I heard Kirk took her back though, fixed her up yet again. He forgave her and now they're still together."

"Who's still together? Kirk and Mia or Sediko and Mia?" Kellie could feel her eyes stinging.

"I'm sorry to say Kellie, but both."

So this Mia had meant something to him once. But it was obvious to her now that Sediko didn't want Mia. How many times did he have to dis' her?

"It's about time I pay that bitch a home visit," Kellie said walking off, leaving Mandy wondering if she had said too much.

Six

YES MR MARSHALL, everything will be within the deadline." "It fucking better be. Don't let there be any more surprises, what am I paying you for? Shit!"

Sediko ended the call and kissed the tall dark skinned woman with big breasts sprawled naked beside him on her bed. He couldn't remember her name. He had met her 45 minutes earlier and she had practically begged him to come up to her flat just minutes from where they had met.

"Listen, I gotta jet," he said rolling out of her bed after he had fucked her senseless.

"Alright. Will you call me?" She sat up and wrapped the sheet around her body, a smile painted on her face.

"Yeah." He didn't have her number and he didn't want it.

"When?" She sounded hopeful.

"As soon as I get home." He jumped into his trousers; he couldn't wait to get out.

She got up from the bed and stood in front of him letting her sheet drop to the floor. She tried to seduce him into staying. Her arms went up around his neck.

"Listen," he avoided her name, "I gotta go." He shrugged her off. The sex hadn't been that good. And she had begged him not to use a condom, of course he had, those were the ones that wanted to trap you or share their disease.

"How about coming back later?" She rubbed her hands up and down his chest.

"Yeah, good idea." He had no intentions of ever seeing her again.

"Good, about eight then?" She kissed his neck.

He buttoned the last button on his shirt.

"Don't fuck with me though Two-Face, if you're not coming just say so."

This bitch was getting serious. He pulled on his Nike trainers. "I'll be back," he said, slipping through the door. He ran down the stairs and went to his car, he could hear her calling after him. Quickly, he turned on his engine.

"Wait, wait. You haven't got my number!" she called.

Sediko waited for her to get close to the car and then sped off, laughing.

First Sediko drove home to shower and change his clothes. He had business to see to, people to check on. Had to make sure things were running smoothly. Then, feeling fresh and ready to handle business, he drove west towards Ladbroke Grove. Destination: Smalls's house.

Sediko jumped out of his car and went to what was left of the crumbling block. He got in the lift and pressed 20. He didn't trust this lift, but he didn't trust his legs to walk up twenty flights of stairs. He went up and got out, slowly walking along until he came to number 220. He banged on the door police style. Shuffling. He stood to the side, out of view from the peephole.

"OPEN UP!" he shouted, banging again.

"Is that you Two-Face?" Smalls's voice, shaky and hopeful.

"Yeah man." Sediko laughed. Smalls opened the door on the chain and peeped out.

"Double checking," he said closing, then opening the door. "Why didn't you phone first?" He backed up so Sediko could enter. "If you would have called me I coulda had things ready." He staggered behind Sediko into his shit hole.

"Open some fucking windows man." Sediko kicked past rubbish and went into the messy front room.

"Yeah yeah, I was just about to." He darted to the window, pulled at his dusty curtains then struggled to open the window. "Yeah, like I was saying, I woulda set things up." He gave up with the window and stood with his hands in his pocket.

He was 26 years old, well over 6 foot and skinny. Scars plagued his whole body, as trouble was his first name. Nervously he began to clear rubbish, stuffing cans and Chinese containers into an already full black bag. The small flat was dirty, dark and it had a damp stale smell.

"So…" Sediko started, casually searching the corners of drawers and looking around, "how's business boy?"

"Yeah yeah, everything's cool." Smalls loaded more shit into other full bags.

"How much you got for me then?"

"Well, I didn't get rid of as much as I thought, so I haven't got all of it. Duncan owes me 150." He stopped cleaning. He looked visibly tired now.

"I know Duncan?" Sediko kept looking. He went to the kitchen adjoined to the front room. Smalls watched him closely.

"No."

"So what you telling me that shit for, I don't do business with him." Sediko had decided to toy with him. He looked at his watch: 6:30 pm, plenty of time.

"Yeah, I'm just saying."

"So once again, how much you got for me? I'm not here for a fucking social visit." Sediko knew where the money was– in his lungs.

"I didn't get rid of that much, plus minus the £150-"

"What's all this plus minus bull shit! If you haven't got the money then where's the merchandise? I'm looking but I can't seem to find it." Sediko stopped looking and looked at him.

"I think about £200." Smalls began to sweat.

"Aha, you're taking man for a fool then?" Sediko laughed then became deadly serious. He wasn't even angry, he'd known for years that Smalls couldn't be trusted. Smalls wasn't sly, he was stupid.

"No. No. I'm ill d'ough, that's why I haven't been out there, you get me? I'm suffering."

"Well alright my boy, I'll allow you this time. I might have a job for you soon. You can work off what you owe me. Keep that £200."

Sediko used him without him even knowing. Smalls almost smiled.

"What, what about the money?"

"Like I said, you'll pay me later." Sediko slapped him hard but playfully on the cheek. "So don't forget, when I call you, you come running."

"Ah thanks Two-Face. You can trust me, I know I'm always fucking up. Whatever it is, I'll make it up to you." Smalls tried to hide his big grin. He looked as if he began to relax.

"So what's wrong with you anyway? What illness you got?"

"Well, it's not really an illness." He began to fidget.

"What fucking illness?"

"Yeah well, it's a.. it's a STD, innit."

"What? Come again." Sediko laughed aloud.

"Some crab shit."

"Crab what? What's that? I don't even want to know. I'm out, don't want any of your creepy crawlies. Erg you little dirty dosage boy!" Sediko laughed, moving for an exit.

Any woman that gave him disease in *any* shape or form, he would kill.

Seven minutes and a shaky lift later, Sediko was on his way to Sara's. Forty-five minutes later, he parked across the road from her house and phoned her.

"You busy?"

"Not that busy. Give me five minutes." She cut the call.

Sediko sat waiting as usual.

In the car, Mia and her shocking news played on Sediko's mind. Kellie would be pissed but he would talk her around. He was happy. He would be a dad. He hoped for a boy, a son.

Sara's door opened. A nigga came out– shirt open, zipping his pants and trying to push his foot into his shoe. Sediko watched him go, then went in through the open front door and into her bedroom where she lay naked on her bed.

"What's up Negro?" she said. A spliff hung from her lips.

"Shit's cool." He walked around the bed. She wasn't spectacularly pretty, but she had the best body he'd seen in a long while. Everything perfect. Full breasts, long legs, big firm ass and small cute feet.

"Come, sit then." She patted the big empty space beside her.

"Come on now, you know man ain't messing with you; business right now." His eyes were glued to her body.

"Why you always fronting like you don't want me? You see me see you watching me." She had wanted him from the first time she had laid eyes on him.

"You just *had* a session."

"Maybe you owe me because you interrupted me."

"Man like me take pride in their body. Don't want any uninvited guests. Get my drift?" Sediko grinned, thinking of Smalls.

"Just because I enjoy sex that don't mean I'm a Jessie with disease you know."

She got up and went to her wardrobe. Sediko watched her. She took out a box.

"So why can't you enjoy sex with one man?"

"I like variety, what can I say. Like you." She sat back on the bed.

"I'm a man, innit." He laughed. He had always liked her, looked at her in 'an on the side' sort of way.

"I'm sure a man like you would satisfy *all* my urges."

"Come on." Sediko chuckled.

"Okay I'll stop, let's do business." She could still feel Sediko's stare. Sediko felt safe enough to sit on the bed while Sara emptied the box.

"Shit. What did I tell you about counting that shit!" He looked at the hundreds of notes spilled on the bed, crumpled and uncounted.

"How about well done, you gave me more E's than usual and I still got rid of all of it," she moaned.

"That's because you're probably buying the majority of them for yourself. I know bitches like you love to fuck on E's."

"So?"

"Alright. Well fucking done. Now come help me wrap this shit into one hundreds."

"Actually, I'm going into the bath." She jumped off the bed.

"I'm off then, I'll deal with this at home. I'll send someone tonight with the next load." He stood by the bathroom door as she bent over to run her bath.

"At least send someone nice looking this time. Bone, whatever his name was, fat bastard. Send someone fit," she said seriously.

Sediko laughed. "You're a joker."

After five other successful visits, Sediko drove back to his house. He was glad to be home but wished Kellie had been there to greet him. He took out all his money, built a spliff and began counting his money.

Later, he looked at his watch. It was 12:59 am and he was still counting; he was well past 25 g's. All he had would be put into the club. He owned 80%; Path, Bones, Sparrow and Image had 5% each. Their share wasn't legal, but they had his word. That was enough. They were helpers.

As he strapped £1000 into a neat bundle, there was a knock at the door. He switched on his surveillance and saw Brenda looking up at him. Shit. He wasn't in the mood. She kept knocking; he kept counting.

He was annoyed. Nearly every Friday night she did this. His phone rang beside him.

"What?"

"Two-Face, let me in please."

Brenda smiled up at the camera. She looked sexy. Tight skirt. Cleavage spilling from a low cut top.

"Listen, I'm busy."

"Busy doing what?" Her smile vanished.

"What you doing here at this time?" He spoke through his hands-free set while he counted.

"Why can't I come in? What you doing? Counting your drugs money? Weighing powder? I know what you doing so you might as well let me in," she said turning away from the camera.

"I don't deal in drugs." Sediko cut the call. Why was that bitch talking so hot on his phone? He would have to get rid of this number, he was paranoid like that.

Sediko kept counting. He had to get his money to the safe deposit box. He'd been using it since he was 18. It wasn't a real safe deposit box but a ghetto one. Every month he put in at least £200 without fail and he had only ever taken money out twice: the club and his mother's funeral. His mother, Joy.

Joy had died when he was 19 and it had killed him. One late night she had sat him down and told him that she had cancer. Weeks later, she was dead. He had watched her suffer a short bitter end. A confusing bitter end. He would have done anything to take her pain away, he wished that he had understood her illness, maybe it might have helped him at the time. He felt so angry at being so helpless. And when she had closed her eyes to the pain, he had been with her.

At her small funeral, a few close friends had come to pay respects. But no family. His grandparents had both died and she was an only child, as was he. The remains of his family lived in Jamaica. He had never met any of them. His dad, Malcolm, didn't come to the funeral either; he had taken Sediko's threats as seriously as they were meant.

Malcolm had abused his mother in every way he could until Sediko was 14 and towered over him. His dad had left then. The only reason Malcolm was still alive was because Sediko had promised his mother to let bygones be bygones.

Again, there was knocking on the door.

≈≈≈≈

So you've got nothing to tell me Marie? Nothing at all." He looked down at her lying in their bed reading Jackie Collins. "I said no. Honey, what's this all about?" She clearly wasn't paying him an ounce of attention; she hadn't lifted her eyes from her pages.

"Put that fucking book down!" He grabbed it and threw it onto their cream two-inch-thick Italian carpet. Marie sat up instantly, her mouth fell open.

"I'm sure there's no need for that Bill, using language and throwing valuable reading across the room. Have you been drinking?"

"Have I been drinking? So what if I have, I'm trying to talk to you. So have I got your undivided attention now? Have I?"

"Darling just spit it out. Say whatever it is that's on your mind. I noticed at dinner that something was bothering you." She looked at him with sad eyes.

"Alright. I know all about your little phone call!" He was enraged by her calmness.

"What phone call?" She looked baffled.

"She told me alright! What gives you the right to go poking around in my business? And then, then, try and play innocent!" He paced up and down the room.

"Bill calm down and explain this to me. What phone call? What business?" She got out of bed in a long blue see-through negligee. She was trying to seduce him. He would not let her off the hook. He pushed her roughly onto their bed.

"Ahh!" She let out a little scream. "Are you crazy?!" She choked between tears.

"Start talking, where did you get the number? How?" He approached her where she lay shrivelled into a shaking ball.

"I still don't know what you're talking about. I promise. I swear Bill, I don't have a clue." She was crying hard now.

He hated liars.

"I'll give you a clue. Lisa. You accused us of having an affair! How could you?" He towered over her.

"What, you're having an affair?" Slowly, she sat up . Shock now covered her face. "Bill what is going on?" she was almost shouting now. Her face held thousands of emotions. Shock, worry, anger, confusion and pain were only a few.

At that moment, Bill knew. He knew by that look on her face that it she hadn't made that call. She didn't have a clue what he was talking about. Her face and actions told him so; he knew his wife. But now it was too late, he had said way too much.

"Well, who's not talking now?" Marie's face was red and broken. She waited in silence, then continued. "You came in here shouting about some business, some phone call, breath stinking of alcohol. And then you push me and carry on about an affair and Lisa! And now, now, you're silent! I demand to know what is going on!" she shouted. The argument was hers now.

He needed another drink.

"I just thought that you had messed up a deal, that's all. Cost me a lot of money." That was all he could think of with such short notice. He sat down on the bed while Marie towered over him.

"Right, business with Lisa." She nodded. "The one from the dinner party?"

"No."

"Yes, Bill. And someone found out about your dirty little secret and called her for confirmation." She was crying now, not in fear but in anger.

"Marie, honey, you're jumping the gun," he said calmly. She had got it spot on, why hadn't he thought of that?

"Don't you dare patronise me! You've come this far in breaking up our marriage, you might as well just finish it off!"

"Marie, sit down," he sighed.

"No, I will not. You wouldn't sit down and talk rationally when you accused me of phoning your mistress. Please Bill, give me some answers." She brushed her tears away.

"Marie, that's why I was so angry, because it's not true."

"What's not true?"

"Me, having an affair."

"How long has it been going on?" She was testing his patience.

"Nothing's going on!"

"So why did someone call her? They must have had reason to think that you were having an affair. It must be someone I know, they said that they were me didn't they? Didn't they?!" She stood waiting for answers.

"What do you want me to do? Should I admit to something that I'm innocent of?" He was running out of ideas.

"So why did you say that it was a business deal that had gone wrong?"

"That was true, a business deal had. Look," he sighed, "I've had enough!" He lay back onto her side of the bed. "Good night."

"Bill. You can't do this. How could you do this? Just tell me if you're having an affair. You're my husband, you owe me the truth."

"You're sounding more and more like these soaps that you watch all day long. Go to bed." *What was he going to do? He wasn't ready to tell Marie the truth. He didn't want a divorce. He didn't want to choose.* "Marie, I'm sorry that I accused you."

"So who was it then?"

"I don't know." Bill spoke the truth for once.

"Well don't worry, I will find out." She took her dressing gown and marched to the door.

"Where are you going?" Bill sat up.

"You're right. Where *am* I going? *You're* going to sleep in the guestroom. You're not taking *me* for a fool." She took his dressing gown off the chair and threw it to him.

Slowly, Bill got up and left the room. He had really fucked things up this time. He tried to settle in the cold bed. Someone was out to get him. Must be Sally, she was always sticking her nose in his business–

74

eavesdropping or trying to push her body up against him. Tomorrow he would deal with her. How could Lisa be so stupid? Someone had tricked her and it was costing him his marriage. Eventually, he fell into a light sleep.

It was Thursday morning, 5:00 am. Bill shaved, showered and dressed in his normal ritual. Marie was nowhere to be seen until he went downstairs at 6:00 am to find her fully dressed and drinking coffee.

"Morning honey. You feeling better?" He sat beside her at the breakfast table. She stayed silent. "No breakfast?" He looked around; she ignored him. She was still mad. "Well then, I'll have some toast. Want some?" He hadn't made his own breakfast in years. "Where's the bread?" He looked into the fridge. No answer. "Alright fine. I'll grab a baguette from Pret a Manger on the way to work."

"I'm coming with you." She stood up and straightened her suit.

"What?" He stopped in his tracks.

"You heard Bill, I want to see Lisa. Speak to her."

"Have you lost your mind? You're not coming anywhere."
Bill took his briefcase and left.

"Morning Bill," Kellie's voice sang to him.

"Thank god it's you. Come into my office." He felt sorry for himself.

"What is it?" Kellie sat on the leather sofa instead of the usual chair.

"When was the last time we sat and talked, you and I? You started the modelling part time, now we hardly communicate."

"Who am I, your therapist?" Kellie joked, moving to the chair.

"This is serious. Marie's found out about Lisa."

"Oh, so you're admitting it now?"

"What? I never hid it from you."

"But you never actually said it. Who let the cat out of the bag?" She grinned. He could see that she wanted to laugh.

"I did."

"Hah. Very noble."

"Someone called Lisa pretending to be Marie. I asked Marie about it and said too much."
Bill waited for Kellie's good advice.

"But have you actually admitted to it?"

"Gosh no. She'd divorce me."

"So who told?" Kellie probed.

"I don't know. Sally?"

"Sally? I don't think so. Who else?"

"I don't know. It's not that easy. Now Marie's going to start poking around, finding things out."
There was a knock at Bill's door.

"Come in." Sally walked in with a stack of papers.

"Sir, I have all those tapes on paper." She smiled proudly.

"Yes. Put them on Kellie's desk. She can go over them."

"Sir, they just need signing."

"Whatever. I need to have a quick word with you."

"Yes Mr Laymend, but is it urgent? I've got tons of work to do downstairs. I'll be free to come up this afternoon, if that's okay."

Bill nodded. She turned and walked out.

"It was definitely her," Bill said pointing at the closed door.

"Be careful Bill. By accusing the wrong people, you're letting them into your little secret," Kellie said before leaving.

Bill threw himself back into his work.

≈≈≈≈

W hy would you lie to me after everything that we've been through?" They stood in her small two room flat– front room, kitchen and adjoined bedroom and a bathroom.

"I think I'm just late."

Kirk stood in front of her. His eyes were sad. She couldn't admit it to him. She didn't want to break his heart more than she already had.

"You're pregnant and it's Sediko's?"

"When have I had time to see him? You're always with me or I'm at home," she stuttered, lying.

"Mia. We can get through this. But you need to be honest with me. You're telling me you're not pregnant, so how come you're being sick most mornings. You must have put on a stone. I know you. I know you better than him."

He held onto her as he poured his heart out. No matter what she did he always said sorry to her, then forgave her.

"I'm sorry," Mia said first, because she really was. She didn't want to hurt him. "I tried to keep away from him." Tears fell down her cheeks because they had been here so many times before. Except this time she was sober and thinking straight.

"So is it Sediko's then?"

"No." She just couldn't say it. Even though they both knew.

"Who then?"

"You don't know him." Maybe it would hurt him less if it wasn't Sediko....again.

"Does he know that you're pregnant?" His voice was calm.

"No, I haven't told him," she lied again. She would lie forever for Sediko.

"It's alright Mia, it's alright. I still love you." He continued to hold her; she pulled away gently. "Do you love me?"

A knock on the door. Mia rushed to answer. It was Charlene.

"Hiya," she said with a smile.

Mia felt saved by the bell.

"We still going shopping?"

76

"Oh yeah, let me just quickly get changed," Mia said, smiling widely and rushing to pull a tracksuit from her plastic wardrobe.

She went into the bathroom. Kirk followed.

"Here, take this, spoil yourself." He gave her £100.

Mia smiled. Spoil herself with £100? Was he joking? Sediko would have given her no less that £400.

"Ready, Char."

Mia came out of the bathroom. She couldn't wait to get out of the house. She kissed Kirk quickly. Since starting back with Sediko, she punished herself every time she let Kirk touch her.

"So how's things going?" Charlene asked as they walked up Ealing High Street.

"Not good," Mia sighed.

"Kirk loves ya. He looks after you an' you're carrying his child. What's not good about that?"

"It's not right, Charlene."

"Why?"

"Because I don't love Kirk," she admitted. She couldn't help her feelings.

"So why ya with him?" She frowned angrily.

"Like you said, he loves me."

"So you're with him through pity?"

"No. I do have feelings for him. He helped me out a lot, I owe him. I could never forget what he's done for me but I was a different person back then." Mia felt like shit.

"What about Two-Face?"

"I still see him," Mia admitted.

Charlene stopped dead in the middle of the busy high street and turned to her, shocked.

"I thought you said you were done with him."

"I love him. Same way that Kirk loves me."

"Two-Face treats ya like shit."

People tutted as they had to circle around them.

"If I was his woman things would be better. I know it and he doesn't treat me like shit, no one understands him. We've been together on and off for over 11 years-"

"Yeah on and off, mostly off!"

"…that's a long time, I don't expect you to understand. We were both 14. I'm 25 now and I still love him. I don't think that I'll ever stop."

"How you gonna be his girl if you're carrying Kirk's baby?" Charlene asked.

Mia looked at her.

"Oh Mia, please don't say it's Sediko's. Does Kirk know?"

"He knows it's not his, that's all." Mia felt dirty.

She pulled Charlene to the nearest quiet spot. They sat at the empty bus stop.

"Ya told Two-Face?"

"Yeah, he's happy."

"Has he told his girl?"

"I don't know. I asked but he's not saying nothing." Mia wanted to change the subject.

"Anyway, all I can say is good luck. You're gonna need it. We sitting here when we got shopping ta do."

Charlene was a good friend.

"Exactly, shopping to do." Mia smiled.

After a long day, the cab dropped Charlene to Camberwell. Mia then directed the cab to Battersea. She called Sediko.

"I'm outside, you busy?"

"Na."

As the cab pulled up outside, Sediko came out to pay the cab fare. They went inside and kissed by the door where they stood. He really kissed her. He hadn't been so loving in a long while. He stopped, then rubbed her stomach.

"You're happy?"

"Yeah, mans is in a good mood. Things are getting better and bigger. My club opens soon."

She followed him into the front room where he was watching a black movie.

"You're opening a club?" she asked in doubt.

"Yeah what, you think I'm too ghetto to have my own business?"

"No. I'm happy for you. That's boom. Where is it?"

"So, how's the baby?" He switched subjects.

"He's fine, I'm almost 4 months." Mia felt he was all hers.

"How you know it's a boy?" He smiled at the idea.

"I'm just hoping. I got a scan coming up soon, you wanna come with me?" She prayed that he would say yes. That would show how committed he was.

"Course. Just remind me closer to the time. I'm gonna be there for my baby."

"I'm not worried, I know you'll be there for us." She sat beside him.

"Not you, my yout' I'll be there for my yout'. Don't start this shit again."

"Whatever." Nothing was going to upset her. She was having his baby, they were going to be connected forever. "I love you Sediko."

"Yeah," he sighed.

Mia sat and listened to him for over an hour talking non-stop about his club. She smiled and nodded. Spoke when questioned. This was where she wanted to be. Eventually, he stopped talking and leaned over to kiss her. At last. She responded. She wanted to satisfy him. She wanted to be better than her.

Three hours later, Mia dressed quickly, before Kellie came.

"I'll call you." Sediko kissed her cheek. That meant don't call me, I'll call you.

The cab honked outside.

"Here, pay for the cab." He gave her money.

"Fifty pounds to pay for a cab to Gypsy Hill?" She laughed.

"I like to spoil you." He gently pushed her towards the door.

"Bye."

As the cab reached the bottom of the road, Kellie passed in her car. Their eyes locked momentarily. Mia sunk down into the back seat. On the way back she was all smiles. She didn't feel guilty going back to Kirk. She could bare him for weeks after one night with Sediko.

When she finally got home Kirk was asleep in the chair which also doubled as their sofa bed. He awoke.

"Hello, I thought you would have been home ages ago," he said sleepily rubbing his gorgeous eyes.

Mia looked at him. How was she going to break his heart?

Seven

"POSITIVE." HER DOCTOR smiled.

"Oh my gosh." Kellie was happily surprised. She had Sediko's child inside of her.

"Congratulations. It seemed only the other day I told you that you were pregnant with Samuel."

"I know." Kellie was almost speechless.

"Make an appointment at the front desk for two weeks time, we'll have to keep an eye on you. Your last pregnancy was quite stressful."

Outside the surgery, Kellie called Sediko. She arranged to meet him for lunch at Chester's Café in Tower Bridge; she couldn't wait to tell him the news. On the way she listened to her Coffee Brown album.

Kellie entered the American-style restaurant and spotted the father of her unborn child at the back. She stood by the door and looked around the busy café. Women watched Sediko, gave him eye contact, practically threw themselves at him. A tall dark woman approached his table. Kellie moved further out of view. The woman sat down and seemed to speak angrily to him. He ignored her and looked around nervously. The woman reached for his hand; they began to talk. She laughed. He smiled.

Kellie stood rigid. She could be a friend, a cousin, maybe one of his friend's women. Then the woman leaned in and kissed him. Gently, fully on the lips. Sediko's tongue snaked into her mouth.

People telling you was one thing, seeing for yourself was another. He was sitting here waiting for her and he was kissing some bitch! Kellie was furious. She moved from her position and went to the door. Had he looked up he would have seen her, but he was too engrossed in his kissing conversation. Mia she could handle, but random hoes? Definitely not.

Kellie left the café, jumped into her car, switched on the engine, switched off her phone ringer and sped off toward home.

Knock, knock.

"Mo's not here," Tex answered and slammed the door shut.

Kellie's mouth dropped open. She knocked again. He opened.

"Where has she gone?"

"Call her and find out," he spat and went to close the door in her face again but she pushed her foot in.

"What is your problem?" Kellie asked baffled.

She didn't see eye to eye with Tex but this was ridiculous. His arm relaxed on the door.

"You know what? I don't want you in my yard. Simple." He pushed her back out. She tripped backwards and just about caught her balance.

"And why not?"

"Cos you're a fucking crackhead."

"What?"

"Don't act like you don't do it. I don't want that shit round my sons."

"I am not a crackhead," Kellie denied.

"First sign is denial."

"Kellie!"

She turned to see Mo who was clearly happy to see her. Kellie hugged her and kissed her two sons in turn. Tex watched at the door.

"You staying for dinner?"

"Yeah, if Tex don't mind."

"Don't be silly, come on," Mo said.

Tex was fuming.

Kellie helped Mo manoeuvre the massive buggy through the door past Tex.

"Well I'm off." Tex leaned in and kissed her.

"Alright, I'll save your dinner. Don't come back too soon," she joked winking at Kellie.

Tex left and they settled into the living room.

"So Kel, how you been?"

"So-so, you know how it goes. Where you coming from?" Kellie asked her as Andy came to her shyly.

"I want to play with Samuel," he interrupted and then ran back to Mo.

"I'll bring him back round soon," Kellie promised him.

"Yeah so, I'm just coming back from the doctors. Ronan was coughing but he's alright. Doctor just gave me some Calpol. Where you coming from?"

"You don't want to know," Kellie sighed.

"Actually I do, I want to know what you've been doing. I haven't seen you in ages; spice up my boring life with tales of your exciting one," Mo pleaded with a smile.

"Well, I've been to the doctors today as well."

"I know that look Kellie. Come on, spit it out. You ain't pregnant?"

"Yes," Kellie confirmed.

"Oh, I thought you were going to say no. Congratulations." Mo hugged and kissed her. "I can't believe it. What did Sediko say?"

"I haven't told him yet."

"Why, what's wrong?" Mo undressed Ronan who was sleeping soundly.

Kellie told her about the kissing conversation she had seen that day and about seeing Mia go off in a cab from Sediko's house. She told Mo about what Mandy had told her, about Sediko's new club venue and complained about all the women that were always ringing his phone. Mo sat and listened. Kellie went on about her fears with Samuel and her taking drugs. Drugs that she could once handle and the drugs that were now a part of her everyday life.

"Why don't you just stop now?"

"Yeah, much easier said than done."

Holding Kellie's hand Mo asked bluntly, "So is it easier to know that what you're doing can harm your baby?"

Kellie sighed.

"It's not in your lifestyle, how can it be? It's Sediko's lifestyle."

"He didn't force me," Kellie defended.

"No, but he gave it to you. Tex has never offered me a spliff. Sediko knew you didn't smoke."

"I'm not an addict. You're talking as if I'm half dead and selling all my shit."

"You said it, not me. Maybe you don't want to quit."

"Maybe.....I can't."

"Maybe you need to think about your baby and not yourself. Okay so you want to quit. But now that you've got another life to think about, you *have* to quit. Please Kellie, stop now."

"When Mandy told me about what happened to Mia, I felt as if Sediko had mapped out my life with him. He knew what he was doing. He's made me walk in her footsteps. Now that I know, I can't even face her. She's fine now and look at me. Look what happened to her when she let the drugs take over. Sediko left her."

"But you won't be doing it for him. Do it for Samuel," Mo told her.

Kellie shook her head. It felt so good to talk to someone, no holds barred.

Hours had gone by. Kellie's phone vibrated in her pocket. "Shawna" flashed up on her phone.

"Kellie, usual t'ing, about an hour?"

"Call me back in 10 minutes." Kellie cut the call.

"Who was that?"

"Shawn."

"Who's that?"

"Just a friend. A good looking one." She couldn't tell Mo that she was a drug dealer as well as a messed up pregnant drug taker.

"Well, just be careful. And don't leave it so long next time. It's always nice to catch up with you."

"Definitely. We should go out for a meal."

"Yeah, you can tell me all about this Shawn geezer." Mo smiled her pretty smile.

"Here take this, it's for the boys." Kellie stood up, then took £300 from her purse.

"No, I can't take that." Mo looked at the money, shocked

"Good cos it's not for you, it's for the boys. Just tell Tex that you won bingo," Kellie winked and pushed the money into her hand.

≈≈≈≈

K ellie walked through Brockwell Park to the usual place. She spotted Shawn standing with his back to her on his phone. This man intrigued her. Kellie walked softly and tried to get closer so that she could hear his voice, figure out who he was talking to. Just as she got within earshot, he closed his phone, pushed it into his pocket and turned around.

"Hello beautiful," he greeted. He was very well spoken and today he wore a business suit that suited him to a tea.

"You alright?" Kellie greeted, trying to relax in his mysterious presence. She handed him a small gift-wrapped box. "You got a little extra in there."

"Why?"

"I quit."

"I didn't know you was a.... I mean-"

"No, I said I quit." She felt smaller than small.

"Well, here's yours." As usual, he passed her an envelope which she slid into her bag.

"So, what you doing now? Anything special?" He bit his bottom lip.

"Why? What did you have in mind?" *What! What was she saying?*
A smile curled on his lips.

"Oh. So now you're ready to give me some of your time? After I been trying to spend time with you for ages. Well, I'll be busy tonight. I'll call you when I'm free." He walked away.

Shit, he had just blown her out; she had practically thrown herself at him.

Two girls began to follow Kellie as she walked slowly to her car. She threw her bag in the car then turned to them. They looked as if they had a chip on their shoulders.

"Why were you just chatting with my man?" the first nappy head asked. She had weave and acne problems.

"Why don't you ask him?" Kellie wasn't in the mood.

"No. I'm asking you. Why were you just chatting with my man?" Her face was screwed tight. The other stood, hand on hip, waiting for Kellie to spill the beans.

"I don't know you. Don't ask me my business." Kellie was ready to kick this girl's ass. Especially as Shawn had just blown her out and this was one of his girls!?

"You're rude innit? All I'm saying is keep away from my man, yeah." She looked and acted a little young to be his girl.

"No. I won't keep away from your man, you will get out of my face before I kick your little fucking head in."

"Whatever, you must be sucking his dick anyway."
This girl was getting too brave.

Kellie turned to get into her car. She didn't want to be seen arguing with these hood rats; she didn't want to lose her temper. Suddenly Kellie jerked forward. A blow to her head. *The fucking bitch hit me!* She touched her head and turned to face the girl who was holding a smashed Bacardi Breezer bottle. Kellie looked down and quickly shook glass from her hair. She sighed angrily, then went for the bitch.

Grabbing her weave, Kellie punched her face repeatedly. The girl fought to get free of Kellie's grip. When she finally did, she left her ponytail in Kellie's hand.

"Call Fixer! Go call him!" she shouted to the friend.

Kellie pushed her up against her car then head-butted her. The girl's eyes rolled up and her nose gushed blood. She then threw her to the floor and stamped in her face. The girl slapped sluggishly at Kellie's feet, she was already barely conscious. Kellie kept kicking, even when she noticed that the girl had stopped moving. The second girl tried to help. Kellie stopped attacking girl one and gave her friend a backhand that sent her flying. She then went back to girl one on the floor– the one with all the mouth.

Kellie kicked and stomped. She lost count how many times. Tears began to roll down her cheeks as she let out all her anger. Blood covered her feet, hands, face and hair.

"DON'T...FUCKING...QUESTION...ME!"

She kicked harder with every word.

"DON'T...FUCKING...QUESTION...ME!" she shouted again.

Kellie could now sense people all around her. She didn't care. She carried on; using her arms to increase the impact. This bitch had crossed the line. She felt someone drag her. She resisted, then surrendered, she'd had enough; she was exhausted. She looked down at the girl before they dragged her away. Her pink Capri suit was stained red; her face was unrecognisable.

Kellie was dragged into a car. Only at that point did she realise that she'd been arrested. In silence, she let them drive her away. Her hands were cuffed behind her back, her head ached and she felt dizzy. Shit. She had been arrested. Her heart thundered in her chest. Kellie hoped the girl would be okay. She didn't want to even consider the possibility of going down for attempted murder, or even murder.

"Do you have anything illegal in your possession? If you do, I suggest you tell us now. It will save us some time." The desk officer spoke to her as if she was a known criminal.

"I haven't got anything," Kellie murmured.

"Sure. No weed, crack, needles maybe?" He was taking the piss.

"I...said...I....haven't...got...anything. Understand?" Kellie spoke very slowly. She could take the piss too.

"Alright. Empty your pockets."

"None." Kellie shrugged.

She wanted to go home. This was the first time that she had been arrested and she didn't like it one bit.

"Name?"

"Kellie, with an I E Palmer with an E R." The bright light at the desk hurt her eyes.

"Age?"

"Twenty-three." Almost, she thought; her 23rd birthday was a month away.

"Address?" He kept his eyes down.

She slowly gave her address.

"Any Jewellry?"

"Ruby ring. Gucci watch. One pair of platinum earrings. One gold anklet. One platinum chain," she answered quickly. She wanted this over with as soon as possible.

"We'll call for a doctor to look at you."

"Is the girl alright?" Kellie asked as they led her into a cell.

"Not that you really care, but we'll let you know as soon as we do." He slammed the heavy door shut.

Kellie stood in the dusty room. She looked around the confined space. A bed and a stinking toilet; she felt sick. At first she refused to sit down. As soon as she got home she would sniff four thick lines. That would be her last time. She deserved it after the night she had had and was still having. She needed it.

Walking up and down the small room, she began to feel hot and tired; she began to feel the confinement.

"SHIIIIIIIIIIIITT!" she screamed out in frustration. She had totally forgotten that she was pregnant.

"How could I?" she asked herself. She should be in hospital right now, not in a Brixton jail cell. She began to cry. She took off her jacket, spread it onto the plastic mattress and reluctantly lay down and closed her eyes. She couldn't believe that she had lost her temper like that. How would she explain to Sediko that she had a fight in the street while carrying his child? How was she going to explain this to Shawn, or Fixer, as the girl had called him. What if the girl pressed charges? What if she was in hospital? In a coma? What if she was dead? What if she went to prison? What if she had her baby in prison?" Kellie screamed at herself. She was torturing herself with all these 'what ifs.'

"Sleep, sleep," she told herself.

The heavy door opened. Kellie sat up quickly.

"Come on Palmer, the doc's here. After that, statement time. Let's make this quick; we all want to go home," he said standing by the door. Kellie stood and stretched. The old doctor came and went; she had no major injuries. She took her jacket and followed the officer unsteadily out.

"This way."

She followed him into another room. He explained some formalities, then pressed record on a small cassette.

"PC Carter and PC Dave interviewing at 3:35 am," he said looking at his cheap watch.

Kellie couldn't believe the time. She had been here for hours.

"Could you please state you name?"

"Kellie Palmer." She settled back in the chair.

"You denied the presence of legal representation when earlier asked. Correct?"

"Yes."

"Can you briefly tell us what happened at approximately 7 pm today in Brockwell Park car park?"

"I was about to get in my car, when these two girls tried to rob me. They said they wanted my jewellry and car keys. We argued. I turned to get in my car when she hit me in the back of my head. So I kicked the shit out of her in self-defense." She crossed her legs.

After the statement they took her fingerprints, DNA samples from her mouth, and walked her back to the desk.

"The lady has decided not to press charges. You're lucky young lady." The desk officer spoke to her like a head teacher.

"I'm not surprised. She tried to rob me. It should be her standing here."

"Maybe if she could stand, she would be. And you don't beat crime with violence."

"You should tell that to some of your colleagues," Kellie retorted.

"Okay, okay, sign your release paper."

As Kellie walked outside, she felt dizzy. She rubbed her stomach and sighed. Maybe she wouldn't tell Sediko about the baby just now. She sighed again, angrily this time, as she realised that she had locked her car keys in the car. She walked to the nearest cab station, waited five minutes, then had to argue with the cab man because she couldn't pay at the base.

Eventually, she got in a cab heading for home.Three months pregnant and she was fighting in the street. Sediko would never forgive her. Once they were at her house, she sat in the cab baffled. How was she going to get in to pay the man? Her keys and money were in her car. She turned to the driver. He stared at her expectantly.

"Wait there," she told the driver as she jumped out the car before he had a chance to lock her in and demand his fare. She kicked off her bloody shoes beside the door and prepared herself to climb through one of her windows. She didn't have a clue how she was going to do this. Then her door opened. She looked up quickly, mouth open, not knowing what to expect.

"Where you fucking been?" he half shouted. He was fuming.

"There's a cab outside. Got £20?" she asked quickly. *What was he doing here?*

Sediko went back in to get the money. Kellie pushed the bloody shoes out of view. He came back and she paid the driver.

"So?" he said as soon as she sat down. "It's after five."

"I got arrested."

"What?" A smile of relief washed over his face. "What happened?" He relaxed. Interested.

She decided to tell him the same lies that she had told PC shithead.

"Two girls tried to rob me. She bottled me so I fucked her up. The next thing I know I'm being handcuffed and flung in the police car." Sediko smiled as she told her story. She put her feet up over his legs.

"So is that what happened to you earlier on today?" he asked rubbing her feet.

Kellie put her feet down slowly and sat up.

"Yeah," she lied. Visions of Sediko kissing another woman flashed before her eyes.

"What did you want to tell me?"

"Oh, just something about work. Babe, I'm tired." She stood up. She wouldn't tell him about what she had seen or what she was carrying.

"Alright. I'll be up in a minute." He offered her a spliff.

"Er, no. No thanks."

"Why not?"

"I quit today."

Kellie rushed upstairs before she changed her mind; tomorrow she would go and see her doctor, she was worried about the life inside her. She was worried about her job once she started to show. It was just one thing after another.

Sediko had kissed that woman in the café today. There was no denying it. But what would be the point in asking him? They would just argue. He'd lie, or even worse, admit that something was going on. She would have preferred it to be Mia, she had known about their on and off thing. This café episode just proved that neither she nor Mia was enough for him and he was spreading his wings.

Kellie's head spun.

≈≈≈

Ballers!" Sediko shouted throwing his arms in the air. He smiled broadly as he stood with his boys behind him. They looked up at the purple neon sign hung up high above the entrance. Sediko's heart was racing. He was where he wanted to be.

He pulled opened two heavy, solid iron doors. They walked up a few stairs, then to a massive dance floor. It had two floors and three fully equipped bars armed for every alcoholic need: cocktails, alcopops, bottles beers, spirits, liquors, champagne, shots, the whole shit. The ceilings were covered in mirrors. Big brown leather lounging chairs dotted one corner. Large silver tables with chrome stools dotted another closed off area. The two bars downstairs - each twenty foot long - sparkled with silver surfaces. There was a high box stage for the technics. Beside a massive wall-to-wall mirror were spiral stairs that led to the VIP area which was half the size of downstairs.

As Sediko led them up. They all wowed at the long catwalk with dancing poles, more lazy chairs, a table and chairs and dance floor. A VIP bar stood in the corner stocked with fine wines and expensive champagne; purple, dim spotlights above.

"Well?" Sediko turned to them. He had had full control of renovation and interior design, which he had kept secret until now.

"I can't fucking believe it!" Path moved towards the poles, nodding and grinning. "I can't believe that this is the same place. Shit, Two-Face, you smashed it." Bones nodded in agreement.

Sediko went and stood behind the bar.

"And it was quick!" Sparrow grinned.

"There are a few more surprises. What you man drinking?" Sediko offered.

"Sex on the beach," Image said sitting at the bar.

"I wouldn't even know where to start, man can't make cocktails. Henessey?" Sediko suggested and poured them all drinks.

"Don't drink it yet. Follow me."

He took the spiral stairs back down to the main dance floor. They stood in front of the wall to wall mirror directly beneath the VIP area. The stairs to the right slightly hid a portion of the mirror. Sediko took a card from his pocket and pressed it onto a small black box. Part of the mirror slid smoothly and silently out, then across.

"That's my favourite part," said Sediko, smiling proudly.

They all praised him. They were all impressed. Neither of them had ever imagined that Sediko had been this serious. So much effort, so first class. They all separately wished that they held more than their 5% each.

They walked inside the medium sized room. A glass round table stood in the middle, five sofa chairs around it.

"Gentlemen. Sit." Sediko held his arms out as he stood at the head of the table where he could see the main dance floor, the main bar and the entrance.

They all took their seats. Path and Bones sat beside him.

"To all the big fucking ballers in Ballers," Sediko toasted.

They all held up their glasses. They finished their drinks and talked about the club.

"Now come, my niggas."

Sediko stood up and went to the door behind him. He opened it and waited for them all to go through so that he could see their faces; see if they loved it as much as him. He led them through a dark corridor, then flicked on the light.

"Two-Face, what you do to get all this shit?" Sparrow asked. "Man knows this shit ain't all legal, you're too *il*legal." Everyone laughed, including Sediko.

"It don't have to be legal, as long as it's making money and it's all mine, then I'm straight."

He pushed a bar to open a back door.

"That's just the alleyway at the side of the club. Managers only entrance."

He slammed it closed, then jogged up the stairs. They followed.

"Room 1: Naked sexy hot strippers, this is their changing room." They looked in.

"Image gonna be in there all night," Bones joked.

"Room 2: My private room." Sediko stood by the wall."

"Where?" Sparrow asked.

"Good. They done a good job."

Sediko moved on. They all looked to each other, baffled. They walked on through to the entrance and exit of the catwalk. Together, they must have walked around the club about ten times. Every time finding something else that they loved.

They talked business straight through the night— drinking and smoking, no one mentioning exhaustion they were all so excited. The big opening needed planning. But before all that, they needed workers. The first interviewee was due at 9 am that morning.

The club was to open on Kellie's birthday, the 25th of July.

At 8:55 am there was a knock at the door. Sediko staggered over to the entrance.

"Come on you lot, fix up!" he shouted behind him. The rest were all sprawled out in the lounging chairs.

He jogged down the few stairs and unlocked the door.

"What's up Jimmys?" Sediko clinched his fist and touched them both. They were two big burly twin brothers, both as black as tar. No one ever knew which one was Jamie, so they were both Jimmys.

"Come, come." Sediko closed the door behind them. "Come meet the boys," Sediko invited. They followed him, both wearing black suits with black t-shirts and wobbled up the stairs bulging muscle.

"You hired," Bones said as soon as he saw them.

"Shit, that the bouncers?" Path asked coming from the toilet. Jimmys ignored everyone else and turned to Sediko.

"We got a few more in our crew. You pay us, we pay them. And we only 'ave one boss," Jimmy said, his accent a thick east end.

"I think we understand each other. I'm the boss. I want you here on the 25th. That's our big opening night, it's gonna be a birthday bash." Sediko smiled proudly to himself.

"What time we got license to open till?" the second Jimmy asked.

"I have license till 5 am." Sediko stressed the I.

As soon as the Jimmys left, a stream of different people came and went. Sediko's good mood had disappeared. He hadn't advertised the jobs properly and people were coming in without basic knowledge of bar work or an ounce of education. They just wanted a piece of the new bashment club.

All but one, sat in the office. Smalls sat outside sending them in. They had no trouble with numbers, people were coming in from everywhere.

"Two-Face, I'm off." Bones stood. "Ma bed's calling me."

"Yeah," the rest agreed.

Sediko watched them leave, a spliff hanging from his lips.

They had seen at least twenty people and only one applicant seemed promising. He needed 10-12 bar staff– at least 2 fully qualified, 10 dancers all qualified, 1 small cleaning company and girls to work the cloak room. The only thing Sediko had sorted was the MC, DJ's and bouncers. He wandered out of his office while waiting for the next hopeful. He looked around yet again, imaging it full of sexy women and ballers.

"Hi, are you Sediko?" he turned to a pretty thing.

"Who wants to know?" he asked smiling.

"I'm here for a job."

She looked nervous but least she had dressed for the part; she wore a navy suit.

"Good. Come into my office."

Sediko led the way. He heard her gasp when he opened his mirror slide door.

"Sit."

He took his seat at the head; she sat beside him.

"My cousin Justin told me to come. He said you might be needing bar staff." Her voice was hopeful.

"You done it before?" He leaned back in the chair while she sat forwards on the edge of hers. Her long hair fell on her shoulders like Kellie's.

"Yeah. I used to work in Corks wine bar up until two weeks ago. We had a disagreement and I left," she explained vaguely.

"Can you make cocktails?" he asked her.

"I'll show you, if you like." She waited for him to give her the go ahead.

Sediko gave her the nod. This was good, she was confident.

She stood, went over to the mini bar in the corner and looked in the mini-fridge.

"Let's go to the other bar, not much choice in here," she said softly trying not to offend.

"Ready?" she asked from behind the main bar. Sediko gave her the go-ahead.

Professionally, she shook and mixed drinks, then poured two tall glasses. She was very fast. The end result looked brown and creamy. She sprinkled chocolate flakes on top. He lifted the glass to his lips and sipped. She watched and waited.

"Umm nice. What is it?" He sipped again. It was nice, different.

"Well, it's a secret recipe. If I get the job I might consider giving it to you." She leaned over the bar facing him.

"Right. You're hired." He backed the rest of the drink.

"So when do I start?"

"July 25th. Be here by 6 pm."

"I'm Jade by the way. See you then."

Jade left, but it seemed she had left him good luck. By 4 pm he had hired all the people that he needed and more.

Sediko left the club exhausted. He called Mia. They spoke and agreed for her to meet at his house.

"Where's Kellie?" she asked cautiously.

"Don't watch that, just come to my yard." Click.

Lately he wasn't caring if Kellie caught him with Mia; she already knew about them. If she didn't know then it was more fool her. But she was, and always would be, his first lady.

Being faithful to Kellie stopped over a year ago, the day that he had seen Mia in Whyno's in Brixton. If she allowed him to fuck Mia, then he could fuck other bitches too. He drove towards Battersea where he knew Mia would be waiting.

Eight

BILL OPENED UP his morning paper. He flipped straight to the sports page.

"Morning, Daddy." Carrie pranced into the kitchen.

"What are you doing here? I thought you and Jeff were staying out?" His head stayed in the pages.

"No. He's not here. We broke up." She moved around the kitchen.

"So how come you're so happy?"

Bill closed the paper and looked up at her. She had dyed her long brown hair, light pink. She had also straightened her masses of curls. Her make-up was dark as if she was in mourning. He wondered why she had a curtain wrapped around her body.

"Because I've realised that I don't love him. And I don't want to talk about it."

"Well it's lucky that I didn't let you go ahead with the wedding. We'd be speaking of divorce."

"Yes, you've said that a million times and we stayed together this long." She poured fruit juice.

"I presume you're moving back in?" Bill was glad and hoped it would be permanent this time. The two had decided to get a place together and had moved out just three days ago.

"Yes, if you don't mind."

"Of course I don't mind."

Bill wanted to know what that tramp Newman had done to upset his daughter. He wanted to congratulate her for getting rid of him, even if it was yet again. But he knew better than to bad mouth Jeff, that would only make her defend him.

"Where's Marie this morning?"

"I have no idea. I didn't hear her leave."

Bill reopened his paper to the sports page. It was Friday morning and Kellie had told him to lie in. She had said that she would be fine without him for a few hours, so he had taken her advice. It was 9:30 am and for the first time in years, he was at his breakfast table on a workday.

"So you haven't read that paper that you're holding. Centre pages." She tried to keep a straight face.

"Why? What is it now?" He opened the centre pages, blinked and looked again. His heart skipped a beat and his mouth dropped open. He couldn't believe what he was seeing. There he was. Broad as daylight. The picture was in colour and crystal clear. He was at a hotel in Leicester, he remembered clearly the day. With Lisa. Their arms were locked around one another and they were sharing a passionate kiss!

"WHAT THE HELL!" he shouted in a delayed reaction.

"Allow me."

Carrie took the paper from him. She began to read like a newspaper reporter.

"Headline reads: LISA BEDS BILL

Since the sexy Lisa brooks split with long term hubby, (who can not be named for legal reasons) she has been seen with a string of our British bachelors but none stayed long enough to be crowned partner to luscious Lisa....until now. The luckiest man alive some would say as Lisa Brooks was crowned world's most sexiest female by FHM and Loaded, two bestselling men's magazines. Bill Laymend, manager to a highly regarded, fast up and coming fashion company is currently married to his second wife Marie Laymend who is sadly nothing but an equation in this sordid love triangle.The attraction between Lisa and Bill can clearly be seen in this picture that was taken in a Leicester hotel only days ago. They were said to be open and passionate. The pair's relationship blossomed when she was a rising model that brought Laymend's and herself into the big wide world of fashion. A source from Laymend's Fashion Company in Soho said the pair's affair had been going on for years-"

"STOP!" Bill shouted. *What is happening to me?*

"Daddy, I think it's safe to say that Marie has seen this morning's paper."

"What paper is that?!" he bellowed jumping out of his seat spilling his coffee across the table.

"Does it matter?" She darted to grab a cloth.

"Get me their number! They won't get away with this! What do I tell you and Marie about these papers! I'll sue the fucking pants off the bastards! Whatever happened to privacy in this damn country!"

"Daddy, isn't that you?" She wiped the table.

"So what!" he bellowed. He paced the kitchen. He ran his hands through his hair.

"You're kissing?"

"Just pass me the phone!"

He grabbed the paper from her. The picture had been taken last weekend. *Last weekend!* he shouted in his mind. Lisa had begged him to go. He read on.

"Another source, close friend to Lisa Brooks confirmed
the pair's affair and said that Lisa was deliriously happy.
She told of late night meetings and their open exchange
of togetherness.
Mrs Laymend is said to be oblivious the ongoing

93

affair."

Bill closed the newspaper.

"What kind of rubbish is this? Deliriously happy! Exchange of togetherness! This is a load of rubbish! Who reads this?! Tell me!"

He looked to Carrie for answers. She took the paper from his tight grasp.

"Daddy, look, read this part." She gave him the phone.

"No!"

"'Hunk Italian Bill,'" she giggled then read on, "'…is definitely having his cake and eating it.' Look." She pushed the page in front of him. It was he and Marie at some film premiere. Marie looked beautiful. Her long hair that was usually in a bun was flowing near her ass. She wore one of his favourite dresses; he almost had to force her to wear it. It was strapless with a split to the thigh. She had stolen the show that night.

"They think you're a hunk, isn't that funny?" She laughed then stopped.

Bill ignored her and almost ran to the privacy of his office. He paced up and down holding his phone.

"Morning, Laymend's Fashion, Bill's office, Kellie-"

"Yes, yes, it's me."

"Can I help you?"

"I hope you can."

"Oh Bill, have you seen the paper this morning?" she asked excitedly.

"Of course I have."

"There are journalists everywhere," Kellie laughed.

"This isn't funny. What am I going to do?" he asked, still pacing.

"What else *can* you do but smile to the cameras? You were caught red handed. Just be grateful, the phones are ringing off the hook!"

"Really?" He stopped pacing.

"Yes Bill. Your tone's changed."

"Well, what's good for the business is good for me, and you." He was smiling now and in a hurry to get to work. It didn't look good getting to work at this time.

"Well, what has Marie said?"

"Nothing. She left early this morning." He began to pace again.

"Maybe tomorrow's headline will be 'BILL GETS DIVORCED, BILL MARRIES TOP MODEL.'"

"Don't say that. Marie's my wife through and through. I won't loose her over this."

"Okay well, I'll see you when you get in, I've got work to do. Bye." He called Lisa.

"I've got reporters camping out in my garden. I can't leave my own home."

"This is your fault. A string of bad luck since you received that phone call, it was your idea to go to that hotel!"

"I didn't ask for this. You're calling from home, Marie not there?"

"How do you know if I'm calling from home?"

"I called your office as soon as I saw it, Kellie told me you were home," she explained.

"This is fucking madness! Did you read what they said? A source from my own company!"

"Well, that could only be Kellie," she said convinced.

"No, it's not her," he said irritated. "We have to keep it low now, maybe even break it off for a while." He couldn't believe what he was saying.

"If that's what you want."

"I'll see you soon Lisa," Bill promised and cut the call.

He wasn't ready to break it off with Lisa. And he had promised himself that if he ever did have to stop seeing her it would be *his* choice– this was the exact opposite. But he loved Marie and would do anything to save their marriage. He dialled her mobile number.

"Hello Bill," she answered flatly.

"Marie. Where are you?"

"Where am I? You're worried about my whereabouts when your face is slashed all over the paper!"

"I'm sorry, I'm sorry. It was only the once; I had a drink she had a few and one thing let to the other. Where are you, I'll meet up with you, we'll go to your favourite restaurant and we can sort this mess out," he gushed breathlessly.

"I want a divorce," she said simply.

"What?" He hadn't heard.

"You heard. I want a divorce."

"What are you saying? You can't make a decision like that without talking with me first! I'm your husband for christsake!"

"I'm with my solicitor. Don't fight it, Bill. I've had enough of you, and your daughter. You, you bastard!" she swore.

He couldn't believe that she had sworn, this was more serious than he had initially thought.

"Marie please, don't go saying things that you'll regret later. Let's just meet up and talk about it, before you make any rash decisions. Think about what you're throwing away. Please." Bill tried to handle the situation; he usually could.

She hung up.

Marie would come around. At the end of the day, she loved him. They had been married 14 years. Since that day, Marie hadn't had to do a single day's work. He loved and looked after her.

Bill opened his door to leave. A handful of photographers took his picture. They pushed big fluffy microphones into his face and threw questions at him.

"Are you still seeing Lisa Brooks?"

"Will Mrs Laymend ask for a divorce?"

"Is it true that your wife first heard of you affair in this morning's paper?"

Bill walked to his car.

"Are you and Lisa in love?"

"I love my wife," Bill stated before getting into his car and speeding off. Shit, he hated when news travelled too fast.

He called Marie's phone again.

"Marie don't cut me off. We need to talk."

"Yes, you're right, we do. But we can do it through our separate briefs. We'll settle everything."

"What do you mean settle? You'll get nothing of mine. You already signed," he reminded her. He was in shock. He shouldn't be having this conversation with his wife.

"I want nothing from you! How dare you? You're the one who's been committing adultery for years. It's hard to imagine yes, but you made it a reality. And you made it public knowledge. You've made me feel and look like a fool! And worst of all, you have broken my heart."

"Marie come on, it isn't all that bad, you've only read what the paper and gossips have had to say, you haven't given me a chance to explain. I love you. We need to talk." He drove steadily to work, one hand on the wheel, the other on the phone; one eye on the traffic ahead and the other looking out for the police who would nail him for 'mobile whilst driving'.

"Yes, you had plenty of time to tell me! I asked you right out if you were having an affair. You had a chance to come clean but...but you lied through your back teeth!" She was sounding more and more distressed.

"And I'm sorry. Please, please can we meet somewhere? Just to talk," he begged.

"If it was just a one off, I probably could have forgiven you. But through years of our marriage?" she sobbed.

"Marie, I said it was only-"

"No, it's too late," she cut in, then continued, "You can't even admit the truth, even now, with our marriage on the line."

"Okay, okay, but..hello? Hello?"

≈≈≈≈

Kirk! Back off, man." Mia sat on the sofa bed. "I love you! Don't that count for nothing?" He stood in front of her.

"I need a break, I want to be alone."

"How can you want to be alone at a time like this? You need support! You fucking need me!" he shouted.

"I need to be alone!" she screamed back.

"He don't love you like I do."

Kirk stood handsome and tall. He was a good man. Just not the one for her.

"Who?"

"Come on Mia! You're carrying his child! How is that affecting me? You ever thought of that? No. But I'm still here, after everything I'm still here, been here whenever you've needed me. You know what? You're fucking selfish!"

"If I'm selfish, leave me! Go!"

"That's not what I mean. Remember when we first met? You wanted a gentleman. I used to make you laugh."

Mia sighed loudly. He looked hurt. Pain lingered in his eyes.

Kirk nodded slowly. "You don't want me no more. I done fix you up and now you don't want me. Ha. You were just some skinny crackhead bitch, fucking for money-"

"I did not!" Mia shouted, shocked.

"That's what you wanna go back to? Well fuck you then, go on! It's a good thing that bastard baby ain't mine!" He backed up toward the door, then left.

Mia lay on her bed and looked down at her stomach. She had nothing to worry about. She was having Sediko's child; they would be together. She was a bulging 5 months pregnant. She took her scan out of her draw. Sediko Junior. She smiled at the picture.

For the next 7 hours Mia waited for Kirk to come back. Strangely, she was missing him. At 3 am she had finally accepted that Kirk wasn't coming home. She was crying; she missed him. Everything that he had said about her had been true. But if she had to sacrifice one...

≈≈≈≈

Kellie awoke to the soft sounds of Erika Badu. Sediko came in with a tray.

"Happy Birthday, babes!"

He put the tray beside her. She sat up. Her bones ached as she looked at the fried dumpling, fried plantain with saltfish and callaloo.

"Thank you. What time is it?" She smiled, then yawned.

Sediko leaned in to kiss her. She looked at the food, not feeling hungry– only sick.

"Nine o'clock. Listen, I gotta leave you, I gotta set up shit for later."

"Set up what?" she asked interested in what surprise he had for her this year. Last year he had taken her to Jamaica for a week. He had kept it from her until they had gotten to the airport. He had told her they were collecting a friend. When he had finally told her about the trip, she was upset with him. He had packed her suitcase, and they had to run around the duty free shops buying all the things she knew that he had forgotten.

"Don't worry. I left a little something downstairs on the side. Enjoy yourself until later and make sure you look sexy when I call you." He kissed her again.

"What time should I be ready?"

"Now you know better than that," he said before he left.

Waiting until she heard the door close, she took the food and flushed it down the toilet. She went to her mirror and lifted her nightie. Four months pregnant and her stomach was as flat as it had ever been.

Kellie called Samuel, his little voice was so sweet. He sang *Happy Birthday* to her with such love. She cried silently; she told him how much she loved him. Guilt washed over her as she imagined herself sniffing; she needed it after that call. Maybe Sediko had left her some; he did say he left something on the side. She rushed downstairs. There was an envelope. It was probably Charlie; it wouldn't hurt to just have one go, chip it into a spliff.

She opened the envelope.

Money.

"Shit!" she shouted, throwing £2000 around the room. She realised how much she had wanted it to be the drug that she had been trying to quit for the past month.

Kellie ran to find Sediko's personal stash, and without thinking, she layered then sniffed. She cried immediately after. Dressing quickly and spontaneously, she drove straight to her doctor. She didn't give herself a chance to think about it.

Kellie looked around at the other sick people sitting in the waiting room, they looked at her as if she had 'crack mother' tattooed across her forehead. She wanted to get up and run, but her bones ached.

Two hours of 'emergency appointment' waiting later, she finally sat in front of Dr Ashlon. She sat opposite him, sweating and shaking.

"The hardest thing is not thinking about it. The more I try not to think about it, the more it goes round and round in my head. Everyone out there was whispering about me. They know about me?" Kellie shakily wiped light sweat droplets from her forehead.

"Kellie, you've got so much adrenaline going through your body that it's making you paranoid and shaky. What happened to the leaflets that I gave you? Did you contact the Start Team? There are some excellent drug councillors, they can help you. Please try to understand what you're putting your body through. Cocaine increases your heart rate and can cause high blood pressure, even fits. It can also damage the membranes in your nose-"

"I don't care about me," she cut in.

"Your unborn child is also in danger. You're well aware of the risk in using crack cocaine– brain damage or worse."

"I didn't contact the Start team and I lost the fucking leaflet. Can't you help me? Tell me what to do?"

"I've done a few courses but this isn't my field, I can't begin to tell you everything. I would prefer that you saw a professional substance abuse advisor. I can write you a referral letter."

"No. Please. I don't want to make a big thing out of this; it doesn't rule my life and I don't want it to start. I've got a son and a, and a job, a modelling career. My life is just starting!"

"Alright. I will give you advice, not guidelines. But...you have to promise to do three things first. Like I said, eventually you will need to see a professional drug counsellor and you also need to have regular scans make sure your baby is growing healthy. If you continue to take these drugs it will be unlikely that you'll have a safe, natural birth. Finally, I want you to leave a urine sample. If you agree, it will be tested each week in the toxicology department. It will help me to keep up with you, know what's inside your system. Understand?"

Kellie nodded.

"Whenever you start to think about using, remind yourself why you want to quit. Lose contact with your supplier, stay around friends and family who don't use, try to find things to occupy your mind and time. It does get easier."

"Is that it?"

"I'm afraid so. I'm not a professional drug counsellor, that's what you need."

"How the fuck is that gonna help me!?"

"Only you can help you."

"It's my birthday today you know," Kellie said sadly.

"Happy Birthday."

"Happy Birthday, Kel." Mo hugged her. "What's wrong?" she asked as Kellie retreated back to her snug place on the chair with her thermal blanket.

"Nothing."

"It's your birthday, come on cheer up. It's boiling hot out there and you're sitting here with a blanket. Tex is looking after the kids, so you've got me for the whole day. It's 2:30, I thought we could hit the shops. Look, here's your present."

Mo took a gift-wrapped package from a bag.

"What's this now?" Kellie smiled weakly. She opened it to a long silk night-dress. As she lifted it out the box, it looked extra big.

"It's massive!" Kellie laughed.

"Yeah, soon that will be the only thing that will fit you." Mo laughed in return.

Kellie's smile dropped. Two fat tears fell quickly down her cheeks.

"What is it Kel?" Mo asked again sounding concerned.

"The longer I leave it, the harder it gets."

"What, you haven't told him?" Mo asked surprised.

Kellie was actually talking about her quest to quit drugs.

"No, not yet. I don't know what it is. Something just don't feel right."

"No you're not right, you have to tell him. You're four months, how could he not know?" Mo pushed.

Kellie stood and lifted her night dress to show her stomach.

"You sure you're pregnant?" Mo looked with wide eyes, searching for a lump or a bump, some kind of visible proof that she was, in fact, pregnant.

"Of course. I had a test at my doctor's. I even tested myself again to make sure. I wasn't like this with Samuel. Sediko's not *meant* to know." Kellie sat down.

"I thought you two were okay?"

"We are. Well, *he* thinks we are. It's not just him, it's everything– work, Samuel. I'm just finding things hard. Suddenly my life started moving too fast. I guess I just got to sit out the ride."

"Listen, it's your birthday not your funeral. I came to make sure you have a good day. Just think of things this way, you're with a man who loves you, you have a dream job, you'll probably be a famous model soon and you're having a baby. Samuel will be happy to hear that he's going to have a baby brother or sister." Mo held her hand.

"Is it that simple?"

"If you want it to be."

"I'll get ready shall I?" Kellie bounced off the chair.

Two hours later they were shopping in High Street Kensington. Kellie's phone rang as she and Mo laughed, packing bags into her boot.

"Happy Birthday." An unfamiliar voice.

"Thank you, who is this?"

"You don't recognise my voice? Maybe that's because my usual line is 'usual place.'"

"Shawn." Kellie smiled uneasily. Did he know about what had happened in the park?

"Yeah. You enjoying your day?"

"Yes, I am thank you, I'm out shopping with my friend. How did you know it was my birthday?"

"I know everything about you." A short silence. "Anyway, I'll see you later."

"Bye."

"Who was that?" Mo asked as they both got in the car.

"His name is Shawn. That one I was telling you about."

Kellie told her about the night she had spent in the police station. Mo was in stitches.

"You're fighting in the street now? First Mia, then this. You're a regular boxer now. What did Shawn say?"

"I don't think he knows. She took the piss anyway, she hit me first.

All that was going through my mind when I first saw her was, that can't be his girl. The reason he probably hasn't said anything is because he's ashamed of her."

They both laughed while Mo nodded in agreement.

"So what you doing tonight?" Mo asked as they sat in traffic.

"I don't know, Sediko's got this big surprise thing. I think it's the club's opening night. I'm gonna wear that suit from Levi's."

Kellie awaited Mo's reaction.

"You can't wear that! You're a pregnant woman!"

"Nobody knows that but you and me. Are you coming?" Kellie looked hopeful.

"Well, maybe."

"Come on you old bag, have some fun. It's gonna be good."

"Yeah, I've heard quite a few people are going. That Marion what's her face is going with her man. It's her birthday as well, remember?"

"Yeah, that bitch."

By 8 pm Kellie was ready. All she had to do was put on her clothes and take out her rollers. She looked down at the micro-mini faded jeans skirt and matching jacket. Her shirt was white with ruffles to the neck. She looked at the shoes, which cost her at least six times more than the suit and shirt together– Manolo Blanket's. She dressed slowly and stood in front of the mirror wearing her Gucci belt with matching Gucci bag.

"Well?" She turned to Mo.

"You look well sexy," Mo admired. "You'll look even better once you've taken your rollers out," she added with a laugh as she went through Kellie's jewellry box.

"What about this?" She took out a thin silver chain with a blue feather. "Or this?" Mo delicately lifted out her ice chain.

Kellie sprayed on Poison by Christian Dior, then chose the ice chain with matching bracelet.

"Shall I wear my Emanuel glasses?"

Mo nodded.

"So you're sure you don't want to come?"

"Na it's alright, it's you and Sediko's night."

"No, it's my birthnight."

Kellie picked up her ringing phone.

"I'll be there in ten minutes, make sure you're ready, alright?" He cut the call.

"Shit, Mo quick, my hair! He's on his way."

"All you have to do is take out your rollers and shake your hair; it's that boom."

"I hope it don't look buff."

As they took out the curlers, the door slammed downstairs.

"That was a quick ten minutes," she said to him at her open bedroom door. He stood leaned up against the frame. He looked even better than he did the day that they had met. He wore a black suit with a white scarf and white Kangol hat.

"So, you're wearing the shoes."

She looked down at them.

"Yeah, cos they go wid the suit. Do they look alright?"

He looked down with his foot to the side.

"For £250 they *better* look alright."

"Shit babes, is that how much you paid?" He came close to her. "Babe, you look boom. I love you." He kissed her softly on the lips, his hands went up to her curlers.

"Thank you. Don't look too bad yourself," she replied in kind.

"Hiya Sediko," Mo waved.

He nodded.

"So, where we going tonight?" Kellie asked.

"Are you ready?" asked Sediko grinning and looking at the few rollers still clamped to Kellie's hair.

"Yes. Just give me and Mo a minute."

"What you need Mo for? And don't walk strapped. Leave that shit in the top draw," he cautioned as he walked back downstairs.

Kellie stood in front of her full-length mirror.

"Mo, you sure that you can't notice?"

"No. Come on, take out the rollers."

Mo began to tug softly at them.

By 9 pm they were parked outside Ballers.

"Sediko." Kellie sucked in her breath at the beauty of the club. A queue outside stretched to well over 100 heads. Another line for those on the guest list stood at over 50. Girls glared at Kellie as she walked, hand in hand with her man, past the line and toward the side of the club.

"Where we going? Ain't we going in?" Kellie turned back to the excited lively queue.

"Back way."

Sediko knocked twice and it was opened quickly by a tall skinny man.

"Yes, Smalls." Sediko touched his fist with his own.

"Two-Face, how long do I have to stand back here? It's dark and man can't hear the music," he complained, his eyes glued to Kellie.

"First, take your eyes off my woman before I shoot 'em out; second, you will fucking stand up there until I tell you to move."

They continued down a short corridor. Sediko took out his keys and opened a door. As soon as she walked in Kellie was in awe.

"What kind of gangster shit is this?" Kellie laughed. She walked past a round table to the back of the large room. She stepped up to the wall-to-wall window and looked out at the people filling up the big venue.

"Can they see me?" she asked. The place was already half full with drinkers and dancers.

"No. It's a mirror on that side."

Sediko sat at the head of the table.

"This is just, I can't believe it. You. This place is.. I give it top, top marks. I can't believe how you turned this place around. It doesn't look like the same place. You own a bar! A club bar. Ballers bar." Kellie turned to him. He stood up and went to her. "I just can't believe it!"

"Yeah man, feels good, you get me?" He smiled proudly. "And tonight, it's all yours."

There was a knock at the door and in came Path with Mandy. She looked sweet in a baby blue DKNY dress.

"What's up girl? Happy Birthday," Mandy greeted, then came around the table to hug her.

"Thanks. Glad to see you. Is Keisha and the rest out there?" Kellie asked her.

"Don't worry Kellie, wifey's only up in here," Path said to her.

"So nigga we hitting that bong?" Sediko asked his boy.

"So, how's things?" Mandy asked her.

"Good as it gets." Kellie didn't want to talk about life, she just wanted to have fun.

"You two ready?" Sediko asked them both.

Sediko and Path led them through the back and upstairs through to the VIP suite. In one corner Kellie spotted Keisha wrapped up in a group of unfamiliar girls. She looked down to the crowd below; already it looked more packed than it was just a moment ago.

The MC wished her a happy birthday over the mic. Thirty minutes later Sediko came up behind her with a glass.

"Here babes."

"What's that? A cocktail?"

"Yeah, it's special. New shit, it's called, 'Two fucked you.'" He began to laugh. "Get it?" He laughed again.

"Are you high?" She turned to him; his eyes were red balls.

"Do you want the drink or not? Shit."

"No thanks."

"Why? Come on, it's your birthday." He held the drink up to her face.

"I can't, I'm on these antibiotics, I'm not meant to drink," she lied.

"What for?" He looked at her; his eyes focusing on her pupils.

"Look, can we talk about this later?"

"It's your birthday, come on. You gots ta get high man." He grinned.

"Just go get me a can of coke and a weed spliff."

"Alright babes. You wanna bong wid we man?"

"No."

"Alright, back in a hot minute."

He slipped away and Kellie turned her attentions back to Mandy.

"So, you still smoking then?" Mandy asked.

"No. Well, I quit white. I smoke weed sometimes."

Kellie thought about this morning, when she had done a line before rushing to the doctor. She wrapped her arms protectively around her stomach. She was quitting. She *had* quit.

"Why'd you quit?"

Kellie looked slowly down to her own stomach and then slowly back to Mandy.

"Oh."

"You have any?"

"Almost, once. Lost her at 5 months," Mandy said gently.

"I'm sorry."

"Na it's alright, it was a long time ago. So what you gonna do?"

"I'm keeping it," Kellie said shocked that Mandy would think she would dash her belly for no reason.

"Why hide it then?"

Keisha joined them."What you two chatting about?"

"Nothing, you enjoying yourself?" Kellie spoke to her like a child.

"Dis shit is wicked. Two-Face said that I could start working in 'ere next weekend. I'll be behind the bar," Keisha informed her excitedly.

"Good for you." Kellie held her laugh but Mandy let hers out loud.

"So what about you Kellie? You gonna work here?"

"No, I've got a job as you well know," she said slowly.

Sediko came over with a spliff.

"Oh yeah, I read about your boss and that Lisa Brooks. That bitch man-thief," Keisha cursed.

"Keisha, I think one of those girls is calling you," Mandy informed her.

"Back in a minute," Keisha said before moving away.

"Come on, let's go check out the dance floor." Mandy pulled her arm down the stairs. Kellie caught Sediko's eyes on the way down. "Love you," she mouthed to him. He winked in reply before she walked out of view.

Kellie was fast beginning to like Mandy. She was pretty, confident and down to earth. As the two danced the night away, two men approached them. The taller of the two leaned in close and spoke into Mandy's ear as the music was blared out of multiple speakers. Mandy smiled, then turned to Kellie.

"They wanna buy us a drink."

Before Kellie could answer, the other leaned towards her ear.

"Want some champs?" He held up the bottle.

Kellie leaned in even closer.

"Two-Face, the owner of the shit is watching you from the VIP suite. That's my man. Watching you stand so close to me is probably burning him. If he gets angry he'd shoot you before you get to the exit."

The man flinched back, his eyes darted around the club. He tapped his friend who was leaning too close to Mandy and whispered something into his ear. They both ducked out. Kellie and Mandy laughed and carried on mashing up the dance floor.

≈≈≈≈

This is a surprise."
It was the Monday night after the opening. Kellie smiled widely at the white rose in her plate and wanted to burst when she looked around them at the hundreds of candles surrounding their table situated in the middle of the dance floor. The muted flickering light was beautiful.
"Yeah, took me ages."
"It's lovely."
Just then soft music began to play from the speakers and waiters came out from the back to pour wine and offer a menu.
"What you having?"
"I have a choice?" She took the menu and looked inside. White wine was poured into her glass and his. "I'll have the Salmon and new potatoes please."
Sediko stared at her.
"What you staring for?"
"I'm just watching your smile. You know that I love you."
"Yes, I do."
As Sediko raised his glass to toast, Kellie raised hers. Suddenly, he put down his glass and hers, grabbed both her hands and looked deep into her eyes. She trembled slightly as the look that he gave her produced a strong surge of love in her heart.
"No, for real Kellie, sometimes man does certain things and you might think that I don't care but I do. No gal can get between us! None. And any man that tried to take you, Kellie I'm telling you, I'll kill him. Cos you're *my* bitch, *mine*. And I know that you'll always be mine."
"I know that I'm yours," she said to him as if in a trance.
"No one will take me away from you, I'll always be yours. I just wanted you to know babe, that you're my favourite girl and I love you. It's just the two of us. Just me and you."
He smiled.

Exactly a week later the club was just as packed as it had been at its opening, if not moreso. The vibes were everywhere. Kellie stood in the VIP suite while ladies behind her danced topless for gentlemen. She looked onto the crowd below. She thought she had spotted Shawn but before she could see properly Sediko pulled her to him for a slow dance and he was a man who could do that well. She threw her arms around him the way she knew he loved and he wrapped his arms tight around her. They whined to Berres Hammond like true lovers. It felt like the right time.

"Sediko, I got good news," she said into his ear.

"What's that babe?" he asked, then turned his attention to the dance floor below. People were moving and giving way to a crowd. Police Sediko indicated to Path who had already spotted them. They both went down the stairs to the main dance floor. Kellie watched from the top of the stairs. An officer went right up to Sediko and tried to pull his arm behind his back. For Kellie, everything seemed to freeze. She knew what would happen next. Sediko shouted something. People rushed the door as two officers turned to four. Kellie scrambled down the stairs.

"Sediko Marshall, I'm arresting you." He pulled Sediko's arm again. Sediko punched him square in the face. All four police officers were on him in a blink.

"Get off him!" Kellie shouted as they tried to restrain him. Sediko punched out as Path knocked one to the ground.

"Path! Stop!" Mandy screamed.

A police woman tried to move Kellie away, she headbutted her to the floor and she hit the ground hard. Kellie couldn't believe that this was happening. Bones pushed his way through as more boys pushed their way into the already half empty club. Sediko kept punching out, they couldn't hold him down. Sediko finally pushed them off him and stood back. His breath was coming fast and hard. Somewhere along the line, someone had turned off the music.

"Okay, Sediko," one of the officers said panting and puffing. "Alright, just come with us."

"FUCK YOU! YOU COME IN HERE TRYING TO FUCK UP MAN'S SHIT!" Sediko stood back. Five bull stood in front of them; four more held Path, five held Bones.

"Sediko, we don't want this to get nasty."

"PUSSY! YOU DONE COME IN HERE AND MADE SHIT GET NASTY!" Sediko was bellowing.

The two bouncers joined the group. Kellie was shaking. Sediko was bleeding from somewhere.

"We're not leaving here without you," the same bullman said. Slowly Sediko handed a bunch of keys to Kellie. The same bull that Kellie had headbutted stood behind them and shocked Sediko with a stun gun. Kellie screamed as he fell to the floor. Path shouted something out as he watched his boy fall to the ground. Once there, all the officers moved in and took turns in kicking Sediko while he lay unconscious.

"I'm arresting you for intent to supply a controlled drug and suspected possession of a concealed weapon."

"And assaulting a police officer," one said to Sediko's limp body on the ground.

Bones struggled to get free but was already handcuffed. Kellie screamed as they then picked him up by the legs and dragged him out. His head bumped and scraped the floor. By this time, the club was empty but for a few. Mandy found her hand as they followed them out to four waiting police vans.

"How can you drag him like that?! You're dragging him you fucking bastard! You think I'm gonna let you get away with this shit! " Kellie looked to Sediko as they lifted him into the van.

"Sediko! Wake up! Please wake up! Wake up! Let him out! He needs an ambulance!" Kellie screamed to a woman bull.

"He's fine, it's just a shock, now move away."
They left him slumped on the van floor. Four officers got in after him, then they slammed the door shut.

"Where you taking him? If anything happens to him all of you can kiss goodbye to your jobs cos I will make SURE that you don't get away with this! Assault, that's what it is!" "I'll meet you there babes!" she called to Sediko as they drove away with Bones and Path in separate vans. She stood out in the night and watched the vans speed away. She turned and went back into the club.

"Ain't we going to the police station?" Keisha cried to her. Kellie blocked her out.

Sediko had given her the key. Where were Image and Sparrow? She walked straight over to the DJ booth and took the microphone from its stand.

"Everyone get the fuck out!" she said then threw it down and walked across the dance floor towards to the office. She opened the slide door beside the VIP stairs, went in and sat down.

A black girl came in the office through the back followed by Mandy and Keisha.

"You in charge?" the girl asked.

"Didn't you hear me, I said get the fuck out!"

"I work at the bar, I done the takings." She put a grey bag on the table. "What about next week?" she asked.

"Be here for 7 pm on Friday." Kellie couldn't let the club suffer. Sediko would probably be home by then anyway.

"Will Sediko be here?"

"Listen, I said be here for 7. Tell the rest of the staff."

"What about-"

"Just get out! Are you fucking deaf?! I've told you what to do."
The girl turned and left. Kellie returned to the dance floor. She looked at her watch. Two hours ago the club had been full and she had almost told Sediko her news.

"I said out!" she shouted to the bouncers.

"'Ave ta listen ta our boss miss. We got our instructions if anything like this should 'appen," he said.

"And what instructions are those?"

"Wait till 4:45 for the cleaners and don't leave till you've locked up carefully and safely."

"Oh."

A tear welled up in her eye, but she didn't let it drop.

"Here, I think you need this." Mandy approached her with a spliff.

"Thanks."

Kellie sat at the bar. The cleaners came and went. They gave her the entrance takings and the coat booth takings. She locked up behind her.

Kellie, Mandy and Keisha sat in Bones's jeep. They drove straight to Sediko's house. Keisha sat in the back crying with Mandy beside her as Kellie drove silently at a steady 80 mph. Once there, Kellie jumped out. She let herself in and punched in his security code. She took his drugs box and stuffed it in a bag to take. She cleared all evidence– Rizla chipped cigarettes, Charlie residue on surfaces. She went to his secret place and took out the gun he always left in his house. Finally, she looked in his moneybox. Empty. She locked up and went back to the car with the bag.

They drove on to Bermondsey.What had they said? Drugs, weapons and assault. In reality he was guilty of all counts ten times over, but he couldn't go to prison. He had just opened his new club and she didn't have time to run it for him. Kellie reached home in silence with Keisha still crying in the back. She ran in and hid the bag beneath her bed, then ran straight back out to the car. She pulled on her seat belt.

"You alright?" Mandy asked her.

"Yeah. Did you hear them charge Bones and Path?"

"No," they both said.

"Where did Sparrow and Image disappear to?" Kellie asked next.

"I saw them leave just before the police came," Keisha said leaning forward.

"Well, that's fucking convenient."

Kellie parked up outside the station.

"You two stay in the car. Let me go see what's going on. If we all go in there blazing, they won't tell us anything," suggested Mandy looking to Kellie for agreement. She nodded weakly. Mandy jumped out, Keisha immediately followed. Mandy gave Kellie a 'where is she going?' look. Kellie sat and waited. Twenty minutes later, they returned to the car.

"They've all been charged for intent to supply and something else, suspected guns or some shit. They all got to go to court. They'll go to jail on remand." Mandy tried to hold back tears but they betrayed her and two fell.

Kellie sighed, then pulled out. She dropped Keisha and left Bones's jeep outside. Mandy and Kellie waited at a cab station. It was 7 am, Sunday morning.

"Where you going?" an African cab driver asked them.

"Wanna come to mine for a coffee?" Mandy asked her.

"Yeah, why not."

"Fulham, please."

"This is my humble home," Mandy said outside her door. She used a thin card to open it.

"Looks like breaking and entering to me." Kellie chuckled.

"I know, it's this new key card business, apparently it's American." Kellie walked in behind her. The flat was small and nicely decorated. It reminded her of her bedroom as a teenager, but on a bigger scale– the pink and purple walls, the posters of her favourite artists, a big plastic sunflower in a massive vase. The front room was smaller than her whole bedroom, but was clean and cosy. One big 'L' shaped sofa stood against the wall taking up half the room, a kitchen door ahead of it. Mandy disappeared as Kellie pulled off her jacket. She came back in wearing an oversized t-shirt.

"Tea or coffee?" she asked walking through the open kitchen door.

"Coffee. Got to stay awake."

"You can stay for a bit if you want, get your head down for a few hours. You shouldn't even be stressing in your state."

"I should go home, Sediko might phone."

Twenty minutes later Kellie sat in a cab heading northeast, back to the club. On arrival, she got into Sediko's Porsche and drove it home. At 10 o'clock Kellie laid her head on her pillow with the phone beside her head. Hours later the ringing phone jolted her out of sleep.

"Sediko?" she answered.

"Yeah babes." She could almost see him.

"Are you alright? Are you hurt?"

"I'm safe. Did you deal with the club?"

"Of course. I collected the moneys and locked up."

"Good. Baby I'm going down on remand. Couple of weeks max." His voice stayed strong, Kellie couldn't find hers.

"Baby you there?"

"Yeah, I...I..."

"Don't worry, it will only be a few weeks, I promise."

"What am I gonna do? What about the club?"

"All you've got to do is be there, everything's set up to make it easy on you."

"Sediko I can't, not without you, I need you. Can't Sparrow or Image do anything?"

"Don't let them pussies into my club you hear me!"

"How am I meant to keep them out!?"

"There's two big motherfuckers, Jimmys, they'll take care of shit like that, they'll protect you babes. Listen, I gotta go. Remember that I love you. Don't let any man in while I'm away. I'll bell you at work tomorrow."

"I've got this meeting with Samuel's gran and the social worker in the morning; I'll be back at work in the afternoon." The phone went dead.

Kellie sighed and threw herself back on the bed. How could this be happening? Why was this happening? Why had the police just come to the club like that? Something wasn't right.

≈≈≈≈

Sediko stepped out the van with Path, Bones and six other men. They all walked silently through the corridors of Wandsworth prison and were instructed to stand on a faded yellow line in front of a desk in a big room. The head officer stood in front of them.

"Stand still until your name's called!" he shouted, looking at them all one by one.

Ten minutes later, Sediko was called. He followed an officer into a room where he was told to stand in a marked yellow square.

"Name?" another officer behind a desk asked. It stank and the room looked like an old hanging hall.

"Sediko Marshall."

"How long you serving?"

"On remand."

"Canteen or phone card?"

"Phone card."

"Wait over there in the holding cell," he pointed while another officer led him through. Bones was already sitting in the small cold room with two others.

"What's up nigga?" Sediko sat beside him.

"Cool," Bones sighed and bowed his head.

It was obvious that this was his first time in. Sediko knew what that was like, he had served four months for GBH just after his mother died. He looked around the small room. No windows, one door. From there they were led to the medical office. He stood alone in front of the 60-year-old barely alive doctor.

"Step on the scales," he croaked.

He weighed 14 stone.

"Mmm. Are you on drugs?" he asked next.

Sediko nearly started laughing. If he were to shout "boo!" loud enough this man would properly die.

"No."

"Any illness?"

"No, Doc." He hadn't seen a doctor in years.

An hour later they were all allowed to shower. They were then led back to the holding cell. Three of them declined food, the others ate quickly. Later they were led to the cells through two high iron bar gates. Sediko looked up, it was at this moment that you really had to admit to yourself that you going to live here for however long that they gave you. You were no longer in control of your life.

They all sat in a big cell waiting to be led to their private suites. That's when Sediko pulled out his bag of weed and a King L ready-rolled spliff.

"Yeah nigga. I was just about to ask for a cigarette." Path smiled for the first time since they had been arrested. "Cos look." He pulled out a big bag also. They all laughed.

"Mans thinking about Sparrow and Image you know," Bones said seriously which was rarely his personality.

"We'll talk about that tomorrow, we got plenty of time." Sediko lit the spliff.

"So what which man wants to share a cell?" Path asked them. "I'm gonna go talk to the Guv."

"I need my own shit." Sediko pulled hard on his Crow skunk. It stunk.

Path went the door to speak through the pigeonhole. When Path returned, he informed Bones that they would be sharing.

"You niggas had my back, no doubt. But don't worry about a thing, you know Two-Face always got ideas," Sediko assured them.

"Why, what you up to?" Bones asked instantly cheering up. Bones trusted Sediko, he always came through in the end. He always knew the right man or the right man's wife.

Two hours later they were led to their cells. Sediko stepped into his slowly, all suited up for prison life. A bed, a sink, a small table and chairs. What luxuries. He lay on the bed with his hands behind his head. Thinking time now.

Being in the jail cell didn't bother him too much, he loved his own company, he was his own best friend. The only thing that would drive him mad was being away from his baby. Being away from the woman that he loved, the woman that changed him for the better, the one woman that he trusted with his life and almost trusted more than his boys. She was sweet and sexy, she was strong and vulnerable. She was a hard worker and left plenty of time for him. His wifey for the past two-and-a-half years– Kellie. He cleared his mind of her.

Sediko had to go over everything. When he had been arrested they had found a small blade– four inches. He had said that it was for protection, they had said assaulting an officer, his solicitor would say self-defence. Suspected of being in possession of a gun. No gun, no evidence. They would try to get him with intent to supply, they said that they had a witness. Sediko didn't know who it was but his solicitor would deal with that.

Mark Whale had been his brief for years. He was a white, young, English, smart, Eton boy. Mark's only problem was that he was addicted to the white powder that Sediko supplied. He wasn't worried, they would all bust this case. The boy them knew it too.

That's why they would try and keep them on remand for as long as they could.

He fell asleep wondering if Kellie was looking after his car.

At 7:30 am a screw opened Sediko's door.

"Wake up, breakfast!" he shouted banging the door.

By the time he opened his eyes he had decided to take this time as rest time.

"Wake up you fucker, I said breakfast!" He banged again.

"Alright chill, I'm up, shit." He sat up and rubbed his face.

"Can I make a phone call, Guv?" He pulled on his t-shirt.

"Yeah, just a soon as you've had your breakfast." He marched off to wake some other poor sucker.

Sediko stepped out the cell. Bones and Image slumped out of theirs.

"Shit, I can't take these early morning rises," Bones said rubbing his big belly. "I'm starving," he said yawning.

"Be careful what you eat," Sediko said laughing.

"Two-Face, that you nigga?"

Sediko turned to the familiar voice.

"Johnny. What's up?" Sediko touched fists with him.

"When you land? Last night?"

"Yeah, look at you, all crooked out."

Johnny was on a life stretch for rape and triple murder. He ran the whole prison. Anything you wanted he was your man, Shawshank style– from drugs to spades, a blow job, or a cup of Courvoisier. He was in his early 30's, dark short and stocky.

"So how long your bird, king?"

"On remand, rude boy. I'm out soon, they been tryin' to hold man for long now. Someone try gee man up, you get me? But it's all good though, you know mans got his own hater's fan club." They both laughed and nodded.

"Breakfast girls!"

They all walked towards the breakfast hall. Sediko skipped breakfast and went straight to the phone.

"Yeah," he said as Kellie anticipated that it was him. He spoke to her for a few minutes before cutting her off to phone Mia.

"Sediko?" she asked before he even spoke.

"Yeah."

"Are you alright, where are you?" He could hear tears in her voice.

"Wandsworth jail house. I'm alright though. You can bring some things up for me Wednesday morning."

"What do you want?"

Those were the words he wanted to hear her say. He reeled off his list, then cut the call. Had to save his credits. He dialled Mark's office number.

"Who said you could use the phone?" demanded a voice behind him. He hung up and turned around.

"My man over there said I could," Sediko answered. He felt like a school kid. That was the last time any one had spoken to him like that.

"You had breakfast?"

"Na." Sediko was slowly getting pissed off.

"Well get in there and eat." The screw stood with his hands on his hips.

"Fuck you."

Sediko turned, look at his phone card and walked past him towards his cell. The guard put a hand on Sediko's shoulder. Kissing his teeth, he shrugged it off and kept walking. This was meant to be relaxing time.

"Well get in your cell and starve then, suppose you won't be having any dinner either," he called to him. They were trying to make him angry; they had nothing on him so they were trying everything.

When he got to his cell he dropped to the floor and did 200 press ups, he had to release his energy.

Nine

BILL SAT IN his best friend's large chair. He lived in Chelsea in a nice, small, two-bedroom house right by the river. He had all the essentials even though it was a small place. A dishwasher, a giant freezer, a small bar in a good sized front room, wide screen flat television, a PC and a bedroom fit for a bachelor.

Burt Congal. He was an actor, whose latest and biggest job was as a local thief in a popular evening soap called Northenders .

"Yes, I know what it's like," Burt sympathised.

Bill sat with the papers open wide in his lap. 'Bill begs wife. Mistress begs Bill. Wife dumps Bill. Bill dumps Mistress,' he read. The papers were making a mockery of his life, a joke out of his marriage and public knowledge of his sex life.

Last week he had stupidly met up with Lisa. They had again agreed on the separation. The tabloids slashed it all over the paper two days later. That alone dashed any hopes of him getting back with Marie. His personal life was crowded with cameras. Only this time he was at the zoom end.

Recently he had been asked to attend a celebrity man sale for cancer charities. He hadn't agreed. More publicity was the last thing that he needed, even if it was for a good cause. On the up side, his business was the best it had been in 24 years; he was thinking of expanding.

"So what are you going to do?" Burt asked him sipping champagne at 2:30 in the afternoon.

"About what, Marie? What more can I do? I told her that Lisa and I were separated. She knows, I've made it clear. Since she's listening to the tabloids more than me, they will tell her. She's still going ahead with the divorce proceedings. Multiple adultery they call it."

"What about Carrie?"

"Well, Marie was right about one thing, she is a scheming little so and so; nothing like her mother. It's these new hip grunge people. She asked me for 12 thou. I said I wouldn't give it to her unless she told me what it was for. She already gets an allowance, and at *her* age for god sake. She wouldn't tell me. Then she said that she would sell her story to her favourite magazine for double that price. After that, she said it was a joke, but what kind of a joke is that at a time like this, ay?"

"Wow Bill, little Carrie's all grown up. What happened to that little sweet girl that ran into her room and slammed the door when she couldn't get her own way?" He slapped his own knee and shook his head.

"I wish I knew. I ended up giving her 8 thou. Bribery– in my own home!"

"You're not drinking your bubbly. You need something stronger?" Burt stood and went to the bar. He was a small man with a big mouth.

They had been friends for as long as he could remember. His bleach blonde hair fell on his shoulders. At 45, he had the impressive physique of a 25 year old.

"Yes, I need something stronger. In fact, I need a holiday. A week away, somewhere hot. Somewhere remote." He looked up, imagining a small deserted island, population 200, no tourists or clicking cameras.

"Don't we all." He came back with two tall glasses of something red and creamy.

"What's this?" He didn't expect cocktails for lunch.

"It's a little special of mine, used the blender and everything and made enough to last all week."

Bill sipped his. He had only been here a little over 2 hours and already they had finished a bottle of wine, a bottle of champagne and now they were on rock and roll style iced cocktails. The thick liquid burned his throat as it went down. He had never tasted anything like it.

"This is nice, I'd love to serve this up at one of Marie's dinner parties." He smiled at the thought of them all rolling around drunk out of their heads. "So how's Albert Road?"

"Well, I haven't got many scenes. Apparently my character needs a build up." He began to slur his words from too much red creamy drink. He was gulping his like orange juice.

"So, how's Belinda?" Bill lifted his eyebrows and smiled. Burt had been a bachelor most of his life, never married and no children. Recently he had gotten engaged to a twenty-something black beauty.

"She's great, gone shopping," he said quickly and downed the rest of his drink. Bill sensed a problem.

"Listen old friend I know I'm going on about my crisis, but I've still got ears."

"Well, if you don't mind my going on. I love Belinda. She's so beautiful and funny, but she's so hard to please. She hates everyone and everything. Last week I brought her a Renault Clio, new reg; this week she wants something bigger and better. She's still refusing to sleep with me until the wedding night. She wants a big affair, money for the dress, money for flowers; I just can't keep up.

Clubbing every weekend, champagne all night. She's got me into this obsessive drinking, you noticed? She's so good to me though, always buying me little things to show that she thinks about me. She says that she loves me. Sounds full of for me. It feels good. She even wants my kids. I'm 45 for christsakes, except *she* thinks I'm 35." Burt talked and talked. He was a great listener but once he started…

Bill downed the rest of his drink in one swift gulp. *If you can't beat 'em, join em.* Burt carried on.

"Even worse, Sharon hates her. She thinks Belinda is only after my money."

"Sharon's been interfering in your relationships since your first girlfriend when you were twelve. She's your twin, she would."

"Talking about me were you?" Belinda came in. "Hi Bill. Burt got you on his cocktails as well?" She sat beside Burt. "Pour me one please hon," she asked with the right amount of sweetness. Burt stood to pour her and them another.

"Bill, you've turned into a right little celebrity. Newspapers, magazines, pictures of you taken by someone hiding behind a bike shed," she remarked laughing.

Sitting across from her, Bill couldn't help but to admire her body. She wore a tight short mini-skirt. Her legs were slightly open but he couldn't see far enough up. Her big breasts spilled out of a low-cut fluffy pink jacket. She watched him watch her.

"Not by choice. I hate every minute of it. I was just telling Burt, they've taken away my privacy. It's a nightmare," he sighed.
Burt came over with a jug of the drink.

"So what did you buy?" he asked as if he didn't want to really hear the answer.

"Go get my bags out of the car and I'll show you."

When Burt returned from his third trip there were around forty bags. She took out clothes, shoes, bags, make up and whatever else she could find. She also had a story with every item; a rude cashier or an unhelpful helper.

"I brought you something Burt." She rummaged around the bags and minutes later produced a small black box and handed it to him. Burt opened it to a pair of platinum cufflinks. He kissed her.

Drinks later, Bill called Marie. Burt and Belinda had disappeared for a moment.

"Yes Bill."

"Would you consider coming out to lunch or dinner with me?" he asked softly. Trying to pour his love from his words onto her.

"My solicitor thinks that's not a good idea."

"Fuck the solicitor, will you come to dinner? Please Marie, just dinner."

"Bill you're drunk, stop phoning me." She hung up.
Shit, he would soon give up on Marie. There were other beauties in his life besides Lisa and Marie.

≈≈≈≈

She had decided that today would be the day. Sediko had been in for 17 days and by the time he came out, Kellie would be off the scene. It was the second week in September and Mia's 7 months looked more like 'overdue by a week.' She dialled Sediko's home number knowing that Kellie would be there. When Kellie saw her stomach there would be no denying. And she wouldn't dare hit her; Sediko would kill her. The phone rang 3 times.

"Hello?" "Hello?" Mia couldn't speak.

"This must be one of Two-Face's hoes. Come off his line, he's just playing you bitch, he's got me." Kellie laughed an evil cackle.

"It's Mia, we need to talk." Her turn to be silent. "Hello, Kellie?"

"What would we have to talk about?" she spat.

"I need to tell you a few things, but not over the phone."

"We haven't got nothing to talk about. You ain't with Sediko and nor am I."

"I think you'll want to hear what I've got to say. And don't be misunderstood, I am with Sediko. Maybe not at the moment but as soon as he lands."

"You're one crazy bitch. If that was true, then how come I'm the one in his house, how come it's me who's got the keys to his club and car? As always you will come to the same conclusion, he is with me! What the fuck are you doing except running his ass down? You are beyond dumb Mia and I feel sorry for you."

"I'm on my way to you." Mia cut the call. She wore a tight top and the blue tracksuit that Sediko had left there.

Mia sat in the cab on her way. Why was Sediko letting her stay there? Fair enough Kellie had been on the scene for a few years but she had been there first, before the club, before all his money. They were teenage sweethearts, they were each other's first love. That had to count for something.

She paid for the cab and knocked on the door. No answer. She stood waiting. The bitch had gone out, Sediko's car wasn't in its parking space. She knocked again and again, still no answer. She hadn't come all this way to just turn back. Mia took her keys out of her pocket. She had a copy of his Yale lock but wasn't able to sneak in again to get the bottom Chubb lock – that was a special cut.

Mia didn't really *want* to let herself in. Kellie would tell Sediko and he would kill her, baby or no baby, but she was desperate. She knocked again, praying that Kellie would just come to the door. What was her problem, why had she left? Maybe Kellie already knew about Sediko Junior.

Hoping that the bottom lock was open, Mia pushed her duplicate key into the hole. The door clicked open. She went in quickly and punched in his security code– his mother's birthday combined with the date of her death. She closed the door behind her, it felt as if she had stepped into forbidden territory.

Kellie's things were everywhere, more than usual. She walked around slowly. Then, there on the table, she saw it– her scan picture. So she knew. But Mia didn't remember giving Sediko a copy. She wished she could find some evidence against Kellie. Maybe she was bringing a man here. She picked up some photos from the speaker box and looked through them. Pictures of them. Pictures of Sediko and Kellie's bastard son. Why did he want to take on another man's child? Maybe in the same way that Kirk had been prepared to?

Mia waited for over an hour. Finally, she decided to go. Maybe she would come back tomorrow, or even later on that night. A door slammed. Mia stood rigid in the front room waiting for Kellie to pounce. She held her stomach.

Kellie gasped when she saw her. Then both sets of eyes fell on each other's stomachs. Mia heaved as she saw Kellie's small bump; she couldn't believe what she was seeing. Her head felt light and she couldn't catch her breath. She tore her eyes away from Kellie's stomach and to the scan that she had seen earlier on the table. The name in the top righthand corner read: Ms K. Palmer. Her legs gave way beneath her. Her world went blank.

Mia awoke in a hospital bed. Her head ached but it was nowhere near the pain that her heart felt. Why hadn't Sediko told her? They had no secrets.

"Visitor?" A nurse asked peeping her head through the drawn curtain.

"Who?" It couldn't be Kellie.

Charlene stuck her head through. Mia sighed relief, she was happy to see her friend.

"Yeah thanks, but no one else please."

Mia sat up and Charlene sat at the end of the hospital bed.

"How'd you know I was here?"

"Kellie called me."

"What?" Mia's eyes opened wide.

"So who do ya think brought you here? What happened?"

"Where's my bag?" Mia looked around.

Charlene took it from the side cabinet. Mia grabbed it and took her keys out. Kellie had taken the duplicate.

"What's going on? Come on, I'm baffled here. What were you and Kellie doing together?"

"I went to Sediko's house to confront her. To show her, to tell her that he is my man, my future. I had a copy of his key so I went in and waited. When she came back Charlene, you won't believe... I saw her belly..I just can't believe it, I couldn't believe it." Mia began to cry.

"What?"

"Kellie's pregnant."

"Ohmygod!" Charlene's hand covered her mouth in shock.

"She's pregnant, why didn't Sediko tell me?" She began to sob, her shoulders moving up and down fast. "What is it Charlene? What is it with me? Why is she pregnant? That fucking bitch!" Mia shouted.

"Calm down, think about *your* baby, not hers. And really, it's not her fault. She brought ya here and stayed wid you until they gave ya the all clear. Then she phoned me. To make sure you wasn't alone."

"Right, so she's a fucking saint now? Whose side are you on?" Mia's face screwed up in pain as her baby shifted positions.

"I ain't on any side. I think ya both mad. But how do you think she feels, looking after her so called man while he's in the pen, then find out he's got another girl preggers. No. I would kill a man for that shit. She can't be all that bad, if I were 'er I would have dragged you out the house and left you. You broke in her yard and she still brought ya and waited to see if you and baby were alright."

"She wasn't so nice the last time we saw each other."

"You were both hot headed, and not pregnant."

"Charlene, all this boils down to one thing. Sediko. And I can't give up on him."

"So what you gonna do when he lands?"

"I'm gonna be with him, that's it. Can you leave me, I want to be alone now."

"Why do you always push away people who care for you; just when ya need 'em."

"I don't."

"Seen Kirk lately?!"

"Kirk is old news."

"He loved ya you know and now he's gone. He don't even want to see you you fucked him up so bad. I come here ta support ya and you wanna be alone. Who you gonna talk ta now, Kellie?"

Mia cried as Charlene spoke. She stood to leave.

"Wait Charlene. I'm sorry. Don't go yet."

Charlene came and hugged her tight.

≈≈≈≈

Kellie walked in the door, coded in, and went into the front room. Her heart skipped a beat as she saw Mia standing in the living room. What the fuck, how did she get in? Kellie's mind raced. Her eyes fell to Mia's stomach maybe a month or more bigger than her own. Mia's face seemed to crumble and her breath came short. She fell to the ground. The bitch had fainted.

For about 5 minutes Kellie looked at her lying face up on the rug. *Mia was pregnant. Pregnant.* She picked up her bag and emptied it onto the floor. *Mia was pregnant.* She should call the fucking police and charge her with breaking and entering, trespassing. Then she saw her key. Angrily, Kellie tugged it off the bunch. How the fuck could he give this bitch a key? She didn't have time for this, she refused to get upset, this was her and Samuel's day. She waited. Ten more minutes went by before Kellie started getting worried. Even though Mia was a waste of space and she would be happy if she were dead, she had a life inside of her just as she had.

Why was this pregnant girl lying on the floor in front of her? She never believed that she really had the bottle to come, and now here she was. She would have to speak with Sediko. Maybe it wasn't his child. Mia's got a man, why can't it be *his* child? She wouldn't argue with him over this until she knew the facts. Plus, the thought of her splitting up with him was too much to bear. She needed him more than ever now. And now that Mia knew she was pregnant she had to tell Sediko before she did.

Kellie hadn't been to visit him. He had said he didn't want her to see him locked up. Really, it was the other way round. In those 2 weeks her stomach had blossomed; she was now 5 months pregnant.

Kellie bent slowly and grabbed Mia under the armpits. Slowly she dragged her out to the car, stopping every 5 seconds to catch her breath. Getting her in was the worst. When she woke she would feel cuts and bruises everywhere. Kellie smiled at the thought.

In the car, she pulled on Mia's seat belt. She looked at her closely; her eyes were shut firmly. Kellie's hand went up to feel her stomach. It was harder than hers, lower too. Was this Sediko's child? Mia's head was rolled towards her, she *was* pretty cute. She remembered when she had first laid eyes on her; she had thought that she was a little girl that could cause no harm, no threat. Now..now she was carrying Sediko's child. Maybe his first child. Kellie started the engine and drove to the hospital.

Kellie waited 45 minutes just to hear the doctor say she was fine.

"The baby's heart is beating normally now. They should both be fine, we'll keep her overnight just to keep an eye on them. Is there anyone that you'd like to call for her? Her mother or the father of the child?" the doctor asked.

The words burned her. The truth burned her.

"I'll try and call her mum."

Kellie moved quickly towards the waiting room. She should have left her, now she was stuck doing her arch enemy favours. She took out Mia's phone and went through her phone book. Eight numbers, two of which were Sediko's. This girl was a loner. She chose Charlene and dialled the number.

"Where are you? I been waiting ages."

"This ain't Mia," Kellie said bluntly.

"So who's this? Where's Mia?"

"She fainted, she's in hospital. First George's in Tooting. She's alright but has to stay the night."

"Who is this?"

"Kellie."

She hung up as she heard Charlene gasp.

With the phone call made, Kellie immediately left the hospital. She jumped into Sediko's car and looked at her watch: 1:59 pm. She had an appointment at 2:30 at the other end of town. She put her foot down and glanced at the back seat full of toys. It was Samuel's birthday and whether he came home with her or not, he would get all of them.

Ten minutes to spare; just what she didn't want. She didn't want any time to think, her mind would always ask too many questions. She sat waiting in the big room.

"Miss Palmer?" a voice asked behind her. She turned to an extended hand in a blue suit. She stood and shook it.

"Hello, I'm Anne Herr, Samuel's social worker. Would you like to come this way?" Kellie followed her.

"It's nice to finally meet you Kellie, Samuel talks about you a lot," Anne said still walking. They ended up in a small conference room. Samuel sat beside Carol. His eyes quickly fell on her now noticeable lump.

"Hello Carol. Hiya Samuel."

Samuel jumped out of his chair and ran to hug her. She held him tight, overwhelmed by his affection.

"Take a seat," Anne offered.

"Alright, we are all here for one reason. We all want what's best for Samuel. At the moment he stays with you Carol. And Kellie, his mother, is desperate to have her son back with her. We've been evaluating the situation and-"

"Have you evaluated that she's a drug addict? Come to me Samuel," Carol said angrily. Samuel slipped off Kellie's lap.

"I'm not on drugs. I've got a good job, I bring home more money than you." Kellie kept her cool. Every word that Carol spoke pushed her further and further away from her son.

"I know you are. I've already told Anne that I've a good witness. You're most properly high now. You're not fit to be a mother."

"Yes, you said that last time. That's why last week I had a full drugs test with my doctor." Kellie took an envelope from her briefcase. She passed it to Ann. Carol's eyes blazed.

"The father of that unborn child is in prison. What kind of example is that?"

"It's that son of yours, Stuart, that's giving you all this false information. What is it with you lot? What have I done to you? We used to get on."

"You killed my son," Carol spat.

Kellie sighed. "I wasn't even there! I hurt too you know! I loved Simon and you know it! But this isn't about him is it? It's about Samuel and he's mine. I made a mistake and I'm sorry, but I'm still his mum. I can take care of him. I'm successful-"

"That you are. A glamour model, running a strip bar and working for a convicted adulterer. Simon wouldn't have wanted that for his son.

He would have wanted it this way. You used to be such a sweet girl."

"He can't replace Simon, he's gone. The way it hurt you when Simon passed, is that what you want for me? Would you cause me that pain?" Kellie hadn't spoken Simon's name in years.

"Is my room still at your house?" Samuel interrupted.

"Yes. And it always will be."

"I wanna come home now," he said simply.

"He doesn't know what he's saying." Carol held tight to him. He squirmed uncomfortably.

Anne spoke up.

"Well, as it stands Kellie we really have no reason not to let him go home with you. This proves that you don't take drugs." She handed the envelope back to Kellie.

"What?!" Carol almost shouted.

"Carol of course you will still see Samuel, we will all make sure of that. We'll hold meetings at least once a month just to make sure that Samuel is happy and comfortable."

"What are you saying?" Tears began to well in Carol's eyes.

"Listen Carol, I'll let him stay until the end of the week. You can inform his school that he will be leaving," Kellie said smugly.
She was getting her son back, she hadn't expected it to happen so quickly.

"When you get bored, you'll bring him back."

"Really? We'll see. Are we finished here? I've got to get to work." Kellie beamed.

"I'll send you the paperwork Kellie. It's always a pleasure to reunite parents with their children. Only once in a while do the parents actually want the child back with nothing but love and good intentions rather than to get back at a spouse or to claim money. I hope it all works out for the best. I'm sure it will."

"Can I have a moment with Samuel? We'll be just outside." She beckoned a smiling Samuel to her. Outside she bent down on one knee to look level in his eyes.

"You sure you want to come and stay with mummy?"

"Yes." He nodded vigorously. "Are you gonna have a baby?" he asked curiously.

"Yes, we are." She pulled him close to her. "I'll collect you on Sunday, alright?"

Fifty minutes later Kellie was at work. This was going to be a long day.

"You sure you want to do this?" Sally asked her.

"Why not? It's nothing new." Kellie sat with only a towel covering her. She was doing nude shots for a big fee.

"But you're pregnant."

"Really? I didn't realise."

"But why didn't you say?" Sally couldn't hide her shock. Kellie gave her an 'as if' look.

"Miss Palmer, I'm your photographer, Ben. I take most of the controversial photos for Penneton," a short scruffy man said proudly.

Make-up and hair artists buzzed around her. She remembered her first time with Lisa, back then she had felt in over her depth. Now she was a natural. This modelling had gotten her face in magazines and papers. She never looked at any, nor did she read about herself. Most of the time she forgot that she was a minor celebrity. Last summer she had cringed every time she saw the double billboard posters of herself in a white thong bikini. Men had followed her around for ages. This would be different though; she wasn't thin and sexy, she was pregnant and beautiful. Some people would think that what she was doing was wrong. Sediko especially, and that's exactly what she wanted.

"This is Deke, he'll be your male model for the evening." Someone pushed him towards her. He was the most handsome white man she had ever seen. Better than Brad Pit, taller than Tom Cruise, sexier than Al Pacino. He had long, thick, dark, European hair. His chest was well built, as were his legs. A towel covered his modesty.

"Still think it's a bad idea?" Kellie whispered to Sally whose mouth was on the floor.

Kellie extended her hand for the sex god to shake.

"Hello Deke, so you're the one?"

"Hi Kellie, you are definitely the one," he said nodding his head.

Deke had begged for this job. At 18, he was ready for the modelling world. He had been following Kellie's short career from day one when she had done a men's magazine spread with Lisa Brooks. Kellie had taken his breath away. And pregnant women - who flourished instead of flawed - turned him on, even moreso if the baby was nothing to do with him. He couldn't and wouldn't handle being a father.

"How long you got?"

"Thirty minutes to go and counting; no pictures yet."

"Well don't worry; heard that he gets his best pictures in a hurry." Deke smiled, showing a perfect set of white teeth.

"You have beautiful hair," Deke complimented touching her long dark ringlets.

"You too." She touched his long dark hair in return.

"RIGHT! CLEAR THE STUDIO!" Ben shouted.

"Good luck," Sally lied to her. "And nice to meet you." She shook Deke's hand.

The studio emptied half way.

"GET IN THE BACKGROUND!" he shouted to them. *Were all photographers deaf in one ear?*

Deke dropped his towel first to reveal skin coloured thong briefs. Kellie dropped hers to her own total bald nudity.

"Position 1! As was shown."

Behind them, on a giant wall stage, were photos and photos of babies of all races. They both sat in an oversized sofa and gazed into each other's eyes. He sat behind her holding onto her perfect stomach just the way the photographer wanted. He snapped around 15 times, seeing the perfect couple through his lens.

"Excellent! Position 2!"

They both stood while the set was quickly changed. This would be the shot the world would judge her on. An oversized bed was brought on, the backstage was taken off. A real looking bedroom stage decorated with soft pinks and sky blues was brought in.

Deke helped Kellie onto the tall bed. She relaxed in the biggest, fluffiest pillows she had ever laid her head on.

"You alright?" he asked as he lay beside her.

She nodded. She felt as naked as she was, but loved the feeling. And as wrong as it was, she loved the way Deke's eyes followed her, even in her 6th month of pregnancy.

Ben sat looking uncomfortable at the head of the long bed, just above their heads.

"Do what comes naturally! We have 15 minutes, so just be creative."

Kellie climbed on top of Deke. She held her arms in the air, she scrunched her hair and shook it, she fingered his chest all the while keeping her eyes on his. Deke sat up slightly, his pecks bulged. He came up slowly and kissed her lips gently.

"PAUSE!" Ben shouted, jumping off the bed and running around to a different position. Deke kept his lips firmly on Kellie's while he sat up on his elbows. Both sets of eyes were closed.

"Okay, continue!"

Deke was fighting himself physically and mentally not to get excited. This had never happened to him before. He could feel it rising, he tried to clear his mind.

"GOOD! SWITCH PLACES!" Ben shouted. *Shit,* Deke thought.

It was too late, his penis was as hard as a rock. Kellie looked down at him. He bit his lip and grimaced.

"Er, sorry," was all he could manage.

"It's alright, honestly," Kellie reassured him. "Just hurry up and sort it out," she teased him with a smile. Slowly, hiding his erection, they both switched places. His head lay lightly on her stomach.

"No, no, no good; it looks like he's squashing you! You alright Kellie? Swap back. Both were sitting up. As you were when you kissed. No, no, do spoons!" he instructed.

"You still alright?" Deke asked. She nodded again. He positioned himself behind her. This was much worse for him, this was his favourite position.

To finish up she lay across his legs while he stroked her stomach and hair.

"That's it then!" Ben shouted. Two towels were thrown their way.

"Sorry, again."

"It's fine, you were a natural."

"Really, you too." He tried hard not to sound like the lovesick fan that he was.

Kellie was helped off the bed and dressed quickly.

"Thank you. E-mail me."

She rushed off true diva style.

In the car she looked at the time: 7 pm. She drove home to change. Her day had turned from shit to great. Mia had tried to sway it but it hadn't worked. Samuel was coming home. Carol had tried to bring her down but it hadn't worked. And best of all she hadn't touched any crack cocaine or Charlie. A weed spliff passed her lips only now and then; her doctor had informed her that there was less of a threat to her unborn child from smoking cannabis. Sediko's phone rang. He had left her in charge of everything, not just the club.

"Kellie, it's Smalls."

"Yeah, meet me round the back of Haydon's. About nine-ish."

Once Kellie got home, she showered and washed Deke's touch from her body. As she stepped out there was a knock at the door. She answered, dripping wet, to Mandy. They had been spending a lot of time together since their boys had been locked up.

"Before we go to the club, I need to sort out a few things, you wanna come?" Kellie said to her once they were in her room.

"Well as long as we go, I didn't dress up for nothing."

"Yeah, we'll go a bit later. Jade can cope till I get there." Kellie rushed around getting dressed. Since Sediko had been gone she had almost split herself in two she was so busy. Always had something to do or someone to see. She put on her elasticised Henney's pinstripe business suit.

"It suits you," remarked Mandy.

"Thanks, got it in Henney's.

"No, I mean pregnancy," Mandy corrected.

"Thanks. Oh, my son will be home next week."

They talked as Kellie got ready. Kellie told her about the Mia episode that morning.

"Well I can't say that I'm surprised, but I can't believe that she had the nerve to let herself in."

"Right I'm ready. You ready?" Kellie asked her as they pulled up outside Haydon's.

"For what?" Mandy asked. Kellie took a desert Eagle handgun from her briefcase and slid it beside her.

"Shit, Kellie. What the-"

"Just come on, or stay here." Kellie stepped out the car.

Inside the shop she spotted Image and Sparrow at the back by the

125

stairs. The rest was packed with Afros and fades, mostly talking or watching MTV Base on a big screen. Kellie walked straight up to them, Mandy followed close behind.

"Sparrow, you got anything for me, I know I was meant to come long time but I been busy."

"Who me? I ain't got nothing for you Kellie, except this." Sparrow groped his groin. They both laughed. She looked at him unamused and serious as a slit throat.

"I've just come to collect for Sediko. Come, lets go talk upstairs and keep our business to ourselves," Kellie suggested trying to be reasonable.

"Talk up what stairs? You ain't welcome up there no more. If anything, Two-Face owes *us* money, 5% worth," Image spat at her.

"Fuck that, I'm here about the money from here and the games machines you've been emptying."

"Bitch, what you on!? Oh yeah, crack." Image and Sparrow laughed at her again. "Just take your pregnant self back home, go sit down, and you and Mia can compare baby notes." The laughter continued. They were really taking the piss now. She sighed. She wouldn't let Sediko down; he had come too far.

"I didn't want it to get to this."

Kellie stepped up close to Sparrow who sat in a barber's chair. She took her gun from her swollen waist and slapped it hard across his face. The laughter stopped immediately. He jumped out the chair and stood directly in front of her. She pushed the gun into his chest and flicked off the safety catch.

"Bitch you mad?!" Sparrow looked at her.

"What?! What the fuck you got to tell me now? Don't make me nervous cos I'm liable to blow your fucking heart out! Just like Sediko taught me."

"Alright calm down, mans just having a joke."

"Whatever, now let's start again. Sparrow, have you got anything for me?"

"Image, give her the fucking bag! You turned into a real super bitch, innit? True you got Two-Face to back you."

Kellie moved closer to him and placed the gun below his chin. He could feel her anger, he dared not move.

"Do you see Two-Face in here? I don't, unless he's grown a pussy and two breasts!" she whispered to him. Mandy laughed from somewhere behind her.

"Kellie?" asked a male voice behind her. Kellie turned with the gun still in place, every eye in the place was on her and her corner by the stairs.

"Who the fuck are you?" Kellie spat with a look to kill. Sparrow was still stiff, he knew that Sediko would make sure his girl had a fully loaded round.

"Smalls innit, you remember me?"

"You can't be Smalls, I told that nigga to meet me the fuck out back!" She turned the gun from Sparrow to Smalls's trouser zip.

"It's cool, it's cool; I'm outside already," he said while backing up to the door. While her back was turned, Sparrow jumped away from her. Image came down the stairs with a Nike bag.

"It's all there." He handed it to her.

"Excuse me for not listening to a fucking lying word you fuckers say. Count it."

"There's over 7 grand, I ain't counting that shit."

"Oh really?" Kellie waved the gun toward Image this time.

"Alright maybe minus a grand, but that shit will take ages to count," Image moaned.

"Do I give a fuck? No. Upstairs now; both of you."

"What? This ain't the movies bitch."

"No, no it's not, if it was you would be the black man that dies in the beginning. Now don't let me prove to you that I'm not scared to use this shit." They both went slowly to the staircase. Kellie watched them go. They reached the top and looked back to her standing at the bottom. She laughed loudly.

"Look at you two pussies, being sent upstairs by a pregnant lady. You think I'm gonna miss one shitty grand. I hope you smoked it cos I'll take pleasure in telling Sediko all about it." Kellie turned to leave.

"I heard Sediko got a 10 bird," one of them called.

Out the back, Smalls waited for her. She felt so in control, so powerful.

"I collected 35-"

"35 what? Grand?" Kellie hid her shock.

"Yeah, I know it's not all of it but-"

"What's all this shit. Everyone trying to take out cash here and there as soon as Sediko's back is turned! How much more do you owe?"

"Five," he muttered.

"Alright, get to the club."

"Kellie, you had them shitting bricks. Sediko will be proud," Mandy said to her in the car as they made one more stop before leaving South London.

In the car they talked and talked about every and anything. Kellie chose not to tell her about the nude pictures just yet, if everyone was going to hate her, she needed to be prepared for it. And she was still reeling from Deke's touch.

"So I'm finally going to see him on Monday. I'll break it to him slowly that he may have two kids born at the same time."

"That's madness Kellie. You think that it's his?"

"I hope not, but realistically, even if it is, my plans are gonna stay the same. We're gonna move in together and bring up our family."

"Well, good luck."

"So, where we walking to now, aren't you tired after all that? Mad break-in, dash to hospital, work, home, then collecting your shit true gangster-bitch style *and* you're pregnant." Mandy admired her strength.

"No time to be tired, I'll relax at the club."

"You got work to do at the club."

At 11:20 pm they walked past the spot where she had almost beat Shawn's girlfriend to death and was arrested for the first time. That seemed so long ago, when everything was simple. She had had the chance to tell Sediko about the baby then, but she hadn't.

Shawn stood with his back to them.

"Is that who you're meeting?" Mandy asked too loudly. And as usual, he turned before she could creep up on him.

"What's up?" He turned and embraced her quickly, then looked down to her stomach. She pulled away from him. He looked at Mandy who stood a few feet away, then spoke into her ear.

"So how are you?"

"Pregnant."

"Yeah and looking extra good."

"What's all this, you know I'm-"

"Yeah, in a hurry," he finished her sentence.

"My girl's waiting, you want this?"

"No." He bit his bottom lip.

"So what then? Come on," Kellie urged, she thought he would have been distant when he saw that she was pregnant.

"Alright, but I don't know if you're gonna like it... I like you."

"Yes Shawn, you've made that clear and I told you that I-"

"You told me that you had a man," he finished for her again.

Kellie smiled this time. She turned to see that Mandy had made herself scarce.

"I've got to get to the club, I haven't got time for these games. I drove all the way from Central London for you to tell me that?"

In a way she was fuming, because if this had been a year ago she would have fucked him just to show Sediko that two could play his game.

"What's the rush? I know right now you must be feeling lonely." He stood so confident, so manly and handsome.

"Not really," Kellie lied.

"If you want someone to come and keep you warm tonight, who knows….like they say, while the cats away…"

"Won't your woman miss you?"

"What woman?"

"The one you must have visited in hospital a while back. She must have told you."

128

"She did. That's when I knew that I had to have you." He had an answer to everything. "Maybe I might see you a bit later tonight?"

"Tonight where?"

"Ballers of course, unless you want a home visit."

"Bye Shawn."

As she turned to walk away he gently pulled her arm just as Sediko had two-and-a-half years ago. Instead of shrugging him off she allowed him to pull her gently towards him and kiss her tenderly on the neck.

"I'll be there to protect you, beautiful," he said before walking away.

"From what?" she called after him as he walked into the night. *What did he mean by that?*

Kellie walked back to the car where Mandy was waiting.

"Love was definitely in the air," Mandy teased.

"Speak for yourself. What, you want a hook up?" Kellie got in the car slightly annoyed that Mandy was putting two and two together and making five.

"Path is my man, I don't need a temp, that just makes things complicated and oh, I was gonna say, I've seen that man's face somewhere. Who's his people?"

"You know what, I don't know nothing about him, don't know where he's from or what car he drives, all I know is his baby mother is ugly."

Mandy laughed.

"So how did you meet him? Through Sediko?"

"Well that's what I first thought. It was about 6 months ago; he just phoned me." She really didn't know how he had gotten her number.

"Well I'm telling you, I seen him before. Yes that's it, he was in Ballers the night they got arrested. He was talking to Sparrow."

Kellie went deep into thought while Mandy kept talking. She remembered that she thought that she had seen him that night too. *Why didn't Shawn say that he was there?* She looked at her watch, she was running late.

Once they got to Ballers, Kellie went straight to the office and sat around the table to do the accounts. This was her so-called 'resting time.' She'd work all week - half in the office, half doing modelling around London - then she'd go home and have lonely, sleepless nights. No Sediko. No Samuel yet. She just couldn't relax alone anymore. At Ballers everyone danced around her without a care in the world; it made her relax.

"Kellie, this keeps going round and round in my head. Do you think that Sediko knows Shawn?"

"Don't know."

"Yes or no?"

"Probably not," Kellie was forced to answer.

"Right then, if he don't know Sediko then how did he get your number and what was he doing chatting to Sparrow in the club? Plus you obviously sell crack to him. And the police say they've got a witness to say the guys sell drugs. Come on, suspect or what?"

Kellie sighed loudly. She went to the door and called to Smalls. As she sat back down, her baby kicked. She kept on forgetting that she was pregnant. With Samuel it was feet up, wrap up, in the house 24/7. This time was the total opposite.

"But why would Shawn fuck with Sediko?" Kellie asked herself aloud.

Five minutes later Smalls knocked and came in.

"Sorry Kel, I had to shit."

"Too much information you nasty fucker. And don't call me Kel. Go get Jade."

That night Kellie didn't sleep well.

The next day she sat alone in the office, thankful that the club was only open on weekends. Jade came in wearing the new shirts that Kellie had Laymend's design. It was black and fitted with a big silver B on the back written in old italic writing. On the front was a single pocket over the left breast with Ballers bar written small in the same silver writing.

"You like it?" Kellie asked her.

"Yeah."

"Good."

Kellie went back to her work. Jade stood there.

"What?" Kellie looked back up to her.

"Just wanted to tell you that the orders have come, everything's there apart from the cocktail sticks again. I went and brought some for tonight. I took money from the petty cash and left the receipt in there."

"Get the suppliers on the phone. Make sure there is double for the next delivery. Anything else?"

"Yes. Keisha isn't doing any better. I don't think the course helped. She's broken 3 glasses already."

"Alright just leave her with me. Sit down for a second, there's something I've been meaning to tell you."

"Am I in trouble?" she asked quickly.

"You've been doing quite well. You're basically running the bar and the staff so I'd just like to change your job title and obviously your salary."

"None of us have been paid yet, or know how you want to pay us."

"What? Didn't Sediko sort all this out?" Kellie asked shocked. This was the club's second month and it was doing well. Now it looked like they were lucky to still have staff. "What about the dancers?"

"I think they just keep what they get."

"Alright, we'll get this all sorted out tonight. Don't worry."

"I never did. And thanks. And congratulations." Jade nodded towards her stomach before leaving.

Kellie had tried to help Keisha but she was useless, she should have made her the cleaner. Kellie's mind drifted between thoughts as she found herself doing more and more thinking.

Samuel would be home on Monday, something had to give. She would have to make time for him, she wanted to be a good mother again. Monday would soon be here. Visit Sediko, collect Samuel. Bill was asking questions about the future, the modelling. She had decided having two children shouldn't ruin her career, she'd be back in shape within 6 months. She thought about Deke. She had felt his lust radiate from him and yes, she had enjoyed it. Sediko, that bastard. Mia was pregnant. She couldn't be angry with him yet, and Mia, well, she probably loved him just as much as she did.

Kellie looked up to a tapping on the window. Mandy stood waving franticly at her own reflection. Kellie let her in, smiling.

"What you doing here?"

"Look who's coming; she was behind me."

Kellie closed the door and looked out. She saw nothing but faces in a packed club. "Where?" As soon as the words passed her lips she spotted her, light skinned, small frame and a bump beneath her breasts.

"What the fuck is *she* doing here?" Kellie spat as she walked with another girl towards the glass door.

Mia tapped gently. Kellie went right up to her, Mia couldn't see her of course. She looked straight at her. What was it in the girl that Sediko liked so much? She was totally different to her. Not ugly, just different.

"Are you gonna let her in?"

"Yeah, but I want to talk to her alone."

"Okay, but don't do anything stupid."

Mandy slid the door open as Kellie went to sit down in her chair. Mia walked in and Mandy nudged the other girl away from the door as she left. Kellie watched as Mia came and sat beside her. *What was wrong with this girl?*

"Thank you. For bringing me to the hospital," blurted Mia.

"What you doing here?"

"We've got to talk-"

"Again, the last time you wanted to talk you were face up on my floor."

"Sediko's floor. I was just shocked. We can't fight Kellie and we can't ignore what's going on."

Mia didn't want to be here but Charlene had forced her to try and sort things out.

"I know what's going on, my man got another girl pregnant. We'll get through it," Kellie said emotionless.

"But that's not it Kellie, as much as you'd like to think he's yours, you've got to be realistic. He only got with you because he was on the rebound from me. We were split up only for a few months before you came on the scene. We were childhood sweethearts. Me and him, through and through."

"Yeah, cute. But that was the past Mia. You've got to try and understand that Sediko is my man now. Yes it's wrong for him to use you but that's exactly what he's doing. He doesn't care about you. I know about what happened to you when the two of you broke up the first time— he dissed you. Not surprising, you were all cracked out and looking run down; of course he didn't want you. His standards have gone up since then. If he loved you wouldn't he be with you? Why would I even be in the picture?"

"Because you stole him from me!" Mia shouted.

"You're just impossible. And don't raise your voice, you said you wanted to talk. I won't hesitate to throw you and your friend out the front doors."

"Fuck you." She stood to leave.

"The truth hurts doesn't it?" Mia sat back down at the other end of the table. "That baby probably isn't even Sediko's, you've been sleeping with your boyfriend haven't you?" Kellie challenged.

"No. We broke up ages ago. This baby is Sediko's. He told me on my last visit that he doesn't love you."

"He told you that to shut you up. We almost live together, got a business together. When he was on road he was with me every night, when did he have time to get you pregnant?" Kellie chuckled then continued. "Now listen Mia, me and you are never going to agree and Sediko will soon be out. Here's what we're gonna do. If he comes out and tells me that he wants you— fine, I'll cut him off. Cos I don't play second best like some. If he tells you that he wants me, you have to back off. We're gonna have to trust each other on this, it's the only way that this will work-"

"This is stupid-" she interrupted.

"Shhh. If you break your end of the deal, I'll kill you Mia, because I've had just about enough of you. I'll come to your house and I'll fucking kill you, your baby, your man, your sister, even your little sket bredrin out there! Just so me and Sediko can live in fucking peace!"

"What's that meant to mean? You trying to threaten me?" Mia asked. Kellie sighed loud and angrily, then shook her head. This bitch was so lucky that she was pregnant.

"Mia. I *am* threatening you. Are you that dumb that you don't know!? I'll get rid of you understand? If you push me, I can see myself breaking your fucking neck." Kellie could almost feel herself diving towards her neck and killing her dead.

Mia looked visibly shaken. She stayed silent while she took it all in, then she said, "What if he chooses me?"

"Please. He won't." Kellie shook her head.

"But if he does?" Mia tested.

"Like I said earlier, I'd leave you and him to it."

"What about your baby?"

"Our baby. Not that it's any of your business but I don't need a man to bring up my own. Believe it or not it wouldn't be the end of my world if we split," Kellie lied.

"Would you tell Sediko that it's not his?"

"What? Then whose would it be?" Kellie leaned forwards. She sensed that Mia was up to something.

"Shawn's," she said.

What was going on? How did she know him? How did she know she knew him?

She played cool.

"Who's that?"

"Deal or not?"

"But that's false information, you're chatting shit. Unlike you, I've been faithful to Sediko from day one; you had a man."

"So no deal?"

"Hell no, you little bitch! Anyhow you try and tell Sediko that I'm fucking someone— You see, that's why me and you can't agree!"

"Alright, forget it."

"You damn right forget it! Get out!" Kellie stood angrily.

"No. Nothing's been solved."

"Solved? How can it be when your trying to brandish my name?!"

"Okay, forget that last bit."

"You are just! Oh, I can't even find the words. I don't trust you but we'll go ahead with my plan. But if he says he wants me and you still hang around, girl I will deal with you proper. That last time you didn't get nothing, next time— just give me a next time. Get out now, I don't need to see your face again until Sediko makes his decision when he comes out. Stop hounding me now, I told you once before to step away from my relationship! You remember that?"

Kellie showed her the door.

As soon as Mia left, Kellie dropped into the chair. What did she know about Shawn? It seemed everyone knew everyone before she came on the scene. This wasn't good. And just as he came into her mind, there he was on the dance floor. Two girls walked beside him wearing next to nothing. She looked at one of the girls closely; it was the same bitch that she had beat down. Kellie went up through the back to the VIP. She spotted Smalls drinking and laughing with two of the dancers.

"Get up you fucking idiot! Is that what Two-Face pays you for? Come. Keep your eyes on me," Kellie said. One of the staff passed her a glass of water; they did that frequently. She drank it down.

"Everything alright?" Smalls stood to attention quickly.

"Just do what I said."

133

She gave him the empty glass and went to the top of the staircase waiting for Shawn to spot her. He did straight away. She looked around for Mia but couldn't see her. *Please let her be gone.*

She looked behind her toward the tables. Three big ballers tonight–playing cards, hundreds of pounds between them. She turned to Smalls who was looking away.

"Did you hear what I said?"

"Yeah I was-"

"Shhh." Kellie turned back to the dance floor. Shawn stood watching her at the top of the stairs, he motioned her to come to him. He stood alone, his two dogs off in the crowd somewhere. Kellie looked again to Smalls, then to Shawn, and started down the stairs. A black woman jumped in front of her, looking a little embarrassed.

"Can you sign this please Kellie; it's for my little sister." She handed Kellie a small poster.

"What's your sister's name?"

"Tasha, I mean Shola." Kellie quickly signed it and gave it back. Shawn watched her, amused.

"Thanks." She rushed off.

Shawn leaned in close, "Look at you, signing autographs."

He looked nice in a khaki iceberg suit. Kellie looked again at Smalls, he looked straight back. She felt very uneasy.

"What's that gal doing here?" Kellie demanded.

They were standing so close she could feel his breath on her, but if she moved away, she wouldn't be able to hear a word he was saying.

"Who?"

"She ain't welcome in here."

"Let's go talk somewhere."

"Why don't you take her home?"

"Come." Shawn pulled her arm gently, this time Kellie stood firm. She looked him straight in the eye. His arms found her round waist, she pushed his arms away, half holding onto his strong embrace. He felt her resist.

"Alright. I'll go."

"Yeah and take her with you."

He backed away from her into the crowd. She went back upstairs.

"Who was that?" Smalls asked angrily.

"Don't fucking question me, how dare you?" She went and sat in a big leather chair and watched the dancers.

"Two-Face did tell me to watch you." He followed her.

"Do you want me to tell him that you're fucking all our dancers and giving them fucking viruses? Tell him you're always late for work? What about the money you were short of yesterday? Or shall I tell him how you allowed Sparrow and Image to dis' me while you just stood back like a pussy? Your choice." Kellie couldn't believe that she was talking like this.

"Alright." He moved away without another word.

Just as Mandy was approaching, Kellie went back to the confines of her office. She needed to think.

Ten

"GOT A VISITOR!" Mr Mullets called one Friday morning. Mr Mullets was safe, he always allowed Sediko late-night phone calls.

"Who?" He jumped up just short of finishing his 200 press-ups. He boxed at the air, sparring alone.

"Your solicitor." Mullets used his chain full of keys to open his door. Sediko followed him down the hall to the special visit room.

"What's up, Whale?" Sediko greeted and pulled up his trousers before sitting down. Mark sat opposite him. On the small table was his briefcase, a cup of hot coffee and 20 Benson & Hedges.

"Everything's going as planned. Your court date is two weeks tomorrow. They may push it back due to lack of evidence but there is nothing to worry about." He opened his briefcase and gave Sediko a wad of papers. "The police reports. They haven't got a leg to stand on."

"Yeah and when they call up their so-called witness, he'll remember that he made a mistake, innit."

"So… we still got our deal?" The cat in him scratched out.

"I ain't out yet, I been here 2 whole weeks." Sediko took the cigarettes. "So who was it?"

"No names, just information. From what I hear, look close to home."

"I know who, don't worry."

"So our deal?" Mark pushed for a straight answer. Sediko had promised him a fat delivery if he and his two friends walked free. That was an easy deal for him, as his aunt's husband was the arresting officer in the case though he dared not tell Sediko that. Officer uncle had a few secrets that he didn't want Auntie May knowing about. This was kid's play for Mark; no work involved.

"Yeah yeah, that's the least of your problems," assured Sediko.

"That's it for now; I've got to go, I've got a meeting with one sexy client. Keep the cigarettes." He left giving Sediko a reassuring pat on the shoulder.

Monday morning Sediko sat with Bones in the breakfast hall, while Path stood in line.

"I thought you said that shit was cool. Two-Face, I'm getting da shakes in here, I miss Keisha, man." He shook his head slowly and shoved food into his mouth.

"I said that and I meant it; give it a few more weeks."

"A few more weeks!? Nigga that's long." Path joined them with his tray.

"Remember I'm here with you, man; don't like it here no more than you, but we have to ride that shit. The good news is, when we get out of this shit you two are up 10% each. Anyway, I'm seeing Kellie today. She's been looking after the club proper like; it's gonna kill her when I tell her about Mia and the baby."

"Nigga you fucked up there, you should never 'ave breed Mia, fucking leach." Path sipped foggy water.

"Boy, there's nothing I can do now."

"So what about that nigga, what's his name?" Bones asked.

"Who, Kirk? He's a batty."

"So what, the yout' can be his."

"That nigga can't have yout's," Sediko explained.

"So. Bigger miracles have happened." Path thought his boy was being naive.

"I don't know."

Sediko stood and approached the officer to take him back to his cell. Mia's baby had to be his. He wanted a son, a miniature Sediko. Or a little baby girl who no one could touch. He'd spoil her with everything he had. Of course he would have preferred Kellie to be the one to give him his first child, his new family, but it was Mia; she wasn't so bad. Maybe he wouldn't even tell Kellie about it. He didn't want to have to choose between his child and Kellie, blood was always thicker than water.

Sediko sat behind his door and waited for his visit. He had shaved his facial hair and head. He looked fresh again. He wore the latest Nike 120's and a Reebok tracksuit that Brenda had bought for him.

His name was called and his heart raced as he followed the screw to the visiting area. He sat at his table and waited. Minutes later, he watched as she looked around the big hall. Something wasn't right. She spotted him and walked extra slow towards him. Something was wrong. He looked her up and down, then up again. Then he looked at her stomach. Suddenly he felt a sick feeling. He grimaced. No, he must be seeing things. She came closer and it was visibly clear.

"Sediko." He stood to face her, shocked out of his mind. He hugged her tight. As he felt her lump, his heart raced even faster. He let her go and they sat, neither one knowing what to say next.

"You're not mad?" she asked cautiously.

"Mad? How can I be mad? I can't fucking believe it!"

"I just couldn't tell you," she half explained, taking his hands into hers.

"Ah shit...Kellie." He definitely couldn't tell her about Mia now!

"You're gonna be a daddy."

"Kellie, I love you babes. You know you've always been my number one, from day one."

"So who's number two?" She kept hold of his hands.

"Well, I've got some news-"

"It's alright, I already know." She didn't want to hear him admit it.

"No, you don't, I had a-" he was about to tell her about his meeting with Mark Whale.

"–I saw her Sediko," she said in a low voice as if someone was listening.

"Saw who?" *What was she going on about?*

"It's alright, we'll get through it together, if that's what you still want." She looked so hurt. He pretended not to look shocked as Kellie told him the story of Mia and the break-in. He listened silently.

"Baby, I'm sorry. I didn't give her a key, would I be that stupid? She must have taken it and had it cut. I'm sorry." He really was. There Kellie was, trying to keep his business afloat for him, and Mia was trying to fuck it all up.

"You sure it's yours?"

"No," he lied. He hadn't a doubt in the world that Mia was carrying his child.

"Why didn't you tell me about her, why did I have to find out like that?"

"Why didn't you tell me about you? To tell you the truth, if I would have known about you, I would have dragged Mia to the abortion clinic. Why didn't you tell me?"

"I was going to, the day I asked you to meet me in Chester's Café," she answered.

Sediko thought back. Perhaps it was his sense of guilt, but it sounded as if Kellie had seen him there. Maybe the arrest story had been a lie and she had caught him with the girl that afternoon.

"Can't we just forget the past shit and move on? I still can't believe that my baby's pregnant. How did it happen? What about your pill?"

"I may have forgotten a few times. So what you gonna do about Mia?" Kellie pushed.

"I'll deal with it."

"Alright."

"I love you babes. Shit, I know you're overdoing it and it's all my fault. How can I have my pregnant wifey running up and down doing all my shit?"

"I'm fine."

"So how many months are you now?" He leaned over to touch her stomach.

"Five months and counting."

"And I didn't notice that shit?"

"I only just started blossoming, I carry in my back."

She filled him in about the club. He felt as if life was passing him by.

"So, you sure it's me and Samuel you want and not Mia? No more in between; me then her, her then me. I can't take it no more."

"Stop stressing.

"I been stressing."

"Daddy will be home soon."

They chatted more and laughed. Sediko couldn't wait to get out and be with her. Couldn't wait for her to have his baby; what a bonus.

"VISIT'S OVER!"

"We'll talk about my salary when you get out," she joked, standing up to leave.

She was so beautiful and all his, Sediko thought. He hugged her; she smelt so sweet, so clean and pure.

"I love you." He held her face in his hands.

"Stop Sediko." A tear fell down her cheeks. "It's so lonely without you." She cried silently into his shoulder.

"Soon, babe, soon." He stepped back as he felt himself getting emotional. Now that his baby was pregnant, two weeks in jail felt more like two years.

As soon as his visit ended he was allowed to use the phone.

"Hello?"

"Mia, have you lost your fucking mind?!"

"What? Sediko what?"

"Don't act the fucking fool! Why you trying to mash up Kellie and me? I done told you, time and time again, that I ain't leaving her!"

"But what about the baby? What about us?"

"What, do I have to spell every shit out to you? I don't want you. If you wanna be my side t'ing, then that's cool, anything else it's a no go area for you. I'm taken."

"But why?" she cried.

"No Mia!" he shouted.

"Why?" she repeated herself.

"Bitch, why you always got to beg?"

"I'm not begging. It's just that I know something about Kellie that might change your mind about her."

"Phone me when the baby's born. Don't contact Kellie and keep your fucking nose out of my business!" He slammed the phone down. Now that Kellie was pregnant he regretted to the max that Mia was as well. Mia had trapped him just like she said she would. He would make sure that he and Kellie made it through.

He dialled the shop number.

"Haydon's Barbers, what's up?" Jayson answered.

"What's up with you?"

"Oh, you alright?"

"Yeah yeah, shit's cool, everything running smooth at your end?"

"No, it's a Ben for that still." Jayson spoke in a code that Sediko understood.

"Dem man still cotching there?"

"Yeah."

"Alright one." Sediko cut the call.

He stood by the phone booth with a queue behind him. He had come to the final conclusion that Sparrow and Image were taking him for a punk. They were wannabe gangsters working for their own enemy. If someone wanted him off the scene, who better to help them than two frienemies.

What did they want? His club? His name in blood? Kellie? He had much to lose but shit to give. When he finally reached road he would treat them like white strangers. He'd shoot Image in a blink. Sparrow had shocked him. But he'd make sure they both knew why he was doing what he was going to do. Once you cross your boys, there's absolutely no coming back.

For now, they were sitting up in the barber's; they had heard he had gotten 10 years. Next, they'd be trying to take over his club. He couldn't leave Kellie to deal with them in her state and the only other boys that he trusted were beside him.

"Candy," he said to himself, dialling her number. He knew it by heart even though he hadn't dialled it in over a year. He'd met her in his young boy days when she had come from Jamaica to his school in the 3rd year. Candy and Mia hated each other from day one. Candy was a bad bitch, she was like a female brother to him. Back in the day she was always up for sneaking out and breaking into the cemetery where they used to smoke weed into the night. He had seen her take down plenty of men. She was short dark and fit and used to be into gym and acrobatics. The only thing that was wrong was that she was a lesbian. Sediko had fucked her once– took her virginity. He was the first and the last.

Sediko thought back briefly to a time when the two of them had travelled to Leicester, bunking on the coach to go and see Saxon Sound, their favourite Jamaican reggae group at the time. They were clashing with Bodyguard Sound. The two had refused to miss it, money or not. They were both 15 and had no way of getting home.

Once there, they had enjoyed themselves. They sold ash, weed, skunk and E's– got rid of all the drugs they had come with, then started on a bottle of champagne. About 7 am they left and went to find a cab station. As they walked, three men had followed them into an alleyway.

"Oh you niggers! What you doing down our way?!" one laughed drunkenly.

Sediko had punched one in the face straight away. He scuffled with the man, trying to take him down. When he finally did, he turned to see the other two rolling around on the floor. Candy and Sediko ran like hell and were chased for about 45 minutes. Candy kept up with him all the way. They passed a woman pulling out of her driveway and Candy pulled her out. With the keys still hanging in the running engine, she drove 80 mph all the way home, then dumped the car.

"Two-Face dat you?" her voice rang familiarity.

"Yeah woman, what's up?"

"Bomboclat!" she shouted happily in her Jamaican accent. "How comes you always leave it so long? Mi ear say yuh ave big club?" She laughed thinking of the young boy that he used to be.

"Yeah, me and my woman."

"Not dat likkle bitch?"

"Na man, but she having my yout' still."

"Trapped, that's all I 'ave to say 'pon that situation. So who's the new girl on the block?"

"It ain't like that, Kellie's my long time baby."

"Seen that long hair one that you told me about?"

"Yeah. So what you on anyway?" he asked her. He knew that she knew where he was, she heard about everything.

"Nothing but the usual cats."

"Can they take a break? A two week break?"

"Alright."

"Phone the place and get a visit by Friday. God knows what gal you shack up with now."

"Wouldn't you just like to know?" she asked before hanging up. Sediko didn't have a problem with two women sharing each other, especially if they wanted him to join in.

He went back to his cell wondering how Kellie would take Candy. Kellie was a new, improved lady; Candy was an old time yardie bitch and she knew what mans had to go through. That's what mostly separated him from Kellie, the past, his past.

≈≈≈≈

Bill sat in his office alone. For a minute, he didn't know where he was, at home or at work? He sat up and spun his chair around to the window. Trees. He was home. He would have preferred to be at work. He missed Kellie and Sally.

But it was Sunday and he was home alone. Carrie said she would come around later in the evening, 7:30 she had said; he would be starving by then. He looked at the time– 2:50 pm. Still early and he was half drunk. He wanted to call Marie again but she had called him a stalker on their last phone call. He missed her, didn't she understand that? This was killing him. He called Lisa at home instead.

"Lisa," Bill breathed.

"Who's this?" A male voice. Bill hung up quickly.

Two seconds later, his phone began ringing.

"Hello?" Bill answered.

"Did you just call here?" the same male voice asked.

"No," Bill lied.

"Well someone did." He sounded irritated like he had just been interrupted.

"This is a big place, anyone could have called," Bill lied again.

141

"Oh, okay." The man put down the phone. Bill slammed his down too. Who the hell was that? he asked himself. Was she seeing some one else already or was he jumping the gun?

Bill left his office wearing his suit. He went to his bedroom and into the walk-in closet he and Marie had previously shared. His on the right, hers on the left. They used to love choosing clothes for each other and then watching the other dress. Her side used to be a long full rack of dresses, shirts, skirts, slacks, everything. Fur coats, suede jackets, over a 100 pairs of shoes in a ray of different colours, even with most of her clothes gone, her side still looked fuller than his. His was mostly greys and blacks, whites and dark blues. Maybe 15 or more of his suits were the same, some different only in colour. His shoes were all black except for one pair of Nike running trainers that Marie had brought him. He dug his only tracksuit out of this cupboard and put it on. He felt ridiculous, he probably looked it too. He heard a slam of doors. It was only 4 pm, Carrie wasn't due yet. He went downstairs to find Carrie and Jeff in the kitchen.

"Evening Mr Laymend," Jeff greeted without looking at him. Carrie stood in the fridge.

"Hello Jeff. Carrie, you alright honey?" He touched her shoulder and tried to turn her so he could see if she was tearful. Her eyes were red.

"Hi Daddy, I'm fine, we decided to have dinner here that's all." She took cooked chicken from the freezer. The last that he had heard the two were finished and she was going to her mother's mum for Sunday roast.

"So how was Granny Mary?" he asked softly.

"I did go Daddy," she busied herself.

"Alright then, I'll get straight to the point. I thought that you two were separated?"

"What, like you and Marie?" She banged pots around the cooker.

"This isn't about me, it's about you. I'm just going by what you last said." He sat beside Jeff.

"Well, we're fine now."

"Should I go up to your room?" Jeff asked Carrie.

"No, you will not," Bill told him.

"Alright, then I'll go." Jeff stood.

"No you're not, we've got things to discuss," Carrie hissed to him.

"But I think you father wants to talk with you." He swallowed looking uncomfortable. "He doesn't want me here."

"He didn't want you here before, that didn't stop you," Carrie challenged. He sat back down.

"What makes you think I don't want you here?" Bill asked wondering what was going on between them.

"Well, what you said."

"I asked my daughter a question that's all, I want to know what's going on. You're in my house, I have a right to know." He looked at them both in turn.

"Jeff…" Carrie started.

"Carrie! You promised." His face screwed up as if he was in pain.

"Promised what?" Bill was now interested. Jeff was sweating.

"Daddy, I can't." She turned back to the dinner preparations.

"Oh yes you can and you will right now. And Jeff you don't say another word!" Bill went and stood by Carrie and blocked her view of Jeff.

"Jeff is doing expensive drugs and it's tearing us apart!" she cried and threw herself into Bill's arms.

"Yeah and it was you who called Lisa Brooks!" Jeff shouted in a tit-for-tat reply.

"What?" Bill backed away from her.

"Jeff you promised!" Carrie screamed. Her hands went up and covered her face in fear that her father would slap her.

"So did you?" he asked weakly. She stood silent.

"Jeff get out of my house now! Carrie sit!" he bellowed. He didn't want to admit that his own daughter had caused his marriage and affair to crumble.

Jeff almost ran out of the kitchen, slamming the front door behind him.

Bill didn't know where to start. He paced behind her as she sat on the stool biting her nails.

"Daddy?"

"Carrie, you will go upstairs and pack your things. You are leaving this house. You're a traitor and a blackmailer. No child of mine." He didn't shout but his voice was course and serious.

"Daddy," she stood quickly, "where will I go? To Jeff's, is that what you want?"

"I don't care. I'll be stopping your allowance today. What's left is yours after that you'll have to find a job. You'll not get another penny out of me until the day I die." He remembered when he had accused Marie. He should have known better.

"Daddy it was just a joke, I've known for ages about you and Lisa. I didn't mean to hurt you."

"Hurt me! What about Marie? Ever think about her?"

"Did you?" She was crying now.

"Once again, this isn't about me. That's your problem, keeping your nose out of my business!"

"I won't leave." She stood defiantly.

"You're almost 21, old enough to stand on your own two feet. If that means you living with Jeff then so be it. Isn't that what you said you always wanted, isn't that what you fought tooth and nail for? Well now you got it. Whatever, you will leave today!" He turned on his heels and walked out before she could grovel.

He grabbed his car keys and mobile before leaving the house in his tracksuit.

143

"Hiya mate," Burt slurred as he led Bill into the sitting room where Belinda sat– her hair plaited in two, her short shorts once again giving a sneak preview of her bottom, her sporty bra doing wonders for her cleavage. Burt saw him looking. He smiled and nodded towards Belinda proudly.

"What's up Bill?" Belinda greeted, sitting back and crossing her slender brown legs. Bill nodded a 'hello' and slumped into the chair.

"Don't look too clever mate, what's wrong?" Burt asked going straight to the bar.

"Well, it was Carrie. It was her that called Lisa back then, remember?" Burt nodded. "That simple phone call has led to a disastrous chain of events that will eventually lead to my divorce." Bill grabbed the drink that Burt held towards him and took four gulps. He winced as the familiar red drink burned his throat. "That little…" He stopped himself before he said too much about his once sweet little girl. "I blamed Marie, almost hit her. And after all that damn therapy."

"What did you say to her?"

"I've kicked her out and stopped her allowance. What more can I do?"

"Well you've still got your business, that's doing well," Belinda encouraged. "Kellie Palmer and that guy. Real nice. I've got something that will cheer you right up," Belinda offered. She took a roll-up cigarette from her bag. "Here," she offered to Bill, "spark it."
Bill turned to Burt who was grinning.

"I don't smoke," Bill admitted.

"So. It's not a cigarette, it's super skunk, a.k.a Colombian crow," she clarified, her arm still extended.

"Really?" Bill was amazed. "Where did you get that, it's illegal."

"Never mind where I got it, do you want it or not? We are behind closed doors."
Bill looked again to Burt who nodded to him reassuringly. He took it, then requested a lighter. The first pull and Bill had a fit of coughs. Belinda and Burt laughed. The second, and he had forgotten about everything.

≈≈≈≈

Mia sat in a chair beside Charlene outside the courtroom. She could feel Kellie's eyes on her. *I have a right to be here too,* she thought.

"You alright?" Charlene asked her. Mia nodded weakly. "I don't even know why ya bothered coming."

"I don't need this. Why did *you* bother coming?" Mia whispered angrily.

"I came here to support you when Two-Face says that he don't want ya," Charlene screeched.

Her opinion of Kellie had changed. She liked the way Kellie handled things, and she wasn't scared to do just what she wanted.

"Keep your voice down. He only said that to Kellie cos she was pressuring him." Mia looked over to Kellie standing alone.

"How much longer?" Charlene moaned.

"Fifteen minutes."

"So, what do you thinks gonna happen?"

"He will walk this. He always does," Mia hoped out loud.

"Marshall, Jones and Fitzroy– Court Room 5!"

Charlene stood up; she looked down at Mia who had a frightened look on her face.

"Come on then."

"Shit Char, I can't go in," she panicked.

"Just come on, it will be alright," Charlene gently urged. She watched Kellie walk in through the doors, her head held high. She didn't look in their direction. She looked sophisticated in a blue dress and long blazer, her long hair swept up in a pin. Mia looked down at her own clothes. Nike tracksuit bottoms resting beneath her stomach and a woolly jumper barely covering her condition.

"I'm not going in. You go."

Charlene walked ahead through the double doors.

Mia couldn't bear to see Sediko look lovingly into Kellie's eyes. She looked expensive and nice. Mia was, and looked like, the ghetto chick on the side. She felt her baby kick and it reminded her that there was hope for them. So what if she was pregnant too, that didn't cancel out *her* baby. Even if he did choose her, he would always be there, he had told her that. Kellie could threaten all she liked. If Sediko chose her, she would make sure Kellie was out of the picture for good.

Mia looked at her watch. Twenty minutes had gone by in a blink. *What was happening?* Another 20 minutes went by and still nothing. Five minutes later, Charlene came out. Her face was expressionless.

"Well?" Mia stood up quickly.

"Don't know the details but he's out tomorrow; he's serving one more day cos he failed his piss test last week. Let's go." Charlene linked her arm through Mia's and they walked quickly towards the stairs.

"He's out tomorrow?"

"Yes."

"Yes! Yes, yes, I knew it." Mia smiled. She stopped to hug Charlene tight on the stairs even if she didn't share her enthusiasm. She thought about Kellie, who too, must be on cloud nine.

Outside Lavender Hill Court heading toward Brixton, Mia and Charlene sat on a 345 bus. Mia had a grin that wouldn't go away. Everything was going to be alright, Sediko was coming home. She sat by the window and looked out. She watched the mothers with their prams or buggies; most of them walked alone, no daddies walking beside them. She watched a light-skinned woman struggling to push her double pram into a shop doorway. In the end she gave up and continued her journey. The two babies started crying but it didn't faze her, she just kept right on walking, her head held high.

"I wonder what you're thinking about?" Charlene said from beside her.

"What?" Mia turned her attention to her friend.

"Looking forward to tomorrow?"

"Course. Did you speak to Kellie?"

"Why would I do that?" Charlene asked.

"Did you?"

"No." Charlene looked guilty as sin.

"No? Remember, it wouldn't be the first time," Mia accused.

"Just concentrate on Two-Face, not her. You got some tidying up to do in your flat, shopping to do. You want him ta come to your yard looking like that?"

"Like what?"

"Your gaff's a mess, innit."

"A bit, I *am* pregnant you know. Anyway forget that, don't be trying to change the subject. What did you say to her? I know when you're lying."

"I said 'hello' to her," Charlene admitted.

"What for?! Just now you said that you didn't talk to her!"

"What is your problem? What has she done to you? It should be Two-Face you're angry at!"

"So you're defending her now. Miss Goody two-shoes is she? You don't even know her."

"I know she is a successful black woman. She's famous for godsake! Where's your job?" Charlene couldn't admit that they had spoken for 20 minutes while waiting for the judge to arrive.

"So what! I can't believe you just said that! Kellie Palmer is a ho!" Mia shouted for the whole bus to hear.

"What makes her a ho?" Charlene asked as they stepped off the bus and walked to the number 3 bus stop outside Iceland supermarket.

"She's fucking some nigga called Shawn."

"Now you know that's not true."

"So."

They got on the bus.

"Mia don't chat shit. I'll tell Two-Face *myself* that ya lying. I don't know how Kirk ever did put up with you," she spat.

Mia burst out crying. *Why was Charlene treating her like this?* Kellie was turning her man and now her best friend against her.

"I'm sorry." Charlene put an arm around her. They travelled the rest of the way in silence.

At home at last, Mia thought as she put her key in her door. Charlene had been right about one thing, her flat was a tip.

"I think you're making a mistake with Two-Face. Check it, you and Kellie are in the same boat. Both loving a man who's cheating. Open your eyes, you had Kirk, he would have looked after you and the baby. He never *ever* gave you woman troubles. That fucking Two-Face has been mashing up your life for years."

"I'll call you later."

"What, you want me to go after I followed you all the way here?.... Bye."

Charlene left and she began to tidy up.

≈≈≈

All charges against Sediko Anthony Marshall, Alepath Warren Jones and James Fitzroy have been dropped." Kellie sat calmly and watched the big grin on all their faces as they stood in the witness box. Sediko shook Mark Whale's hand vigorously.

"Congratulations," Charlene said to her.

"Thanks. So you'll tell her 'tomorrow?'"

"It won't kill her, it's only one more day," Charlene said as Mark approached them.

"Hello Kellie." Kellie turned her attentions to him and shook his hand. "He said he'll meet us at the back."

"Thanks Mark." She watched them all led back through the doors; she couldn't wait to get outside and hold him.

"See ya." Charlene left.

Kellie left the courtroom feeling relaxed. She took out her mobile, switched it on, and called Mandy at work.

"Hello Sophikut Hair can I help?" answered a young female's chirpy voice.

"Can I speak to Mandy please?"

"Hold up. MANDYYYPHONE!"

"Kellie?" she asked hopefully a few seconds later.

"I'm going to get them as we speak."

"Ahh!" she squealed. "Come pick me up!"

"Alright girl, see you soon."

Kellie walked through to the car park, Mark in tail. And there he stood, free as a fucking bird. They all stood laughing and joking. When he saw her he stopped and came to her. She could feel butterflies in her stomach. She wanted to just run over to him and have him pick her up, just like Johnny and Baby in Dirty Dancing, but she waited and eventually his arms found her and she inhaled, then exhaled into him.

"Whoops." He loosened his grip. "Sorry babes."

"I love you," she told him. She had missed him so much– his touch, his smell, his voice.

"Did you bring the car?" Path called from behind.

"Yeah, Mandy's waiting for us to come pick her up from work."

"Yes, that's just what I wanted to hear." He smiled clapping his hands.

"What a shame for you," Bones laughed as Keisha ran towards him. "My wifey is right here, we're jumping in a cab." He laughed as she ran into his arms smiling and crying. "See ya." And they were gone.

"So shall I call you Wednesday?" Mark asked Sediko.

"Na, you can bell me later."

"Good." Mark smiled, then went to his car.

"Come on then, man wants his wifey too. Which way to the car?" asked Path, grinning.

By 2:30 pm they had dropped Path off and were lying naked in her bed.

"I'm so sorry," he told her.

"For what?"

"For leaving you alone. For Mia."

"You know you need to tell that girl to step back."

"You know I can't do that."

"Why?" she asked softly. It was very rare that she could talk to Sediko like this.

"My yout', no matter what happens I'm gonna look after both my kids, treat them the same. Love them the same."

"Are you sure that it's yours? You said you weren't sure before."

"Yeah, just as sure as I am about you," he said honestly this time.

"Will you have a blood test when her baby's born?"

"Will *you*?" he asked seriously.

"If you want." She didn't have any problems with that.

"I don't want. I said I'm sure of you both."

"Alright, then we both will."

"If you're paying for them."

"Fine."

"Just forget about her, she's not here is she?"

"Only because she thinks you're coming out tomorrow, otherwise she would have been banging the door down long time."

"Why's that?"

"Cos I wanted time alone with you. I need you to choose."

"Choose what? You know I want you, who the fuck is she?"

"Yeah, but you need to tell her that. Tell that bitch that you don't want her, and tell her about the blood test."

"Yeah," he sighed. "How's the club?" He changed the subject.

"It's going well," she said proudly. "Every weekend we have to turn people away. We're on demand for Sunday and Wednesdays. Our VIP suite is *real* VIP now. I got a few of my celeb friends up in there."

"*Our* VIP?" Sediko smiled.

"I sorted out everything, the club works itself now. I got your books together and I got these new-" she rambled on about her new hobby.

"What about you?"

"What *about* me?"

"I seen you in the paper."

"Have you?"

"Nothing to say?" His face was expressionless.

"It's just modelling," she murmured. Deke flashed into her mind.

"It's alright, I liked it."

"What?"

"You looked sexy. What, you expected me to go mad? That man looked gay anyway. One white dude in jail wanked over your poster every night."

"Nice." Kellie grimaced.

"It's alright though cos I got the real thing." He kissed her.

Kellie got up for work. It was Friday– work, then club. Her favourite day of the week. She turned to Sediko who lay asleep in the bed. The other love of her life toddled sleepily into her room. He stood just over 3 feet tall; his tan pajamas from Gap Kids clung to his skin as he rubbed his eyes.

"Morning Mummy."

"Morning." Kellie smiled at him. He had been home for a week and had settled, all but for a few nightmares. She heard the front door close downstairs, everything was back to normal.

"Come on, Buffie's here." She held his hand and led him downstairs.

"Morning Kellie. Samuel, come here my darling."

"Right, I've got to go, tell Sediko."

"He's out?!"

"Yeah, didn't you see him yesterday? Yes, both my boys are home."

"Oh."

"Don't sound too excited."

"Why, should I be pleased? You want Readybrek, Sam?"

"Just tell him that I had to leave for work, and if he wants to go out he has to take my car and-"

"Why don't you leave him a note?"

"Why can't you just give him the message?"

"Alright, I'll tell him to phone you when he gets up, if I'm still here."

"Thanks. Bye Samuel, have a nice day at school."

Driving to work Kellie finally felt complete. Everything was perfect. She had everything that a woman fights for: A good job, a family, a nice home, two great friends, looks, a perfect figure that she hoped she'd get back, a hobby which made her money, an almost perfect man (almost would do, as no man was perfect), and a drug-free life. What more could she want? She answered her ringing phone.

"What?"

"Who said that I wanted you to go to work?"

"I took the day off yesterday; I do wanna keep my job," Kellie replied, laughing.

"What about pregnancy leave?"

"Maternity leave? Not yet, I'm only coming up to 7 months. When the time comes I will, alright babe?"

"Alright, what time you finish?"

"I'll be back about 4:00, then tonight Ballers."

"You ain't going."

"What you mean, course I'm going. I been thinking, you need a proper manager, I'm the girl for the job," Kellie said without thinking, but liking the idea.

"Don't go getting carried away."

"I'd still be working for you. When you see how well I've been doing…"

"–We'll talk about it later."

"Have them two left yet?"

"God knows and trust me that gal ain't looking after *my* yout'."

"Why? She's alright."

"I just don't like her."

At 8:30 am Kellie parked her car in the car park. She took her briefcase and walked into the building.

"Great pictures Kellie," someone said.

"Yes," a few others agreed.

In her office, papers were piled high on her desk. Bill came out.

"Kellie good news. A friend of mine from *Cosmopolitan* called wanting to do a double page article on you. They will triple your pay if you wear just your birthday suit with Gucci shoes and a Gucci watch! Something about them owing Gucci a favour." He grinned.

"Right, slowly now."

"Kellie, you're a hot potato. They love you they want to interview you. I said you'd call him back to finalise the decision."

"That's assuming I'll take the job," Kellie teased.

"This is it for you. Aren't you happy?" He threw his arms wide. "At least *your* life is going alright."

"Feeling a little lonely at home?"

"Well, a bit. I was going to maybe pass by your club tonight," he half asked.

"You? I mean, yeah, if you like."

"Well I'll be coming with other people too, one of which I want you to meet."

"New girlfriend?"

"I wish. No, she's with a friend of mine, Burt Congal. Just want you to check her out, see what you make of her."

"Okay fine. Tonight's going to be packed."

"Why, special event?"

"No, it's always packed. Just give your name at the door. Four passes?" Kellie's phone began ringing.

"Hello Kellie, I've got a Richard Deeking on the line," informed Sally.

"Fine.... Yes?"

"Hello Miss Palmer, this is Richard from Cosmo, a friend of Bill's."

"Hi."

"Has he discussed the details with you?"

"Yes, he did." She would play hard to get.

"Well?" he urged rudely.

"I'll think about it."

"If you want more money it's no problem but we do need a answer today."

"Well I don't-"

"Alright, don't say no. How about lunch? The Ivy, West End, next Wednesday, 1 o' clock. Can Bill make that date?"

"Let me check my diary. Hold, please."

"Kellie?!" Bill turned red.

"I don't want them thinking I'm easy," she said laughing before returning to the phone call.

"Yes, that date is fine and Bill will accompany me."

"Great. I'm looking forward to it."

"Brilliant," Bill said as she put down the phone.

"So tonight, you bringing anyone?"

"Who can I bring?" he sighed. "What time should we get there?"

"Best time? Anytime, we open at 10."

"Alright I'll e-mail Burt. Do you watch Northenders?"

"Yes it's my Sunday ritual. Why?"

"You'll see." He went back to his office.

Kellie picked up her phone and dialled an office below.

"Hello, Mr Frank's office, Sally speaking."

"Hi Sally, any messages for me?"

"I'll come up before lunch."

"Thanks."

Everything was moving so fast– Gucci, *Cosmopolitan*. She thought back to a meeting that she had had with Lisa, Lisa's date and Bill. They had almost forced her to model and now her career was really taking off. Her phone rang.

"Laymend's Fashion, Kellie speaking…"

"Hi Kellie, my name is Tracy Date, celebrity director from *Now* magazine. I was hoping that we could meet up for lunch, maybe discuss a possible article?" She spoke very fast.

"Contact my agent," she said before slamming the phone down.

"Bill!" she called.

"What is it?!" he said running in. "Shall I call an ambulance?"

"No, no calm down, it's not that. We've got to do something. *Now* magazine just called, they want an interview."

"Well that's great news."

"No, not great. This is Laymend's Fashion Company not Kellie's Modelling."

"What are you saying?"

"I'm saying I'm going to need some advice on how to manage the business side of things– an agent. I wouldn't even know where to start, you've sorted all that in the past."

"Look no further."

"You?" She laughed.

"What's wrong?" He looked temporarily hurt.

"Haven't you got a business to run? Have you really got time? I don't think so, the best you can do is help me find a decent one."

"So that means you'll leave here?"

"Not necessarily."

"You'll be a supermodel with a PA job, I don't think you'll fit in with the rest of the celebrities." He stood up and paced her office.

"You know that I'll always be here for you," Kellie said softly.

"Shit, it's all my fault anyway, I pushed you to model and now I'm losing you."

"I'm not dying, Bill." They both laughed.

At that moment, Sally walked in, her hair was swept up in the same way that Kellie had hers.

"Morning, Sir. Morning Kellie. Good news."

"For me or Kellie?" Bill asked.

"Well, for Kellie, Sir."

"I'll be in my office then."

Sally waited for Bill's door to close, then sat opposite Kellie at her desk.

"An agent from Oman Cosmetics called. Oman Cosmetics, you know Davis Bozen's Oman? They want to speak with you. Isn't that just wow!" Sally clasped her cheeks with her hands.

"When the money starts rolling in, then it will be big wow. Back to today's work."

"Will Bill be looking for a full time PA soon?" she asked hopefully.

"If and when I do leave, you'll be the first that we'll offer it to. You had a rocky start but the job's grown on you; Bill said so too."

"Really? Thank you."

They talked for a further 20 minutes, then she left.

Kellie typed a few letters, did two hours of audio tape, then decided to leave. She went to say 'bye' to Bill.

"Leaving already?" he asked, seeing her holding her jacket.

"I'm feeling cramped in here. I'm going home to relax and get ready for tonight."

"Yes. Burt e-mailed me back, they're definitely coming."
"So, are you bringing anyone yet?"
"Still no. What should I wear?"
"Whatever."
"Shall I expect VIP treatment?"
"Of course, nothing less."

Eleven

SO MUCH SHIT to do, Sediko thought to himself as he lay on Kellie's bed. He had been gone only two months but it felt like forever. He had lots of people to see. He wasn't even sure that he wanted to go to the club tonight. Maybe Kellie was right, he should leave her in charge, she did have a better business mind than him. The second week of the club opening and he was arrested. After he had put in so much work. He hadn't even had the chance to see it develop.

Sediko saw the door open and looked up. Buffie stood looking scruffy in a blue tracksuit. She stood staring at him.

"What?!" he shouted to her.

"Just checking in," she whispered.

"Checking what? Get out!" He rolled over to get the ashtray.

"Got anything?" She talked low as if someone was listening.

"Hell no! Not for you. Remember the money that you already owe me!"

"I haven't got it." She bowed her head.

"Well then, neither have I. Now get out!" He was annoyed.

She stayed put.

"If you wanna come in, come on?" He grinned and lifted the quilt from his naked body.

She ran from the door.

"Bitch!!" he called after her and dialled Candy's number.

"Who's this?" she asked.

"What's up gal? You do what I asked?"

"Yeah nigga, course I did. When did you land?"

"Couple days ago. So?"

"Yeah, she was cool, she can run t'ings, innit."

"You talk to her?" he asked.

"Hell no. You going tonight?"

"She is going but I don't know if I'll go. Man kinda feels out of place."

"How could you feel like that in your own shit? It's a boom turnout. I suggest you jump back on the bandwagon before it lef' you. Anyway, I gotta go. Gal like me is busy, I'll see you there. You can introduce me to Kellie properly."

Sediko jumped out of bed. Time waits for no man. An hour later he was dressed and waiting for Path to pick him up. He sat at Kellie's table and smoked a spliff while music played in the background. While he had been away he had been thinking about buying a house for Kellie and their new family; he wanted to make things more official, more grown up. His phone rang.

"What?"

"Sediko?"

"Yeah."

"You planning on coming to see me?"

"Is my yout' born?"

"What's wrong? Don't block me out." She started to cry.

"Mia, let's not go through this."

"Through what?"

"Why are you calling me? I said don't contact me until the yout' is born!"

"I gave up everything for you once! I could've been in Canada with my family but I chose you!" she shouted.

"Don't start getting the story mixed up. Your family didn't want you, cos you were a crackhead. Shit to do with me."

"I loved you back then."

"I know."

"I was there for you when your mum died, I loved you through it. When you couldn't cry to anyone except me, when you wouldn't see any one except me. It was me, right there beside you."

"Yeah I know." She always used that one, but it was the whole truth and much more.

"Please Sediko, don't let me go! Don't put her in front of me."

"Mia I got nothing more to say to you. I refuse to get angry with you and be emotionally blackmailed into playing your shitty games. I've told you time and time again that I love Kellie; I cannot stress that enough." He tried to talk gently. She went silent. "Mia?" Silence. "Mia!"

"Yeah," she sniffed.

"How much longer?"

"About two weeks."

"You alright?"

"Yes." She sniffed.

"I'll come see you before then."

"Alright." Her voice cheered instantly.

As he ended the call there was a knock at the door.

"Yo," Path greeted when Sediko opened the door. "Come."

Twenty minutes later they were in a rented Mercedes heading to Haydon's.

"No long talking. If they are there, it's on."

"You think they'll be there?" Path asked at the wheel.

"Jayson said they were there yesterday, I'm praying that they still are."

They drove the rest of the way in silence. Once he got there he would show them who run t'ings. He would show them what happened to people that crossed Two-Face.

They pulled up outside and jumped out the car. The shop had been repainted to a dark blue. He spotted Image straight away, he was half-way through having his hair cut. His eyes were closed and he was tapping his fingers to the music.

Sediko moved the barber aside and took the clippers from him. Jayson stood beside him with a worried look on his face, cutting another head. Path went straight upstairs to look for Sparrow who was nowhere to be seen.

"What you waiting for nigga!" Image opened his eyes to see Sediko standing behind him.

"What's up?" Sediko growled. "I can give you a boom fade, what's wrong?"

"Let me finish my cut and then we will sort shit out."

"What! Sort what out?"

"I'm just saying, you get me, just let man just finish his hair, innit." His eyes darted around the shop for some kind of help.

"Get up."

Sediko pushed his shoulder hard enough for him to jerk forwards. He stood slowly and Sediko followed him up the stairs.

"Yo Jayson, if Sparrow comes in tell him that Image left, don't let him upstairs," Sediko called to him.

"How am I meant to do that? What if he wants to come up?" Jayson asked panicking.

"Stop being a pussy!!" He ran up the rest of the stairs and went into the back room where Path was already grilling him as he was trying to explain himself.

"How long Path? You know that I'm your boy."

Sediko walked right up to him as he stood by the window. He punched him to the floor first of all, his nose gushed blood as he picked himself up.

"Two-Face, what's going on man?" His voice was shaky.

Sediko headbutted him. Again, it sent him to the floor; his nose swelled instantly.

"Shit!!" he shouted with pain and frustration. Blood poured down his shirt.

Sediko punched him twice more, just in case he hadn't felt the others. Image fumbled around in his pocket and pulled out a handgun.

"Back the fuck up!" he cried, tears running down his cheeks. Sediko and Path stood back and waited. Shakily, he pointed the gun at them both in turn. "SHIIITTT!! What da fuck is this about!" he shouted as he wiped his bloody nose with his shirt sleeve.

"What da fuck you gonna do with that shit, you pussy?! You try get man set, innit? I know that you man were involved. And you try dis' my woman!" Sediko charged him and pushed the gun to one side grabbing it over Image's hands. One shot went off and Image dropped the gun like it was a hot potato. Sediko punched him three more times and he crumbled to the floor, this time he didn't get back up. He stomped on his face and smiled.

"You- try- shoot man!" Sediko kicked him with every word as he lay on the ground.

"My leg, hole up my leg!" he shouted.

Sediko kicked harder and harder and harder still. No one could understand his rage! This pussyhole had tried to cross him! He kicked and kicked.

Path stood back for a while, then pulled him off. Sediko shrugged Path off and continued to kick. All the rage in him had a chance to come out. Who cared if Image had nothing to do with half of it, at least he could get all that prison anger out! Out! Out in every kick that landed on the poor soul at the other end of his foot.

Sediko's breathing slowed and Image immediately began to crawl towards the door. Sediko watched him sliver to the stairs.

"Tell that Pussy Sparrow that he is next!" Sediko kicked him to the bottom of the stairs he rolled down backwards then forwards. Sediko stifled a laugh.

The boy that had been cutting Image's hair came running over to his crumpled mass on the floor. He tried to pull Image up.

"Leave me! Leave me! My fucking leg!" he cried.

"Who da fuck are you?" Sediko asked him.

"Who the fuck are you?!" the boy shouted in return. He stood with his chest high like he was considering backing Image. Sediko gunbutted him with Image's gun. The slap across his face sent him spinning into the chair.

"You're questioning me? You ain't ready!"

"That's my cousin man," the boy whimpered holding his cheek. "I don't want no fucking beef, let me take him home."

"Yeah, you *better* get da fuck out of my shit." Sediko waved the gun. "Here, take this piece of shit." He emptied the pegs onto the floor before slapping it hard into the boy's palm.

Image tried to sit himself up. Sediko laughed at this half-cut head.

"My rib," Image moaned as the cousin dragged him to his feet and pulled him toward the door.

"You should have known better Image."

"Tit wa Patrrow," he gurgled from the door through his swollen mouth.

Sediko ignored him and turned to Path.

"Feel better?" Path asked.

"Na man, we don't know shit yet. We need to find Sparrow before Image."

By one o'clock that morning, Sediko and Path had pulled up outside Ballers. Sediko wore a simple Armani linen suit and Gucci shoes that Kellie had surprised him with. He would never even think about going and buying a pair of shoes for 700 pounds; he could feed his whole estate with that! He grinned to himself. His phone rang.

"What?"

"Babes, you near the club?" Kellie asked.

"Yeah, I'm outside."

"I'll come meet you round back; someone is here asking for you." Her voice sounded agitated.

He opened the back door where Kellie waited. "Some girl called Candy," Kellie said before turning and leading them to his office. Inside, Candy sat in his head chair, her feet up on the round table.

"Get your feet down," Kellie spat. "And you're sitting in my chair."

Candy looked at her. She looked sexy in a mini, light-purple dress and baby blue Timberland boots. Her breasts were firm small and braless; her skin as smooth as Kellie's. She had cut her hair short. It was bright red and spiky. She stood and turned to Sediko.

"Wha gwan!" She hugged Sediko tight, then turned to Path."Hello you."

"What's up Candy gal, what you doing here?"

"You mean you ain't happy to see me?" she asked him, smiling happily.

"Any man would be happy to see you." Path laughed, admiring her rarely seen curves.

"Yeah and I hope you're happy to see your girl who's waiting upstairs for you," Kellie snapped.

Path excused himself. "Man's going upstairs to the VIP, there are some nice fit dancers up there Candy," he said laughing.

Kellie sat down in Sediko's chair.

"Kellie this is my long time bredrin Candy. Candy this here is my wife, Kellie." His hands snaked around her neck from behind, then onto her stomach. "You alright babe?"

"Yeah."

"Sit down na gal," Sediko said in patios to Candy. She sat to Kellie's right.

Sediko wandered over to the window, looked out at the many faces, then turned back to Kellie.

"Yeah man. Kellie, this is my tight bredrin, known her nearly all my life. I want you two to get on, you get me?" He looked to them both in turn.

They looked at each other. Candy cut an eye and Kellie raised an eyebrow.

"I got guests upstairs, I gotta go. Did you think about what I said?" asked Kellie.

"What was that?"

"The job that I'm perfect for." She smiled at him in the way that he loved.

"Yeah, it's all yours." He hadn't really thought about it, but she was already doing it. "But I'm serious you two, get on, no screw face business, I know how you women stay. I might have to get wicked on *both* of you."

"Please," Kellie and Candy said at the same time.

They smiled at each other, then Kellie left to her guests.

Sediko smiled.

"What's that grin for?"

Candy stood and walked slowly toward the window to join him.

"Look at you; you look sexy."

"Got to be a lady *some*times."

He had never even seen her in a skirt, let alone this micro-mini extra skin-hugging dress. He shook his head.

"What you shaking your head for? Am I making you sweat?" She grinned at him.

"Come on, you know that I've always checked for you, but you decided to go down Dyke Street; what could I do?" They both laughed.

"So what's gwaaning wid dem boys?" Candy changed the subject and got serious.

Sediko filled her in about the ruckus in Haydon's with Image.

"So who they wid now? Sparrow and Image couldn't have set that shit up alone."

"Fuck knows." Sediko stood beside her.

"So who you got beef wid?"

Sediko laughed at her question.

"Who haven't I got beef with. You know how it is, I'm always in beef."

"When was the last time you really fucked up someone's shit? And what was it about?"

"Boy, that was a while ago still, man's been a good boy, you get me? We caught a little luck with a few keys of shit. One nigga called Fixer was meant to be hunting for me." He remembered what the naked man had said when he had shot him in the foot. "But I don't hear nothing on that front. Or it could be this next nigga called Mat that took my fall. Ha, I'll tell you about that later. Or this other dude; I fucked his gal then his sister-"

"Stop, stop. Two-Face yuh na easy!" She laughed.

"I'm a bad man, you get me? Ole dawg like me we hafi ave dem inna twos an...." He and Candy began singing an old ragga tune that they both had loved way back in the day when they used to go to nothing but bashment dances.

"I'm gonna find Sparrow and find out what I need to know. Anyway forget all that shit for now, what you been on?"

He went and sat at the table. She followed and sat beside him.

"I been here innit, these sides."

"Any other news? Was Kellie behaving when man was locked up?"

"She was cool. How lucky are you to have two pally, pally, baby mothers."

"What you mean? Mia was here?" Sediko asked, well intrigued now.

"They were chatting in here for about 20 minutes."

"What am I gonna do about that gal? You know, I'm fuming that she's breeding now. The bitch is running me down– breaking into my yard, phoning Kellie, fucking coming in here…"

"But why you always go back with her I don't know, when you got Kellie, you don't need that."

"I know, I wish I was getting that advice before the bitch got pregnant," Sediko moaned.

"You want me to go visit her?"

"Na man, Candy, she's breeding."

"You sure that's your yout'?"

A knock at the door.

"Come!" Sediko called.

Jade came in wearing a tight-fitting, sexy, black shirt. It was unbuttoned just enough to show a perfect cleavage in a silver bra.

"Nice." He twirled his finger in the air. She spun around.

"How are you?"

"Neat, neat. I hear you've been promoted?"

"Yeah, bar manager," she said grinning proudly.

"So whadda you want?"

"I wanted to talk to Kellie about some orders."

"She's upstairs."

"Alright, see ya." She turned and left. Sediko watched.

"I see you haven't been tamed." Candy had looked too.

"Ain't nothing wrong with looking."

His eyes turned to her cleavage and a flash thought of her and Kellie rolling around naked, made him grin.

"Only if you're not thinking about touching." She raised her eyebrows.

Sediko wished that he could have her.

"Member?…" he asked her.

"Remember what?"

"Me and you, long time ago." He tried to stop himself from smiling.

"As if I could forget."

"Was that you're last time with a man?"

"Maybe." She looked away from him and her shoulders raised when she went shy.

"What's maybe? Man don't wanna hear that. I thought I was the only one." He pretended to look hurt.

"You were and you know it. Change the subject."

"Was I so bad I turned you to gal?"

"No, it was the opposite, almost." Her shoulders lifted and she looked away again.

"Was I good then? Stallion man?" He laughed lightly pushing her to talk.

"Who can remember the details? That was time ago."

"So why do you hate man?"

"I don't hate men."

"So why you with girls?"

"Because that's what I like."

"So it must have been shit with me then, innit? You can say. It won't hurt my feelings. You try not talk about certain things when I ask. You know you can ask me anything about anything. Earlier you try change the subject."

"What you wanna know?" She looked him straight in the eye.

"Did you check for me back then? Was it cos of me that you love pussy? Did I fuck up your head?"

"Whoa, whoa. You're not that important, not anymore anyway."

"What's that mean, 'not any more?'"

"Why you pushing me? What's up?" She tried to laugh, he stayed serious.

"What can't niggas talk about anything?"

"You sure you wanna know?"

"Whadda you think?"

"I did like you back then. From time I first lan' in this country, you showed me certain things. We were bredrins, initt? I didn't want to say shit about feelings and spoil things. When we did have that one night I think it meant more to me than it did to you. Next thing I knew, straight away you got with Mia. We were nothing but pickney, I don't blame you, but I knew I wouldn't find any man that made me feel the way I did when I was with you that weekend," she confessed.

Sediko stayed silently shocked.

"You and Mia were tight, so I backed off. I did have a few sexless relationships with men after you but they did nothing for me or ran off when I didn't wanna fuck, so I went to the next best thing and liked it. But don't worry because that was years after you." She turned back to him without looking him in the eye.

"Why didn't you say shit?"

"Boy you were too gally, gally,. I would have had to tame you, you wouldn't have liked that."

"You don't know what could've been."

"Then we wouldn't be as tight as we are now, you're my nigga. Only cos I'm dress up you feel the need to hit on me, when you see me tomorrow wearing the same track bottoms as you, you'll forget all about me."

A knock at the door.

"What?!" he called, vexed at the interruption. They would definitely have to finish this conversation.

"Smalls."

"Come."

Smalls came in with a shadow in tow. Sediko stood. His eyes focused on Sparrow and he instantly forgot about his deep conversation with

Candy.

"He come looking for you." Smalls pushed Sparrow in front of him then left.

Sediko laughed lightly and looked at his ex dog, his nigga. Sparrow stood still, the silence was killing him. Finally he said, "Why you fuck up Image earlier?"

"You seen him?"

"Na, just heard. Wa gwan?"

Sediko came close to him. Sparrow edged back.

"You done the right thing coming here; I was gonna find you. Sidown."

"I don't wanna sit down Two-Face; I just come to sort all this mix up."

"Man don't do business standing up. So sit the fuck down in my chair; it's the last time you're gonna get that privilege."

Sparrow sat opposite Candy.

"Go on," Sediko urged, still standing.

"What happened was, I did owe one nigga some dough through something one night. That bitch passed the debt onto someone else– one credit card nigga."

Sparrow was sweating like a convict in an interview room. Obviously he had practised this vague deadbeat story, thought Sediko to himself. Candy studied him, searching for lies.

"So cos he had this other nigga that owed him, he confiscated this big shipment–"

"Hol' up, stop. You lost me long time. I don't hear you mention any names."

"Names yeah? You gonna have my back when I start chatting man's names?" he asked looking distressed.

"Got your back!? You fucking crazy? Just finish the fucking story in names." Sediko lit a ready-made spliff that was behind his ear.

"It was Pun that I owed the money to, at first anyway–"

"Pun? What for?" Sediko cut in, he wanted to know everything.

"Boy.." Sparrow hesitated.

"What for?" he repeated.

"A card game."

"A card game?"

"A card game, 15 grand IOU," he confirmed then continued, "I couldn't pay that nigga, we weren't making that kind of dough back then, so for his own reasons, like I said, he passed the debt on to someone else. That someone else was Fixer. He the one, the credit card nigga. Fixer is the kind that people always owe him shit. I couldn't pay that nigga either. I met up with him and while we were reasoning one night, a white boy came on the scene. He owed Fixer too, so Fixer took over this white boy's crack base as a payback. This white boy talked too much and gave me too much information and that's the place that we robbed."

162

"What?! Nigga, what the fuck?"

"We weren't meant to go that far, just take what we could and leave."

"But hol' on, why you didn't tell me that shit back then? Why didn't you tell Path or Bones? And we meant to be boys!"

"What I was planning to do was pay Fixer back with his own money, you get me? But by the time we cut that shit up and shared that shit between us niggas, I still couldn't pay. Fixer and that nigga was adding interest, trying to take man for a fool. Later, he found out that it was us that raided his shit. Man started coming down on me and Image hard."

"What has Image really got to do with this?"

"Nothing! He just helped me get the info for that hit, that's all. That's why he didn't deserve that shit."

"Na, he got what you should have got, the mistake Image made was keeping your little fucking secret; man should have came and told me straight away, you get me? Man would have given you the money. Fifteen Gs?!"

"I thought I could sort it."

"You obviously thought wrong! Just continue."

"So then he found out that it was me, you, and the rest of the niggas"

"So how'd he find out it was us?"

"Don't know. He started asking me bare questions about you. About Kellie and the club."

"What did he want to know 'bout Kellie!"

"All different things."

"You mudafucker!"

"He just asked a few questions Two-Face."

"And you told him, yeah? What fucking questions?!"

"Her number, her address-"

"You little pussyhole!" Sediko turned and banged the table.

"But we didn't know nothing about boy dem coming up in here! That same night he came in here looking for me and his money. So I said that he could take it from the safe, just the money that I owed, not from what we made. I didn't even clock that it was Fixer until afterwards. Trust me I-"

"Wait, I can't believe all this started from a fucking card game that you lost?!"

"It's not my fault though. It ain't like that."

"I can see what's it's fucking like! You tried to fuck me over to get yourself out of trouble! When man was in jail I didn't see you or Image come and visit. You man were cotching up in Haydon's and collecting man's money. Worst of all nigga you try dis' my wife! Now you talking about got your back and...and fucking card debts! I don't believe that shit! Why didn't you tell me from the jump?"

"It was only a little money problem at first."

"So when we raided my man's place why didn't you show me then?"

"Cos I was dealing with it, like I said. I was gonna pay that nigga back with the money we made from the hit. I had to do something, that nigga was on my back!" Sparrow was sweating and his eyes were looking pleadingly.

"So what, you think that this Fixer is badder dan me?" Sediko asked him.

Candy stood and went to the mini bar.

"Drink?" she asked.

"Yeah," Sediko answered. He went around and sat beside Sparrow.

"So what, you didn't hear what I said?"

"I'm not saying he's badder than you; it's not about that."

"Yeah, but you do anything to get that nigga his money, even rob from your closest niggas. You wasn't scared to do that shit to me but your scared shitless cos you can't pay some pussy a measly 15 grand, who wasn't even involved in the fucking card game anyway!"

"I'm telling you what you want to know ain't I? I'm crossing his path now, even after you done said you haven't got my back! I'm fucked anyway!"

"So what you tell him about me?"

"Nothing really, just where the club was, nothing big!"

"Nothing big?! You go chat my business, steal from me, dis' my wife! You know what you fucking shit face! You played your last fucking card game!" he shouted.

Candy passed him a Southern Comfort.

"Smalls!" he called.

Smalls came in immediately, grinning at Sparrow who put his head down and muttered something under his breath.

"Get Jimmy."

"Two-Face, I wouldn't be here if I didn't want to sort things out! You're my boy, you get me?" Sparrow pleaded with him, while Sediko sipped his drink.

Path entered the room.

"You, you little punk," Path spat at him, walking round to spud Sediko.

"Fuck you," Sparrow said in return.

"Man ain't got no respect for you," Candy said sniggering.

"Innit. Man's taking out his anger on you," Sediko said laughing with her.

One of the Jimmys came in.

"Woz up boss?" He stood like a black human snowman.

"Take this nigga and meet me at the spot."

"Two-Face, what'd we just say? Fuck! Why do you think I'm here? I'm your fucking boy! I came straight here! I come straight here to sort shit out, I coulda run, I coulda dussed out the area but I came here cos you're my boy. Ah, fuck man."

"I don't trust you no more! You done fucked yourself up! You thought what, I'd let you get away with this shit after I sat in jailhouse for two months! Two months for a fucking card game! A fucking card game!"

"But Two-Face, my man was on my back! Try and understand that."

"You're gonna be on your back forever now you little pussy!"

"Ask Image, I tried to sort this shit out! I didn't knock man!"

"You did! You even told that nigga shit about Kellie! I can't believe that shit! You're over. You try put man's wifey in harm's way? Watch."

"Two-Face." Sparrow rested his head in his hands. He knew there was no point talking. He and Sediko had taken plenty other niggas to the spot. And they were never on the return trip.

"Alright, Guv." Jimmy towered over Sparrow and hauled him out the chair.

"Soon come." Sediko pulled on his jacket.

"Satisfied?" Path asked him as he turned to leave.

"Na."

Twelve

BILL DROVE AROUND Soho in an anonymous car with darkened windows. He was searching for Lola, a prostitute from Puerto Rico with whom he had spent many nights and notes with in the past. Just as he knew he would, he spotted her straight away. She looked just like the slut that she was, dressed in a tight red mini-skirt, a white cloth top, and ugly high boots. Her long hair was flowing over her shoulders and thick make-up covered her beautiful face. He drove up to her. She sauntered to the window. He wound it down just enough for her to see his face.

"Bill!" She opened the back door and got in.

"Long time no see." He looked at her through the rearview mirror.

"No wedding ring?" She was very quick.

"Reading the newspaper?"

"No," she answered as he drove off.

"Got a few hours to spare?" he asked her.

"Got a few hundred?" She smiled and looked into the large Selfridge's bag on the seat beside her. She peeped inside wondering what would be in the bag this time.

Slowly, she took off her clothes, making sure his rearview mirror showed her good side. She took face wipes out the bag and wiped her face clear of all make-up, just as he always liked. She took a long, pearly, cream dress out of the bag. He sure had taste. With barely enough room to swing a cat, she fought to slip it on gracefully, and managed. Next, she took a strappy pair of sandals out of the bag and slipped them on.

Bill stopped the car in an area unfamiliar to her; she came out and sat in the front seat feeling like a princess.

"You like?" he asked, pulling off again.

"I love," she replied with a huge smile. She never wore clothes like this, she couldn't afford to. She never kept the clothes but she didn't mind, she just waited for him to come again. And, for a very long time, he didn't.

They drove towards the motorway.

"Where are we going?" she asked gently.

"I'm taking you somewhere special tonight; it's been so long, I've missed you."

"Missed me? Really?" She had missed him too. It had been a few months but she always knew that he would come back, he always did.

"We'll check into a hotel later, not the same one."

"Oh, but I used to love that hotel." She smiled, remembering the crisp white sheets and the beautiful shower.

"This one will be better."

Bill loved taking her for the night; she was always so grateful, so easy to please, never demanding; a continuous one-night stand.

"So how have you been?" he asked, realising they were in for a long drive and he had never really had a conversation with her.

Bill had met her two years earlier. It had been his first time going with a prostitute and she had made his fantasies real. He wasn't a dirty man, in fact he hated prostitutes, but when he took away Lola's slut mask she was exceptionally beautiful. He had tried his hardest to get her in front of the camera, but to no avail. He would never go to another prostitute and he didn't really think of her as one. Once she slipped into the clothes that he always brought, she could match up to Marie on most counts.

"Fine. Things are a bit slow." She took a brush out of a bright pink bag. She was definitely leaving that behind.

"Why's that?" As if he really wanted to know.

"I got arrested on Monday– me, a few other girls and four customers." She brushed at her long, dark, thick, hair.

"Well never mind all that tonight. We're going to the country. Ever been there?"

"No. What's in the country?"

"Hills, trees, quiet pubs, cows, peace, fox hunting and a casino." She would be his luck charm.

"Wow, casino! I have no money."

"You will by the end of tonight. I may even have you until tomorrow morning."

"Really?" She was pleasantly surprised.

Usually it was a quick drink and a fuck in a private but exclusive hotel room, then home to Marie before 11:30. But that was when he wore a wedding ring– before his wife left him.

Five hours later they were in Wales and he had learned a lot of things about her that surprised him. She had a five-year-old son in Puerto Rico, and was studying Criminology and English in the evenings at university. Now in her second year, she prostituted and performed in strip clubs to pay her tuition fee and for her son's ticket to join her.

Bill wondered if this was all true.

"So, you have family in London?"

"No."

"So how did you get to this country?"

"I saved up for my ticket even before I got pregnant. When I eventually did get here I came straight to London, I had one bag and about £50. I met Pips on my first night. My English was good so we spoke and he took me in. That very same day I met you."

"Really? What a coincidence. Well, here we are."

Bill looked at her. She looked around at all the flashing lights like a child at a fun fair. A valet stood on hand ready to take his car.

"You ready?"

"Do I look alright?" she asked him.

He turned to the bag and took out one of Marie's favourite perfumes. He spayed it lightly over her. Next, he took out one of Marie's hair clips, quickly and professionally, he pinned her hair up. She looked beautiful.

"Perfect."

The next temporary gift would definitely get him into trouble with Marie. But Marie had left him. He took out a box.

"What's this?"

"It's for you, for tonight." She opened the box and awaited her reaction.

"Oh, I can't wear this Bill, it's too beautiful, so perfect." She looked at him then back to the nugget sized uncut diamond on a white gold chain. It had sat just above and between Marie's breasts only once. When he had given the gift to Marie she had been upset because one of her girlfriends had exactly the same design.

"You must." He took it from its big box and slipped it around her neck.

"Thank you Bill. It's the most precious thing that I've ever seen." She kissed his cheek. Like Richard Gere in Carrie's all-time favourite film *Pretty Woman*, Bill never allowed tongue kissing.

The valet stood waiting.

"Bill, I must tell you my real name is Latina. Lola's not appropriate, I think."

"You're right and it's a lovely name, Latina. Come on Latina, we've got money to win."

As they walked up a royal red carpet, Bill could almost smell the money behind its walls.

"Evening Mr Laymend," someone greeted him.

"If anyone asks, you're just a student."

"Of course." She smiled sweetly.

At their card table an hour later, Bill was on a winning streak with two other gentlemen millionaires. Already, thousands had passed the table between them. Latina sat patiently at his side, not complaining about wanting to go shopping or wanting to go and watch a special addition of something or another, she just sat and brought him luck.

"Where's the champagne?" he asked to no one in particular.

"Just coming Mr Laymend."

"Can I join?" a familiar voice said from behind.

"Evening Mr Laymend. How are you?" Cape Newman loomed over him, then took a vacant seat at the table.

Bill kissed his good luck goodbye.

"Great," Bill said aloud and then stood. There was no way he was sharing his card game or his winning streak with this man.

"Please Bill, don't go on my account, I need to talk with you."

"I *was* in the middle of a card game," Bill shot back annoyed.

A full head of grey hair and clutching a solid gold and mahogany walking stick, the old man stood up in pursuit.

"Please excuse us gentlemen, have a drink."

Bill walked away from ears at the table.

"What are you doing out here?" Bill asked.

"I may have heard that this was a regular place for you and your lady friends."

"And your point is?"

"It's about the children," he huffed.

"Children? I think not. Your son is a bad influence on my daughter; you know he's on *drugs*? What is it with your family?"

"What's the meaning of this accusation?!" Newman said angrily.

"No accusation, he practically told me himself."

"Again, we will keep that information between us. But ultimately we both want the same thing."

"Yeah, tell Jeff to back off and find another young innocent girl to play with."

"Fine," agreed Newman.

"Fine," Bill confirmed before walking away. "Come on Latina, we're going," he called to her. She scrapped his winnings off the table and ran to catch up with him.

An hour later Bill and Latina stood outside one of his small secluded cottages. This one he had rented out for years until the couple recently passed away; it had been empty ever since.

"This is wonderful," she said as they walked to the old door. "You used to live here?"

"No, not really." He took a key from inside a hanging plant pot.

"How old are you Bill?" Latina asked as they stepped inside.

"Forty-two," he said without thinking. He should have said thirty-two; he looked it.

"Wow, I thought you were thirty-one or thirty-two at the most."

"Am I too old for you?"

"No, of course not. I'm more than half your age; I'm twenty-four.

"Twenty-four? You're just a few years older than my daughter."

"Am I too young for you?"

"No." He kissed her forehead.

"So," she looked around the large front room, "you have two houses?"

"A handful of houses and a few villas around Europe."

He lit up the fireplace. She took off her shoes and came and stood on the fluffy rug.

Twenty minutes later they both sat in a large chair by the fire. She snuggled up beside him and it felt good. He needed a woman, most of the time more than one. He needed a woman's touch.

"So what about tomorrow?"

"What about it?" she said without turning to him; she just watched the fire as if it was the television.

"I want you to stay with me."

"I can't, Bill."

"I'll pay you, you know that."

"I have to go home to Pips every morning and I've got university in the evening."

"I'll pay you."

"It's not about the money, I just can't okay?"

"What's wrong?"

"Can you get me back by 9 am?"

"Why?"

"He'll want tonight's money."

"I thought you said the money is for tuition and your son's flight ticket?"

"That's true, I save all I can, but Pips has to get half."

"Half?!" Bill sat up. She was sounding like a guest on America's Jerry Springer.

"Yes, he has done so much for me." She stood, unzipped and let Marie's dress fall to the floor. Her naked, firm, toned, brown body shined at him in the flickering light.

"Why can't you just get a job?"

"I have a job." Her nakedness relaxed them both.

"But you've got so much going for you. Where do you live?"

"With Pips in White City."

"How much have you saved?"

"Well I did have £700 but Pips borrowed half of it. He'll pay me back." No one had ever asked her so many questions.

"Only £700 in two years?" Bill said sadly. "Why don't you move away from him; it sounds to me like you've paid your debt."

"Where would I go?"

"You can come home with me," he said without thinking. If Burt could have a younger girl then damn it so could he. No one would know that she was a slut.

"Bill I..."

"What's wrong? Don't you want to?"

"I do, of course I do, but Pips would kill me," she said in a frightened voice.

"How would he find you? He won't know where you are. You would never have to see him again," he pushed. A tear fell down her cheek and a glimmer of hope sparked in her eyes.

"I knew that you would be the one to save me Bill." She approached him and sat softly on his lap. Their faces almost touched and she kissed him square in the lips.

His tongue was eager to find hers.

≈≈≈

Phone Sediko!" Mia shouted as she held her stomach. Charlene rushed around behind her making sure that everything was packed.

"Do you really want 'im there Mia? You haven't even seen him."

"Please!" Mia huffed and puffed.

"Alright."

Charlene found her phone and dialled his number. Mia watched. She hoped to God that he would answer, she hadn't seen him in a month.

"Mia's having contractions and the ambulance is on its way.....Kings Hospital...alright......I will.. Bye"

"He said he will meet you there, he said he promises."

"Good good cos I can't take this pain. Ahh!! It's coming back! Charlene, it fucking hurts!"

"You're alright, just breathe girl breathe. In-out, in-out." Charlene breathed with her.

"I can't fucking breathe, where's the ambulance?!"

A knock at the door. Charlene led in two paramedics.

"Hello. My name is Helen and this is Steve, how are you doing?" she asked coming over to Mia.

"I'm alright but the pain keeps coming back," Mia whimpered.

"That will be the contractions. How far apart are they now?"

"I don't know."

"About 8 minutes," Charlene answered for her.

"That's fine, lets get you in the ambulance then. Is your friend coming with you?" Mia nodded.

In the ambulance Mia sucked on gas and air, thinking about Sediko and their baby. He or she would soon be in the world.

"This is it, girl," said Charlene warmly, as Mia sat in the wheelchair heading for labour ward. She screwed her face as another contraction came on.

"Gas and air?" the nurse offered, seeing her pain.

"Anything! Anything." She grabbed the tube and sucked in. "It's still hurting! It's not helping!" She began to cry as a tightening pain came over her swiftly. "Where's Sediko?" she half cried, half laughed.

"He's on his way," said Charlene walking beside her.

"You sure?"

The pain passed, her head felt light.

Moments later Mia lay on the delivery bed sweating and in pain, waiting for Sediko and her baby. A doctor examined her while Charlene waited outside. Minutes after the doctor left, Sediko walked in.

"Sediko!" Mia cried. He came and hugged her.

"You alright?"

"Yeah, I am now. Ahh! Shit, Sediko call the doctor, I wanna push!" she shouted in pain yet again.

"No don't, wait! Let me call him, just wait one second."

"I can't!" she shouted after him as he ran out the door. She didn't know she would be in so much pain; her stomach was almost burning. She had never felt like doing a big shit so much in her life. What a time to want to go toilet; she couldn't get up now!

Sediko, the doctor, the midwife and a nurse came walking back in.

"I need to go toilet," she moaned, tears falling down her cheeks.

"You're 10 centimetres dilated Mia, you're ready to have your baby." The doctor beamed up at her through her open legs.

"Ahhh! Can I push, should I push?"

"It's alright Mia, you're doing good," Sediko encouraged, one arm around her shoulders the other hand in hers.

"When you're ready, push down onto your bottom," instructed the doctor.

"I can't!" She felt like she hadn't slept in days. Who was she to think that she could ever be strong enough to have a baby? She felt like she had just run fifty miles and her lower region felt as if it was about to explode! She pushed down hard as the urge was stronger than her exhaustion.

"Very good Mia, when you're ready give another push, one big push," the doctor encouraged her.

"I can't! I can't!"

"You can Mia, you *can*. One big push, babes." Sediko's voice made her relax, it was like music to her ears and she did as he told her and pushed down long and hard with all her might, screaming out in pain. Seconds later, she heard a long soft high pitched cry. They laid her baby onto her stomach.

"A boy!" Sediko said excitedly. They offered to let him cut the cord and he did so, proudly.

"We'll just take him for a second weigh, wipe him down and get him wrapped up warm," said the nurse.

"Congratulations to us," Sediko said kissing her, then him, as the nurse took him from her.

"A 7lb 4oz very healthy baby boy born at approximately 10:14 am," announced the the midwife before handed their son to Sediko.

"What we gonna call him?"

"Sediko Jordan Braithwaite Marshall," she said tiredly, her eyes barely open.

Charlene came bounding in.

"Congratulations to you both. Ahh, he's so cute," she said looking at their son's tiny face. "Boy or girl?"

"My son." Sediko gazed down at him, bursting with pride.

Charlene left them alone for a while as Sediko sat with Mia watching their son.

"I gotta go just now, I'll be back later. And I know it's not the right time, but ask the nurse for some information about having a blood test done."

"What for?" Mia sat up, feeling distressed.

"You know what for, but don't worry I know he's my son, I can feel it. It's to prove to the rest of the world. I'll see you soon. By the way, Candy said 'hi.'"

"I didn't know you two stayed in touch."

"There's a lot that you don't know about me. Take care of my boy 'till I get back. You want anything?"

"No, just make sure that you come back," she said weakly. He kissed his baby and left.

"I heard you screaming and I was praying for ya out there," said Charlene, all smiles as she came back into the room.

"Kellie told Sediko to ask for a blood test," Mia said to her without taking her eyes off her Sediko Jordan.

"Well, it *is* best ta know definitely."

"It's Sediko's; this is Sediko Jordan Braithwaite Marshall," she said proudly.

"I can't say that I see a resemblance." Charlene leaned in close to study her baby.

"Give it time."

"You spoken to Kirk?"

"Why would I?"

"No reason."

Mia looked closely at her son. His skin was very light, just like hers and his dark hair was slicked to his tiny head.

"We're gonna show everyone, prove it once and for all. Call the nurse."

The nurse came in with a tiny bottle. She held it to his small mouth.

"Hold him in the bend of your arm, close to your chest," the nurse advised. She did as she was told.

"He's not taking."

"Just take it slow, he'll catch on. Just press this button if you need anything." He pointed to a button above her bed.

"Could I have some information about a blood test being done?"

"Yes, I'll tell Dr May to come and see you."

"Thanks," Mia said turning her attentions back to Sediko Jordan. Finally the baby opened his mouth and sucked.

"He's drinking," Mia said proudly to Charlene. "I'm so tired." She yawned.

"Well done, he's beautiful. I'm going now. I'll be back tomorrow," promised Charlene.

Mia watched her baby suck from his bottle. His eyes began to close. He was a picture of his dad.

A few hours went by and Mia fell asleep leaving Sediko Jordan in his temporary cot.

"Hello, can I come in?" asked a woman's voice.

"Mmm." Mia sat up sleepily and turned straight to her baby, he was lying silently awake.

"I'm Pam, the health visitor. Sorry to wake you but you're my last round for today and I wanted to say hello and congratulations." She walked around to Sediko Jordan. "He is gorgeous. How much did he weigh?"

"Seven pounds, four ounces."

Mia felt like she hadn't slept a wink. A mixture of exhaustion, awe and love washed over her.

"Very healthy. How are you?" Pam asked, her large, round glasses covering most of her small face.

"Alright, just tired."

"Of course, it's only natural. Can I have a hold?" She was a short lady with shoulder length hair, dark brown. She wore a brown anorak with an ankle length tartan brown skirt. Mia took him out of the cot and handed him to her wrapped in his blue blanket.

"What's his name?" She held out her arms.

"I haven't decided." She didn't know why she lied.

"Right, well there's plenty of time. Have you got the necessary things at home for him?"

"What?"

"Nappies, a cot, baby clothes?" Pam sat in a chair beside the bed.

"Not yet."

"If you want I can sort out a few things for you. Sometimes ladies from the clinic leave a few bits? Second hand, but approved conditions," she offered with a gentle smile.

"It's alright, his dad is out getting the things as we speak."

"Fine, just let me know if you change your mind. Do you feel alright with changing and caring for the baby?"

"I'll cope."

"The nurse mentioned that you wanted information about a blood test?" She rocked Sediko Jordan in her arms.

"Er yeah, it's mainly for his parent's sake, his mum never did like me. How long will it take?"

"It can be done today but it will cost, and we obviously need the father."

"Money is no problem, and you can get blood from the father later on today." Mia held out her arms for her baby back.

≈≈≈≈

S o, what's he like?" Mo asked her.
"Alright, American. He knows what he's talking about."   "So is he coming with you to lunch with *Cosmopolitan*?"

"Well he *is* my agent now." She smiled proudly as a new life loomed ahead of her.

"So what's his name?"

"Chad, Chad Delaware."

"So you're gonna do it?"

"Of course. Help me up." She wiggled forwards and Mo pulled her up. She was now eight months pregnant. She waddled to the toilet.

"So how much you think you'll get?"

"God knows? The main thing is I get to keep the Gucci shoes and watch."

"Wow! I know you like that. Was that the door?"

"Get that for me, I'm bursting."

When she came back down, Sediko was standing by the kitchen door.

"You alright babes?" He came and hugged her.

"Yes." Kellie hugged him back tight. It seemed every time that she saw him, she fell in love with him over and over again.

"Where's Samuel?"

"His gran's."

"She give you any hassle?"

"No she's cool. Guess what?" Kellie pulled at his collar.

"Kellie I'm gonna cut you cos I've got to go," said Mo. "I told Tex that I'd only be an hour. Look at the time, it's after ten; he's gonna kill me. I'll call you tomorrow?" And she was gone.

"I got something to tell *you* first," Sediko said when they were alone.

"Go on." Kellie went and sat down. By the look on his face she might drop down if she weren't sitting.

"Mia. She had my son today." He half smiled.

"Right," she sighed. "You seen her?" Her nightmares were all coming true.

"Of course."

"Mmm...you tell her about the blood test?" Kellie felt sick.

"Took it already, we have to wait a few days."

"Why, can't you get the results tomorrow?" she pushed.

"Listen! I did what you said, alright! Drop it." He pulled a baggie from his pocket.

"Did you two talk?" She watched him empty skunk mixed with Charlie onto the table.

"Course we talked, what's your problem?" He began the billing up process.

"I hope you didn't-"

"Didn't what!?" he shouted "Didn't what!? Fuck her beside our baby on the hospital bed! Shit Kellie, what *could* I have done?"

175

"I'm just asking! I have a right to ask and I wouldn't put it past that girl to take you up to the toilets and get her pregnant all over again!"

"You know what, you just worry about your yout'! Not mine."

"Fuck you."

"What!" He lit his spliff and stayed silent for a few minutes, calming almost instantly.

"What did you want to tell me?"

"That I got an agent and I'm doing more butt naked pictures!" She rolled out of the chair and went to the kitchen, her stomach making it impossible for her to do anything quickly.

She could tell that this night would be full of his Jekyll and Hyde two facedness. Whenever he smoked Charlie he just couldn't be himself.

"You ain't doing it!" he shouted to her in the kitchen.

"Really!" she shouted.

He followed her into the kitchen and stood looking at her, his eyes were fireballs. He grabbed her arms, spun her around and pushed her into the door frame.

"YOU AIN'T DOING IT!"

"Let me go!" she shouted, shocked at the strength that he was using.

"You ain't doin' it you hear!" He still held her, digging his fingers into her skin. She shook her body and his arms dropped.

"I am doing it. I done it before and I am again next week." Her face was almost parallel with his.

"You did it before yeah, that was before, I wasn't on road then!" She moved from in front of him into the front room. He followed her and pushed her onto the chair. She held her stomach to protect her unborn.

"ARE YOU CRAZY SEDIKO! What's wrong with you!" She cried out in fear.

"What's wrong with you!" he asked, standing over her.

He left seconds later without another word.

Kellie wanted to call him back, wanted to shout his name and tell not to walk out on her. But she stayed silent, talking to him when he was like that was impossible.

Tears fell down her cheeks as he slammed her door shut. She was trying so hard to be happy for him, trying so hard to be a good girlfriend so that he didn't stray back to Mia. She tried so hard to be a good mother for Samuel, like he deserved, and trying to be a good manager at the club, but the truth was she felt like she was just along for a ride, her feet hardly touching the floor. Then Sediko would come along and make all her hard work seem fake. Because without him, she didn't want any of it.

She would go to the meeting and she would do her photo shoot. The old Kellie would. The old Kellie was looking forward to it; her new agent was opening doors for her. She would attend all celebrity parties and go to all invitations to famous restaurants, and she would put

Ballers on the map through simple word of mouth. Sediko would just have to live with it. Just as she had to live with Mia.

A week later Kellie was sitting in a studio six times the size of Laymend's. Bill stood in one corner with a pretty Puerto Rican woman, Chad stood in another corner with her interviewer and Mandy sat beside her. Kellie sat in a towel with her hair in large curlers. A gay stylist brushed her face with powder to cut shine. The fashion and picture editors rallied around, waiting for action. Chad walked across the studio towards her.

"Hey, you ready for your interview?" he looked like a blonde beach bum in a suit.

"Whenever you are. Where are my shoes? I want to see my shoes," Kellie demanded. Seconds later someone brought them to her. The sandals were barely there, only a loop for her big toe and a thin studded ankle catch.

"They are beautiful!" Kellie whispered.

"Hi, I'm Cameron, I'll be interviewing you. Just relax and don't say anything you don't want me to print," he said laughing and sitting opposite her in a Burberry suit. Mandy had made herself scarce as they were being photographed and filmed. Cameron leaned in keenly.

"First, how do you feel about interviewing in only a towel?"

"I feel great, it feels natural." She felt someone pulling at her curlers.

"You're a sex symbol at eight months pregnant, how does that make you feel?"

Her hair bounced in her face, she giggled.

"I feel flattered. I wouldn't say that I am a sex symbol but I think it's great if men find pregnancy attractive, it's natural too."

"Does it feel strange to be recognised in the street?"

"Definitely, but it doesn't happen that often."

"So how do you manage being a mum, a wife, a club manager, a model and still find time to work part-time at Mr Laymend's side?"

"When you say it like that I don't know how I manage," she replied laughing. "When you enjoy what you do it takes all the hard work out of it I guess. I love being at the club, that doesn't even feel like work half the time, Bill is a good friend of mine and I enjoy being in the fashion industry. And I love my family very much. Believe it or not we do get to spend a lot of time together."

"So was it when you first modelled with Lisa Brooks, is that when you realised modelling was for you?"

"Basically yeah, it went from one 1 hour session a week, to long hours 3 days a week. I used to love just facial shots, quick and easy."

"So when your baby is born will we definitely be seeing you on our catwalks?"

"That's my aim, but we'll see what happens. Who's to say I'll loose my baby fat. One line of cellulite could ruin my career." Kellie laughed

177

along with half the studio who also laughed at the sick truth.

"Has stardom changed you?"

"I'm Kellie now and always will be."

"Whose body are you most likely to have after the baby is born: Geri Haliwell's yoga toned bod or Angelia Jolie's Laura Croft ripples?"

"Neither, I'll be me."

"What do you do in your spare time?"

"I have no spare time, in my free time I'm with my family."

"Alright, I'm going to ask you ten quick questions; one answer only please." His eyes dropped to her bare leg as her towel slipped.

"Favourite colour?"

"Er, anything in Gucci."

"Favourite dish?"

"Jerk chicken."

"Best album?"

"Angie Stone."

"Worst habit?"

"Um. Pass."

"Worst feature?"

"Legs."

"Really? That's your *best* feature."

"Thank you." Kellie smiled her winning smile.

"Best looking body part?"

"Hair, most definitely, or my feet in my Jimmy Choos, sorry that's two."

"Favourite male celebrity?"

"Samuel Jackson."

"Female?"

"Me. Or Jada Pinkett."

"Favourite alcoholic drink?"

"Malibu and milk when I'm not pregnant."

"And last but not least, how about me and you going out for dinner somewhere, alone?" He smiled, Kellie laughed. "No really, if you could have anything in the world what would it be?"

Kellie thought to herself. If she could have anything in the world it would be for Sediko to change, or maybe have her brother come from America or maybe for Mia to disappear from the face of the earth.

"Well?" he repeated, breaking her thought.

"World peace," she simply said.

"Good answer and one last. Sum yourself up in three words."

"Nude, ambitious and loving."

"And charming and sexy and I could go on. Thank you, that's all for now. You ready for the camera?"

"Yep," she said and looked over to Mandy who totally accepted what she was doing.

She stood and dropped her towel.

By the time she got home she had six messages. She pressed play.
First message, received at 12:53 pm: 'Kellie where you at!? I need to speak to you and your fucking mobile is off.'

Second message, received at 1:37 pm: 'This is Al Newman a friend of Chad, I'd love to invite you to a dinner party this weekend, there will be a lot of career moves. I'll e-mail Chad.'

Third message, received at 1:49 pm: 'You ain't back?'

Fourth message, received at 3:59 pm: 'I hope you're on your way to the studio, don't be late. And I have a full diary for us just as soon as your babe is born!'

Fifth message, received at 4:35pm: 'Fuck Kellie man, pick up your shit!'

Sixth message, received at 5:38pm: No message. Last message.

Kellie looked at the time: 5:40 pm. She sat on the sofa, switched on her phone and dialled Sediko's number.
"The mobile phone you have called may-"
She could hear in the message he'd left that he was mad about something. He was probably phoning to make sure she didn't do the modelling.
Six o'clock came and Buffie arrived with Samuel. He ran towards her clutching a painting.
"Hiya son. Had a good day?"
"Yes. Mummy, I want to buy some bulbs from my teacher, can I? And I painted this for you." He thrust the painting into her hands.
"Wow, this is nice. Did you do that all by yourself?" He nodded vigorously, smiling proudly.
"So who is this?"
"Me, you and Buffie," he answered. Kellie smiled behind him in admiration.
Buffie left them minutes later watching *Beauty and the Beast*.

Kellie heard a key in her door and turned quickly. Sediko came in. She had never given him a key but somehow for over a year now, he had been letting himself in.
"Kellie, who's Shawn?"
"Sam go to your room sweetheart, I'll call you in a minute and we can finish watching the movie alright?" He looked at her sadly and went upstairs.

"Are you gonna leave my door wide open?" She stared at her open door then went to close it when he didn't budge. .

"What, you not listening?" His eyes followed her.

"Have you come here to argue? I don't see you in days and then you wanna argue? Well I don't. Samuel is upstairs and I don't want him upset. Anyway, I don't know who you're talking about." *What was he doing asking her about Shawn!?*

"Don't make me get mad! That nigga has been putting money in your hands for God knows how long and you don't know what I'm talking about?!" He was shouting at her– high and vexed, his eyes red.

"I can't talk to you when you're high."

She turned her back. He spun her around, opened his hand and slapped her - the hardest she had ever been hit - across her face. She flew across the room onto her computer table by the door. It smashed to the floor and she fell to her knees, hugging the table tight for support. Her mind went blank for a second as her head hit the corner. Her heart was racing, she could feel and smell the blood running down her face. Slowly, she pulled herself up. *What the fuck was going on!*

Kellie pulled herself up onto the desk chair. She raised her hand to her face. Busted lip and head, bleeding nose, teary eyes.

"Kellie," he sighed, his face screwed up as if it was he who was in pain.

She looked up to see Samuel watching from the top of the stairs. He met her stare, then ran back to his room. He saw the blood drip from her face and onto her white and brown woolly jumper. She didn't wipe it, she just sat with her mouth open, her eyes sad. Blood and tears dripped.

"Kellie, I'm sorry babes, I'm sorry."

"Fffuck you," she whispered. Her eyes felt swollen.

"Come, let me clean you up and make this all up to you," he offered still standing behind her but making no effort to comfort her.

"No. How are you gonna make this alright? Surprise me? Well let me surprise you. There's nothing you can buy for me that I can't get for myself."

"You want me to leave?" He stood like a young schoolboy waiting to be punished.

"Yeah, get out." Never would she have thought that she would say those words to him, to her love.

"Let me just get you something-"

"No, just go."

"You're acting like a fucking angel but when man was in prison you were running up and down wid next man!" he defended.

"How dare you sit there and say I was running up and down with next man when there's a little bitch out there with your cunt son!"

"You know it was Shawn that put me in jail?"

"What?"

"Yeah, why didn't you tell me that you knew him? How'd you two meet?"

"We-"

"Remember, you don't know him. But it's all good. You want man to move over to make space for you and Shawna? That's what it says in your phone. It's cool." He turned and left with the last word.

Kellie stood slowly. Like a zombie, she walked up the stairs and peeked into Samuel's room. He lay asleep on the floor; he must have cried himself to sleep. She walked further down the corridor, entered her own room and pulled off her clothes. She stepped into the shower and let the hot water splash over her, stinging her lip. Blood and water streamed through the plughole.

Shawn. Shawn? Her mind raced, what did Sediko mean when he said Shawn put him in jail? How could he have? How had he found out about their connection? Mia no doubt. What did she tell him? Why was he blaming him for putting him in jail? What had made him hit her like that after two-and-a-half years? Did he hit Mia like that? That would be the last time that he did that to her.

Kellie felt tired and her head ached. She stepped out the shower, dried off and climbed into her bed. Her eyes began to close and she dozed off.

"Kellie I'm hungry." She heard a whisper. Her mind would not allow her to wake. She could hear the phone ringing but her head ached and she slipped back to sleep. An hour later it seemed someone was nudging her.

"Wake up, wake up, you alright Kellie?" It sounded like Buffie, what was she doing here at this time of night? Her eyes fluttered as she woke.

"Samuel said that you're not well?" she asked full of concern.

"What time is it?"

"Eight. What happened to your face? Ain't you going work?"

"Work?" Kellie asked disoriented, it couldn't be morning.

"Sorry, I was late."

"Shit. I must have dozed off about seven yesterday. I don't remember cooking dinner or anything." She struggled to sit up.

"It looks as if a little four-year-old boy helped himself down there. He said he made a sandwich and a drink, watched a video then fell asleep with his quilt on the sofa. That's where I found him."

Kellie wasn't listening. Sediko had hit her, her face felt sore and she relived the moment. Sediko had hit her.

"I'm not going to work."

She lay back down and pulled her quilt above her head.

Friday and Saturday went by without Ballers. Kellie called Jade and told her that she wasn't coming in. She didn't want a confrontation at the club, she wouldn't let Sediko make a fool of her in front of her workers. Sediko hadn't called her or even tried to apologise. She had decided that no matter what, she wouldn't give up the club for him. For now she would just lay low until she had her baby. No way she'd let Sediko take the club from her when she had been the one to lift it off the ground, keep it up and keep it going. She had even invested some of her own money.

Monday morning Kellie felt a twinge in her stomach. She smiled, she had already waited too long to see her baby. She couldn't wait to go shopping for baby clothes though she had a few things stored away at Mo's. An old wives' tale said it was bad luck to keep baby items in the house before the baby came. Her door slammed downstairs. She sat up in her bed where she had stayed for most of the weekend.

Sediko barged into her room, his eyes once again full of anger. But this time *he* was upset, his eyes were tearful. He stumbled into the room, he was drunk and probably high, too.

"What's up?" he said half smiling, half crying.

"What's wrong?" she asked full of concern, standing to console him.

"You bitches are fucked up!" His tears reached his cheeks and she backed away and sat back onto the bed.

"Is this about Shawn again?"

"No! Exactly some different shit, every fucking time!"

"Whose blood is that on your shirt?" She rolled off the bed away from him.

"Its Mia's."

His face went hard, he stumbled out the room. She heard him go noisily down the stairs and followed him warily into the kitchen. She stood by the door and watched him sniff four lines. He never sniffed before, not like that. She watched the effects of the familiar white powder.

"What happened?"

"What, can't you guess? It's just what you fucking wanted you bitch!"

"Listen, I'm not her." Kellie felt sorry for him but her dream had come true. "The blood test came through then?"

"Course it came through! What do you think! Shit! She told me shit about you too! Shit about that fucker inside you!"

"What!?" Kellie was going to fucking kill that bitch.

"Don't play innocent! You lied about knowing him! Had his phone number under a girl's name! Mia just confirmed my thoughts!"

"Sediko don't do this! For fuck sake, see sense! Can't you see what that little bitch is doing?!"

"See what?! She try give me a bastard son, so why not you too? What, you gonna tell me that you didn't fuck Fixer?"

"I ain't sleeping with him you fool! You're the one that had the affairs!"

"Yeah, you got all the fucking mouth you little bitch!"

"Are you trying to say that I'm carrying a next man's child?!"

"What are you dumb?" He walked towards her. She backed up slowly. *Not again, no not again!*

"Sediko....*please*," her voice shook.

He lunged himself at her. She turned to run but her legs just would not carry her. He grabbed her hair.

"Where the fuck you running to? Why you fucking running? What you got to hide?!"

"No!!" Her hands went up to her ponytail, which was wrapped around his hand. "Let go!!" He released her hair then grabbed her arm.

"You trying to take man for a fool?!" he shouted drunkenly.

"I didn't sleep with him! What do you want me to say?" she cried, her heart racing. He opened his hand once again.

"You ain't bringing no man's child into our yard!" He seemed to take a step back first, then punched her square in the face. Her eyes rolled up.

Thirteen

KELLIE'S EYES WERE barely open and she couldn't hear or see properly. It felt like she was in hospital; it smelt like she was. Her eyelids were weights and she struggled to keep them open. Doctors stood around her. What's wrong with me? she tried to ask. My baby, I'm pregnant! she tried to shout. They didn't hear her, they just moved around her speaking in mute. Faintly she could hear a bleep..bleep..bleep, then her eyes closed and her mind shut down.

Again Kellie tried to open her eyes, again she tried to speak. Faintly she could see her baby, someone had her baby. She wanted to hold out her arms and be a mother once more, she tried with all her might to sit up. 'Come baby,' she wanted to say, but nothing happened. She lay dead still, and her baby faded away. She wanted Sediko, she needed Sediko. She wanted her baby. Again, her mind fell asleep.

When Kellie finally awoke, she lay in a hospital bed in a small single room. Bunches and bunches of colourful flowers were all around her. She lifted her head to see her stomach. It had gone down, her baby was born. She tried to sit up but her body seemed paralysed. Her mind was blank as she tried to remember how she had gotten there. Her arm was hooked up to a drip. She was so confused. A friendly face came slowly into the room.

"You're awake Kellie, how are you feeling?"

"Dizzy, disoriented, where's my baby?"

"Kellie, I'm deeply sorry," the doctor began.

What do those words mean?! 'I'm deeply sorry.' Sorry for what?

"Where's my baby?" she asked again.

"We tried everything that we could. We had to give you an emergency caesarean. I'm afraid her heart had stopped beating before you arrived."

"No. Give me my baby, this is a sick joke!" Kellie grimaced.

"We tried, we were working with her for over thirty minutes." He looked sadly down at her.

Kellie sighed and struggled to pull herself into a sitting position. Her mind was screaming but her heart didn't understand what was happening.

"What are you saying? That my baby is-"

"I'm sorry. Really very sorry. You gave birth to a beautiful baby girl, we all really did try to revive her-"

The doctor kept on talking but Kellie wasn't listening, she couldn't hear. Her baby couldn't have died, she had seen her; what was happening?

"Would you like to see her?"

"Who?" Kellie asked frightened, she couldn't possibly bare to look at her. "I, I can't." She was violently shaking with fear now. "I do want to."

184

She was totally confused, she had all this love ready to give but it was fear and sadness that surfaced. This had to be a bad dream.

"Is there anyone I can call for you?"

"No," she replied dry-eyed.

The doctor left the room.

Kellie looked around at the cards and bunches and bunches of flowers scattered throughout her room. Her breasts felt sore. She looked beneath the hospital gown to see breast pads that she hadn't put there. Milk. She didn't need it anymore. She realised now that she was wide awake; this wasn't a bad dream. This was a living nightmare!

The same doctor came back in with a bundle wrapped in a thick pink blanket. Silently the doctor placed the baby in her lap.

"You had a name for her?"

"Chanelle."

"I'll leave you alone for a bit."

Kellie stared at the closed door for seconds, possibly minutes–anything not to have to look down at what was in her arms. To look down at Chanelle.

Finally she looked down at her still bundle. Her heart leapt, her eyes couldn't blink. She stared at the beautiful brown face, the tiny mouth, the two perfect eyes, shut tight as if asleep. She had a head full of beautiful curly brown hair. She looked like Samuel; felt and smelt the way he did when he was new born. Except there were no smiles here, no happiness, no high-pitched baby cry, no feeling of unexplainable love.

Her tiny mouth was partly open. Slowly Kellie opened her shawl; she wore a pink baby gown. Her fingernails were almost blue. "Mummy loves you Chanelle." Kellie kissed her lips, then her forehead. She couldn't cry. She couldn't believe that this was really happening. *How are you supposed to feel when your baby dies?* A part of her was missing.

Why had her baby been taken away from her? She looked down hoping to see movement; she knew that she wouldn't. She wanted desperately to hear her baby cry. Right now she should have been caring for her, maybe changing her nappy or rocking her to sleep. Instead, she was looking down at her still body; her small perfect little body.

Maybe she deserved this loss; they say everything happens for a reason. Samuel was taken from her before, so maybe she just wasn't meant to have children. Fate always worked, even moreso when you tried to change it. And she had changed. She barely resembled the person that lay in this same hospital and ward almost five years ago. Then, she hadn't taken drugs to jeopardise Samuel's life, she wasn't with an abusive partner to spoil Samuel's chance before he was even born. She looked down at her punishment. How could something have been inside her alive and well, then come into this world and die so suddenly. Her soul had been taken so suddenly and now she was left with just a shell.

Half an hour later a nurse came in to take her baby away. Kellie began to panic.

"Please just a bit longer, just a bit longer," Kellie begged.

She would never see her again, never get to hold her again. Samuel would never see his baby sister and he would want to know why she isn't here. She would never have to separate brother and sister silly squabbles. She would never take her newborn to the clinic for a routine weigh, or to a park with swings. Chanelle would never get a chance to take her first step nor would she ever say 'mama'.

She was dead.

Fourteen

SEDIKO STOOD AT the mirror and Candy lay naked on his queen-sized bed. He looked at his handsome reflection– 6'1", smooth dark skin, a perfectly trimmed goatee and a bald head.

"Yuh vain, eh?"

"It's not that," he sighed then rubbed his head and joined her on the bed.

"Just phone her if that's what's bugging you. And so it should," she advised him.

He ignored and began to kiss her. She pushed him gently away.

"Don't force yourself."

"I'm not, I want you." He kissed her again, then stopped. He just wanted to feel good. He had been fucking Candy and called Kellie's name twice. Candy had pushed him off right in the middle just as he was about to spin her around and- and now she wanted to talk.

"Just call her at least, just to see if she's alright."

"She is alright."

"How do you know? You *did* lick her."

"Yeah but-"

"But nothing! Is the baby alright?" Candy asked him seriously. She may have been in bed with him but she liked Kellie.

"I don't know!"

"You ran out didn't you?" Candy sat up.

"What was I meant to do? Wait for the boy dem?!" Sediko began to get angry.

"Yeah at least wait to find out if your yout' was alright! I can't believe that you haven't even called the hospital after, as you said, you did lick her." Candy looked at him in disappointment.

"I was fucking high! I told you! I didn't mean it. I don't beat my women, I look after them."

"Same way you look after Mia. You bus' her lip as well, innit?"

"Yeah, but she deserved it! She try give me jacket! I don't want no bastard yout'! I should have killed her!" He was getting angry because he knew that he had done the wrong thing! The wrong thing by trusting Mia, the wrong thing for not listening when his boys and Kellie told him to dis' her. He was wrong for hitting both of them, especially Kellie.

"What about Kellie?"

"You know what Mia told me, and remember Fixer contacted her for months, she didn't tell me. That punk Sparrow! It's him that started this shit and then Mia tells me *that*."

"And you believe her? No. I know you don't. Kellie's yout' is yours and you know it!"

"So what am I gonna do now. Fuck what I've already done, that shit ain't helping me now!"

"I think you should go to the hospital and find out if they're both alright."

"You wasn't saying that shit before when you wanted my-"

"Don't get vile! We're only here because Mia and Kellie are out of action and you needed someone else to be close to, someone that was already close to you. You're upset, I shouldn't have taken advantage. I'm sorry that I used you while you're all vulnerable; I just needed some dick."

She looked him straight in the eye, then cracked a smile. He burst out laughing.

"Good, lighten up."

"You're right. About going to see Kellie," Sediko said jumping up off the bed, "I'm gonna go to my family."

Candy rolled two spliffs, then started getting dressed.

"Where you going?" he asked her.

"Out."

"I'm not gonna be long."

"What, you want me to lock myself in your house until you decide to come back?" she asked.

"Basically, yeah."

"What's got into you?"

"Why can't you wait 'til I get back?"

"I got shit to do. I'm not you temporary wifey while one is unavailable. It won't happen."

"Alright, where you going?"

"To Shiffer's."

She was almost dressed.

"What's that?"

"That's my girl."

"She can stay too."

"Is that what you want me for? To fulfill your boyhood dreams?" she said smiling and pulling on her Timberland boots.

"I've fulfilled that dream plenty of times, I just haven't fulfilled *you* plenty of times."

She laughed. "Your hot boy talk is too much for me."

Two hours later, Sediko was in a crowded lift in the hospital. It stank and he felt slightly nauseous. He exited on the maternity ward; someone in blue pointed him to Kellie's room. He stood by the door, he didn't know what he was going to say to her. For once in his life he didn't know how to explain himself.

Sediko watched her through a gap in the curtain. She didn't look happy or sad, she just sat there with their baby in her arms, staring downward for the longest time. He waited and watched his family. He loved her, he loved Kellie, no matter what. They would just need time to heal their wounds.

About thirty minutes later, a nurse came back to take the baby. Was it a boy or girl? Who did it look like? A little girl with Kellie's beautiful smile and bright eyes? Or a boy, handsome like his dad? He waited anxiously for the nurse to come out of the room.

"Excuse me. I'm the dad," he said as soon as the nurse came out and closed the door. The nurse gave him a strange look. A strange, sad look. He had seen that same look when his mother had passed away. Those looks of pity, those looks of 'I'm glad I'm not you.' The look that screams death. He turned and ran.

Sediko ran down the stairs, through the corridors, out the door and straight to his car. Quickly he switched on the engine and began his drive home, his thoughts on Kellie. He hadn't hit her that hard, or maybe he had. Yes, he had. His mind retraced what happened. He had punched her in the face. She had fallen to the ground. His mind kept on telling him that she was carrying another man's child, he was almost convinced that she was Mia repeating. He was mad. While she was lying unconscious he had kicked her in the stomach. As soon as he had done it, he'd bent to hug her, had kissed her lips over and over again wanting her to wake up. In the end he had called an ambulance, then left.

"Shit!" Sediko shouted as he slammed his foot on the brake, almost crashing into the car ahead stopped at a traffic light.

I'm turning into a shit driving woman beater, he thought.

Once he arrived home and closed his door behind him, he cried. Tears filled his eyes as he howled long and hard, then stopped. He hoped to God that Kellie didn't find out. He hadn't meant to kick her, his body had just hit out. He loved her, he was in love with her.

Two days later and Sediko was bored and lonely. He hadn't heard from Kellie or Mia, thank God, or Candy. He phoned Brenda. He could always count on her so show him some love.

"Two-Face," she said happily.

"Yeah, what's up?" he growled.

"Shit, I can't talk-" He could hear her parents' voices in the background.

"This is Brenda's father. Mr Two-Face or whatever your name is, if you contact my daughter again in any way I'll be forced to call the police and have them arrest you for harassment and I'll have a restraint order put out against you.

"-Dad!"

"We've booked Brenda into the best rehab clinic for detoxing, she will no longer have any contact with a drugselling nigger!"

"-Dad, how dare you!?"

"I hope you've got the message." Click.

Sediko, Path, Bones and Jade sat in Ballers' office a week later.

"I need Kellie, you lot won't even know what I'm chatting about. Things are going downhill already. Everyone is asking about her. What can I say? *I* don't know and you won't say nothing," Jade spoke up.

"We're not discussing Kellie right now," Path spat at her.

"We *have* to discuss her cos without her this place is going nowhere but south."

"What exactly is the problem here?" Sediko asked, after all it was his club.

"First and most importantly, Kellie usually does most payments by direct debit through her own bank account. She hasn't been here in nearly a month and we are now running seriously low. Secondly-"

"One thing at a time, yeah," he sighed.

If he closed his eyes right now he would be able to see Kellie gliding around the room and giving orders, knowing just what to do.

"No, it doesn't work like that, I wish it was one thing at a time. The accounts need doing and our new dancer is a thief."

"How much do you need?" Sediko asked.

"I need you and all your entourage to stop drinking from the bar without paying. You lot drank nearly every bottle of champagne downstairs without paying!"

"How much do you need?" asked Path this time.

Sediko stood and opened the safe. He took out a bundle of money.

"It's not about how much I need. I can't do everything!"

"Here's three grand. Use it for whatever. Phone Kellie and ask her what to do, it's gonna take me a while to find another manager."

"Kellie's not coming back?" Jade asked, surprised.

"No." He threw the money onto the table towards her.

"Hurry up and get out Jade," Path spat. "We big people wanna talk."

Jade cut her eye towards Path, took the money and walked out.

"I'm sorry about Kellie and the baby nigga," Bones said to him full of sympathy.

"We got business to sort." Sediko sniffed and moved on with the conversation.

"We don't expect you to just bounce back so quick. You might as well say you lost two yout's," Path said uncomfortably.

"My personal life is *my* fucking business. Kellie and me are done, Mia's disappeared and my money is more important. M.O.B nigga. You lot stay idle yeah, pass me the phone, life never stands still."

He dialled a bitch's number. No way would he sit and wait for a woman; he never had and he never would.

"Hiya babe," her voice purred.

"I need a phone number. Now."

"Anything baby, just say the word."

"Pun, you know gambler Pun?"

"Yeah hold up…one second…07949089243 or 07991372596. Now,

what do I get?" Sediko cut the call.

He phoned Pun.

"Who dis?"

"Two-Face."

"What's up?"

"Couple months ago you played a card game wid one of my niggas?"

"And?"

"And them fools owed you a couple gran. Why'd you pass that shit on to this Fixer? Your debt is your fucking debt, you get me!"

"What you talking about?"

"What, you can't remember? Alright, I'm coming down your sides."

"Hold on, I remember now. I passed that shit cos Sparrow is a broke ass nigga. I don't gamble for fun, I do it for money, you know man's got eight yout's to look after. I needed them notes so I passed it on to a nigga who could pay me. So what's up?"

"You hear all the drama you caused?"

"I heard that Sparrow's on a long holiday. I didn't put you in this shit."

"So who is this nigga?"

"People always owe him shit."

"Yeah, so I heard." Sediko cut the call.

Bones shook his head. "Forget about that fool, for now. Go look after Kellie."

"Look after Kellie? It's because of that nigga why me and Kellie are done! That nigga is up to some shit! Member man put us in jail! And why was he calling Kellie?"

"You need to ask her that," Bones answered.

"I would if I could."

≈≈≈≈

In his bed, Bill held Latina tightly in his arms .   "I'll have to get up in a minute, got calls to make at work. I'm sure I can find you something to do in the building. You can use a computer?"

"Of course I use them at college."

"Good! Get dressed."

"What will I wear?"

"There are a whole bunch of dresses in the closet, wear any one."

"Where is she?"

"Not here, that's all that matters. Come on, shower and dress, we leave in 30 minutes."

"Sally this is Latina, she'll be helping you out in the office. Make her busy."

"Yes sir, I'll find her something to do."

191

He excused himself to his office and left them to talk.

At his desk, Bill phoned Burt.

"Burt here."

"It's Bill."

"Hiya old boy, lucky you caught me, I'm on my way to work."

"Just confirming it will be a foursome this weekend."

"What, you with Marie?"

"No, actually it's a young fine Puerto Rican lady."

"Not Lola," he replied in shock.

"Actually, it's Latina."

The day went by with Latina doing a perfect job. Sally was glad to have someone else to boss around and Latina was grateful for the job.

After a successful day at work, they returned to the house. As they entered Bill could immediately feel another presence. He silently closed the door and listened.

"What's-"

"Shhh!" He put his index finger to his lips. He walked toward the stairs.

"Carrie!" he called out.

"Bill, it's me."

His heart was in his mouth as Marie's voice came from the top of the stairs.

As soon as she saw them she stopped in her tracks. Then slowly she glided down the stairs. Her long brown hair that was usually in a bun had been cut to shoulder length. It suited her, made her look younger. Bill looked to Latina who stood scared, beside him.

"Who is this?" she asked at the bottom of the stairs.

"Marie-"

"Bill please, who is this? It's not Lisa!"

"This is-"

"What are you doing in my clothes!" Marie shouted to her.

"Marie I-" Bill started again.

"No Bill, this I will not tolerate! First you're having an affair for God knows how long! Now you've got this tart walking around in my house in my clothes!"

"I won't have you calling my guest a tart, and in case you have forgotten you don't live here anymore, you wanted a divorce," he reminded her. His arm found Latina's waist.

"It's alright," she sighed, lifting her head high. "Your little tramp can have my old clothes, that will save me going to Oxfam."

"Marie!"

"Hasn't she got a mouth of her own? Or doesn't she speak English?"

"Actually yes, I do speak English," Latina spoke up.

"Well then you can understand this, Bill and I have been married 15 years. How long have you known him? Longer than 5 minutes? I

192

doubt that even. That is my husband!"

"Marie, what are you saying?"

"I'm saying Bill," she moved closer to him and ignored Latina, "I'm saying that we have been married for a long time and I still love you."

"But you said...you made it clear, that you wanted a divorce. You refused to see me." His arm dropped from Latina's waist.

"Maybe you two want to talk. Bill, I will be upstairs." She left with her head held low.

Marie turned to watch her walk away.

"Bill, I will be upstairs," Marie mimicked her accent. "I can't believe this, you're replacing me already! Again!"

"I need a drink."

Bill walked to the living room, Marie followed. He poured a scotch.

"You're right, I didn't want to see you, not at first. I needed time to think. If I would have known that you had already started seeing some one else-"

"It's not like that." He downed his scotch and poured another.

"So what is it like? Is she not walking around in my clothes?"

"Yes, but-"

"So how am I supposed to feel?"

"If you would just let me speak.

"Bill do you love her?"

"Of course not." He downed another drink.

"It's no good getting drunk. I'll just leave you to it." She turned.

"Wait." He couldn't just let her leave. "Listen, maybe we can sort this out, she means nothing to me."

"Like Lisa meant nothing?"

"Are we ever going to move on?" he sighed.

"Will I be able to just forgive and forget?" Her back was still turned to him.

"I hope so."

"So tell her upstairs to leave, right now. If you want me to forgive and forget," she challenged.

"I-I-"

"Goodbye Bill." She began to walk away.

He didn't call her. He couldn't just put Latina out on the street, her pimp would kill her. She needed him and he had already told her that she could stay. He heard the door close. He loved Marie, why hadn't she contacted him earlier? He had tried like mad to get her back.

Latina tiptoed in wearing her ugly red mini that he had picked her up in.

"Go change!" he barked at her.

"I thought-" she began.

"I will not talk to you when you're dressed like that! Now go change into something nice." He swallowed more drink. She turned and left the room. At least she was obedient, listened to what he said.

It was his turn to be happy, Marie and Carrie had been nagging him for years, eating their way through his good side, making him spend too many late nights at work and not appreciating the comfort of his own home. When they had first moved in, he loved it, he was comfortable. After a while it became the nagging zone– both Marie and Carrie going on about clothes, make-up, wanting money or moaning about their so-called friends. Then they would be at each other throats, both trying to pull him to their side. He did his best to keep out of it.

Latina came back in wearing only his work shirt.

"Better?" she asked.

"Perfect. Come have a drink."

"Thank you."

"Don't worry, you're not leaving."

"Your wife, she's very pretty."

"I've got good taste, gets better every time." He smiled at her and poured her a drink.

Latina sat on the sofa. She was falling in love with him; she had always held a torch for him. He was everything girls like her wished for: a rich, handsome, educated man. She had to try and keep hold of him, her life depended on it now. Latina rose from the sofa, walked beside him and gently began to massage his shoulders. She then took his hand and led him upstairs.

Bill followed her up; she wasn't Marie but she was very sexy. Everything that a man wanted: a great body, adventurous in bed and very obedient. It wouldn't hurt to just enjoy it for a little while. As they lay in bed, his mind went back to the night that he had accused Marie of phoning Lisa. Now he had lost both his girls, Marie *and* Carrie.

"Latina, I'm tired." He turned as she tried to touch him.

"Okay, Bill." She was so understanding. "Was I alright at work today?"

"Fine."

"I love you, Bill," she said to him.

"*Shit*," he thought to himself.

≈≈≈≈

So what happened to your face?" asked Kirk looking down at her. She wasn't listening, she wanted to forget all about it. She thought that Sediko was going to kill her, literally take her life.

The doctor had come into the room. Looking smug, Mia couldn't wait to see the blood test results and prove herself right. She had held Sediko's hand and he had squeezed hers tight, ready to play the proud father role. But it didn't turn out like that.

"I'm sorry Mia, the blood type is different. This man isn't the baby's father."

Sediko had walked out of the room, she had followed him.

"I'm sorry, wait! I'm sorry, I didn't know." She pulled his arm to stop him going down the stairs. "I love you!"

He stopped and turned to her– his expression fixed, arms at his side, hands fisted. He had a look in his eyes and she backed up against the wall. She didn't want to remember what had happened next; she had deserved every punch.

"Well, what happened?" He stood proudly rocking his son whom he had renamed Karim.

"Nothing." She laid in her bed feeling sick. All she could think about was how she had let Sediko down and how she had handed him straight to Kellie. She could imagine them playing happy families, she'd soon be due.

Charlene had phoned Kirk to tell him the bad news, but good news for him.

"Daddy is gonna take care of you and mummy," he said to Karim looking at her in the corner of his eye. How could he say that after the way she had been the last time they had spoken. She had made it clear that she didn't want him and here he was still trying to please her. He would never be able to take care of her. She looked at her baby and felt guilty resentment towards it. Why wasn't he Sediko's? Why wasn't he Sediko Jordan? She asked herself this every time she looked at him.

"I bought a few things for the two of you as soon as I found out." He kept his eyes on his son. Mia looked toward the many boxes: Moses basket, baby bath and bumper sized packets of nappies. "You like them?"

"Yeah, thanks."

"Yeah just went out and spent bare money."

"Good."

"Anything else you need just let me know."

"I'm tired, I'm gonna lie down for a bit."

"Go on, I'll be alright." He sat to change him. Mia couldn't even watch. Kirk was his father, Kirk would be the one in his life, the one in her life– forever. Sediko would never take her back after this. Every second that went by she missed him.

"You alright?" Kirk asked as a tear fell from her eye as she lay staring up at the ceiling.

"Yes."

"Was he at my son's birth?"

"Who?" She turned away from him.

"What's up with you? You might as well speak the truth, you've hurt me enough for it not to hurt anymore."

"Alright, he was there, is that what you wanna hear?"

"No. But it's alright cos he ain't coming nowhere near my son again."
He left her alone and sat at the other end of the room with his son.

What did he want her to do? Smile and pretend that everything was alright, play mummies and daddies? She looked at him. He was handsome– hazel eyes, light brown curly hair. He was good looking but he wasn't Sediko.

Fifteen

TWO DAYS LATER Kellie was allowed to go home. She lay in her bed all alone in her home with no baby cries ringing in her ears.

She had sent Samuel back to his gran's, just for a while, 'til she sorted herself out. Carol had phoned her to give her apologies and offer a helping hand. Samuel hadn't wanted to go; he didn't say anything but she could see it in his eyes. But she was too weak to take care of him.

Kellie and Samuel had held a small funeral for Chanelle to help him understand where his sister had gone. He had watched the tiny box go into the ground with a confused look on his face. Since then, she had only left her room once, for a package. Other than that she hadn't spoken to anyone for two days.

Her future had been changed. What was she meant to do now? What would she do with the time that she would have used caring for her newborn baby? She had taken 6 months maternity leave. She had MotherCare vouchers, Baby Gap vouchers, Next Kids vouchers and those few things at Mo's. Her breast milk was still coming.

Who was going to help her? Who was going to tell her that everything was going to be alright? Why hadn't Sediko come to see her? Why had he left her to suffer the death of their child alone? Why wasn't he here telling her that everything would be alright? Why hadn't he even come to the hospital!?

She looked over to her package on the dressing table. One thing would make it alright, one thing would make her *think* that everything was alright. An ounce of Charlie sat there waiting for her to sniff. She had been watching it for two days, temptation trying to break her down. It was still sitting there because she had quit. She had made a conscious decision to quit.

Her phone rang, she made no attempt to pick it up. She just sat up in bed, her eyes distant. The message came on:

"Kellie deepest regrets and right now this may sound crude, but Oman Bowie wants to meet you, she says that your face is 'perfect'– her exact words. My motto is, 'when in doubt make money.' Come on Kellie, I know that you're there, I'm your agent for christsake! You can get through this, you don't want people walking around on egg shells, show-"

"Hello Chad."

"Well hello, so glad to hear your voice. So whadda you think?"

"I am on six months leave."

"Right, you are, but this is Oman! She wants you to be the new face of Oman beauty products."

"When does she want to meet?"

"Adda girl! I'm proud of you. Next week some time? I know it's soon what with your loss-"

"It's fine, I think I need to keep busy."

Four days later, 14 days after she had lost her baby girl, Kellie was still in bed, her mind still working overtime about her loss and still looking at the package on the table. Chad was due to phone her for a meeting today but she wasn't up to it. She still hadn't cried for her baby and she felt guilty. She hadn't phoned Samuel and she felt ashamed. She hadn't spoken to Sediko and she felt lost. She hadn't been to the club in two months and she felt defeated. Oman wanted to meet her and she felt ugly.

A knock at the door. Chad was early.

"Hi." She opened the door in her dressing gown.

"You're not ready?!"

"Twenty minutes."

"You seen the paper?" He walked into the living room.

"No."

"You're slashed all over it. Lots of condolences, praises and business."

"Right. I'll be down in a minute. Drinks in the fridge if you want."

Upstairs, she showered and dressed quickly. She looked good in her trousers suit and Jimmy Choos, but when she looked in the mirror at her face, it was drawn and grey looking. Her eyes were sunken and it looked as if she had been crying for days. She carefully applied her make-up and that took care of that, but she still didn't feel pretty or confident.

She went to her dresser and opened her package.

"THAT'S HALF AN HOUR NOW!" Chad called up. She jumped.

"I'm coming!"

She chipped off a small piece with a razor and began to chop at it like vegetables. She held back her hair and using a solid gold straw that she had bought for Sediko, she sniffed up each nostril. Immediately she felt refreshed. She went back to the mirror. She looked great and felt great.

A knock on her bedroom door.

"Ready or not, here I come." Chad came into her room.

"I'm ready. One minute please."

"Oh, sorry." He left the room. She did two more lines and slipped some in an envelope for later.

Kellie sat in Moon's Chinese Restaurant three days later, wearing a tasty little Laymend's Fashion black dress– spaghetti strapped, figure hugging, no underwear. Bill sat beside her, Chad opposite and a petite Chinese woman sat beside him.

"I enjoy this country." Her English was barely recognisable although she spoke an almost perfect English vocabulary. She looked at Chad lovingly.

"Don't worry, it won't last," Bill said laughing. "Let's make a toast. To Kellie's future." He held his champagne glass high and they all followed. Kellie smiled a successful smile, as Oman had loved her and wanted her face on her products. She had signed a six-month contract. Chad was over the moon.

They sipped and talked. Kellie mainly listened, and picked at her food, not really eating. She was happy about her new contract, it would keep her busy. Keep her from the obsessive thinking that she was doing. Thinking about her daughter and son, or Sediko, or the club.

"Kellie?" Bill nudged her gently.

"What?"

"We were saying, why finish the celebrations here? Let's all go to Ballers. I quite liked it there the last time."

"Ballers?"

"Yes, that's alright isn't it?" Bill asked her.

"Yeah of course, Ballers then."

An hour later, they pulled up outside Ballers in a limousine. Chad, Mina, Bill and Latina stepped out. Kellie looked up at the building, then stepped out herself. The two Jimmys spotted her straight away and one came over to greet her.

"Good ta see ya Kellie. You back?"

"Maybe." She felt a slight surge of power come back to her as she re-entered her club with her friends in tow.

"Is he here?" she stopped to ask the other Jimmy. She would know just how to handle this, as soon as she went to the office and did a line. He shrugged his shoulders.

She led Bill and the rest of her celebration pack upstairs to the VIP and went alone through to the dancer's changing rooms.

"Kellie!" one screamed.

Kellie ignored her and went straight to the bathroom. When she came back out she was so at ease. She went back downstairs to the main floor and stood at the massive mirror. He was in there, she could feel him staring at her, watching her– shocked, surprised and happy that she was there. The side mirror slid open and Kellie walked in.

"Hello." He came towards her slowly, looking at her from head to toe as if drinking her in. She didn't meet his stare. Instead, she went over to the bar, ran her finger across the table and looked at her finger. Dust.

"Thought you wasn't coming back."

"Did you?"

"I'm sorry," he said quietly.

Kellie pulled out the chair at the head of the table and sat down.

"I want to come back to work," she found herself saying. It was just what she needed.

"What?"

"You heard right."

"Yeah course, forget the club for a minute. Kellie, I've been worried about you; I been calling you."

"And?" She looked him straight in the eye. He looked away and stood to go to the bar.

"Drink?"

"No thanks. I'll be back next Friday. I'm upstairs anyway, I'm celebrating, just got a new modelling contract," she told him as he drank Stone ginger wine from the bottle. She stood to leave.

"What about me and you?" he choked.

She stood quickly, she had to get out. She could feel her hard exterior vaporising, her heart softening. She left the room quickly without turning back. She rushed up to the VIP to finish her celebrations. On the way she spotted Mandy, trapped in a boring looking conversation.

"Kellie." She looked sadly at her, then grabbed her into a meaningful hug. Kellie pulled away.

"Are you alright? Should you even be out drinking?" She looked to the glass of champagne that one of the bar staff had pushed into her hand.

"Why not? I'm not pregnant now. Finally, I can have a drink." She downed the glass and nodded along to the music.

"You sure you're alright?"

"I'm good, come meet some friends of mine." Kellie led her away from the condolence chat. Her heart felt hard and empty.

"Kellie!" She turned to see Jade. "Good to see you. At last you're back to sort this place out."

"She's a supermodel now, she can hire people to sort things out," Chad said laughing.

"Yeah Jade, but not now. Early Friday we'll get this shit back to normal."

Kellie turned to Mandy who was staring at her strangely.

"And what's up with you?" Kellie asked her.

"I was gonna ask you the same question."

"I'm here to celebrate and look to the future; I want to move on. If I don't, life will just go on without me." She smiled. She *had* to smile, she couldn't tell anyone that she couldn't cry for her baby. What was the point? It wouldn't bring her back. Her eyes began to sting. "I'll be back in a sec."

Kellie left the VIP through the back and went outside for some fresh air. Outside she inhaled, then exhaled and fell back against the wall in the dark, quiet, side street. Finally, with no warning, she began to cry. The tears started to fall, all the tears that she had locked away. Her shoulders were heaving up and down, her whole body was shaking as the tears came harder and louder. Her hands covered her face as all the tears that she ever wanted to cry flowed up and out of her. Rocking herself back and forth, she cried, remembering the hurt that she didn't deserve, losing a baby that she should have had. She had lost out on being a mother! Just three years of being with that man had caused her a lifetime of pain.

Six weeks into their relationship when he had left her alone in Whyno's to sleep with that tramp bitch Mia, she forgave him. The love was nowhere near as deep then as it was now. She could have left him then, but she forgave him, and that's how it all started. He showed her a life of drugs with her son suffering the consequence. Throughout most of their relationship he had been fucking Mia, then he got her pregnant, then didn't get her pregnant. He fucked off to jail and left her to deal with everything alone– Mia breaking in and stalking her. Then he had hit her and her baby girl had suffered the consequence; her precious, innocent newborn had suffered.

Barely able to take a breath, she cried on, wrapping her arms around her flat stomach as if holding herself up. It was as if she hadn't even been pregnant. Her tears kept choking her, and kept her from seeing Sediko who was watching her from the shadows. She snivelled and couldn't stop. He came toward her; tears in his eyes too.

"I came to see you you know."

"What?"

"In, in the hospital. At first I thought that you were alright, the two of you. I waited outside."

"Why didn't you come in?" Kellie asked him still sniffling.

"Cos, cos I was scared that you and the baby wouldn't forgive me. She was wrapped in a, in a pink blanket. And you, you were wearing the white gown thing. When the nurse came out and-" He began to cry and Kellie pulled him into her arms.

"I'm sorry too," Kellie cried with him.

"No, *I'm* sorry baby. Kellie I'm so sorry, please believe me. I didn't mean to hurt you. You know I would do anything for you, you knew how much I loved you, and I still do. I shouldn't have put my hand on you, and you know I'm not about that, hitting women and shit. I just went crazy for a bit and I'm sorry, all that shit I was saying about my boy and you. I know it ain't true."

"Fixer?" she asked surprised.

"Yeah Fixer. I don't know what it is with you two but I don't care, I trust you."

"Good," was all she could manage.

"I've been holding this in my pocket for a while now." She looked down to the ring in the box. "For real this time, ask me anything you want and I'll tell you. I'm wide open. I'm a man now Kellie, I done grown up and realised that I can't live without you. Every day that went by and I thought you wasn't coming back, it fucked me up, don't leave me again. Will you marry me?" He looked sincerely at her. His hands found hers and he stared into her eyes and waited.

"Just like that?" she asked.

He nodded.

She looked deep into his eyes, searching for a glimmer of deceit. All she could see was love pouring out of him. She knew that he loved her and she knew that she loved him and at this precise moment she couldn't find one reason to turn him down. She loved him.

"Yes." She nodded and began to cry again, this time through happiness. He pulled her close to his chest and held her tight. No one but themselves knew the truth of what had happened and no one else mattered.

"I love you Sediko."

"I know. We can do this straight away."

"I won't rush you."

"No, I want this. Man's twenty-six now, getting old. I'll marry you quick before you change your mind."

"Sediko," Kellie began. Mandy came out the back door with a worried look on her face.

"Here you are. I've been looking all over for you. You alright?"

"Yeah, we're getting married," Kellie squealed.

"Oh, congratulations. Come on then, now you got two reasons to get drunk."

They all laughed and went inside. Sediko didn't leave her side once she introduced him as her fiancée. They danced together all night and did 6 lines of Charlie each. Things were starting to look up. She forgot all about being angry with him, forgot about punishing him.

"This is my fiancée," she introduced to Bill and Chad.

"Hi." Chad held out his hand to shake. Sediko nodded and ignored Chad's extended hand.

"Very cheerful," Chad said frowning. A frown that reminded her that their problems hadn't gone away with baby Chanelle.

"Kellie, haven't seen you in a while." Prevor smiled at her from behind.

"Yeah, I been tied up."

"You know, I'm sorry."

"Life goes on."

"And I hear congratulations are in order, heard about the Oman offer."

"Already? News travels fast."

"I'm a celebrity," he joked. They chatted for a while, then she moved on to mingle. Everyone wanted to talk to her or buy her a drink. She spotted Sediko talking to Candy on the ground floor. They talked and laughed while Sediko sipped champagne.

The following day Kellie sat in a small bar in Knightsbridge. Shawn sat opposite her. He had called her and she needed some questions answered. If Sediko was serious about marrying her, there had to be no secrets.

"How are you?" he asked as she took off her jacket.

"Fine, thank you."

"I was sorry to hear about your loss. I wanted to come and see you but I knew that Two-Face would be there-"

"I really don't want to talk about it."

"Okay, so I finally get to take you out." He sat back comfortably in his chair, his left hand on his glass of Southern Comfort.

"I'm here because I need to talk to you."

"I'm here because I like you."

"Well I think you're out with me because for some reason you're using me to get at Sediko." She put her own two with two and hoped for four.

Shawn took a ten-pack of Bensons from his pocket, offering Kellie one first. She shook her head. He took one out, lit it, then turned to the table behind him for an ashtray.

"Why do you think that?"

"First, I know now that you don't know Sediko, so I don't even know how or why you got my number. But you do know one of Sediko's boys cos you were seen chatting to him in Ballers. And Sediko said it was because of you that he got arrested. I don't know what you think you're going to gain by buying crack off me."

"You've been a proper little detective." He grinned and nodded.

"Are you gonna lie?"

"I haven't got reason to lie. I don't like that nigga true, he fucked with something of mine a while back. But I'm not using you; I like you."

"So you keep saying. What did he fuck up of yours? Why didn't you tell me?"

"What for? It's wasn't really your business."

"We had agreed to keep our meetings quiet, why tell Sediko if you're not using me to get at him?"

"I *didn't* tell him, I was the one who didn't want him knowing," he dodged.

"Was it you that sent them to jail? If it was, we will never see each other again; he won't have it."

"That fool can't stop me from seeing you."

"He's not a fool."

"You two still together?"

"Yes, why?"

"So has he stopped sleeping with Mia? Oh yeah, I heard the yout' wasn't his." He blew smoke in her direction. She sat forward.

"That was my next question. How do you know her?"

"Shouldn't you be asking your man all these questions?"

"I'm asking you."

"I used to go out with Mia's aunt."

"Her aunt?"

"Yeah, I'm 28 innit, a big boy. I used to be around her and Two-Face

203

but I didn't know him too good. You know Pun?"

"No."

"Your man don't tell you much, does he?" he asked. Kellie stayed silent. "Forget him. What about me and you? I've waited long enough."

"There is no me and you. Me and Sediko are getting married."

"Getting married?!" His turn to sit forward.

"Yes."

"My man's been disrespecting you the whole time you've been together and you're getting married? He probably asked Mia the same shit!" He sighed, sat back and smiled to himself.

"What do you know about me and him? Anyway she was then, I'm now," she defended weakly.

"That was what a month or two ago, how you so sure that they're finished?"

"Like you said, the yout' wasn't his."

"He was probably happy that her yout' wasn't his, he don't need her running him down every minute the brat gets a cold."

"This isn't your business!" Kellie shouted.

"I'm just trying to look out for you. Anyway, you're the one that wanted to talk."

"Yeah but-"

"But nothing. If you want to talk to someone you have to be prepared to listen. It's called conversation." His hand found hers on the table. "A boy like that will just hold you back. You deserve better than him, you deserve to be loved like the woman that you are. Why are you crying?" He brushed the tear from her cheek.

"I don't know." She hadn't even realised that she was crying. She sat back and let go of his hands. She knew why she was crying, she was crying because Shawn was right about Sediko. As much as she loved him, he had been having his cake and eating it freely for too long.

"You wanna come to my house? Somewhere quiet?" he asked. She nodded yes without thinking.

They left the bar in his car, leaving hers in the car park.

"Can I ask you a question?" he said while he drove.

"It's a bit late to ask me that, isn't it?"

"True. Why, why do you stay with him and you know that he's sleeping with another woman? Not just any other woman, a woman that he cared for, for years."

"I love him. It's all about love. I bet that's something that you will never understand."

"Feels like you're judging me. I know about love and if you love someone, *really* love them, you don't sleep with your ex-."

"I know."

"So you're saying you love him but he don't love you?" He kept driving.

"He loves me!" she cried out.

He looked at her sadly.

"Maybe he did in the beginning, but the day that he slept with Mia, that's when he stopped loving and respecting you." He was saying all the right things to make her see sense.

"What do you care anyway?"

"What do I care? How long have I been trying to show you that I care?"

"So what makes you any better than him. You're trying to get me into bed and I've told you I'm engaged!"

"I'm not trying to get you in bed. Yes I want you to be mine, but I want you to be just mine, I would never share you with him, even if I could. What you need is a man and I'm looking for a woman like you."

"A girl like me who lets her man fuck out on her?"

"Kellie it's him doing the wrong, not you."

"Enough."

"Kellie-"

"No! I've heard enough!" she shouted and they drove the rest of the way in silence.

Finally they pulled into a driveway, then into a massive garage.

"This is your house?"

"Yes."

They got out the car and went through a side door which led to a massive kitchen almost bigger than the whole first floor of her house.

"Wanna tour?" He held out his hand and she took it.

They walked through the kitchen door into the lobby. It was a big space with black and white tiles and a coat stand by the door. Opposite the massive double front door was a wide winding staircase just like in the old movies, off which were three big archways leading to three different corridors. He took her to a hall on the other side of the staircase. Rows and rows of pictures hung on the wall. Basketball stars, rappers, actors, all strong, black heroes. They went into a dining room. It was cold and almost empty aside from a crystal chandelier and a six-person dining table.

"Through there are the cleaners' rooms." He pointed through another pine door.

"Cleaners?" She turned round and round, unable to hide her shock. Was this really his house? Maybe he was housesitting.

"Yeah, no way would I be able to keep all this clean and tidy. Come on." He took her hand again to lead her to yet another room.

"Where are we?"

"In the dining room."

"No, what area?" She smiled as they went back through the hall of fame.

"Green Park."

He led her into what looked like a trophy room.

"These all yours?" she asked from the door. He didn't show her in.

"Yeah, course. Football, basketball, swimming. I loved sports." He closed the door. "I got a basketball court out back, I'll show you that later."

"You live here long?"

"About 4 years, but I'm mostly at my other flat in Hackney."

"Next room." Kellie was enjoying her tour even if he was lying. She found herself relaxing as he led her up the extra wide staircase toward the three arched corridors.

"My suite of rooms," he indicated, looking left. "Couple guest rooms," he pointed out on the right. "Ahead is the sports library, the office and something else; you'll love it when you see it." He waited for her to choose her route. She walked straight ahead to the library.

There were shelves, drawers and cabinets all packed with DVD's, magazines and cards for almost every sport.

"You're a collector," Kellie observed as she approached his office, tried the door and found it locked.

"This way."

They stood at another closed door.

"Be careful." He opened the door. Kellie stood slightly back not knowing what to expect. He opened it to an enormous empty space with a green house ceiling.

"Come closer." He looked down from the doorway. She stood beside him and looked down. No floor. In front of the door was a long thin diving board that looked more like a pirate ship plank. She moved closer to see where it ended. Two floors down it seemed, to a massive indoor pool. "Wanna swim?"

"What...now?" She looked down again; it was a long drop.

Without taking his eyes off her, Shawn began to take off his clothes. He stood in his boxer shorts. He most definitely had a body of a man who loved sports.

"Come on, or I'll jump without you."

He held out his hand. She took one last look, then nodded. She stripped naked; she wasn't wearing any underwear. Kellie avoided his gaze but she could feel his eyes helping her to undress.

"Ready."

She held his hand; she couldn't believe that she was naked in Shawn's mansion getting ready to walk his plank! He walked ahead of her, still holding her hand from behind his back. As soon as she stepped away from the door frame she wanted to turn back and resisted slightly.

"Trust me and just don't look down," his voice echoed around the room. She stepped slowly, one foot in front of the other. Finally, they reached the edge.

"Wait! Don't jump without me," she whimpered. She stood at the very edge, he turned to face her. He wrapped his arms around her waist and she clung to his neck.

"How deep is it? Is it deep enough?" she panicked. "Forget how deep it is; it looks like 1000 feet down!"

"Not quite. I'ma count to three."

"Wait!"

"You trust me?" He looked her in the eye as he held onto her naked body. She nodded. "One....two...three!"

He jumped backward pulling her forward with him. She screamed and held onto him for dear life. Finally, they hit the water and sunk to the bottom. As they both gently kicked with their feet against the water, his mouth found hers as they rose to the top. They both gasped as they reached fresh air. He released his hold and she shyly, slowly swam away from him.

"Like it?" He swam towards her.

"The jump or the kiss?" She tread water and smoothed her hair from her face.

"That was hardly a kiss, that was just lip touching. Come here and let me kiss you for real." He swam towards her and she swam playfully away. He caught up with her just as she reached the side. He grabbed her playfully and held her up against the side of the pool. He leaned into her slowly and put his hands around her waist. His muscular body pressed up against her and his lips were taking too long to connect. Just as they were about to...

"Let's, not," she stopped him. Her heart was beating fast, he had to have been able to feel that, he was close enough.

He swam away on his back; she climbed out and sat on the edge.

She watched him swim the pool length four times before climbing out and sitting beside her.

"You wanna go in the sauna?"

"You're spoiling me."

"Yeah, trying to give you a sneak preview of what it would be like to be my woman." She stood and went to one of the many towel racks and brought them both thick dark blue dressing gowns.

"What, like your other girl?"

"Come on, you really believe that that t'ing was my girl. That was my mistake, everyone can have those. She's my baby mother."

"Baby mother?" Kellie was openly shocked.

"Yeah and she ain't never been here, only my son has."

"How old is your son? How old is *she*?"

"He's 5, she's 23. My girl lied about her age."

"Really?" Kellie asked doubtful.

"Yes, really." He led her to a small looking hut in the corner. "She has tried all sorts of shit to get to me, what she done to you for a starters– or what you done to her. She gets pure money off me for my son but I know she spends that shit on herself. That's why I got my flat in Hackney, to be near him, he lives down the road from there." He opened the door for Kellie. "All that bitch wants is my money," he continued.

"So how come you two came to Ballers that night?"

"I don't hate her. Even if I did, she wouldn't know. I don't want my son to grow up thinking it's alright for daddy to dis' mummy. I keep her sweet by being peaceful."

"Not all women are after your money. Some are independent."

"You're proof of that."

"So wow, this is really yours. Where'd you get all this? What illegal shit are you involved in?" she asked as he shut the door and he sat behind her on one of the benches. She leaned in comfortably between his legs.

"And the good news is, it's all legal. This will never slip through my fingers, it's all mine."

"But where did you get the money? Where do you work if it's all legal?"

"I don't need to work, I'm set for life."

"What, a rich dead aunt? I didn't expect this."

"That's because I don't show off; I don't need to prove to anyone that I'm flossing." His arms went up around her waist. They talked in the sauna for another twenty minutes. As Kellie stepped out she felt dizzy and swayed. Shawn caught her in his arms and picked her up in one swoop.

"It's alright, I can walk."

"I bet you want to shower, wash your hair and shit. Let me carry you upstairs."

"Thank you." She allowed herself to relax in his strong arms.

"I'm trying to keep fit, this is for my own benefit," he joked as he carried her through the hall and back up the stairs.

In his room there was a massive queen-sized half-circle bed. He laid her down and she looked up to the ceiling. A flat screen television stared down at her.

"Thanks. Your house is just beautiful."

"Thanks," Shawn replied, taking off his shorts. She turned away, even though she was naked beneath her towel.

"Where's the shower?" She jumped down from the high bed then stepped off a stage on which the bed was mounted.

There were two arches: one leading left, the other right. Kellie walked left and opened the big double doors to an enormous bathroom.

Seconds later, she stepped into the biggest shower she had ever seen. The shower space alone was the size of a small room. The bath beside the shower was round and big enough for two people to lay side by side. She let the hot water sting her for a second. For a moment she wondered what time it was, but decided that she didn't really want to know. She felt like Kellie again. The young problem-free teenager that she used to be, without a care in the world. She stepped naked out of the shower to see Shawn sitting naked in the empty bath.

"I didn't hear you come in."

"My turn." He got out and stepped past her to the shower.

Kellie wandered around his bedroom then walked toward the right arch. She opened the big double doors. A walk-in oversized closet packed full of clothes, shoes, trainers and jackets. She opened drawers and looked in boxes. At the back was a unit; on top was some super skunk. She took some, then searched for Rizla and cigarettes; she didn't have to look far. She built a ram spliff, took it back into the bedroom and lit up on his bed. She smoked slowly, feeling the buzz go through her body. Half-way through she was fighting to keep her eyes open, she felt tired. She rested the spliff in the ashtray and her head on his pillows.

Kellie awoke in the morning alone in Shawn's bed. She yawned, rubbed her eyes and got up, wearing his oversized t-shirt.

"Shawn," she called from the bottom of the stairs. She listened, heard nothing, but could smell food. In the kitchen stood a woman. Pretty, blonde.

"Morning, I'm Nancy. Shawn's just gone for a swim, you hungry? I'm making pancakes."

"Morning," Shawn said from behind. He hugged her and kissed her cheek. "You met Nancy?" he asked, his arms still around her. She nodded, she didn't like the idea of a stranger hanging around at ten in the morning. "Can I smell pancakes?" He sniffed the air, then let go of her.

"Uh huh," Nancy confirmed, standing at the cooker.

"I've got to go," Kellie said to him as he went to smell his pancakes.

"You're not having breakfast?" he asked turning quickly.

"I don't know, I'm gonna go get dressed." She left the kitchen and waited for him to follow.

"Don't go yet. Have breakfast with me, then I'll drop you to your car, please. And don't change; I love you in my t-shirt."
Kellie laughed.

They ate their pancakes in the dining room. Shawn wasn't the person that she thought he was, he was better.

Kellie and Shawn stood in the car park in Knightsbridge; it was twelve noon.

"So, can I phone you?" he asked as she stood by her car door.

"I don't think that's wise."

"Why not? We can be friends."

"Alright, then I'll call you. I promise."

"A promise means nothing until it's carried out."

"Trust me then." Kellie kissed his cheek and then climbed into the Porsche; she stayed to watch him drive away. The second he was out of view and she switched on her engine, all her problems, losses, excessive thoughts and far away dreams came flooding back. She switched on her phone and seconds later it rang.

"What's up babe? I've been ringing your phone, where are you?"

"I'm-"

"It's alright babe, you don't have to tell me, I trust you. Can we link, I got a surprise for you."

"Alright, I'll make my way to Battersea." She hung up and guilt plagued her. Even though nothing had happened, it could have. Shawn had been a gentleman, he had made her laugh and she had kind of kissed him.

Kellie did like him, but she loved Sediko. No one could change that.

Sixteen

IN A RESTAURANT, where water cost £8, Kellie and Chad sat across from Oman and her photographic manager passing pictures around the table. An exceptionally beautiful Oman looked and nodded or refused to comment.

"I love this one," she finally said. Her photographic manager leaned in to look at the picture she chose.

"Yep, that's the chosen one, you are brilliant!" he sucked up to her; she waved him off.

"Well that's done, I've got to dash, Davis is waiting for me. Kellie, my accountant is late but he can finalise the details. Are you ready?" Oman asked her.

"Yes," she said smiling, with no idea what Oman was really referring to. *Ready for what? Food, modelling, what?*

"It will go out day after tomorrow," the photographic manager informed her.

"That soon?" Kellie asked excitedly; she did look beautiful in the photo.

"I'm so sorry that I'm late, Mrs Bozen, car troubles," her accountant apologised breathlessly as he approached the table.

"Fix it, you get paid enough!"

"Yes Ma'am." He took a seat.

They all talked for a further twenty minutes then left, leaving Kellie and Chad with two envelopes.

"This is it my flower, this is what we work for. You first."

"I know they haven't put a cheque in there."

"No, it's like a sort of pay compliment slip," Chad explained.

They both opened their envelopes and smiled at each other.

"This deserves a toast," Chad said holding his glass high in the air.

≈≈≈≈

I've missed you," Brenda whispered in his ear. Sediko ignored her and smoked his spliff. She climbed on top of him and he pushed her off. She tried again.

"What you doing? Get up!" He pushed her harder this time.

"What's wrong? Why don't you want to fuck me? I'll take an E if you want." Brenda pushed herself up onto him.

"What time you leaving?"

"Leaving? I can't leave, I told my dad that I was staying at a friend's."

"And?"

"And it's four in the morning, how am I gonna get home?" she panicked.

"Get a cab; you're pissing me off."

"I haven't even said anything." She was sounding more and more distressed.

"Pass my phone and I'll call you a cab."

"Can't I stay Two-Face? I won't talk, I'll give you a massage." A massage sounded good.

"Alright." He turned onto his stomach.

As she rubbed his back he thought about Kellie. He had proposed to her. If he hadn't, he probably wouldn't have gotten her back. Marriage. He couldn't back out now. It wouldn't be so bad; Kellie was already his wifey.

The next morning Brenda was out by 7; he didn't want her hanging around. Sediko had given her three ounces of brown to hold for him. She never said 'no' or even moaned about it. By 11:00 he was out of the house and getting into Kellie's Peugeot. *I swapped my Porsche for a Peugeot?* His phone rang.

"What?"

"It's Mark Whale."

"What's up?"

"Can we meet for lunch?"

"I'm busy 'til later." Sediko cut the call.

Lunch? He was having a laugh. He hated when people phoned him for shit, that's why he had his boys, he wasn't the deliveryman. He drove round to Candy's.

"Wha gwan? Soon come," she said through the intercom. He waited in the car. Finally, she came down dressed in a blue Nike tracksuit. She hopped in the car and he pulled off. They got to Ladbroke Grove at 2:16; he called Sara's land line.

"Yeah, I'm outside."

"Alright hol' up one minute." She hung up.

Sediko watched and waited.

"Watch Candy, a man's gonna run out of there zipping up. My girl is a proper ho."

She, too, watched and waited.

A pretty white girl came out tying her dark hair into a band. She bounced to her car smiling.

"Hmm, she's quite fit," both Candy and Sediko remarked.

Sediko stretched his neck.

"Come," Sediko jumped out the car followed by Candy.

Sara had left her door open for him to come straight through. She lay in her bed with only a thong.

"I got someone with me man, fix up." Sediko stood at the end of the bed.

"So, come in," she called to Candy who came in, then stood beside Sediko.

"Come on Sara, I'm in a hurry," he said, taking in her body with his eyes.

"Don't rush me, come sit down." She patted the bed beside her.

"I'm with ma bredrin, innit."

"She can join in too."

"You are one randy little bitch."

"Yes, we had this conversation. Well?" She looked at Candy. Sediko was bursting inside. He hadn't had sex for the longest time and he hadn't slept with Kellie since before she lost the baby. This must be his lucky day.

Candy looked at him and without any coaxing she pulled off her jumper. Sara moved aside on the bed with a big grin on her face. Candy stripped naked and joined her. The two began to kiss one another and he dived in between.

Ninety minutes later, Sediko sat at Sara's desk counting his money. Candy and Sara lay sprawled out on the bed. Sara lay still, her eyes rolled up to the ceiling. Candy's eyes were a sickly red.

"Shit's neat." He stuffed money into three envelopes. "Come on Candy, we're ready."

"Alright, mek mi jus hole a shower first."

"Na man, you've had plenty of time for that shit!" he barked at her.

"Wait. Who you chatting to like that?" She stood up, naked.

"I'm chatting to you Candy, come on." His voice was firm.

"Don't try talk to me like I'm some fool! Have some respect, give me 5 minutes, dat na go kill yuh." She marched out to find the bathroom. Sara sat up with her mouth open in shock.

"Well, that told you."

"Don't you fucking start! You, you're lucky I even *put* my clean hood in your dutty front." He stood and pulled on his clothes. "Dat t'ing will be here tonight, don't go out." He took his envelope and left the room. "I'm waiting in the car, don't take all fucking year!" he bellowed banging on the bathroom door.

Exactly five minutes later, Candy came jogging to the car.

"You calm down now?" she asked him.

"Yeah." He leaned in to kiss her. She leaned back away from him.

"I don't know what you think you're doing." She frowned.

"What? Didn't you say that-"

"I know what you're gonna say, that's why I didn't even want to have that conversation with you. Just because I like you that don't mean I'ma let you use me or fool up my head."

"That's cool."

"You don't need no more gal pressure right now. You heard from that Mia?"

"Na, I want you to move to that gal, still."

"What long time I wanted to bruk that girl's backside. Come, we go to her yard."

"Not now, we got cash to collect. I gotta get my shit to the safe deposit box before 6:00, it's 4:30 already." He pushed his foot down on the accelerator carrying three months worth of hard-earned drug and club money.

They drove around until quarter to six. Business was good, no one fucked with his money and if they did they would rather thief it from their parents than tell him that they were short. He drove to Bond Street.

"Wait here," he said to Candy before jumping out the car and going into the building.

"Ah, Mr Marshall, how are you today?" the account manager greeted him at reception

"What's up, Richie my man." They shook hands. "You know I'm alright if my money's alright."

"Of course your money is alright. In fact your money is very happy here," he chuckled. Sediko followed him to the 12th floor, as usual.

"And how much are we putting in today?" His big ugly face smiled as he turned a key held by only authorised personnel.

"I'm putting in quite a lot."

"Yes, Mr Marshal, you are."

In the room they passed filing cabinets until they came to a drawer where his money was temporarily held. Sediko dialled in a code and used Richie's key to open his drawer.

"One hundred forty gran in these envelopes," he took the seven envelopes from his pocket, "...ten for you in the seventh." Sediko always tipped Richie; if it wasn't for him he would never be able to hold his money here. Richie was a business crackhead. They talked for a further 15 minutes, then he left the building.

"You took your time," Candy said as Sediko returned to the car.

"Yeah, sorry. Work done now, time to relax, where you wanna go?"

"Drop me home. Go take your fiancée out."

"What's that, sarcasm?"

"No."

"So why did you say it like that?" Sediko headed Southwest.

"Like what? You still waiting for me to fall at your feet?"

"Whatever." He chuckled.

"Didn't you enjoy yourself earlier?" she asked.

He nodded and grinned.

"Well so did I, so don't spoil it," she warned him.

She switched on the radio and listened to music the rest of the way to her flat in Wilsden Green.

"So I'll call you later," he said to her as she got out.

"When I see ya. Say hiya to Kellie."

He watched her disappear into her block.

It was 10:30 pm; he had taken Candy's advice and was sitting in a bar in West London waiting for Kellie. She was twenty minutes late; he sipped his champagne while he waited. Ten minutes later she turned up looking sexy in a brown almost see-through dress. She smiled as she saw him.

"Sorry I'm late." She kissed him on the lips. "You been waiting long?" She sat; he poured champagne in her waiting glass.

"An hour," he lied.

One of his phones rang. Kellie sighed.

"What?"

"It's Mark, thought we were gonna do lunch, I'm gasping." His voice sounded irritated.

"You thought wrong."

"So, can we meet?"

"I'm busy right now; I'm with my fiancée." He smiled at Kellie who smiled back. He cut the call. "So," he turned his attentions back to his baby, "what you was doing today?"

"I just went to get my hair and nails done. I- hold on." She answered her phone.

"Hello.....Really!.....Uhh, I can't right now." He watched her, there was a long pause then, "Alright." She cut the call. "Sediko babe, I've got to go. I'm sorry." She stood up quickly.

"What, go where?" he asked, shocked that she was about to leave when she had heard him put her before his own business.

"I can't talk now, I'll come to yours later, or meet me at mine?" She was still standing, pleading with her eyes for him to understand.

"It's a bit late."

"Late for what? If I don't go now, I'll miss out on an opportunity."

"Fuck that, does that shit come before me?!"

"Sediko, don't do this *now*."

"Do what now? Don't this engagement mean shit to you?!"

"Of *course* it means a lot to me, you know I love you-"

"So why you fucking off as soon as we get here? I wanted to talk to you." His eyes blazed into hers. He saw defeat. She sat down.

"Right, let's start our night." He smiled topping up his glass.

"Are you asking me to choose between you and my career? Because that's what it sounds like." Her eyes were still pleading.

"No I wasn't, but now you come to ask– yes."

He leaned in close. He knew how to treat her, he knew how to love her. She couldn't, wouldn't, put anything before him.

Kellie sat with her hands on the table, she hadn't touched her glass. Her phone rang on the table. She looked at it, then to her hands, then back to the phone. Sediko sat back and watched her. She twisted the two engagement rings that he had bought her. She looked at him, slid them both off slowly and dropped them in his drink.

215

"What da fuck!" He sat forward. She answered her phone.

"I'm on my way." She stood. And with tears in her eyes, she left without looking at him.

He sat alone in the bar.

≈≈≈

Well this is nice." Bill sat at his table of good company. Ladonna and Boyd Richie sat in one corner, Fara Palmer Robinson sat in another. Other minor celebrities stood at the bar. At his table was a top fashion designer; Latina, his side beauty; Burt with his sexy young thing; Chad with Mina and supermodel Kellie. They had been waiting for Oman's representative for 45 minutes.

Chad looked at his watch.

"It's alright Chad, just relax," Kellie urged as she ate her desert: a chocolate mousse.

"They're late," Chad whined.

"That food was boom." Belinda nodded and rubbed her stomach.

"Yes, the food was wonderful," added Latina who positively glowed, the good life was good for her.

A gentleman was shown to their table, he stood beside Kellie's chair. "I'm Simon, Oman's agent." His accent was Southern American.

Yeah, one of them, thought Chad who leaned over to shake his hand.

"Chad. Kellie's only agent," he introduced in turn.

"I've gotta a message for Kellie." He didn't sit, he turned to her, "I trust your first payment was sufficient?"

"Yes, of course."

"So you alright?" Bill asked Latina who couldn't help but to look at everything in awe.

"Yes, I'm having a very good time."

That evening he and Latina sat listening to classical music in his living room. He sat in his underpants, something that he had never done. She lay in a brand new see-through negligee bought with her own money. He had had a nice day and now he was settling down to a perfect evening, then hopefully, a wild night.

He jerked forward as he heard the door slam. He had to get his locks changed. Latina stood up with fear in her eyes. Just as he went to usher her out the door, Marie and Carrie walked in. They both looked so healthy and beautiful, he instantly remembered how much he had been missing them.

"How dare the two of you barge into my house?"

"There she is," Marie said to Carrie, totally ignoring him. Carrie looked her up and down with disapproval.

"She looks my age." Carrie shook her head to an agreeing Marie.

"Alright, that's enough Carrie." They had just ruined his evening.

"You were better off with Lisa." Carrie laughed, Marie didn't.

"Will you please have some respect for my guest?" Bill would lose this argument, especially if the two came together.

"It's alright dad, Marie told me she didn't have a mouth of her own."

"Just tell me what you are doing here!" he shouted. He felt a fool standing in his living room in his underpants with his lady friend, his wife and his daughter.

"Daddy, I can't believe you threw me out to bring in an under-aged prostitute. And to think that you tried to warn me off Jeff! I'm here because I'm worried about you."

"You've barged into my house in the middle of the night because you're worried about me? Right." He nodded doubtfully.

"Bill," Marie stood forward, "...maybe we can sort this mess out. I understand you're a man and you have needs." She turned dirty-eyed to Latina, then back to him. "I want our family back; that's why we are here. You had no right to kick Carrie onto the streets."

"The streets? A £500 a night hotel is hardly the streets! And why are you defending her, she calls you a witch! She broke down our marriage!" Bill spat.

Carrie lowered her head before Marie could look at her accusingly.

"Bill, I'll come back tomorrow, let you think about it. And you," she turned to Latina with dagger eyes, "...you're not having my husband!" Carrie marched right up to her and slapped her face. Latina let out a squeal and ran out the room.

"CARRIE HOW DARE YOU!" Bill approached her; Marie stood in front of her as protection.

"Oh, just go put on some clothes," Marie said before turning and shuffling Carrie out the room. Seconds later, the front door slammed. Bill slumped into his chair and got drunk.

Bill awoke in the morning with the headache of the century. He had fallen asleep on the sofa. Latina sat in a chair watching him.

"You're awake? I understand your problem, you love your wife."

"What?" He sat up.

"I'm leaving."

"Right, maybe that is for the best." He pretended to look hurt.

"Yeah." She took a bag from beside the chair.

"Thank you for everything." She came and kissed him on the cheek. Latina left. Bill didn't stop her; he couldn't be bothered. Maybe he *should* stop her, where would she go? But he couldn't get up, his head was swollen. He went to the kitchen, swallowed some tablets and went back up to bed.

≋≋≋

Karim screamed in his cot. Mia sat with a paper clipping in her hand. Kellie had lost her baby. She had lost Sediko's baby. It was a sure sign. She ignored Karim's cries, all she could think about was the second chance she had been given. Sediko most probably needed her now.

She heard a key in the door; Kirk came in.

"Mia, can't you see Karim needs attending to!" He scooped his son up from his cot and he immediately stopped crying. "His clothes are soaked! You change his nappy?" he asked, his voice agitated.

Mia watched him attend to his son.

"You deaf?"

"Course I changed him," she lied. "I'm just going to the shop." Mia stood up, she was already wearing her jacket.

"Whatever," Kirk replied, not turning to watch her leave.

Thirty minutes later, Mia stood in the block opposite Sediko's flat and watched the door. No one came in or out. She waited half-an-hour and then went over and knocked. Her heart was beating, she should have called him first. The door opened.

"What?"

"Can we talk?" She walked into the house before he said 'no'.

"About what?" He followed her into the front room where all his things were packed up in boxes.

"Where you going?" she panicked.

"That's not why you're here."

"I'm sorry to hear about Kellie," she lied.

"Really."

"Are you two er-"

"Finished. Yep."

"Are we?" she asked him once and for all.

"*Are* we?" he asked her in return.

"If you're asking me, then no we're not. You know I still love you, no matter what." She smiled at him. She had missed him.

"You know what Mia, it was you who fucked me and Kellie up," he spat at her. She flinched at his outburst.

"Let's not go there, Sediko. Why can't we just be together, why always point blame. It's no one's fault if we keep on ending up together," she told him.

He laughed.

"What's so funny?"

"You really think that Kellie and me are finished?! Come on, Mia, I've told you time and time again, you will never match up to her! You go back to your two Kirks. That's your family now."

"What!" Mia cried. Tears began to well up in her eyes.

"Get out my yard, me and you ain't got nothing to chat bout!"

"You fucking bastard!" She jumped at him, she hit him with her fists, not caring if he hit her back. She clawed at his face while he tried to hold her arms back.

"What you doing, you mad bitch?!" He spun her around, held her arms behind her back and pushed her toward the door.

"Let me go!" she screamed. He had given her two seconds of hope and then took it away. "Alright, alright, let me just say something, then I'll go." Her voice calmed as they neared the door. At least she could have the last word. "I left you before, I can do it again."

"Go on, then!" he shouted, checking his face for scratches. There were three.

"But you know that you'll come back. Just like you did before, just like you always do. You remember that."

Mia turned and left. Sediko didn't call her back; she hadn't expected him to. Once again, he was pushing her out of his life when all she wanted to do was be the centre of his world. Every time that he left her she suffered, she had loved only him for so long.

They had started going out in secondary school. Both 14, young and immature. They were best friends as well as boyfriend and girlfriend; they grew together. She was there when Sediko used to hustle small. There when he used to ride his BMX around the ends. He was never faithful to her; she had to fight many girls over him, not always coming out on top but always leaving with her man. They went through it all together.

When they were 19, Sediko's mother died. He had taken it badly and she had been there for him. She was the only one that he could talk to, the only one that he could open up to. She watched him cry for weeks and months. She soothed his bad dreams and sat up at night with him when he missed his mother. He took out his anger on the street and that's when he turned from selling small drugs to more heavy stuff. A year after he buried his mother, he was making money and looking after her. She wanted for nothing, he made sure that she had it all. More girls on the side came and went; he had never promised himself to her but he always stayed with her.

At that time she was living in Wandsworth with her mum, Sandra, and her two younger sisters. She was at home less and less, which made her and her mum argue more and more. As she started smoking crack she drifted further and further away from them. She began to argue with them. In her mind, her sisters were jealous of her. They had a different dad and were very dark skinned and fat, with nappy heads and wide hips. She was slim, light skinned and beautiful.

Sandra found out that Mia was smoking crack. She had cried and Mia had moved out– into Sediko's drug house. Piles of money went through both their hands. Sediko had started making her pay for her drugs, he had said that she was smoking too hard. That was the last year that she and Sediko were together - before Kellie - and they were both 23. It was a blur. Drugs, parties, more drugs, Sediko. She had heard that her mum and sisters had gone to Canada without her. She didn't care at the time, she thought that she had Sediko. He had her out half high, half drunk, selling weed for him on the front line and she was at her worst; she didn't blame Sediko for hating her. She weighed 6 stones, her hair was falling out and she had the body of a 12-year-old boy.

Sediko had bought her the small studio flat where she still lived. He had given her £1000 and told her to come off the crack. He had told her to fix up and then come back. A week later, when she hadn't seen him, she tried to contact him but couldn't. Two weeks later all the money was finished and she was still sniffing hard. When she went to his mother's old house it was boarded up and he was gone. Over the next few months she had gone really low, selling most of her things: clothes, furniture, anything that she could. Her flat had been taken over by some drug men she owed money to but couldn't pay. They kicked her out of her place and it was during that time, at her lowest point, that she met Kirk. She had been in carnival with Charlene who had been trying relentlessly to help her.

Mia remembered when she used to lock herself in Kirk's bathroom for up to three days with nothing to eat. Charlene and Kirk would both bang on the door until she answered. Kirk would sometimes just sit outside the door and talk to her. She wanted to die.

Kirk began to warm to her, maybe through pity. He began to make advances and through loneliness she had responded. Kirk was everything that Sediko wasn't: faithful, a career man, someone you could bring home to the family— it was nice at first. But whenever she was sober, she thought of Sediko.

Six months later, she was clean. Kirk and Charlene had pulled her out of the gutter and now Kirk wouldn't leave her alone. He made sure that she was eating again and made her take regular visits to the hospital. Two months later, Sediko had turned up. She hadn't seen him in nearly a year, then suddenly they were back in each other's arms. That had lasted for only a few weeks. Even without the drugs, he was no longer satisfied with her.

Mia went back to Kirk who was always there for her. He never shouted or got angry, he understood. Kirk had fallen in love with her. And even though she still loved Sediko, Sediko didn't want her, so she stayed with Kirk. It seemed like the right thing to do and was better than being alone. She had feelings for Kirk once and still did, but just not the right ones.

After that, she didn't see Sediko again....until she started searching for him. She went to all the spots that she knew he liked, she even went to the houses of friends that they both had when they were together. Then finally that day in Whyno's, she'd found him. And that very day he had proved that he still had feelings for her.

When she had first spotted Kellie, she wasn't worried. Even when

Sediko made it clear that she was his girl, she still didn't care. Girls had come and gone in the past and despite that, she had stayed with him. But not this time. This time she was the loser. This time it was Mia that had to walk away.

≈≈≈≈

Kellie stood with a glass of white wine in a roomful of people that she didn't know. Some barely noticed her, others had heard about her and offered senseless small talk. As usual, Kellie looked beautiful in a figure-hugging, strapless dress. She smiled and sipped as her eyes darted around for Chad who was nowhere to be seen.

This was her celebration party. Everyone there was there to celebrate her success. She strolled outside onto the beautiful grounds. She stood alone, even though the whole place buzzed with life. Music played and everyone seemed to be enjoying themselves. She took her phone from her clutch bag.

"What's up babe?" he greeted her. His voice sounded happy. She didn't expect that, she hadn't spoken to him since walking out on him three days ago.

"I'm sorry about the other night."

"It's alright, I understand. Where are you?"

"At my celebration party," she sighed.

"Sounds like fun."

"Can you come and pick me up?"

"Where's the car?" he asked in a bit of panic.

"It's alright, I left it at home."

After the call, she rushed around to find Chad. Finally she saw him, coming down the stairs with a blonde.

"Chad, I've been looking all over for you! I have to go."

"Go? Go where?" His smile dropped and his girl wandered off into the crowd.

"Home," Kellie said seriously.

"This is *your* party."

"No, it's not my party!"

"Yes, this *is* your party."

"No IT IS not. None of my friends are here! Bill's not even here. Neither is my fiancée and I am NOT enjoying myself. I'm not having fun and my feet are killing me. I didn't wear these £3000 shoes for a bunch of strangers." Kellie stood with her hands on her hips. "Should I go on?"

"No, no. At least let me arrange for some photographs before you leave, you look beautiful."

"I know, just make it quick. I'm bored!"

"Shh..alright, keep your voice down, we don't want to offend any of our guests. Look, you go freshen up then meet me by the statues, okay?" He rubbed her arm gently. She nodded, sighed, and went up the stairs to find the bathroom.

Once up there, she did four lines of Charlie in the big, beautiful, empty bathroom. In the mirror she fixed her hair and make-up, then went to meet Chad. Thirty five minutes later, she was waiting for Sediko in a small, secluded pub.

Kellie watched the door, waiting for him. What would his mood be like? He sounded alright on the phone. Since she had lost her baby, they'd been distant. He had changed a little where it came to his temper and so far it hadn't surfaced again. But things had to change permanently if he really wanted her as his wife. He would have to prove to her in some way that he could be a one-woman man. At that moment she saw him searching for her with his eyes; she waved him over. They stayed in the pub for ten minutes before leaving and heading for her house.

As Kellie put her key in her door, Sediko stopped her.

"I got another surprise for you."

"What?" She smiled and waited.

"Inside."

As always, his face showed no clues. She pushed the door and went inside to see.....big boxes? Suitcases and bags were strewn across her floor. She turned to him confused.

"I'm moving in, babe."

"Moving in?" she asked shocked, then looked again at the boxes and it then made sense.

"What, not happy?"

"No..yeah...I mean, I'd have thought that that would be the last thing you'd want. You used to say the only woman you would ever live with was your mum."

"Well man's just trying to show you that I'm serious. Only if you want."

"Are you sure this is what *you* want?"

"I've just told you innit, I know you're gonna make a good husband out of me." He stood looking serious.

Kellie nodded and smiled, she was overwhelmed. She couldn't believe that he wanted to live with her, live with her so that she could watch his every move.

"Welcome home then!" she said laughing, and hugged him tight.

The next two weeks flew by for her. Ballers was back in her life and taking up a lot of her time. They were now open on Wednesdays which was 'members only' night and Sundays which she had made 'singles night'. Sediko was settled in but they still led almost completely separate lives. He wanted to move, said that he had found a place in Hammersmith, but she didn't want to, she didn't want to move away from Mo, Andy, and Ronan.

Kellie sat waiting in her car at the Brockwell Park car park. He was never late but she'd been waiting now for over twenty minutes, and she knew why– she'd been ignoring his calls. She wasn't even so sure that he would come at all, but it felt so peaceful just waiting. It was nearing 11:30 and Sediko was at home. He thought that she was at one of the many parties that she and Chad often had to attend. She rubbed her eyes and yawned.

A tapping on her window. She turned.

"Sorry." He walked around the car and got in. "You alright?"

"Fine. Shawn listen-"

"What?"

"Stop phoning me. It's making things difficult," she blurted out part of her practised speech.

"Why? I thought we agreed on friends?"

"We did. But-"

"But you prefer him over me." He looked away from her.

"It's not that, it's not a competition. You're a nice person and I had a good time with you that night. Okay, so maybe I'm attracted to you, but I love Sediko. I just want us to be happy and if that means not speaking to you every now and then..."

"Another night like that won't hurt him or you."

"One night may be nothing to you, but it is to me."

"He would never find out," he urged. "I bet he doesn't even know where you are now. Have you ever been unfaithful?"

"No."

"And how many times has he been unfaithful?"

"That's none of your business." She hated these conversations with him.

"I want you. At least spend one night with me." He bit the corner of his lip. The few seconds of silence felt like minutes.

"The only way you would ever have me is if I wasn't with Sediko and that is not going to happen." She had to be blunt.

"Alright, then I'll wait, I ain't going nowhere. And if you ever need me, you know where I am– anytime." He got out of the car without saying 'bye.' She watched him walk away. He was another one that was hard to work out. Where did he get that big house, what did he do for a living? Unfortunately she didn't know anyone that knew him directly, neither did she know why he started buying from her in the first place. He didn't take or sell it.

She drove back home half expecting him to call. He didn't. She opened the ashtray in the car, then licked, dipped and rubbed her teeth. Once again, she was spending excessive amounts of money on drugs. And this time she wasn't getting half of it free from Sediko. He hadn't noticed how out of control she was getting, but she couldn't possibly go to all those important meetings and celeb parties sober; she would feel left out if nothing else. No one in the media didn't have a drink or drug problem. She was taking care not to get too dependent; she had quit once she could quit again.

As she parked her car it seemed strange to see the light on. She was still getting used to it; Sediko was home. As she slowly walked up the stairs ready to surprise him, she could hear laughter, woman's giggles and sweet whispers. She peeked slowly into her room, her mind clear. Two naked bodies: sweaty, happy, giggling. A dark-skinned woman; Sediko's naked shoulder covered her face. Touching, moaning and more girlie giggles. Slowly, she went back downstairs undetected.

Quietly, Kellie took the big brown box which had contained Sediko's clothes and began to fill the box with his things, which were still in the living room as she had refused to share the wardrobe. Six pairs of jeans; four pairs of Nike trainers; three *single* Gucci, Fendi and Prada shoes; his DKNY jumper and all his designer shirts. She wasn't really looking, just silently stuffing. She then went to his aftershaves packed neatly on her windowsill: Blue Jean, Polo Men's, CK, Ralph Lauren, JPG, Iceberg, Valentino and others. With care not to clink the glass, she placed them in the box among the clothes. A pair of women's jeans– in the box; a tight, cheap top, woman's– in the box, his three phones with three chargers– in the box and to top it off his leather Avrex jacket. She went to the kitchen and took his 'oh, so precious' bottle of Jamaican rum and poured it into the box all over his clothes. She looked around for extras. An ounce of weed– in the box, three hats including his favourite bowler hat– in the box. She dragged the box to the door. The scraping was loud but the laughter and happy giggles were louder.

Without a second thought, she took matches from her pocket and set the box alight outside her door. She edged back as a fire rose quickly. In seconds, the whole box was alight. Kellie watched all his shit go up in flames. He was too fucking wrapped up with some bitch in her bed to realise that all his prized possessions were on fire. She went inside and back up to her room.

"Having sex without me?" she breathed. Sediko jumped and spun to her.

"I thought you were going out." He moved away to reveal Candy.

"You! Get the fuck out my house!" Kellie shouted to her as she fumbled around for her underwear. "Don't rush love, he's all yours!"

"Kellie." He pulled on his trousers.

"No! No Sediko! Don't say a word! Not a fucking word, just get out!" she shouted.

"Where are my clothes?" Candy asked Sediko.

"Outside bitch, where you're going!" Kellie shouted. "Come on, get out! Out!" Candy went to pass her and Kellie punched her hard in the face. Candy punched her back and Kellie grabbed for her just as Sediko pulled them apart.

"Yuh lucky. Yuh fucking lucky, bitch," Candy threatened angrily without shouting. She took Sediko's jumper and pulled it on. Her own clothes were sharing the bomb fire with his.

"What the fuck you fighting for?!" Sediko shouted.

"Not over you, that's for sure! Now get out! You fuck a bitch in my bed!"

"We didn't fuck."

"Oh please," Kellie moved away from him as he neared and Candy left the room.

"We didn't, she's a lesbian. We didn't fuck Kellie."

"Does it look like I give a shit? Bye."

"Two-Face!" Candy screamed out from downstairs. Sediko ran down to see what she was hollering about. Kellie followed. As soon as he stepped out the house with Candy to salvage their clothes, she slammed her front door shut.

"Kellie, you burned my shit!" he shouted through the letterbox. Kellie threw herself on the chair.

"All my fucking shit!" he banged at the door. He banged and kicked until Kellie was sure he was going to burst through the door and kill her. "All my shit! You fucking bitch!" He banged and banged. She went upstairs, pulled the sheets off her bed, opened the window and threw it out onto them.

"I should burn these dirty sheets as well!" she shouted down to them. She closed her window and didn't listen to the replies. She ignored the continuous banging.

Kellie looked at her bare bed. She couldn't sleep there now; how could she? How could he? She went downstairs and slumped in the chair with a bottle of E&J. She was tired and the banging and shouting had stopped. Sediko had let her down once again! Yet again! Her phone rang; she ignored it. She poured a glass, drank it quickly, poured another, drank it quickly and continued 'til the bottle was half empty. The alcohol swirled around her head, it swirled around her body. Sediko was fucking Candy in her bed. He had proposed to her, moved in, then he had fucked a dyke in their bed! Her bed! After he had proposed to her! After he had moved in with her! She picked up the phone and called Mo.

"Can I, can I speak ta Mo? Please, Tex."

"You know what fucking time it is?" he asked angrily. Kellie looked at the big digital clock: 1:55 am.

"Sorry. It's urgent."

"It better be.. Mo! It's Kellie...and tell her not to call so late."

"Kellie, you alright?" Her voice was full of concern.

"He...has fucked up again," Kellie cried into the phone.

"Who?"

"Sediko. I caught him fucking Candy." Kellie relived the scene over again in her mind as she relayed it to Mo and downed another few glasses.

225

"Kellie, I don't want to sound cold, but just move on. Sediko is not worth it. You're a famous model, hundreds of people love and admire you."

"I want *Sediko* to love and admire me!" Kellie screamed. "Fuck Mo, what am I going to do? I don't even want to be here; he's all around me! He's under my skin." The drink took control of her speech.

"You leaving him is the best thing that's ever happened to you besides the modelling contract. And you're not short of male company; what about Shawn?"

"Shawn?! Some creep who fucking spies on me. I'm engaged for fuck sake! Engaged!"

"Kellie please! You're lucky to be where you are. You've worked hard and I'm proud of you. A few years ago we were in the same boat, both going college and looking after out babies. Now look at you, you've got a good life."

"Good life?! Who says that I enjoy sitting around having people treating me like clay! To tell the truth I'm tired of it Mo! It's not me. My every move in some magazine, people judging me-"

"You don't read what the papers say."

"I know but-"

"I know you don't, because I do. People admire you and they don't know about your love life."

"I'll call you back," Kellie sighed.

"I know that means you don't want to talk anymore. Just promise that you'll call me tomorrow."

Kellie sighed drunkenly.

Kellie sniffed four lines on the kitchen table, then lined up two more. Mo said that people admired her. "Ha!" That was a joke. Look at the state of her. She bent, did two more lines, then stood up too quickly. She swayed from side to side as she experienced a head rush. She couldn't stand up. She rubbed her nose; it was stinging like mad. It started to bleed.

"Ah shit." She wanted to sober up but she couldn't stand. She began to panic; she felt strange. Her heart was pounding and she felt lightheaded. She stumbled into the front room and slumped into the chair. Her head was spinning and her nose trickled blood. Maybe she was overdosing. She felt almost hysterical inside and had cold sweats on the outside. Her head slumped back and the room spun around her. Her stomach churned and her body felt rigid. Blood dripped from her nose, down her lips and onto her clothes. She dribbled white froth from the corners of her mouth. Her eyes were barely open and her heart pounded harder and faster. She felt close to death and almost welcomed it. She'd lost Samuel, Sediko and her baby, who did she have to try to live for now? Suddenly she heaved forwards to be sick but nothing came out. Her insides burned, her head fell back against the chair. Bleeding, dribbling, crying, gagging. What was happening to her?

Kellie's eyes rolled up.

The next morning Kellie awoke sprawled in the chair. A stench surrounded her as she laid in her own blood and vomit. The smell alone caused her to gag and vomit again in the chair. Her head was pounding. Slowly, she sat up. Sediko and Candy flashed through her mind but she blocked it out quickly. She went to the kitchen; it was a mess. Broken glass and bottles, things knocked onto the ground. She swallowed two headache tablets and began to tidy up. Forty-five minutes later, she showered, washed her vomit matted hair, then crawled into Samuel's bed.

At 8 pm Kellie woke up with a need that went deep into her stomach– worse than starvation, worse than thirst. She dressed quickly, jumped in the car and drove to the nearest cash point. She dialled in her pin; the hole in the wall swallowed her card.

"Shit!" she shouted aloud.

She got back into her car and drove to Ballers. On the way, she sped past two red lights and was flashed by traffic cameras at least five times. Her head ached. She licked her lips and dipped into her car stash– it was empty. "Shit!" Her luck had definitely run out. She had to get to the bank tomorrow. She knew she wasn't overdrawn; she was rolling in money. Maybe she had splashed out on clothes and shoes but nothing too expensive.

Finally, she skid-parked badly outside the club.

"Sediko here?" she asked the Jimmys.

"Na."

She raced past them, moving quickly through the already packed club trying to avoid the talkative regulars and fans. She kept her head down, she had only come for one reason. She went the back way through to the office and closed the door behind her. First she went over to the pane of glass and looked out. People danced, unaware of her stare. She then went to the safe on the wall behind the mini bar and coded in. She pulled it open and looked inside. It was full of everything she needed right now.

Opening her big *Cosmopolitan* bag, she began to stuff in rolls of money. One thousand, two...four....seven... At nine, the office door opened. Kellie froze. Her heart hammered inside her chest. She couldn't turn around. She thought she had locked the door! One hand was in the safe– her elbow holding the safe door open, the other was holding her bulging bag. Half seconds felt like half hours.

Jimmy had said that Sediko wasn't here. There was no way to explain this, no way to explain taking so much. She jumped as the door closed softly.

"Kellie?" A soft voice, a woman's voice.

Kellie turned quickly.

"Shit Jade! Can't you fucking knock!" She slammed the safe shut. Her hands were shaking violently as she zipped the bag. Jade stood staring at her. "I'm sorry. You just frightened the shit out of me," she apologised and laughed nervously as relief washed over her like never before.

Jade smiled. "I didn't see a thing. The bastard deserves it." Jade had never said a bad word about Sediko before.

"Thanks." Kellie unzipped the bag. "Here." She threw her a grand. Jade caught it, smiling.

"Thanks. I just came to tell you that everything is fine I-"

"Jade, I can't stop tonight. E-mail me, use the laptop." Kellie was out the door.

Kellie sped off, she stopped at the light and took the small amount of Charlie she'd managed to find. Sediko must have left it. Her phone rang.

"Chad?" Kellie answered.

"How are you?"

"I feel like shit."

"I'm coming for you right now."

"Chad -!"

"Now that's sounds like negativity. I'm ten minutes from your house. You'd better be in girl." He cut the call.

She had been thinking about dropping him, he had too much of a hold on her schedule. Kellie U-turned and headed home. Every traffic light that she came to, she rubbed a little powder onto her teeth. She got home in just under twenty minutes to find Chad sitting on her doorstep.

Two months had gone by since Kellie had lost her baby. Two weeks had gone by and still she hadn't seen Sediko. She sat in Barclays bank with her bank manager.

"So what are you saying?" Kellie asked him.

"You've past your credit limit on two of your cards and you have thousands of pounds of unpaid direct debits."

"So can my other accounts cover it?"

"Well yes, your savings account. Obviously you can't transfer from your son's trust fund."

"No, no, obviously. So how much?" she asked, scared at the reality of what her bank manager was saying.

"One hundred forty-four thousand." He looked her straight in the eye with a bank manager's smile. "Or, we could discuss a loan."

"A loan?"

Kellie sat behind the wheel of her car. The money that she had taken from Ballers had lasted only three days; she'd had a small crack party with Chad and three up and coming models. Chad had models chasing him now; as her agent, they wanted him. She switched on her engine and headed to Mandy's.

"Who's that?" Mandy asked through the closed door.

"It's Kellie, you busy?" She heard the chain come off and the door opened.

"I got company, but come in," Mandy said smiling, dressed in an over sized t-shirt. She stood aside for her to come in.

"You're busy, I'll come back another time."

"No, I haven't seen you in ages; it's only Path." Mandy led her into the house by the arm.

"So what's up?" Mandy joined Kellie on her sofa.

"You know me-"

"OOYYEER!" Path hollered from the bedroom.

"Hole up. WHAT?!" Mandy got up and disappeared into her bedroom.

Kellie stood and pulled off her brown leather Prada jacket. Path came marching out of the room. He glared at Kellie on his way out, then slammed the door.

"Sorry." Kellie smiled apologetically to Mandy.

"Forget that. I heard about what you did!" Mandy sat beside her again, waiting for her to spill the beans.

"What?"

"What you mean what? The ten grand that you took."

"Sediko knows?!" Kellie silently panicked.

"Course he knows, you weren't exactly discreet. You are one brave bitch."

"What's he saying?"

"He's saying some shit about you having problems."

"Problems?"

"Well, you *are* looking kinda thin."

"Mandy the only problem I have is him fucking dykes in my bed."

"Yeah, he did mention that but no one was surprised. Heard you burned up their shit?" She laughed.

"Yeah, it was mad." Kellie shook her head.

"So you two done again?"

"Yeah, this time it's gonna be permanent. I should've let Mia have him."

"You and Sediko have been through a lot though."

"*I've* been through a lot! He's caused it. The only good thing that man ever had was me."

"Hear you now! I've never heard you say a bad word against him."

"I'm not saying anything bad, I'm just talking the truth."

"So, how's work been?"

"Well I haven't been to Laymend's; I think Bill understands. I just signed a contract with Oman Cosmetics, oh and hopefully some time soon I'm gonna be interviewing Joel for MTV Base. Me and Prevor."

"It's me and Prevor now is it?" Mandy giggled.

"Please," Kellie laughed.

"So when did you start smoking again?" she suddenly asked.

"Let's not go there."

"I want to go there; I thought you stopped. I know you stopped smoking it."

"I don't smoke it, I snort it. What's with you? Please don't get between me and my shit."

"You sold your belongings yet?"

"I'm not an addict."

"Kellie, I respect you but I don't respect what you're doing."

"It's fine, my life is under control. It's just a pick me up."

"Alright if that's what you think. You remember what I told you when I first met you?"

"What?" She could hardly remember last week.

"About Mia."

"Please don't start about that stupid bitch."

"You're walking that same bitches footsteps."

"Why you trying to mother me?!"

"I ain't mothering you, but I should! I told you about what happened to Mia as a warning. And what do you do?! You're just the same as her, the only difference is your money will last longer. But it will all be spent on the same thing, or maybe you've run out of money already? That's why you robbed your own bar."

"Look, don't you worry about my financial position. Just know I make more money than you."

"Please don't go there. You may make more money than me but at least I ain't a crackhead!"

"Oh, I didn't come here for this." Kellie kissed her teeth.

"Look, I'm only trying to look after you, best intentions and all that. So what you gonna do?"

"I'm gonna take one day at a time," she answered slowly. What else could she do?

Three months later and 6 weeks before Christmas, Kellie sat with her new supermodel friend Anna. She was French, super skinny, with long thick dark hair around a pale beautiful face.

"So you think that I should fuck Cameron?" She lay in Kellie's chair, smiling and curling her hair around her fingers.

"No I do not!" Kellie laughed, kneeling on the floor by the coffee table in front of them.

"Why?! Tell me he's not fit."

"He's nice but he's the camera man. Come on, a super model can do better than that." Kellie chopped at the Charlie.

"Oh fuck that, he's niiice. Come on." She sat up. "What's taking you so long you baking that shit?"

"Wait, bitch, wait." Kellie laughed.

"So what about you? You haven't had any dick since, since I don't know?"

"Since '89." Kellie laughed but Anna didn't get the joke.

"For real, you don't wanna fuck?"

"No, I don't actually. I haven't got time for a man."

"Who's talking about a man? A fuck takes 30 minutes, 3 minutes if you're unlucky. You haven't got that?"

"Just come on." Kellie moved aside so that Anna could join her on her knees.

"About time." She joined her on the floor. They both sniffed, then sat on the chair close together.

"That was good," Kellie said minutes later, almost to herself.

"So, you gonna answer my question?"

"What question Anna?"

"About fucking. When was the last time?"

"With Sediko about what..er, four months ago."

"You don't talk about him, what's up with that?"

"Nothing to say. Went out for 3 years and a few months," Kellie sighed.

They talked for another few hours and when the drugs were gone Anna made her excuses.

Kellie sat alone. Anna was a funny person, they had fun, but she wasn't a real friend. She hadn't seen any of her real friends in months. Mandy and Mo had had enough of her. She hadn't seen Sediko, he didn't come to the club anymore. Her free time she spent with Chad and her new friends. Her contract with Oman had run out and they had signed her again, but she wasn't due for any new features for a while.

Here she was, 24 years old. She had a 5-year-old son who lived with his gran. She was a model and a club manager and she was sitting here sniffing her life away with each line. She was going to quit! It was Friday night. She cut up her five credit cards. No money, no drugs.

The next morning, Kellie lay awake in Samuel's bed with cramps. The thought of not sniffing gave her an instant migraine. She stayed in bed. Late afternoon and she still couldn't get out of bed. Slowly, she forced herself onto her feet. She crawled slowly down the stairs, sat in the chair, looked at the table and then without thinking she kneeled and licked dust off the table where she and Anna had been the previous day. As soon as she did it she began to cry. She crawled back in bed. She had no money! Why the fuck had she cut her credit card! She just needed a little money, just to get a little so that she could wean herself off. She cried herself back to sleep, blocking out her pains.

The following night Kellie could take no more and she knew what she had to do. She had made up her mind. She had a habit that she had to maintain. She put on jeans and a t-shirt beneath a black Nike tracksuit. She pulled her hair back into a bun and pulled on a woolly hat. She collected her loaded gun, a small flashlight, and folded a thin black shoulder bag into her pocket. She wore tight leather gloves and left the house at 11:37 pm thinking only of the task at hand.

Hours later, she sat in the car about ten feet from the house, watching with her headlights off. Watching and waiting. She wasn't scared, she was ready. After a while, seeing no movement, she got out of the car and closed the door. She ran towards the house, staying quiet in the shadows. She went around the side and looked through the glass into the empty garage. She looked at her watch: 2:04am. She didn't realise that so much time had gone by. She crept around the back, feeling against the wall; the night was pitch black.

Kellie thought she heard a rustle and slowly turned, pushing herself flat against the wall. She pulled the pen torch from her pocket and pointed towards the sound. Nothing. She continued on 'til she came to a glass door. It was unlocked; she opened it gently. Obviously he didn't think that this was the sort of area where crackheads pretending to be supermodels went shopping. She closed the door silently, slowly, behind her. She stood still and listened out for any noises or signs. Nothing.

Kellie switched on her flashlight. It barely lit the corners of the room but she could make out that she was standing in the kitchen. She tiptoed out and walked down the hallway. Quickly and quietly she crept up the stairs. At the top she turned her flashlight to the lobby below, just to make sure. Nothing. She stood in front of the three arches and paused as her conscience kicked in. He would never find out. She went into the left arch, his suite of rooms. When he'd brought her here before, she'd wandered into his walk-in wardrobe and had discovered some skunk. While she had been looking for the necessary tools to smoke it, she'd stumbled across a small hatch in the floor. She'd lifted the lid and been surprised at what she'd seen.

Now, months later, she kneeled in that exact same spot with a flashlight between her teeth. She opened the hatch, it was all still there, untouched. She took the black bag from her pocket and began to fill it. Six diamond studded men's rings, men's bracelets, three gold watches– one Rolex, some ladies' jewellry and about three hundred thousand pounds.

Kellie replaced the hatch and stood up; she was almost home free. She zipped the bag then heard a definite noise. A fucking noise; just what she didn't need. She switched off the flashlight, then switched it back on; it was pitch black and she couldn't see a thing. She moved towards the door and pulled the gun out of her pocket. She stood against the closet door, flashlight in her left hand, gun in her right.

Stepping out of the closet, Kellie scanned the room with the flashlight. Nothing. Another noise. She knew that she had heard something. Maybe it was that bitch maid. She wouldn't mind killing that bitch, she was most probably servicing Shawn every time he came home. But if it was Shawn and he caught her, what would he do? Kill her? She went back into the closet, picked up her bag and pulled it over her left shoulder, then over her head. She heard another noise and went back into the room with the flashlight. She was stunned, as the flashlight was snatched from her hands.

With the light switched off, Kellie's heart began pounding against her chest. All movement had stopped and she was alone again. She pointed the gun toward the mysterious flashlight thief. Suddenly, from straight ahead of her, the light was on and pointed into her face. It glared into her eyes as she flicked the safety catch off of her gun.

"What the fuck you doing?" A familiar male voice, but not Shawn's. She stood silent, gun still pointing, heart still pounding. *Could it be?*

"Sediko?" she whispered.

"Yeah, what da fuck you doing here?" He moved the light from her face. She could barely see his figure as he stood in front of her.

"Sediko?" she asked again, just to make sure. She needed to calm her nerves, she couldn't think straight.

"Move that shit from my direction!"

"Shh." She dropped her right arm.

"What for?!" His voice level still high. "You hear me, I said what you doing here?"

"What are YOU doing here?" she whispered.

"I followed you. Your turn." The flashlight in his hand pointed towards the floor, the light was flickering. She couldn't see his face.

"I don't have to tell you shit. You lost that privilege when you fucked a dyke in my bed!" she whispered loudly. She wanted out.

"What's in the bag?"

"Don't you question me."

"What, who you talking to!? You don't respect man!" he shouted louder than before.

"Sediko shut up!" she whispered again loudly. "I've got company downstairs," she informed him, hoping that he would want out too. Instead, he began to laugh. He bellowed loud and hard.

"Please Sediko just shut up! You want them to call the police?" she pleaded.

He stopped.

"Call police for what?"

She pushed the bag behind her. She moved toward the door and he blocked her way. She moved to the right and he synchronised her movement.

"Sediko, I wanna leave."

"What for? You just got here. Don't you wanna make yourself comfortable; that's why you're here, innit?"

233

"Sediko-"

"Why you want some of the white stuff? I got some right here."

"Have you?"

"No!" he shouted then laughed.

"What is your problem?" She began to panic, as minutes seemed to be passing by.

"I'ma tell you what my problem is. This motherfucker Fixer is trying to fuck up my motherfucking shit and you know that! We're gonna wait for that nigga and I'm gonna dead him right here and right now! And bitch, you're gonna watch. Then you're coming home with me!" He pulled at her arm and she jerked away. "What you gone you silent for?! Talk man! We got all night."

"I ain't got nothing to say. I just want to go." Her tone hardened. She couldn't believe that he was here standing in front of her.

"What are you doing here and where's that punk Fixer?!"

"You still haven't told me what you're doing stalking me! This is stupid." She had to think of a lie and quick. But why would she be here in the middle of the night dressed in black creeping around in the dark alone?

"Kellie!"

"Alright you want the truth?.... Shawn has just gone to the petrol station. So you'd better just go."

"What?!" He mirrored her thoughts and began to laugh at her story, only louder this time.

"Shut up!" she shouted over his insane laughter.

"You shut up. You the one that's been caught this time. Are you coming back with me?"

"Coming back with you? Are you crazy? I hate you! You're a lying, cheating, fucking bastard!"

"And how you work that one out?"

"Cos you let pussy fuck with your head, and what makes it worse is you think you know how to treat a woman! You only know how to trap them and fuck them up!"

"Have I trapped you?"

"Yes, me and Mia! That poor bitch! She'll pine after you but I'll forget you in a hot minute. I'm glad that we're done, all you know how to do is sell drugs and use your cock! Ain't got no fucking brain!"

"Oh and Shawn has?"

"And and I hope that Shawn comes back and takes your life tonight!" she was shouting in full rage. She forgot all about the money, all about the gun, she totally forgot that she had just stolen tens of thousands in money and jewellry from Shawn.

"Yeah, let it all out Miss Perfect Bitch!"

"You're damn right. I was perfect until I met you! Whatever you touch turns to shit. I left you just in time!"

"Please, look at you! You're a crackhead that's why you can't tell me shit! Your problem is you can't hold down a man!"

"Oh really! Did I even get a chance? How long were we together before you started fucking Mia?!"

"Long enough!"

"You're just a bastard, that's your problem!"

"Yeah that's right, I'm a bastard and you're a crackhead bitch. So tell me something, if I was fucking gal so quick how come we lasted this long?"

"We did last, because I loved you. Stupid fucking me!" she argued with him.

"Well as far as I'm concerned I enjoyed every piece of pussy that I got, including yours!" he shouted and his words dug into her.

"I feel sorry for you. You can't even see when people are there for you. You treat your 'oh so precious' boys like gold and it's them same boys that fuck you up! I've been there for you for so long and this is how you throw shit at me! Who was looking after your shit while you were locked up? Who? Huh who? Who's looking after your club now? And who took you back after you fucked up time after time? Come on who?!"

"What you-"

"Don't say shit to me! I don't even want to hear it! Your nickname suits you. Two-Faced. And this, this is the side of you that I hate! This is the part of you that took our baby!"

"Don't start that shit."

"What shit? What have you forgotten all about her or you don't want me to remember that the nurse told me I had a footprint on my stomach!"

"Kellie."

"Yes, I know what you did! I knew what you fucking did and I didn't say a word!"

"Kellie." His toned softened.

"No! Don't Kellie me you cunt! You made me lose my baby! At least admit it to yourself! You didn't even come to her funeral. It was me one! Me one! Why didn't you follow me then?!" She was shouting out loud now and the tears in her eyes had dropped.

"Kellie," he said softly.

"Don't say my name like that! You can't make this one alright!"

"I already apologised for that!" he shouted back.

"Oh, so that makes it alright?!"

"Kellie."

"Not a word cos I thought I understood you. And for some sick reason I still forgave you! I forgave you! And then you fucked a motherfuckin' dyke in my bed! After all the other shit you put me through you had to fuck up one last time! I can't even sleep in there any more! I can't sleep in my own bed because you decided that it would be fun to fuck a dyke stud in my bed! That, I will *never* forget!"

She was really crying now.

"Kellie, you bottle things up, that's your problem."

"*My* problem! You are sick! You're fucking *sick*! This is YOUR problem! I've moved on and you're fucking stalking me!"

"Stalking you! I fucking love you! I'm here because I love you." He grabbed her arm again and the flashlight dropped to the floor and went out.

"Get you hands off her!" Another voice in the darkness.

BANG!

A gunshot rang out in the darkness.

Sediko! her mind screamed! *Sediko!* She heard his shadow slump to the floor. Sediko! But she stayed silent.

BANG!

This time her finger was on the trigger pointing in the direction of Sediko's shooter.

BANG!

Another fire, then a thud to the ground.

Kellie stood rigid in the silence, her arm still outstretched to where the voice had come from. It seemed liked minutes had passed. No movement, only her heartbeat. BOOM BOOM, BOOM BOOM, BOOM BOOM, BOOM BOOM! That was all she could hear.

At least five minutes went by. She was shaking violently and breathing fast and hard. Finally, Kellie moved to the closet and pulled the switch. Gun still aimed, she turned to where she had been standing. Two heaps: Shawn, not moving; her Sediko, not moving. Shawn had shot her! Shawn had shot Sediko first, so she had shot him, and he had shot her right back. Sediko!

She stood over him. What had life come to? Her mind was blank to today, but yesterday plagued her. How had she gotten here? She held the killer in her gloved hand. She felt dizzy, hurt. Her jumper was ripped, her left side bleeding hard. She turned to leave, holding her injured side, blanking out her future nightmares thinking only of what was to come. Still, she held tight to the bag.

Seventeen

Bill stood at his doorstep ready to go in. He had a funny feeling, but didn't know why. He went straight upstairs to shower and to change into another suit. He then went to his office. He almost screamed! The office door was wide open and the lock had been broken. Inside, the place had been ransacked. He looked to his cabinet and prayed that his solid gold three foot eagle was still there; it was one of a pair, the other was in his work office. It was gone!

Quickly, he left his office and ran upstairs. All his and Marie's jewellry– gone! He couldn't believe it. The finger pointed in the direction of one person. Without thinking, he called the police, then regretted it as soon as it began to connect. He couldn't tell them that his former live-in prostitute lover's pimp raided his house! That would be in the headline for weeks.

"Which emergency do you require?"

"Sorry, I've made a mistake," he blurted out.

He wouldn't let her get away with this. He could replace everything, but it was the principle. He'd tried to help her and she'd left with more money than she had come with! He was going to look for her.

Bill rented his usual tinted window car and cruised her streets. He drove up and down but she was nowhere to be seen. Maybe she was with a client, she was a prostitute after all.

Thirty minutes later, around twenty after ten, he spotted her. She approached the car in front of him and he watched her jump in as it sped off. He followed them. A few roads down, on a quiet side street, her driver parked. Bill parked his car, got out and walked down the dark road. When he approached the car, he banged on the passenger side window. Seconds later, her door opened and a bald old man was pushing her out the car. She toppled out and he sped off.

"Bastard!" she called out after him.

"Bill?" She stood unsteadily. "What are you doing here? You must leave."

He pulled her towards his parked car, she resisted gently. He opened the driver's side, pushed her across the seat, jumped in, then sped off.

"Bill let me out. You're putting yourself in trouble," she pleaded.

"No, you're the one that's in trouble. The police are looking for you right now! How could you? I helped you."

"I'm sorry, it was Pips, I had no part of it."

"You did the worst part by showing him where I live!"

"I didn't, he followed me. I tried to get away, I tried to come back to you," she pleaded.

"So you didn't show him where I lived?"

"Of course not."

"Well, let's go then."

"You'd better take me back! He'll kill you. I'm not worth that."

"Of course you are. We'll go to the country and stay in the cottage for a few weeks." *Why was he taking her back when he had just gotten rid of her? She had robbed him for christsakes.*

"What about work?"

"I am the boss."

Bill and Latina spent two weeks away and soon remembered why he always used to go looking for her on cold nights. On their return home, he promised her for the hundredth time that everything was going to be alright. He had some friends in high places; he could easily get a pimp thief off the street for a few years. Bill listened to 19 missed calls, 12 were from Marie.

≈≈≈≈

One week before Christmas, Mia sat in front of the television. There she was looking glamourous and sexy, wearing twisted fitted jeans, a black glittery top and matching costume jewellry. She looked totally in control, calm and professional as she interviewed Joel about his new album. They laughed and chatted as if they had known each other for years. *Why did she have to come up on top? Look at her laughing and smiling with Joel, the famous millionaire singer.*

Karim was screaming behind her. As usual, Mia ignored him. He was 6 months old and as hard as she tried, and as guilty as she felt, she didn't love him. She didn't even like him. He cried, he stunk and he looked just like his dad. She hated him because he wasn't Sediko's. Karim had ruined her life! Sediko hadn't called her and she knew that he wouldn't. She hadn't contacted him because she knew there was no point. Kirk and Karim had spoiled her chance.

Mia watched the television. She could see why Sediko loved her; Kellie was pretty, famous and now rich. She had his club and she had him. *What do I have?* she asked herself. Kirk and Karim, big fucking wow!

"Shut up!" she suddenly screamed at the baby. He cried louder. "Just shut up! Shut up!" He cried louder and louder twisting himself in his bouncy chair, kicking his tiny legs and waving his arms with fisted hands. His face was red and his eyes swollen from crying. Mia stood up, pulled on Kirk's tracksuit and her jacket, and left the house, slamming the door on Karim crying alone behind her.

Mia walked down the hill, she didn't know where she was going. She blocked out the thought of Karim crying all alone. She just kept walking, walking away from everything. Walking away from a life she would be trapped in. She didn't love Kirk. She couldn't stand being with them both day in, day out! If only she would have guessed that the baby was Kirk's, she would have had an abortion straight away. No one asked her if she wanted to be Kirk's baby mother! Kirk was just a companion to her when Sediko wasn't around. Kirk loved his son, they had each other. They would take care of each other.

She kept walking and didn't turn back. She felt around in Kirk's tracksuit bottoms. His wallet. This was a definite sign, a sign telling her to run far away. Kirk had Karim and Sediko had Kellie. Who did she have? No one needed her here.

Walking made her feel good and she smiled despite the tears that streamed down her face. She was leaving. She searched the wallet. Three hundred pounds. If this were Sediko's wallet it would be more like three thousand. He had two cash cards so she walked to the nearest cash point, emptied both accounts, then hailed a black taxi.

"To any hotel in Hounslow."

"Gonna be a long ride," the driver warned before setting off on her journey.

Mia realised that she was taking this 'leaving' to the extreme. She had no clothes, no passport, but at last she was alone and thinking for herself.

Three hours later, the black taxi brought her to the Spring Grove Hotel.

"Sixty-two eighty, miss."

She gave him a fifty and twenty pound note.

"Keep the change."

"Cheers, love."

Mia stepped out into the unfamiliar area.

After checking in, she sat on the single bed with the phone in her left hand.

"Hello?"

"Charlene?"

"Mia is that you?!" she asked franticly.

"Yeah, I need a favour," Mia asked calmly.

"Where are ya? Kirk is going mad! How could you leave Karim like that?"

"I need you to collect a few things for me. From the flat."

"What? What for? Where are you?"

"Are you gonna help me or not?"

"That depends on what you want me ta do. What the hell is going on?" Her voice screeched into her ears.

"I need some clothes and my passport."

"What you need your passport for? What about Karim? You left him crying!"

"Are you gonna help me or not? Charlene *please*."

"Alright, where are you?"

"When you get my things I'll call you back and tell you where to meet me. Tell Kirk that I'm sorry."

"What clothes you want and where's your passport?"

"Any clothes, in the top drawer."

"So you gonna tell me what's going on?"

"The passport is just for identification. I'll call you back in a hour."
Mia put down the phone slowly and sat alone. She felt so peaceful. No
baby cries here.

An hour later and still sitting in the exact same position, she called
Charlene's phone.

"Kirk! Gimme my phone!"

"–Mia, you bitch!" Kirk shouted, his voice angrier than she'd ever
heard it. "How can you leave my son alone in the fucking yard?! How
can you leave my boy alone?!"

"Kirk, gimmi my phone! Mia call me back-" The phone went dead.
Mia waited 10 minutes before calling back.

"Mia, I got the shit now where are ya?"

"You got my passport?"

"Yeah, yeah, where you at?"

"What's my middle name?"

"What?" Charlene asked baffled at her demands.

"If you've got my passport, then you'll know."

"Monica."

"Alright, good."

"Listen, I'm in a cab outside your house waiting for you to tell me
where the fuck to go!"

"Hounslow– Spring Grove Hotel"

"What da fuck you doing there?"

"Just hurry." Mia cut the call and waited.

Two hours later, Mia waited outside the hotel. Twenty minutes after
that, Charlene arrived with Kirk's Nike sports bag over her shoulder.
They went inside to the bar.

"Explain, *now*," demanded Charlene taking Mia's passport from her
purse and handing it to her.

"Let me just use the bathroom," Mia replied.
She took the bag and turned toward the bathrooom entrance. As soon
as she was out of view she began running toward the exit. Outside, she
flagged down another black taxi and climbed in. As she drove away,
Charlene stood at the door, shaking her head angrily.

"Heathrow Airport please."
Mia didn't look back and eight hours later she was queuing for her
ticket. Destination: Vancouver, Canada. She would surprise her mum
and sisters. She was a different person now, they wouldn't turn her
away. She would apologise for the past and she would live on; without
Karim, without Sediko. Sediko. She would never stop loving him and
one day he would come for her. They always managed to find each

other again, no matter what.

Mia sat all alone, a mother without a baby, and waited for her chance to wave an abrupt goodbye to England.

≈≈≈

The next day, Kellie awoke in her own bed for the first time since another woman had christened it. She was hoping, praying, that she had just had the worst dream of her life. She touched her left side. "Shit!" she cried. The pain proved that she was wide awake now and had been wide awake last night.

Last night! What had she done? It was as if she was being forced to look at her past just like Scrooge's first dream. She felt as if she had just woken up from the longest dream in history. There, on the dresser, the black bag stared back at her. More proof.

Kellie felt sick. She stood up. Her body ached and she couldn't think straight. She slumped back on her bed and winced in pain; she didn't know what to do with herself. Slowly this time, she stood, went to the dresser and sat back down with the bag. She emptied its contents onto the bed. She had gone through with it, she had gotten what she had gone for. Had Sediko and Shawn paid the price for her habit? Were they both dead? Or were they both alive and plotting to kill her? She could have killed Shawn. She *did* shoot him. She shot him. She shot him for Sediko!

This time yesterday she had been pacing up and down in her mind but her body couldn't move. This time yesterday she had had flu like symptoms x 100 and she had to find a way to feed her pain. Last night she would have done anything just for one rock, one pebble sized rock. Today she had the money for the drug that she had needed so desperately but today that was the last thing on her mind!

Why had Sediko followed her? Could he be dead? She began to cry as she tipped the bag onto the bed. It glittered with opportunities. She looked at the jewels and money. Was Sediko's life worth this? What was happening to her? What had she turned into? What happened to her fear and trust in the law? And why the fuck was she taking drugs?

She remembered a time when she had loved her life and she was happy. Happy with Samuel and being a mother, being a mother and working in the office, in the office just being Kellie, being trustworthy and honest, honest and straight up, straight up and caring, caring and open, open and... And now she despised herself. Even her close friends found her despicable and insufferable to be around these days.

Kellie loathed her life because of hate. Hate in the form of Sediko. Hate had been following her, suffocating her, changing and spoiling her for three-and-a-half years now. The more Hate rained love, the more it thundered pain down on her. The more Hate tried to show her desire and passion, the more she allowed ignorance and uncertainty into her life. Hate loved to hurt her, Hate loved to devastate her, Hate loved to disappoint her, Hate loved to hate her, but if nothing else, Hate loved games! She was desperately in love with Hate, and now Hate was gone and forcing her to suffer the guilt, the pain, the nightmares, the inconsolable broken heart– all alone. Hate was gone, leaving her tormented, powerless over her feelings, terrified, angry. Not even Kellie could explain all her mixed feelings. Sediko was gone. So now she would sit for weeks on end, in anticipation.

Trying to shake her head free of thoughts, Kellie stood in front of her mirror; she looked anorexic. Was that the reason she was making it in the modelling business? What would happen to her modelling business if they found out that she was a murderer? No, she thought. She had to stop jumping to conclusions. Shawn couldn't be dead and nor could Sediko. She would keep her eye on the news.

Stepping away from the mirror, Kellie switched on the television; a double murder in Green Park would definitely have made the headlines. Back in front of the mirror, she pulled up her nightie. The bullet had just grazed her, but she could have died! It wasn't as bad as she had first thought, but the gash was deep and still bleeding. The rest of the day she spent in bed, watching the news and flicking channels. She had hidden the black bag and all its contents, in her cupboard, inside one of her hundreds of shoe boxes.

The next morning Kellie awoke waiting for the search party and operation 'Get Kellie' to come bursting through her door to arrest her. They didn't and she stayed in bed. The next morning the recurring nightmares started. A week after that and she still hadn't left the house and her nightmares were stopping her from sleeping.

Someone is chasing her. In self-defense, she begins shooting in the dark. As the mist clears she can see it is Sediko. She shoots him dead. As he dies, he shoots her back, in the stomach, and her baby dies. Her baby dies over and over and over again.

"Open this door now Kellie! I know you're there!" Anna called through her letterbox.

Kellie crept downstairs and waited for her to go away. Instead, Anna lifted her letterbox. "There you are! Let me in!" She kept knocking. Reluctantly, Kellie let her in.

"What's up? Chad's angry with you." She looked at her strangely and went to sit in her chair.

"Come in," Kellie sighed wrapping her dressing gown around her waist.

"Wow Kellie, you look rough! No wonder you're locking yourself away." Anna shook her head.

Kellie patted her hair down with her hands.

"Thanks a lot."

"So, where you been, man? Missed you at Franc's party."

"You know what, I really don't want any company today," Kellie admitted. She never felt like having company again. She was too trusting and too easily led.

"Are you kicking me out?!"

"No, I just want to be alone." Kellie remained standing while Anna still sat.

"Alright, I'll go. But can we go out tonight?"

"I doubt it."

"You're my raving partner now! Please don't let me down, come on! Don't you just want to party?"

"No."

"Oh come on, cheer up girl, what's wrong? This isn't like you. I haven't seen you since, since, I can't remember but it's been too, too, long."

"It's been two weeks, two whole weeks," Kellie said almost to herself.

"Whatever, so you on for tonight? Pleease."

"Alright, come back later."

"Goody!" She jumped up to hug her.

"Alright, see you later." Kellie urged her towards the door.

When Anna left, Kellie began to cry. She couldn't go outside! She hadn't even been eating because she couldn't face going to the local shops! Too many 'what ifs' were clouding her better judgement.

Kellie couldn't help but to remember her last words to Sediko. She had said the most spiteful things, things that she hadn't meant to say, and now she just wanted to say 'sorry.' His three mobile phones just rang and rang. They had separated; she had left him. But now he was out of her life whether she liked it or not.

"Get dressed," she said to herself.

Upstairs she slowly showered and dressed. She had decided to go lunch, then shopping. She stood at her front door looking beautiful and ready to face the world but as she went to open her front door, with her car keys dangling, she just couldn't, she just couldn't. What if Shawn was waiting to kill her? What if the police were waiting and watching her front door? What if an officer called around to give her bad news about Sediko? She ran upstairs and swapped her Levi's dress for her dressing gown.

At 10pm there was a knock on her front door.

"Kellie don't do this again!" Anna called through her letterbox. She went to open the door and made sure she kept out of view. "You're not ready?"

"I'm not going."

"What! Why?!" Anna moaned.

Because I'm a big fat murderer! Kellie wanted to scream.

"I think I'm coming down with something," she lied.

"You detoxing?" Anna slumped in her chair.

"Something like that."

"Well, you should have said. I'm the last person you need to see right now. Oh well, next time."

Anna left.

Friday night Kellie was dressed to kill and standing by her closed front door. With a clear head, she opened it and stepped out. She inhaled, exhaled and went to her car– Sediko's old car. She had to revamp, she had to change and erase the past to a clean slate.

During the past two weeks, Kellie had made some major changes in her life. She stepped out of her brand new Lotus to her awaiting estate agent. She was moving.

"Hello Kellie, so nice to see you again." James shook her hand quite vigorously.

"You too."

"I hope to have better luck this time," he said with a chuckle.

The last three houses she had hated but this one, in Crystal Palace, looked promising.

"Me too. Looks beautiful from the outside."

Kellie smiled happily as they walked up to the miniature castle house, its historic walls made from stone. It stood detached, three stories high, with a pebbled driveway and massive, arched front door.

"It's a four bedroom, as was your first choice. Good sized front room and large kitchen, also as you requested."

"Well, we'll soon see." Kellie smiled at him as he let them in.

"This building used to be a small school hundreds of years ago." They stood in a passage way with high ceilings. "Stairway ahead, kitchen at the end of the hall, but first I'll show you this." He opened the first room door on the right.

"This was the main classroom. Now, the front room." They walked into the massive fully furnished room.

"So?" James smiled hopefully.

Kellie sighed, as if undecided.

"You don't like it?"

"Actually James, so far I *love* it."

That Wednesday, Kellie and her solicitor sat in the Ballers office with Sediko's documents. She was signing the club over to herself. With no word from Sediko, she was doing what was right for her and her only. Ballers Bar was officially hers. Within the same week she had done three live interviews: Graham Newton– funny; celebrity woman sale for Aids charity– funnier and now she was in the middle of her MTV interview with Joel, a famous R&B artist. Her final big change had been her new agent, who had immediately bagged her these three interviews.

Joel was a nice guy and made it easy for her as they talked like they had known each other for years. Prevor directed her as she smiled at the camera. She felt relaxed and at ease and best of all she was as sober as a good judge.

After the interview Joel was whisked off by his minders to a secret destination but not before personally giving her two tickets to his concert New Year's Eve.

"Bring a girlfriend," he whispered in her ear then left.

"So that went well," Tom said smiling.

"Yeah," she nodded, also pleased with the result.

"You're a natural." Prevor winked at her.

"Yeah," she said again.

"You alright?" Tom was ass-kissing at the moment; he was a fresh but efficient agent.

No, I'm still thinking obsessively! she wanted to scream.

"What?" She kept losing track.

"I think she's ready to go." Anna took her hand and gently pulled her along.

"I'll catch you later then?" Tom asked.

"At the club." Prevor blew her a kiss.

"That was brilliant, you are brilliant," someone else said.

"Yeah, yeah thanks," Kellie replied to them all. Anna pulled her gently out and guided her toward the exit.

Outside, she breathed as if she had been choking.

At the end of the two week change, Kellie sat in her new front room on one of her unpacked boxes. Her front door chimed.

"Mandy!" Kellie hugged her. "I didn't think that you'd come." Kellie pulled her in, it had been over three months since she'd seen her last.

"This place is nice Kel," Mandy commented as she wandered into the front room. "Still unpacking?"

"Thanks for coming."

"It's alright. You could have phoned me. A post card? Come *on*."

"Well, I didn't know if you'd come. You haven't been to the club and I haven't seen you in ages."

She had sent a lengthy letter of apology and an invite to both Mandy and Mo. Mo had not yet replied.

"I was surprised when you said you moved. That was quick!"

"Yeah, well I had to make a few changes."

Kellie sat back on her box. She had thrown the old sofa away and was waiting for new modern ones.

"You ready then?" They headed out to dinner.

In her car, a short silence forced Mandy into small talk.

"So how come you moved?"

"Just wanted a scenery swap."

"New car, very nice."

"Yeah, new car, new house and new agent. Most importantly I'm clean now."

"Wow, you *have* been busy. Why all the big changes?"

"Why all the questions."

"Cos you seem different somehow."

"Am I?"

"You seen Sediko?"

"No, why?" She felt butterflies in her stomach.

"He *is* gone then."

"What?!" Kellie slammed her foot on the brake and they both lunged forwards, only their seat belts stopping them both from flying out the window. Luckily, no car was behind.

"Shit!" Mandy shouted. "Are you crazy?! You trying to kill us?!"

"Who got killed?" Kellie asked, her eyes wide, ready to be caught out in her big lie.

"What you going on about?" Mandy asked looking confused.
Kellie just stared at her.

"Kellie, what is up?" Mandy demanded.

"You said, what did you say?" Kellie stuttered. Her eyes were still fixed, her foot still on the brake and both hands were wrapped so tight around the steering wheel that she had to let go and shake her fingers free from tingling.

"I said that Sediko was gone, Path ain't seen him, nor Bones."

"Oh," she whispered nodding.
BeepBeepHonkBeep. She looked in her rearview mirror to a six car back-up. She turned her attentions back to the road and drove on.

"Kellie, you alright?"

"No actually. Would you mind going back to mine and ordering a take-away instead?"

"Course not, let's go."
They drove in silence.

"So where are we going?" Mandy asked her.

"To my house."

"And where's that?" Mandy looked at her as if she was going mad. She looked at the road ahead of her and realised that she was driving towards Bermondsey, toward her old house. She quickly and dangerously u-turned and continued to Crystal Palace in silence.

As soon as they reached the house, Mandy started on her.

"Right, now that we're safe, what is going *on*?"

"Nothing but nightmares." She hadn't meant to say that aloud.

"Forget nightmares, what's going on in your real world?"

"Nothing, I made some changes. I thought you'd be happy."

"I am, don't get me wrong. I'm proud of what you've done but I've spent only a hour with you and I can tell that something ain't right.

Ow." She tripped on one of the boxes and all her shoes spilled out.

"Oh sorry, haven't had time to unpack." Kellie began to tidy the shoe mess.

"Whose are these? Sediko's?" Mandy held up two Rolexes. Kellie just stared at them.

"What's wrong?" Mandy threw them casually into the box.

"I'm fine."

"Yeah, you're always fine. It is alright to talk you know, that's what friends are for."

"I do talk to you."

"But you don't really talk, you don't say how you feel. You say you're happy with these changes but I haven't seen you smile."

"I'm not the same person that I used to be." Kellie paced the room.

"What do you mean?" Mandy's eyes followed her.

"I changed, I had to, I lost touch with the person I used to be well before I even met you."

"So why you act like that when I asked about Sediko? He is gone, innit? Did he do something to you?"

"No," she choked, she was almost in tears. Sediko was gone, she couldn't feel or see him.

"Kellie?"

"What?" Kellie sighed loudly and sat herself down on the cold floor.

"You tell me, you invited me."

"Sediko I- Mandy I- it's so bad," she groaned.

"Go on, what's bad, what's going on? I know it's something. Path and Bones searching for his ass. Kellie, I'm getting impatient."

"I-I-I love him." Kellie bowed out from the truth.

"What's bad about that?" Mandy was disappointed at her revelation.

"It's bad because I'm never gonna see him again."
She held back her tears.

"How do you know?"

"Because he signed the club over to me."

"What? Did he!" She was shocked.

"And.."

"And he said that he wasn't coming back."
She had to secure herself.

"Why didn't you say?"

"Because I don't know where he is." Her tears fell as she spun a web of lies.

"Why didn't he tell Path?"

"How do I know? He's not coming back and it's all my fault."

"Why is it your fault? You're not making sense."

"Look, let's just forget it."

"But it's been weeks, aren't you worried?" Mandy came and sat beside her, then saw her tears.

Kellie nodded. She was worried. Worried and waiting for her

comeuppance.

≈≈≈≈

Bill sat in the waiting room; his solicitor paced the room. He had a sinking feeling in his stomach as he waited for Marie; she was late for her own divorce proceedings. They were about to throw away 16 years of marriage; was he ready for that? He loved his family, he loved living in the family environment. Latina couldn't cook to save her life and she was getting in his way. She tidied the house from top to bottom every day and then asked if he wanted anything else to be done. She was more like his live-in maid. If it weren't for Latina, Marie would have probably moved back in by now! But instead she had kept her distance, as did Carrie.

The door opened and there she was, 90 minutes late and looking beautiful; her new haircut really did take years off her.

"Sorry," she apologised to his solicitor without explanation. She then turned to him.

"Bill I-" "Marie I-" They both began.

"You first," he said quickly.

"I was just going to say, well....ask if you think we're still doing the right thing? We haven't talked about it." He could see love in her eyes and he let her continue. "I keep thinking that after this there is no going back, I'll forever be a divorcee. I still love you."

"And I'm still deeply in love with you." He stepped forward to embrace his marriage. She stepped back.

"We still have a lot to talk about; a lot to leave behind."

"Yes, yes, you're right. We could discuss this over dinner?"

"I hope so."

"Mr Laymend."

"Ms Fletcher-Johnson."

Both the briefs looked at them.

"That's Mrs Laymend to you, this is a married woman," Bill spat at her solicitor.

Thirty minutes later, they sat in a small salad bar.

"So what about that woman?" she immediately asked.

"Who?" He meant which one, but saying that would get him a slap in the face.

"Come on, Bill."

"She's gone."

"Gone where?" She sat beautifully in front of him. "When?"

"Marie, I thought that this was about me and you? Don't obsess alright, she's gone."

"So you're saying it's over between the two of you? Lisa, too?"

"I haven't seen her in ages."

"Oh, so you were faithful to your prostitute but not to me?"

"Marie, please. Maybe this wasn't such a good idea."

"Please what?"

"Don't you want to get through this?" he moaned at her.

"I do, that's why we have to talk, get everything out into the open. I want no more surprises Bill."

"No more surprises, I promise."

"So, how did you meet her?"

"Well she *is* a prostitute, how else do you think we met?"

"I hope you're not saying that she really *is* a prostitute?"

"Well yes, I thought you knew, you called her a-"

"Yes, but I was just- I can't believe this, oh my good god!"

"Marie, really..."

"I'm leaving. You disgust me!" She got up and ran out of the salad bar.

An hour, two chicken salads and a beer later, he left the café and went to Burt's.

"So, you alright mate?"

"Yeah, just fucking great."

"Okay. How's Latina then?"

"She's in the way."

"Oh yeah, the divorce proceedings, how did it go? Cut and dry is it?" Burt asked softly.

Bill filled him in.

"Bummer," Burt said afterwards. "So what you going to do about Latina?"

"I have to cut her loose."

"Best thing to do. You want a drink?" He went over to the bar.

"I need a scotch."

At 4:00 pm, after three hours of heavy drinking, Bill drove towards Soho to his office. Alcohol swirled around in his head; he prayed that he didn't get stopped.

He walked past Sally and into his office. He slumped into his chair. There was a knock on the door.

"Come," he called out.

Sally came in.

"Are you alright sir?" He did look a mess– his tie loose, his shirt open three buttons and his eyes bloodshot.

"I'm fine, haven't you got work to do?" He waved her away but she didn't move.

"Yes but-"

"Go on then!" he shouted and swivelled in his chair to face the window.

"Well you missed your two o'clock and didn't call. You know how

Mr Patel is, he says he's coming right away. That was an hour ago."

"Why didn't you call me?!"

"I tried to call but your phone was switched off," she explained.

"Alright."

"Really sir, maybe you should reschedule; you look, er, rough."

"What?"

"Maybe you should just go home and sleep it off."

"I-" He stopped himself, he couldn't be bothered anyway. He stood to leave.

"You're not driving are you sir?"

"Have you ordered me a chauffeur?"

"I-"

"No! No you haven't!"

Bill left the building; he felt fine to drive. One the way home he stopped for another few drinks, he needed some Dutch courage while telling Latina to leave. After a few more drinks, Bill sat behind the wheel and knew himself that he wasn't fit to drive. But still, stupidly, he began the drive home.

As he drove up his road he could see flashing lights ahead. As he drove closer he saw that the flashing lights were actually police cars and they were parked outside his house. He pulled up behind one of the cars– the entrance to his garage was full of police, yellow tape and all his neighbours. He got out of the car drunk and confused, and pushed past the crowd to get to his lawn.

"Move back, move back!" With his arm, an officer pushed him back, along with his nosy neighbours who, in his drunken state, hadn't yet recognised him .

"This is my house, what's going on?" He raised his voice to sound authoritative but only succeeded in looking frightened and confused. A blanket of silence as they turned to him. "I said what the hell is going on?" He pushed past the uniform and ran to his door.

What he saw lying on the ground made him instantly vomit, right in front of the officer on his doorstep. The image would forever flash in his mind; he would never, ever forget.

"Are you Mr Laymend, owner of this house?" a plain-clothes officer asked him.

"I, yes." Again, he looked into his house.

"Then I'm arresting you-" he began.

Bill felt himself being pulled back. His eyes were locked on the small limp body on the floor, covered in blood. Beside the body was one of his expensive golf clubs. Bill was sick again as he looked at the white substance that clung to it.

"What are you doing!?" They couldn't be arresting him! He hadn't killed her! He did want her gone though, he was just about to make her go. Bill began to cry. He had made a mess of everything. He bawled big fat baby tears as the tabloid cameras clicked.

They loaded him in the car and drove him away.

≈≈≈

It was New Year's Eve and for the moment Kellie sat alone in the Ballers office. The same old nightmares had continued to haunt her. She wore a £3000 designer suit, a pair of £1,500 Manolo Blanket to-die-for sandals and she looked stunning on the outside but inside she was screaming.

Mandy and Mo came busting through the back door, full of laughter.

"Yeah, I am glad that we went," Mo said laughing with Mandy; they had all just returned from Joel's concert.

"You alright Kellie?" Mo asked, turning toward her.

"Yeah, I'm alright but I might go home." These past two weeks were going too well and she hadn't heard anything from that night six weeks ago.

"Home?" Mandy looked worried. "Its New Year's Eve, come on, it's proper lively out there!"

"I don't feel good." She knew a forbidden something that could instantly make it alright.

"Kellie, we know that you've been, well you know, but we're both here for you," Mandy reassured her softly.

"You don't know what I'm going through!" Kellie shouted suddenly.

"Kellie," Mo sat beside her, "I know I haven't been around lately. You lost your baby and I wasn't there, you finished with Sediko, you moved, you've done so much and I wasn't there for you and I'm sorry, really sorry. I'm glad that you've stopped smoking and I can slowly see my friend coming back. So you're right when you say that I don't know what you're going through, but I'm here now and so is Mandy, for, whenever you're ready to talk. I'm still your bestest friend."

Mo had finally forgiven her. But if only she could really tell her the truth, tell her the real pain and guilt that she was feeling. Confess that the way she was missing Sediko was killing her, tearing her apart inside. Every time she thought about him she wanted to burst out in tears, she missed him so much that it hurt. She was constantly looking over her shoulder, and she had almost called the police on *herself* last week. She wanted to go to either of their houses just to check, but she couldn't. She just wanted to know what had happened. Sediko would have contacted her by now, he would have contacted *someone* by now. She was so scared, but maybe deep down inside she didn't really want to know.

"Kellie!" Mandy and Mo called, interrupting her thoughts.

"I'm going home, you two stay and enjoy yourselves. I don't feel good at all."

The New Year brought new obstacles. Kellie had just finished a 7-second advert for Oman products and on the drive home she could still pretend to feel like the successful, smart, beautiful woman that she was. But alone now, the facade slowly faded and she was turning back into lonely, scared Kellie. All the people who moments ago had lavished her with all that attention, all that love, would eventually find out that she was a murderer. She thought of poor Bill, on bail, charged for murder and shivered at the thought.

Nothing could prepare her for what was waiting on her doorstep as she pulled up to her drive. She slammed on her brakes and then blinked to make sure that she was seeing right. Then slowly, she rolled into her parking space. Her eyes locked on the figure sitting on her doorstep– alive and kicking! She sat rigid, her heart thundering in her chest. She wanted to reverse and speed off down the road but she couldn't run from her own home, so she unclipped her seat belt and switched off the engine.

Kellie was shaking and sweating. She felt so hot. And if she had ever wanted rock before, never more so than at this moment! She wanted to shake the feeling of dread that she was feeling. She wished that she was carrying her gun like she had so often in the past, but wrongly she had come to the conclusion that she didn't need it.

Slowly, she got out of her Lotus. He stood. Step by heavy step she moved towards him.

"What...what do you want?" Her voice was shaky and her eyes were locked with his. Maybe this was her time to die. It could happen in just a second and no one would be able to save her.

"What do you *think* I want?" His voice was husky and still sexy.

"I ain't got time for games, Shawn." She went to pass him and he blocked her.

"I think we should talk, don't you? Gonna invite me in?" His voice held no emotion nor did his face or body language.

"You can't come in, I'm busy. Let me pass." Again, she tried to pass and he blocked her way.

"Don't you want to know what happened to your precious fiancée?" he asked her.

She looked up at him. That was the burning question that left her with haunting nightmares, that was the question that she was needing so desperately to know the answer to. Almost two months had passed and now here he was asking her if she wanted to know the truth. And now he was here to finish her off! She had shot him, she had shot him for her precious fiancée. She had to think quickly. She would have to let him in.

"Well? I keep telling you that I've waited long enough."

He stood aside as Kellie took out her keys. As he stood behind her, she waited for his hands to find her neck and squeeze. Or a quick sharp jab in her back. Maybe a single shot to her head that would kill her instantly. She was shaking violently and visibly. She had robbed him, shot him and left him for dead. Why hadn't he killed her already?!

Kellie led him into her front room.

"It's my birthday today," he said standing directly in front of her. She nodded.

"So what do you want? As if it ain't obvious."

"Obvious is it? Well, then why am I here?" He looked serious; he hadn't cracked a smile or offered the slightest glimpse of reassurance. She was done for.

"Well, you've come to get your own back, to deal with me. Well come on then! Don't hold back, do what you got to do!" she shouted; she was ready to die.

She had left a small mark in the world, at least Samuel would know that his mother was successful and known, she thought. No! Shawn wouldn't get away with it! She wasn't going to leave her child motherless, just wait for the inevitable and go out easy! She was smarter and stronger than that. Suddenly she punched Shawn in his face as hard as she could and stepped back.

"What you doing!" He grabbed her, his face full of surprise and now aching. He held onto both her arms as she tried to defend her life. She cried and tried to pull away from his final embrace. "Kellie calm down! What's wrong? Calm down." His grip on her tightened.

"Let me go! Please, let me go, just let me go," she begged her killer and wriggled around in his arms.

"Stop! Stop!" He pulled her into his chest and held her tighter. "I haven't come to hurt you Kellie I promise! I haven't come to hurt you. Just calm down," he breathed heavily into her hair. She went limp in his arms and he held her on her feet. *He hadn't come to kill her! He hadn't come to kill her!*

"You alright?" His voice was full of concern. His grip loosened into an embrace and she stood in his arms. She kept her tearful face held low. "You're shaking."

"Why are you here?" she asked into his shoulder, she couldn't look him in the eye just yet.

"Not to hurt you." He still held her. She sighed in relief but cringed at jumping to her own conclusions.

"Well, then why?"

"I'm here because I've missed you." His words washed over her slowly and slowly she lifted her head to look into his eyes.

"Why?" was all she could manage; she had shot him.

"You said to me once that if you weren't with Two-Face that we would have a chance. Well, here I am now." She pulled away from him.

"But why do you want me?"

"I know that you shot me, ha. It hurt. And now you're trying to attack man. But still, here I am."

"Shawn." She needed a minute to think. If Shawn was standing in front of her, then where was Sediko?

"Kellie?"

"Why did you wait so long to contact me?" she whispered. *All those weeks of long nights wondering, thinking that I was a murderer!*

"You *did* shoot me."

"So what happened, what happened to Sediko?" She almost didn't want to ask, she was terrified of the answer.

"Put it this way, he's gone."

"That's not an answer!"

"You haven't answered *me*."

"Shawn, I thought that you were dead! Then you just turn up here, I thought you were gonna kill me. I've been having dreams and I've been going mad! I can't even think. I still can't believe you're here." Kellie couldn't hide the distress in her voice.

"Baby, baby, baby." He held out his arms for her to return to him but her feet were planted in the ground and she couldn't move.

"Where did I shoot you?" she muttered.

He lifted his shirt to reveal a big, white, bandage.

"Just missed my lung."

"I'm so sorry." Her hand went up to her mouth and tears again sprang into her eyes. She stared at it; had she done that? He dropped his shirt.

"It's alright, I'm alright."

"I don't know what I was thinking. I just pulled the trigger I couldn't see, Sediko he-" she couldn't continue. "Shawn, I need to know. Sediko. Where is he, what did you do?" She flinched as he put his finger to her lips.

"Shhh. Relax, forget the past. It's me standing here now, not him." He came close to her. She felt butterflies in her stomach. She felt emotions that she didn't want to feel. Fear, excitement, anger, relief, guilt.

"Why don't we open a bottle of wine?"

"Wine?! No! How come you're alive?!"

"It was only one bullet; I said I was fine."

"Sediko had only one bullet. Didn't he?"

"Forget the past. You've been moving forwards since then, why stop now?"

"I haven't been moving on! Maybe on the outside but when I'm alone I'm fucking scared! Every day I thought that the police were gonna kick my door down and arrest me! You don't know what I've been going through! Lying to my friends, sneaking around!"

"Two-Face is out of your life, you can be happy."

"You're so sure?"

"If you give me a chance, I can make you happy."

"Really? Well Sediko did make me happy! The only thing I hated was all the secrets and lies, all the private business. We always found out things about each other from other people."

254

"You can't put all that on me, I ain't him, I've got no reason to hide anything from you."

"Please, you've got every reason to hide everything. When I did try and confront you, you were dodging answers. You kept yourself hidden!"

"I kept myself hidden from Sediko, not you."

"Yeah and you were using me to get at him! Just admit it, tell me what happened to Sediko," Kellie demanded.

"You want me to explain everything at once?"

"Take your time."

"You know what's best. When you get that man from inside your brain, call me."

He was leaving. Kellie didn't want him to leave. She wanted him to stay, stay the night just to hold her in his arms. Shawn left the room. She heard her front door open.

"Wait! Shawn wait!" She ran to the door. He stopped outside.

"Don't go, I want you to stay, please stay with me," Kellie said weakly.

"You sure?" he asked.

She nodded and hugged him tight as he came back to her.

Kellie sat opposite Bill at the back of a secluded restaurant, out of view. It was Valentine's night.

"My life is over," Bill moaned. His full beard didn't suit him.

"Have you told the police everything?"

"Of course, the ones that believe me are laughing at me and the ones who don't want to crucify me! Did you see the paper? That picture of me? You see my eyes? Huh, huh? They were bloodshot and evil, I looked just like a murderer! Half her brain stuck to my favourite club. Shit." He looked depressed.

"All you can do is tell the truth."

"The truth is, I was just about to go home and break it off. I was going to tell her that it was over and that it never really began; I wanted to get rid of her."

"You need to watch how you phrase things, Bill," she advised.

They talked for hours. Bill did most of the talking– about Marie and Carrie and how they were both ignoring him now. Kellie sat, listened, and nodded.

On the drive home, Shawn was on her mind. She hadn't seen or heard anything from him since that night, a month ago today. He had stayed with her just as she had asked and he had held her in his arms and allowed her to talk about Sediko all night; he allowed her to talk about the fact that he might be dead. He was the only one that she could talk to and all that time he lay silently beside her. When she had awoke in the morning he was gone. He left no contact number, no note and hadn't phoned, visited, nothing. She wouldn't dare to go to his house in Green Park. Too many memories of madness, too many memories of Sediko. She had put questions about him aside. Shawn's words were 'I wouldn't be here if he was still around.' She worked that out to mean only one thing: Sediko was dead.

The next day Kellie drove to Haydon's barbershop in Battersea. At the back of her mind she was hoping to go in and see him sitting on the barber's chair, or miraculously be waiting upstairs for her. She wished him to just appear, like Shawn did.

"What's up Jayson, anyone upstairs?" she asked him. She hadn't seen him in over a year and he spun nervously to face her.

"Na, I haven't seen anyone in ages. No one's been in, including the customers. I been sitting here for weeks."

"So no customers, no money to collect?"

"Exactly, no rent money. They wrote to say that they'll come and repossess. I'm gonna sell up."

"Alright, whatever. Just contact me in Ballers with the details." She turned to leave.

"What about Two-Face?"

"What about him?" She stopped.

"Don't he get a say?"

"He gave his half of Haydon's to me as a present, you know him and his surprises."

"What about the games machines?"

"You asking way too many questions. Bring the money to the club tonight," she instructed and left.

Tonight she would put herself out there; everyone would get a say. And tonight she would cut loose all unwanted ties.

She made three trips to see Sediko's contacts– the ones that had called her after not being able to find him. They didn't care who gave them the drugs, as long as it was regular. And she had to collect Sediko's money, otherwise it would just stay uncollected. She had contacted his link to his shipment, said a few words, and now all she had to do was collect. It was as easy as that.

When she eventually got to Ballers, she put all the money in the office safe. This time she was filling it, not emptying it.

Thirty minutes later, her unwanted guests sat around her table all waiting for her to sit and start the long awaited meeting. She pulled out her chair at the head of the table. Around the table sat Bones, Path, Candy, Jayson and Jade.

"Everyone's here then," she said then sat.

The mayhem started instantly.

"Where's my boy Kellie? Some funny shit is going on," Path started.

"Your boy's gone," she said calmly and sternly.

"What?"

"Yes Path, you heard, he is gone."

"How you know?" Bones had a worried look on his face.

"Have you seen him?" Kellie turned to him and asked.

Bones shook his head. She looked to Path, then to Candy. They all stayed silent.

"So, I guess we all agree that he's gone."

"So why-" Path started and Kellie cut in, as she hadn't finished her starting speech.

"And he left everything for me."

"I doubt that," Candy spat.

"You, you're lucky that you're even here. I can't even stand to look at you. So if you have nothing proper to say then shut up."

"He gave the club to you?" Path grinned as if this was a big joke.

"Yes."

"Is this a joke?"

"No Path, it's not."

"You're saying that my boy left his whole club to you?"

"Yes."

"So what about my 10%?" Bones asked her.

"What 10%?" Kellie asked him.

"Kellie," Path cut in, "...you know that we had ten fucking percent! Don't play like you didn't know! I can't believe that you're saying he gave the shit to you."

"Did you put any papers towards this? Cos that's what it's all about, innit? Cold hard cash, not a nigga's word. Are your names on any dotted lines?"

"Two-Face wouldn't fuck us like that!" Path shouted and stood to go to the bar. Bones took a ready-made spliff from his pocket.

"Bones, no smoking in my office and Path the drinks are not free," she quickly said before they poured and lit.

"What?" Path turned angrily to her.

"I said the drinks are not free, you and all the rest got to pay." She raised her voice slightly. Path returned to his seat looking to Candy and Bones for answers.

"So Sediko packed up and left, left his club, his boys? For what? To go where?" Candy quizzed her.

"I don't know, maybe you should know. You were the one fucking him! I'm not here to discuss Sediko's whereabouts. I, of all people, wish I knew where he was."

"He wouldn't just go without saying. Not without telling his boys," Bones challenged her.

"What's with you and all this 'boys' talk. What about when his 'boys' Sparrow and Image fucked him up? Weren't they his so called 'boys'?"

"We all rode that sentence!" Path shouted at her.

"Well that's how tight so called 'boys' are."

"What about my ten percent!" Path banged the table.

"There is no ten percent," Kellie said calmly.

"My girl's trying to thief us!" Path turned to Bones begging with his eyes for Bones to agree. Bones nodded.

"Why would I deprive you of a measly 20%? I don't need that shit and you well know."

"You're crazy, you must think that man's a fool! I ain't walking outta here without my 10%!"

"Okay, you're not walking. Well then, you can run, skip, or crawl cos you ain't even getting so much as a glass of water! Not a thing, this is *my* shit! That's what I've been trying to explain to you nicely but you're refusing to listen!"

"What I think they're trying to say is that Sediko wouldn't go without telling them," Jayson offered from his side of the table.

"Did I ask you to fucking translate! Did I!" Path raged at him across the table.

"Alright nigga, man calm down, shit." Bones patted Path's shoulder and he sat slowly.

"You know wha, mek mi put two and two togedder," Candy said in Patios. She stood and walked around to a fuming Path. She rested her hands on his shoulder while everyone awaited her total. "Mia garn." She stopped.

"Gone where?" Path asked quickly. Kellie succeeded to look uninterested while her mind was begging Candy to explain.

"No one know. She jus' up an leave. Lef de pikney wid de fada."

"And your point is?" Kellie tried to keep control of the table.

"Well, they're both gone and it seems like you trying to punish him," Path finished for Candy, satisfied with Candy's story.

If only that were true.

"Yes im garn wid im matey," Candy concluded, laughing at her.

"You know what Kellie? I wanna see papers. I wanna see Sediko's signature signing shit over to you!" Path shouted.

Candy smiled smugly.

"When your solicitor contacts mine you'll see papers, until then, anything else?" She looked at them, she was ready to fall but she had to stay strong.

"So right, now it's your word against his?" Bones asked her.

"What are you getting at?" Kellie sighed.

"Who else has seen them papers? Apart from you," Bones continued.

"I have," Jade spoke up.

"And who the fuck are you?" Path spat.

"I'm the bar manager."

"Do not speak to my staff like that. I think it's time for you to go. I've answered all your questions."

"It's all good." Path stood.

"Let's go." Bones stood.

Kellie stood. Path walked over, stood directly in her face and tried to stare her down. She didn't move back, she stood her ground.

"What you gonna do, beat the 20% out of me? Cos that's what you boys do best, innit?"

"You used to be a nobody and now you're a somebody," Path spat and walked away.

"Everyone out! Jayson, leave my money on the bar."

One by one they walked out, kissing their teeth or muttering something under their breath. Jade gave her a reassuring nod. Bones was last to leave; he stopped on his way out.

"I'll speak to my boy Kellie, sort all this shit out."

"There's nothing to sort out. Like I said, a solicitor is the only man that can help you. It was your 'boy' that got you into this." She closed the door and locked it behind him.

Kellie sat back at the head of the table. Candy said that Mia was gone. Gone and left her baby?! How could she? That bitch! Sediko couldn't have left with her.

An hour later she was sitting in her car outside Mia's flat in Gypsy Hill. She watched the door. Lights on but no movement in or out. She got out the car and went to the door. For once in her life she wanted to see Mia; wanted her to open the door with her baby in her arms. She knocked and waited a minute or two before Kirk opened the door– bare chested, and holding his baby.

"Kellie?" He stared at her.

She wanted to turn back but he moved aside for her to enter. She paused. She was going to walk into the house of the woman that ruined her life. A woman that had Sediko running back and forth like a yo-yo. Kirk stared at her waiting.

"I-"

"You coming in or what? It's cold."

"Yeah," she nodded, then stepped in. He led her into the tiny flat.

"So is it true? Mia's gone?" Kellie came right out with it.

"Yep." Kirk sat down with his son, who was now almost ten months. "Where is she?"

"Canada. Family."

"You hear from her?"

"Once or twice, why? Furthermore what are *you* doing here? Your man ruined my life."

"Yeah, tell me about it," Kellie sighed.

"I loved Mia! I helped her, done all sorts of shit for her, but no matter what I did she just kept going back to him. And now she's left because of him! She was devastated when she found out that I was Karim's dad. She was gutted."

"I'm sorry," Kellie sympathised. She didn't mean for him to really tell her about it.

"Yeah well, maybe it's for the best, at least she's away from him."

Kellie had heard enough. Seconds later she left, unsatisfied. What did Kirk know? Shawn was the only one that could answer her questions and he hadn't given her a straight one. She couldn't just be left wondering forever! Either he was with Mia or he was dead.

That night Kellie lay in bed with Sediko and Samuel on her mind. She missed them both madly and deeply. It seemed that they were a finished chapter of her life. Samuel was six and settled in a life without her. She couldn't haul him out of that again. And Sediko? Sediko! Always leaving her wondering, guessing, on tenterhooks. Once upon a time she thought that she couldn't live without him, but now she had no choice.

Weeks later and her new agent was gone– a good decision gone bad. She was isolated at the moment; work-home, home-work. The only soul that got her undivided attention was her personal trainer who pushed her to limits she didn't know she had.

A knock at the door. Kellie got up to answer it; she didn't have visitors.

"Who is it?" she asked; a finger blocked the spy hole.

"It's me." The voice was familiar.

Kellie opened the door, and unable to see anyone, she stepped out. Hands covered her eyes from behind.

"Who's that?" She laughed playfully.

She spun around to Shawn.

"Hello beautiful."

"I'm not even talking to you." She smiled and walked inside leaving the door open for him to follow.

"How you been?"

"If you really wanted to know you would have come to see me."

"I wanted to give you some space."

"Did I say that I wanted space? Two months worth?"

"You didn't *have* to say. You wanna go out for dinner?"

"You wanna stay in for dinner?" she offered.

Shawn sat down. Kellie watched him get comfortable then sat down beside him.

"Kellie, you know how long I've waited for you?"

"Just waiting?" Kellie nodded. "You been doing shit to pass time though."

"Why can't you just accept that I been waiting?"

"Alright."

"So, you mine yet?"

"I'm no one's." She looked at him.

"It's lonely being no one's. Why don't you want me?"

"You know that I've always liked you."

"So then, what's up?"

"It's hard for me to just move on."

"Move on, it's been what, five months?"

"I need to put certain feelings to rest. I'm not sure you really wanna know."

"Go on. I may not like it but I wanna know what's stopping me from having you."

"Shawn that night, that night I can't just forget, I shot you! And I done it for Sediko. You have to understand that I would do anything for him. That night we argued-" She began to cry.

"I know, you told me you both said some spiteful things."

"Yes, and I still loved him. At that point I would have killed for him."

"What are you getting at?"

"What I'm saying is Shawn, if Sediko is alive... I know that he'll come back for me. I know he will, and if he sees you, you and me together, he'll kill you. And I still think about him, wait for him, wait for him to come and find me just like you did. If you can just reassure me. I want him to be alright, I need to know."

"You really wanna know?"

"Yes. Aren't you the one that wants me to move on? Put the past behind me?"

"Alright, so what your saying is, if Two-Face is dead, then me and you got a chance?"

"Shawn, just tell me! Don't you think I've waited long enough!"

"But if I say I killed him, you'll hate me."

"This ain't about you."

"If I say he's dead you hate me and if I say he's not dead then me and you haven't got a chance!"

"This is about me! I have a right to know, I need to know!"

"There was a lot of shit that you didn't know about Two-Face, things he didn't want you involved in. What's one last thing?"

"Shawn, I'm gonna ask you one last time."

"He's dead," he said simply.

"Wha?"

"You heard right." He stood up. Kellie sat and soaked up the news. He was dead. He was really gone, gone from her for good.

"What did you do with him?" she asked as tears formed in her eyes. She was in a state of shock.

"I don't think you wanna know."

"NO NO NO NO NO!" she shouted out loud. Guilt washed over her as her words from that night played and played in her mind. She had told him that she wished Shawn would take his life! She told him that she hated him and the last thing that Sediko said to her was 'I love you.'

Reality set in the pit of her stomach like cement. She had practically taken over his whole life while he lay dead somewhere. She was collecting his money and he hadn't even had a funeral. She was famous and loved, but his body was rotting away somewhere, a cold corpse. She closed her eyes. Shawn had killed him and she wished that she could blame and hate him for it. But it was all her fault! He had followed her, why did he follow her that night? And why had his last words been 'I love you?' Why did those have to be the words?!

"You alright?" he asked her gently, still standing.

"No, no I'm not." She wiped her tears clear but they kept falling.

"I shouldn't have told you." He kneeled in front of her.

Kellie stayed silent. She wanted to scream out how much she loved Sediko, she wanted to tell him how her heart felt at that moment but she couldn't put all that on him, he would never understand. She stood quickly and ran upstairs to her bedroom. He followed her. She dragged her suitcase from the cupboard and began to stuff the clothes in the bag.

"What are you doing! Where you going?"

"I just need to go for a few days! I need to clear my head Shawn, or I'll go mad, I'll go mad!"

"I can be here for you."

"No you can't! I wish you could understand!" She stuffed the case with tears and visions of a beach in her eyes.

"Let me come with you."

"No!"

"Why?" He followed her from draw to cupboard to bed.

"Because, because.."

"I knew it! You hate me don't you!"

"I.. I.. Hate is out of my life now," Kellie almost whispered.

"Please Kellie, let me come with you. Give me a chance."

"The thing is, I don't blame you, it was all my fault, I'm to blame. You may have pulled the trigger Shawn, but it was my fault that he was there! You haven't even asked me what we were doing there!"

"I don't care, as far as I'm concerned, that was the past."

"I'll ruin your life." Kellie pulled away from him.

"Well, let *me* make that choice!"

"Just leave it Shawn. I'm going alone," she said to him sternly.

"At least let me help you. Where you gonna go?"

"I don't know, anywhere I like. Spain, maybe."

"Alright, let me drop you to the airport and wait with you," he pleaded.

"No! You can call me a cab straight to Gatwick."

"Forget the holiday. I'm taking you somewhere. You'll need clothes, so keep packing."

"Shawn." She slumped on the bed, it seemed now that all her life was to be a constant fight, a constant battle.

"Please Kellie, give me a chance.

Hours later, they were alone in a booth up on the London Eye.

"I thought you said I'll need a bag?" Kellie said, looking over the city of London almost grinning.

"Well, if you didn't like my idea then you probably would have gone to the airport anyway." He grinned.

"This is nice." She looked over at the small lights below her. She sighed and the tears began to fall again.

Months and months had passed without him. Not a day had passed without him in her thoughts and now that had to stop. She had to move on. She would never feel his sweet love again.

"I feel sick." Shawn sat down.

"Do you?" Kellie sat beside him.

"I hate heights, this is too high."

"So why are we here?" She put a friendly arm around his shoulder.

"I wanted to do something to cheer you up, make you smile that beautiful smile."

"Well you have now, thank you." She laughed and shook her head. "We still got another twenty minutes or so."

"I'll be alright, just need to stay sitting."

"You're crazy." She laughed again.

"Yeah, for you."

"You really want to understand?" Kellie asked him.

"Yes."

"Being with you is hard, watching you and accepting how different you are. Little things that you say remind me so much of him and other things you do so differently and I can't help to compare the two. I know I shouldn't, but I can't help it. I loved him deeply. I can see that you want me, and I like you, but.."

"But can I be close to you? You have to understand how I feel. When I first met you, I wanted you. I want to be here for you but I can't if you don't let me. I'll show you what it's really like to be loved."

"But-"

"I'm talking be there and love you as a friend, if that's what you want."

"You're being patient, I know." Kellie hugged him tight.

He couldn't possibly expect her to forget or to forgive herself, but she would practice moving on, with his help.

Eighteen

"NO COMMENT!" BILL pushed past paparazzi dying to take his photograph. He entered his solicitor's building, turned back to look at them, smiled, then walked on. Within minutes he sat in Andrew's office.

"Please give me some good news, Andrew." Bill sat opposite his old friend. He had a strange look on his face.

"Well, it's true that I have news, but it's not good Will." Andrew looked serious.

"Well?"

"The police found a second set of fingerprints on the golf club."

"Yes, that's what I've been saying all along! It's Pips the pimp, well of course that's not his real name–"

"The police," Andrew interrupted him, "the police haven't been able to locate a Pips, and believe me they tried. They have decided to call in others for questioning."

"Good, who?"

"Marie and Carrie."

"What? Why them? What, they couldn't possibly think that, no. I can't even say it." Bill jumped out of his chair and began to pace the room as the reality of what Andrew was saying hit home.

"I don't know what they're thinking, but I do know that we have to discuss further details–"

"Andrew–"

"Do you realise that by the time the police have finished with them it will be your word against theirs?"

"Stop! Andrew what are you suggesting?"

"First, just remember that I'm with you in this, I'm on your side and I'm telling you that the police have probably got them in there right now and they're giving incriminating evidence against you without even knowing it."

"But I'm innocent anyway! Listen they have nothing to do with this so I don't want to discuss it! It's fucking nonsense! Marie only saw her the once."

"The once? In your statement you said they never met."

"Well once or twice, what does it matter! After everything I put her through do you think I want her involved in this as well? She would have been more likely to kill Lisa Brooks than a live-in prostitute!"

"William, that sentence alone gives Marie motive ability–"

"Andrew! This is totally ridiculous!" Bill paced, then stood and worked his temple with his thumb and forefinger. He had stopped doing that years ago, it made him look desperate. And that he was, desperate to clear this whole mess away. Get him out of this eternal black hole.

"William, calm down. Remember, I'm on your side, now tell me what happened when Marie first met her."

"Nothing!"

"Did they say hello? Did-"

"Of course they didn't!" He could just see them now, being dragged to the police station. The two would be scared. He doubted if they had ever been in a cell before. Carrie would definitely be crying by now.

"Was there any malice between them?"

"No!"

"So they were perfectly civilised towards one another?" Andrew pushed him.

"What is this, I thought you were on our side?"

"Not our side, *your* side William."

"Ahh, this is complete rubbish; they'll be questioned, then let go."

"Yes, that's if none of the prints match. Forensic experts are down there now, foraging through your house, examining that golf club, enhancing, scrutinising, probing and investigating."

"Andrew you're not being helpful." Bill continued to pace.

"Alright, if there really was no bitchiness between the two, no cruel or unkind words said, then there will be no vengefulness or evil intention-"

"Marie caught Latina in her clothes, she was upset, but that wouldn't drive her to kill!"

"Maybe she didn't mean to?"

"No!"

"If not her, then your daughter-"

"Now that's enough!" Bill rushed around the table and grabbed Andrew's shirt collar. "Do not accuse my daughter!"

"Alright, alright William." He pushed Bill gently away. "Then it must be you, this is how the police will illuminate-"

"I told you and the police about Pips! That's who you should be looking for; he cleared out my house for christsakes! He took everything." Bill was definitely stressed out.

Andrew's office phone rang.

"One minute," Andrew gestured to Bill. "Yes. Put it through," he said into the phone.

Meanwhile, frantic thoughts still galloped through Bill's mind: *Why wasn't anyone listening? Everyone looks at me like I'm a murderer, or they look at me in disgust for having a live-in prostitute. And now my wife is being dragged into it. She's a murderer no more than I am. And Carrie? Well as soon as they interview her they'll see that she's not capable of doing such a thing.*

Andrew cradled the receiver slowly and looked at Bill gently.

"The good news is that they have released Carrie."

"Thank God. And so they should. And Marie, have they released her?"

"Marie is being held for further questioning."

"What! This is- look, I'm going to find my daughter, call me with anything new." He left, his problems trailing behind him.

Two hours later, Bill sat with his daughter in his car heading for home. She cried softly and her face was red.

"Don't worry, everything will be alright, I promise."

She stayed silent.

They got home and she ran straight to her room. Bill followed her, he needed to know what she had said to the police, he needed to know why the police were keeping Marie.

"Carrie, I know this is hard, a terrible thing has happened. But I need to ask you about the police interview. Did you have a solicitor, was it an informal questioning?" He sat beside her on her big bed.

"It was horrible. They asked me a million questions, I gave them a million answers but still they didn't stop," she cried.

"You and Marie have nothing to worry about, nothing at all, I know who did this and I'm going to find him."

He put his arm around her, he couldn't remember the last time that he had done that and it felt good. She was his little girl. She was a spoilt 22-year-old, younger than her years, but still his baby daughter, despite her faults.

"They asked me about Marie and I told them nothing," she whimpered.

"What do you mean you told them nothing? Well, it was probably for the best, you were without representation. But you have nothing to hide or be ashamed about– you nor Marie. I know who did this. There'll be a simple explanation and Marie will be released. And when she is, I'll sue the fuckers, I will sort this out I promise, I'm just sorry that I dragged the two of you into this."

"Daddy stop making promises!" She jumped away from him and sat at the head of the bed with her knees pulled up to her chin. "I'm not your little girl anymore, you can't protect me so stop making promises that you can't possibly keep." She snivelled and cried. He wanted to take her hurt away; they must have really messed her up in there.

"Carrie, I *will* sort this out."

"How, how?!" she shouted, distressed and overcome.

"You're in the clear, they let you go without charge. Marie will be next-"

"What if they think that Marie's got something to do with it?" she cut in.

"What did they say to you in there? What's working you up like this? Tell me what happened then maybe I can understand better."

"Daddy I-" she started. She was shaking.

"Carrie, my little buttercup." He moved closer to her.

"Mother used to call me that didn't she?" She half smiled but the tears were still falling.

"Yes, she did. And just before she left, I promised her that I would look after you. Love you no matter what, teach you right from wrong, and I have succeeded. I won't let anything happen to you now. But you have to be straight with me."

"It wasn't me, Daddy."

"I know that Buttercup."

"Jeff and I wanted no part of it," she cried.

"Jeff? Please don't tell me that he is part of this mystery."

"No, no, Daddy but *I* was. Involved."

"Involved in what exactly?" He was getting impatient, why did women like to beat around the bush with words, why didn't they just come right out and say it!

"Marie she, Daddy she..... she did it," she whispered looking at him wide eyed and terrified.

What was she saying? Oh my god! He kept a straight face. A poker face, he couldn't let Carrie see how disgusted he really was and she was looking at him, waiting for his reaction. *This just feels like the fucking end! I would have preferred it to be me! Not my wife, not Marie!* His expression was fixed and he was looking straight at her but his thoughts were almost arguing. *Why did you let Latina in! Why didn't you call the police when Pips robbed you! Why didn't you stick to married life! Why is your daughter sitting here telling you your wife is a murderer! But hold on; she's not capable of committing murder. She's your sweet wife that hates swearing.*

"Daddy?" she called his name weakly.

"I'll be in my office." Quickly, he left the room and ran to his office; he could hear Carrie follow him. He raced in and got on the phone.

"Andrew, listen to me carefully. I want you to get a solicitor down to Marie now! The best you can find. I'll meet you back at your office at 4:00." He looked up to see his daughter standing by the door; he cradled the receiver.

"Carrie, were you involved in this?" He prayed, he prayed that she was as innocent as she was 30 minutes ago. She nodded slowly. Bill said goodbye and then put down the phone, rubbing his temple and loosening his tie. She sat down opposite him.

"Please Carrie, just tell me everything." He had tears in his eyes. All this meant that he was in the clear. He could be declared innocent after months of accusation; he should have been joyous, chuffed, happy as Larry. But instead he felt depressed, inconsolable.

"She came to me one day, ages ago– that day you meant to have your divorce proceedings. She told me that the two of you had discussed getting back together over lunch but then you told her that Latina was a hooker! She was devastated, she wanted you two to get back together so desperately. How did you expect her to feel seeing that woman dressed in her clothes. It was as if Latina was replacing her; all her so-called friends were laughing and gossiping. You left her with nothing. She said that she had lived in mother's shadow for long enough.

When she first said what she wanted to do, I thought it was a joke. She said that she wanted me and Jeff to help her, help her get rid of Latina. She was ranting on, I didn't think she was serious, not really. But I went with her. She begged Jeff to come but he wanted no part of it! When we got there you had changed locks. We knocked and Latina opened. Marie was so upset after everything, Daddy that's what you have to understand, she wasn't herself. We went in and they started arguing straight away. Really shouting. Latina was shouting in her language, and I'd never seen Marie so angry, so resentful. Marie shouted that she was still your wife and Latina was saying stuff, dirty stuff about you and her. I just stood there, I couldn't get a word in even if I'd tried, and they were going at it.

Marie stormed off somewhere and Latina was just staring at me. I should have told her to run, but I didn't think she would listen! I was so scared that I couldn't move; I was standing by the door paralysed. The next thing I knew she was on the ground, and the entire floor was bloody. And she wasn't moving. I looked up at Marie and she let the golf club drop to the floor. I begged her to phone you, I threatened to call you myself but she wouldn't let me. Even after we'd left, Marie was worried that she wasn't dead! She wanted to go back and check but she said that I was in too much of a state and we had to get off the road.

At the hotel I cried and cried, but Marie was totally in control, she said that we'd be each other's alibi and when it was all over we could go back to being a family. When we found out that you were being charged, Daddy I was so scared. I wanted to tell you, I really did. But Marie said you'd get off, she said wealthy men like you don't go to prison. She promised me that everything would be alright, she promised me."

Bill sighed. His phone rang.

"Daddy, don't answer it."

"Hello?"

"It's Andrew."

"Yeah, I'll be with you soon. Have you heard anything; you do as I said?"

"William, she's refusing any legal rep."

"What? Get down there and get someone in there. You! Anyone!" He couldn't believe it, Marie had no idea what she was doing.

"She's even refusing to see her *own* solicitor. From what I've heard she's about to sign a confession statement. I'm sorry."

"Don't be sorry! Do something! Can't you just speak to her? She's not thinking straight! Tell them she's depressed, deranged, anything! Andrew I'm serious! Get my wife out of there and do it now!" Bill slammed down the phone.

"Daddy am I in trouble?" She looked drained. "I'm so sorry."

"So you told the police nothing?"

"No, nothing," she said, shaking her head vigorously.

"And Jeff knows about this?"

"Yes," she nodded.

"You should have called the police straight away Carrie, maybe she would have had a better chance. You could have at least told me!"

"Guilty! Guilty! Guilty!" the masked group chanted. She was crying and locked in a cage high above the fiery courtroom, pulling out her hair. Lisa and Latina screamed with laughter as henchmen dragged Carrie away. "NO! WAIT WAIT!" Bill jumped awake from his nightmare. Slowly, he sat up in his bed; he was shaking and sweating.

Today was the day Marie would be sentenced. Six months ago she had plead guilty to murder. She'd been refusing to see him throughout the whole horrible ordeal. He dressed quickly and went downstairs where Carrie was dressed and waiting. She had a distant look as they silently drank coffee at the table.

As they left the house, the photographers - in waiting from early morning - pounced. Bill held Carrie's hand and they walked to the car, ignoring the rapid-fire assault of questions.

"You alright?"

"Yes," she answered, but her body language screamed 'no.' He switched on the engine.

Getting through the courts was much worse. The photographers threw themselves at them, hurled their questions at them, said anything just to provoke a reaction. Bill kept a protective arm around Carrie, who was racked with guilt, as Marie had kept her name out of the confession. She blamed herself somehow and had been staying indoors all day and night, her usual fiery personality gone.

In the courtroom, Bill spotted Kellie and Lisa beneath wigs and glasses. He and Carrie sat facing forward and hand in hand. He was interested in nothing but the verdict. Marie avoided eye contact with him and Carrie cried silently. Hours went by before the court adjourned until the morning.

Bill watched them take her away.

Twenty-four hours later Bill and Carrie sat in the exact same seats. Marie stood in the exact same spot except this time she looked at him. Their eyes locked. And for a second, nothing else mattered. Her eyes were pleading with him to understand, and his were begging an apology. Tears rolled softly down his cheeks.

Why did she plead guilty? Guilty or not he would have persuaded her to plead innocent or temporary insanity. He could have gotten her off, he had connections! But those connections couldn't help her now. If only she had accepted his visits; now it was too late. He prayed and prayed.

"Twenty-five years," he heard the judge say. His head dropped; his heart fell. Marie had entered his nightmare.

"Daddy?" Carrie was distressed.

"No!" he shouted too late. He watched Marie back away, still looking at him, now with a look of dread, dread and realisation. The realisation of what she had done, of what they had done! Latina was dead and Marie was going to prison for 25 years! How he wished he could swap places with her. He turned to Andrew as they both rose from their seats.

"Get her out!"

"I can't William, I'm sorry." Pity was in his eyes.

"Marie I love you!" he shouted.

"Daddy?" Carrie looked at him as if she wanted him to make it alright.

"I'm sorry," was all that he could say.

Nineteen

KELLIE SAT AROUND her table with Samuel and Shawn and watched their friendship grow. "I can mash you up on driver," Samuel boasted, he was 7 years old now and loved computers.

"Well, we will see little man; you don't know about my skills on the game."

"Alright after dinner it's on then," challenged Samuel his mouth stuffed full of rice.

"Yeah, after dinner," Kellie told him with a smile, "Eat up."

Straight after dinner the two rushed off into the front room to play on the computer. Kellie sat alone in the kitchen. Both were staying for the weekend. Shawn made sure that she had her son with her every weekend without fail.

For a year now Shawn had been there for her as the good friend that she needed. They talked and shared feelings; they connected and became almost inseparable.

"Kellie!" Samuel called to her.

"You two play!" she called back to him.

"Quick, you're on the telly!"

"I know."

"Come *on*." He came in and pulled her off her chair.

"Alright, alright." She laughed and followed him.

She sat in the chair in front of the TV. On the screen she was being filmed while she slept.

"What's this you two? What have you two been up to?"

"Just watch." Samuel laughed and sat beside her. Shawn sat beside her, straight-faced as she watched.

"This is my mum," Samuel whispered, "Look at her face, she's famous." She remained sleep. "And this is her FRIEND." He stopped, then giggled, pointing the camera to Shawn who stood behind him stifling a laugh. "My mum fancies him but won't admit it," Sam whispered and giggled, pointing the camera to himself. "Did she say that?" Shawn whispered to him. "No. And we have got a surprise for her but she don't know cos she's asleep." The camera was back on her. "So here it is. Shawn?" He came and knelt beside her at the bed. "Kellie, I love you." Samuel giggled again behind the camera. "Shh....you. This is adult business now," Shawn laughed. "Like I was saying, I love you, I know that we're just friends and a perfect friendship it's been but, well, that's not enough. And it won't be enough to just be your boyfriend." He fumbled around in his pocket. "Erm." "Boyfriend and girlfriend," Samuel sang laughing in the background. Shawn patted his chest pocket. "Where is it?" he whispered to Samuel. "Oh here." Samuel gave him something.

271

"So Kellie, will you marry me?" he said to her sleeping body.

"Yeess," Samuel crooned then laughed.

Kellie looked to Shawn holding up the biggest diamond ring that she had ever seen.

"Now that you're awake, will you marry me?"

"Say yes, Mum."

Kellie was silent. Marry him? She did love him, he had been there for her, had been her rock for the past year helping her to put things to rest. He had helped her to love herself again, helped her to say the name 'Sediko' without feeling pangs of guilt. The name meant nothing but 'the past' to her now. So could she? Had she paid her price? Was she allowed to be happy?

"Kellie?" Shawn looked worried. Her silence meant bad news to him.

"Yes. Yes, I will."

"Yesss," Samuel hissed happily, "I told you she'd say yes," he boasted.

"You don't know how happy you've made me." He pulled her to him and she embraced him. Not as a friend, but as a future husband.

"I'm not really meant to tell anyone, that's part of my contract," Shawn replied as he lay beside her on his big half-circle bed.

"Why?" Kellie asked one night as he let her probe into his past.

"I'm a computer programmer."

"Are you? You mean a computer hacker?" She sat up on his massive bed.

"You shocked?"

"Course I'm shocked."

"Yeah, came out of school with A grades all the way through and went straight to university at 16."

"So what kind of things do you do at work?"

"Things you wouldn't understand. You heard of anti-virus software?"

"Yes, that's what stops computers getting viruses. I'm not completely dumb, I watched Matrix," she defended laughing.

"I know beautiful, well that's a fraction of what I do. Just like Neo, I know computers inside and out, including the illegal side."

They laughed.

The countdown for the wedding was delightful for Kellie; preparations were going well. The six-month engagement turned to four, then weeks into days, until their summer wedding was upon them. They were due to collect her brother Kerion from the airport. He was flying out from America to attend.

"You looking forward to meeting your uncle tomorrow, Sam?"

"Yes."

"You gonna try your suit on?"

272

"Again?"

"Go on, I wanna see how cute you look."

"Alright." He scooted out the room.

"You nervous?" Shawn asked her. "Two days and counting."

"Not at all, I can't wait to be Mrs Jones." She kissed his lips.

"Mrs Jones, Mrs Jones, Mrs Jones…." he sung to her, "we gotta thing going on." His voice wasn't too bad.

"I love you." She kissed his lips again.

"And I love you, Mrs Jones. So, you ready for your hen night?"

"Hmm. And you for your stag?"

"Yeah, as long as we both remember to respect each other's feelings," he crooned in a girlie voice.

"Yes, we both are then, on Friday."

Kellie couldn't wait to wear her wedding dress and of course she couldn't wait to say 'I do.'

"Kellie, Shawn." Samuel came in packed into the cutest little tuxedo suit by Valentino.

"Ahh, look at you." Kellie's heart melted.

"I've tried it on too many times now man, it's not gonna look nice when I wear it on the day," Sam moaned.

"On the day you'll look as handsome as the groom," Shawn reassured him.

"Can I go play computer now?" Sam asked.

"Go on," Kellie said to him with a smile; he was staying for the wedding and then throughout the summer holidays.

"I've checked everything, then double checked." She turned to her future husband. "My hair, nail and make-up people are coming to yours, we're still swapping houses cos me and the bridesmaids need room. Flowers, food, drinks, music, cake delivery, and please God don't let it rain! The limo is booked to take us to the hotel at 11:00 pm. I've got our plane tickets and-"

"Everything's gonna be alright. It'll go smooth."

"You checked your suit?"

"Yep."

"You practice your vows?"

"What vows? You mean speech."

"No, your vows! I told-"

"Yes, I have practised my vows, wanna hear them?"

"No, no. I think that's bad luck." She laughed.

The next day she, Shawn and Samuel waited in Gatwick airport. It had been years since she had last seen him. She was twelve when Kerion left at fifteen; now he was a twenty-nine year old man. They would probably have walked past each other in the street.

Kellie and her family ignored people trying to take her photograph and 45 minutes later she was throwing her arms around her older brother.

"Yo sis, look at you! All grown up." He hugged her tight.

Kellie smiled, touching his face. She felt a love in her heart for this man, her older brother. She had missed being a little sister and was devastated when he'd left.

"This is Samuel." Kellie put a hand on Sam's shoulder.

"Wait, this little man right here?" Kerion looked at him. Samuel nodded shyly. As he bent down to Samuel, Kellie studied her big brother; he looked just like their mum.

"Mum's here?" Kerion asked, holding Samuel in his arms. Kellie shook her head. His skin was dark like hers and he looked very athletic and healthy.

"And this is my husband to be." She turned proudly to Shawn, he put Samuel down and they shook hands.

"Nice to meet you, man."

"And this is Crystal." Her brother turned and a tall light-skinned woman, dressed to kill, stepped out from behind him.

"Oh, I didn't know you were bringing a friend," Kellie remarked straight faced.

"Actually, she's er, my wife."

"Oh!" Kellie didn't hide her shock.

"Hiya Crystal," Shawn greeted before the silence became too much. She nodded a rude hello and turned toward Kellie.

"I've heard so much about you Kellie." Crystal stepped up to her and smiled a stunning smile. Her lips were full and her face was almost a heart shape. She was tall and slender with a toned, athletic body.

"Oh?" *Her brother had gotten married! She had managed to contact him why hadn't he done the same?*

"Yeah, I been following my little sister's career. I'm proud of you. Come here." He hugged her again. "I'm sorry I didn't warn you about Crystal, it was a bit of a last minute thing, you know. Hope there's room."

"Of course there's room."

"Kellie look at ya." Her brother hugged her again.

"Come on, the car's waiting. You got all your stuff?"

"Yeah, yeah." Kerion held her hand as they walked.

"So, you haven't seen Mum?" he asked as they walked ahead.

"No. So you got married? When? You haven't got any kids?" Kellie looked to him.

"Na man, we been married for a few months, but it was nothing big, quiet, you know."

"No, I'm hurt that you didn't call me," she said honestly. "Crystal looks like the ice queen," Kellie whispered with a grin; he laughed.

"You got that right. So what about you? Shawn looks cool."

"He is. I love him."

"So do you like Crystal?"

"I don't know yet but I'll tell you soon enough." They laughed and chatted toward the exit.

In the limousine, Crystal sat next to her. Shawn, Samuel and Kerion chatted away and left them to talk.

"So you're a model?" Crystal asked. Kellie hated her already.

"Amongst other things, what about you?"

"Well I don't work, my daddy is rich." Her make-up was immaculate and her nails were long and French tipped. She was wearing a contemporary French designer dress. Her breasts were almost spilling from her top, but she looked elegant.

"Right," Kellie nodded. She hadn't seen her brother in ages and she was stuck talking to the ice queen.

"So you looking forward to married life?" she asked her.

"Yes. So exactly when did the two of you get married?" Kellie asked her. If she was going to be stuck talking to her she wanted valuable information.

"Four months ago. He proposed, I said yes. Small wedding and that was that." Crystal was just like the pretty girls in the black American movies.

"Did your family go?"

"Yes. Your son is so cute." She turned to Samuel.

"I know," Kellie replied.

The limousine took them straight to Shawn's house in Green Park.

"So you'll be staying in here." Kellie showed Kerion and his wife into the guest suite.

"This is beautiful. Much better than I expected." Crystal looked around.

"Much better than you-" Kellie began angrily. *How dare she?*

"So you live here too?" Kerion interrupted.

"No, I live in Crystal Palace. Right, I got to go get ready."

"Where you going, I haven't even had a chance to talk to you yet," Kerion moaned.

"Shawn's three sisters and two cousins are coming, one of them is the best man, they're coming over for dinner at six."

"Three sisters. Ouch!"

"Exactly. You two be downstairs in the dining room in exactly two hours. And well, Crystal, tonight is my hen; you're invited of course." Kellie rushed out to start getting ready.

Kellie showered with a lot on her mind: her wedding, her brother and his ice queen wife, Shawn's sisters!

Angela was the oldest of the lot, she mothered them all, even Shawn; she was alright. Monica was a few years younger than Shawn and she was easy going. But Sasha, the youngest and Shawn's favourite, was a complete bitch! And they were all invited to her hen night.

"So, I'll see you tomorrow." Shawn kissed her.

"Yes you will." She kissed him.

"Don't be late," he said softly.

"I won't be." She kissed him again.

"Come *on*!" Sasha moaned.

"Shut it you." Angela nudged her.

"You have a nice time tonight. Enjoy your last night of freedom."

"I love you Shawn Jones."

"Lets go! The limo's waiting,'" Sasha moaned again.

"Aren't we waiting for what's her name, Kellie's brother's wife?" Monica asked as they all stood in the lobby.

"I'm ready." Crystal came gliding down the stairs.

"Make sure you look after her Angela," Shawn told her.

"Make sure you look after my brother, as well as yourself. No funny business, going off to France or some shit," Kellie warned laughing.

"No. I'll be right at the altar waiting for you, like I always have. And you look beautiful."

"Thank you, you ain't seen nothing yet, you wait 'til tomorrow."

"We ready?" Crystal said a little too loud.

"And your sure you checked your suit and practised your vows?" she asked him for the millionth time.

"What suit?" He frowned.

"I know your playing with me." She grinned.

"Well, go on then and enjoy yourself." He squeezed her bum as she turned to leave. "Hold on, kiss me again."

At Ballers, Kellie sat with all her girls around her and then some. All, including her, were cheering and laughing drunkenly: Mo, Mandy, Anna, Jade, Crystal and Shawn's three sisters.

They all sat in the VIP lounge and watched fit men strut up and down the cat walk and grind down the poles.

"That one I will fuck!" Anna screamed as a fit dancer gave her a private dance.

"Come over here!" Angela called to him, wanting piece of his action.

"That one's big!" Mo screamed beside her, pointing to his crotch. Mo wasn't really a drinker but she was letting it all go tonight and was knocking back shots.

"Kellie, close your eyes, you're practically a married woman!" warned Mandy laughing, also drunk.

Yes she was, she was practically a married woman. She was twenty-five and an almost a married woman. She was sobered almost instantly.

"What's up Kel?" Mo slurred.

"Nothing. I'll be back."

As she stood to leave, Mandy and Mo laughed at the 'L' sign they had stuck to her back decorated with Durex and diaphragms.

Kellie went around the back, past the changing rooms and headed for her office. A male dancer burst out butt naked. She quickly looked at him from head to toe.

"You like?" he asked.

"No.. Well your nice but-" Her face heated up.

"You're the bride?"

"Yes, the owner actually. Nice show." She turned to walk away from his sweaty, naked body.

In the office, she stood at the large window. She watched people dance and enjoy themselves. They came and spent their money and filled her pockets. The club's anniversary was next month, on her birthday, it was turning 3.

Suddenly her mind betrayed her and she saw Sediko standing in this very spot, proud that he had opened his dream club. But he was gone now and she was marrying Shawn tomorrow. She loved him; he was affectionate, funny, smart, honest, good with Samuel and most of all he was rich and handsome.

"KELLIE!" Mandy and Mo burst into her office. "Come on, what you doing sitting in here? Come on it's your hen night, you'll be a married woman tomorrow," Mo told her.

"An' I think one of Shawn's sister has got the hots for one of the dancers," Mandy laughed.

"Alright, come on then," Kellie replied with a smile.

"And that Crystal is stoosh where did your brother pick her up from?" Mandy laughed.

"I'll soon find out." Kellie threw herself back into the partying mood. This time she was at her own party and she was enjoying herself; people that truly loved her surrounded her.

The dancers had gone and up in the VIP everyone was dancing and enjoying themselves.

"Congratulations." Prevor tapped her shoulder from behind. She turned and smiled at him, a true Ballers supporter from day one.

"Thanks."

"So how about a MTV exclusive on your wedding?"

"It's going to be exclusively *private*," she assured him laughing.

Kellie fell back into a drunken good mood as the night slipped away. She was presented with all sorts of gifts from her staff, supporters and friends. They were all piled up high in her office. Later, when they return from the honeymoon, she'd move them to Shawn's where they would both be living. She'd keep the house in Crystal Palace, it would be a change of scenery for them both when they needed it.

The next morning, Kellie awoke at the crack of dawn and proceeded to wake all her guests: her brother and wife in one suite, Shawn's sisters in another and Mandy, Mo and Anna-her bridesmaids-downstairs in the old maid's quarters. Nancy had long since moved out.

"What time are the beauticians coming?" Mo asked excitedly as all women sat down to an early breakfast. It was 6:00 am.

"7:00"

"It's too early," Sasha moaned.

"Thanks for breakfast, Angela," said Kellie as she tucked into pancakes.

"So you're very calm Kellie?" Monica said to her.

"That's because I'm tired."

"So hold on, I'm confused," Anna said laughing loudly above all the chatter,"Who *are* all you women?"

"That's Mandy and Mo, you've met them. Those three are Shawn's sisters: Monica, Angela and Sasha and that's my brother's wife Crystal. Everyone this is Anna," Kellie introduced.

"You have a brother?"

"Yes and he has a wife," Crystal spat.

"Alright, alright," Anna backed off, laughing.

"I know, I still can't believe that my brother got married."

"Yeah, well he did." Crystal closed her silk dressing gown around her.

"So why did you say that I wasn't invited?"

"It was a quick thing."

"You mean you didn't think about it?" Kellie asked her as the rest of the table stayed silent.

"We thought about it quickly."

"You rushed into it?"

"No! No, it's what we wanted."

"I hope you're making my brother happy, that's what counts."

"I make him happy."

"Good."

This woman had an attitude problem, one big chip on her shoulder and it seemed that she and her brother had had a troubled past too.

An hour later she lay in the gym with Mandy, Mo and Anna, letting the professionals make them look and feel beautiful. Oman's personal makeup artist was doing Kellie alone and trainee's were attending to her bridesmaids.

"Kellie?" someone called.

"Yeah in here, come," she called sluggishly. She felt relaxed as they massaged oil into her back.

"It's only me. Me and Monica are off to the club to check things over for the reception, can you keep an eye on Sasha?" Angela came into view in a granny dress. "Don't worry, I'll change." Angela saw her stare.

"Yeah, yeah. Thanks."

"This is great!" Anna said stiffly as they spread mudpack onto their faces.

278

"Kellie, I feel like it's *my* special day," Mo agreed.

"Yeah, thanks girl," added Mandy.

Later she and Mo sat for a private moment in Shawn's bedroom. She had called it her chief bridesmaid pep talk. Kellie unzipped her wedding dress from its silk case and laid it on the bed to admire yet again. It had been made just for her by Valentino. The rest of the wedding wear was also Valentino: Samuel and Shawn's suits and the bridesmaid's dresses.

"I'm so proud of you."

"Me?" Kellie turned to face her faithful friend.

"Of course you. You've stayed strong. And now look at you, getting married before Tex and me! You're lucky to have a man like Shawn."

"I know, I'm lucky that Shawn waited for me."

"It ain't luck. You made your bed and now it's tidy."

"So, you really like Shawn?"

"Yeah, he's a bit mysterious but in a good way, and he's a gentleman." Mo said the words that she wanted to hear. "Do you really love him? I mean really love him, as much as you did Sediko?"

Mo shocked her with that question. Did she love him that much?

"Well?"

"No. I love Shawn more. I feel secure, more open and able. I don't feel blocked out and I know he's 100% mine and only mine."

"What about his baby mother?"

"Well she ain't making things difficult and God knows she could."

"Good."

"So you haven't heard from Sediko still?"

"No."

"I thought he would have contacted you by now; you think he's in Canada?"

"No."

"So where?"

"I don't know and I don't care."

"But do you think that he's with Mia?"

"Can we change the subject I'm feeling kind of nervous now," Kellie admitted and wandered over to gaze at herself in the massive full length mirror.

Sasha burst into the room without knocking. "The hair people are here!"

"Thanks, we'll be down in a minute," Kellie told her as she invited herself in.

By eleven o'clock Kellie's hair was being washed; it would later be twirled into bouncy ringlets that fell gently around her shoulders.

"That underwear is nice," Mandy complimented.

"Thank you, it's just as important as the dress. I had an agent from

Agent Provocateur come over and make sure it went well with my dress," remarked Kellie, her head tilted awkwardly under the threat of hot curling tongs.

"You know what time it is?" Mo busted in.

"What time? Just after noon probably," Kellie replied as the gay stylist did his magic.

"More like just after 1:00! The car's outside."

"Stop,stop!" Kellie shouted at her hairdresser and jumped from the chair. "I'm supposed to be getting married in thirty minutes, why didn't anyone tell me! Help me Mo, help me get my dress on!"

"Your hair's not done!" Mandy stated the obvious."

"Just get my dress!" Kellie shouted in a panic. She slipped into it with help and looked in the mirror. The top half was a strapless satin bodice that wrapped around her breasts and body like a turban, the bottom half was spotted with real tiny teardrop shaped diamonds which made her dress sparkle. The front of the dress was raised just above the knee leaving her legs bare and the back trailing behind her by 4 yards.

"You seen the fucking time Kellie! Oh you look fabulous!" Anna burst in then admired, slipping on her barley there Jimmy Choo.

Kellie's three bridesmaids stood in front of her in their matching dresses– same style but nowhere near as stunning and without the millions of diamond droplets.

"*Now* can I finish your hair?" the stylist asked.

"No not enough time, gimmi the comb." Kellie grabbed it.

"You're ready. Come on, you're already late." Mo rushed her.

"No, no wait." She swept up her hair in its traditional sweep and left the few ringlets that he had managed to curl hanging down.

"Something old?" Mandy asked her.

"These silk gloves my mum wore when she married my dad." She pulled the long silk elbow gloves.

"New?"

"This dress, new underwear, new husband."

"Borrowed?" Anna asked next.

"No, no. Quick one of you give me something and quick." She looked at them in turn.

"Borrow what?" Mo asked.

"I don't know come on! Someone?"

"I ain't got nothing." Mandy shrugged.

"Here, take this if it's that important to you." Her stylist took off his watch.

"I can't wear a watch!"

"Pin it to your stocking, it's an emergency." He held it out.

"No!" she refused.

"Go on, at least you can time him!" he said and both Anna and the stylist roared with laughter.

"Alright, alright." She took it, lifted her dress and attached it to her stocking. "Now what's next?"

"Blue, something blue." Mo called out.

"Oh for fuck sake, who started with all this?" They were all silent. Crystal came in.

"You know you're late!" Sasha barged in, looking quite respectable.

"That's a bride's perogative sweetheart." Kellie looked again in the mirror.

"I think we're ready." Crystal turned and left the room.

"You'd better be, my brother's waiting."

"Blue, something blue." Mo called out.

"Oh for fuck sake, who started with all this?" They were all silent. Crystal came in.

"Your brother's going mad out there, he says to hurry," Crystal informed her.

"Yes, yes. I need something blue! Now!" Kellie panicked.

"Here." Crystal handed her a blue card.

"What's this?"

"A card," Crystal stated the obvious.

Kellie looked to her bridesmaid.

"That will do."

They all nodded in agreement.

"You know you're late!" Sasha barged in looking quite respectable.

"That's a bride's perogative sweetheart." Kellie looked again in the mirror.

"I think we're ready." Crystal turned and left the room.

"You'd better be, my brother's waiting."

Kerion got out of the limo as Kellie approached.

"Lil sis look at you! You look great." He hugged her tight; Crystal grunted.

"Lets go."

"You ready for this?" her brother asked her in the car as her bridesmaids fussed over her.

"Yes."

"A little too ready, not nervous or excited?" her brother asked.

Kellie poured champagne and drank it down in a few swallows.

"Slow down," Kerion warned her.

"I'm fine."

"Good. And I'm proud to walk my lil sis down the isle. I wish you could have been there for mine." He looked to her, then to Crystal.

"I'm here now." Kellie smiled at him and took his hand. How different would her life have been if her brother had stayed in England?

"Wait, wait," Kellie said, as they were about to enter the doors.

"What's up?" her brother looked at her worriedly.

"Kellie?" Mandy and Anna stopped behind her.

"I, shit." She shook her head.

"What is it?" Anna asked. "You need a little something?"

"No!" Mandy and Kellie chorused.

"Kellie, you alright sis?"

"Yeah, I just need to take a breath before you open those doors."

"You want me to-"

"No, I don't want you to do anything except give me away." Kellie smiled, nodded and reassured them all. "Were *you* scared?" she asked him, hesitating again.

"Very."

"Did you get this deep pit feeling in your stomach?"

"Yes."

"But you made the right decision right? You don't regret getting married?"

"This is about *you*, whatever you want, I'm here. If you love Shawn, then let's continue; if you're having too many doubts, me and you can walk, and you don't have to look back."

"I wouldn't have to look back?"

"Not for a second."

"Kellie?" Mandy looked at her. "You want me to get Mo?"

"No."

"Take your time girl, this decision is for the rest of your life."

"But I already made the decision." Kellie looked over at her older, wiser brother.

"You're right about one thing, *you* make the decision."

"I love him."

"That's a good start."

"There's so much..."

"You can take your time but we have to let them know something." Kerion held her hand.

Kellie stood poised. She was committed to Shawn, she was doing the right thing. She had long since said goodbye to lonely nights and separate lives. She had said goodbye to her anger and was living a normal life. She nodded and smiled at her brother.

As the door opened, the music began. Da dada dum, da dada dum. And every isle was full. Her arm was threaded through Kerion's as she gazed at Shawn standing at the altar. In his formal black tux and tails, he turned to behold her. He smiled widely as she slowly approached him. On reaching his side, she held his hand tight as the worried look on his face vanished.

They both said their promises before God and were then ready to say their own written vows; it had taken her months to find the right words and she couldn't wait to hear his.

"Kellie Anne Palmer, you will now speak your own personal vows." The priest looked at her gently. She swallowed and turned to Shawn. Suddenly her throat went dry. She took his hands in hers and her mind went blank.

"Kellie Anne Palmer, you will now speak your vows," the priest prompted but she couldn't remember a thing. Not a single word came from her lips.

"Kellie," Shawn began his instead, "I have waited a long time for this day. The day that I give you my word of honour to love, support and take care of you forever. From the second that I lay eyes on you, I silently, secretly, fell in love with you. Today I can tell the world and make it official. You were my best friend, my fiancée and now at long last you are my wife. I am forever devoted to you, forever in desperate need of your love. Goodbye Kellie Palmer and hello Mrs Jones. I love you."

He kissed her hand and she tried to hold back her tears but failed. Never had anyone said anything so special to her.

"And now, Kellie Anne Palmer."

"Shawn," she cried happily. "I wed you today with love and devotion, truth and sincerity, honesty and morality. I will love and share with you any unwanted or unfortunate life obstacles, I will stand by you and support you, and you will never in your life be alone again. You have inspired me like a fairy tale, you are my spiritual soul partner and I have faith and confidence that our fairytale will last forever. I love you a little more every single day."

"Now I can make you man and wife, you may kiss the bride." And those were the words that sealed their love.

On leaving, confetti was thrown at them in abundance and it came down on her like dry rain.

"CONGRATULATIONS!" They all chorused.

This was the happiest day of her life, pictures were taken and Shawn, Samuel and Kerion fluttered around her— the three men in her life.

"At last." He smiled and kissed her. "How do you feel Mrs Jones?"

"I feel free, even though I just gave my heart away." She threw her bouquet behind her and Mo and Anna fought for the promise of marriage until most of the petals had fallen off.

After the ceremony they all went to the club. It was closed to the public; open for guests of her wedding only. Rows and rows of tables covered the dance floor. Flowers matched tablecloths, glasses were crystal, champagne was in abundance.

Shawn held her hand as everyone took his or her own personal photographs.

"Is he like my dad now," Samuel asked her.

"Sort of." She smiled down at him.

"You all good girl?" her brother asked her.

"I am now."

Someone gave her a glass of champagne.

An hour later Kellie went upstairs to change into a dress fit for the Oscars. When she came back she stood by the head table while everyone milled around either looking for a table or standing, talking about her beautiful ceremony. She waited for her husband to join her.

"You seen my husband?" she asked Angela.

"Yeah your husband, I think he's upstairs, come take a photo." Kellie followed her.

"You seen Shawn?" she asked her brother as he and his wife settled at their table.

"No. What time is the food coming?"

"Soon."

"It's a bit hot in here can you turn up the AC?" Crystal fanned herself.

"I'll see what I can do, excuse me." Kellie walked off momentarily pissed off with the ice queen.

"Kellie, you know I need a picture with you in that dress." Anna pulled her away. "And *please* introduce me to your brother."

"And his wife?"

"Wife smife!" She laughed.

"Kellie, drink up." She heard someone say laughing; she turned toward the voice.

"Paul! What are you doing here?!"

"Congratulations. I had a hard time getting past your bouncers but here I am, I couldn't miss my first love's wedding."

"I'm glad you're here!" She hugged her first ever boyfriend; she'd been thirteen.

"You look beautiful, I should never have let you go." He laughed.

"Look, get yourself a drink and I'll catch up with you in a bit. Kerion's over there," she told Paul gleefully.

"I thought he was in America," Paul replied, shocked.

"He was. I'll see you in a bit." She excused herself.

"Kellie, where you going for your honeymoon?" Jade caught up with her.

"Bahamas."

"Kellie, should I open more champagne?"

"Kellie, come in this picture," Mo asked.

"Congratulations," Tex offered warmly.

"Thank you," Kellie beamed.

"Kellie, I'm hungry."

"Alright Sam, sit with Angela for a bit."

Her head spun.

"Kellie, the photographer wants to see you."

"Where's Shawn?" she asked an hour later. Every time she tried to find her husband, someone pulled her toward something else. Cameras were flashing constantly in her face and she kept being handed presents which she kept loading behind the bar.

Kellie slipped upstairs, she needed to go into her office for a breather. When she went in, her husband-on his phone with his back to her-stood looking out of the glass. She began to creep up behind him to frighten him, but stopped. She listened as he spoke in a harsh voice and looked out to the many people that were there to celebrate with them.

"Cos I got it all. Just what I told you I would get," he almost shouted, oblivious to her presence. "It's all mine," he continued as Kellie tried to make sense of what he was saying. She was intrigued now. Who was he talking to? He never hid his phone or phone calls, he never left the room when his phone rang. She stood still, she didn't want him to turn around, she didn't want him to stop his conversation. She wanted to hide behind the bar so that she could safely hear every word. At last, he continued, "I got your girl, your club, your whole shit."

His words hit home as she dared not breathe. His words made her almost gag as they echoed through her. 'I got your girl, your club, your whole shit.' Instantly her hand went up to her mouth and she let out a cry. Shawn spun around and his phone dropped from his hands. She watched it fall, as if in slow motion, then smash apart on the tiled floor.

Kellie looked up to him with tears in her eyes. She looked deep into his heart wanting desperately to see into his mind. Her mouth opened but nothing came out. He stood rooted to the spot, as realisation stabbed her through her heart.

"Sediko?...." she whispered.

THE END

FOR A FULL RANGE OF X PRESS

TITLES SEE OUR WEBSITE AT:

WWW.XPRESS.CO.UK